THE LONGEST WINTER

by the same author
THE DISTANT KINGDOM

DAPHNE WRIGHT

The Longest Winter

Doubleday Canada Limited, Toronto

Typeset in Monophoto Sabon 12/13.5 pt

Canadian Cataloguing in Publication Data

Wright, Daphne
  The longest winter

ISBN 0-385-25209-9

I. Title.

PR6073.R47L6 1989   823'.914   C89-094690-6

Published in Canada by
Doubleday Canada Limited
105 Bond Street
Toronto, Ontario
M5B 1Y3

For CWW and AVW
with love

I

Sitting at her dressing-table on Christmas Eve, pinning up her long, dark hair, Evelyn suddenly stopped, looked at her reflection as though she had never seen it before and dropped the silver-backed hairbrush on to the thick carpet. The housemaid who waited on her bent down to pick it up and held it out. When Evelyn did not move, the girl said gently:

'*Baryshnia?*'

Evelyn started, smiled briefly at the maid and took back the brush, saying in her halting Russian:

'Thank you, Annoushka. That will be all.'

The girl looked surprised at the phrase, which had taken her so long to understand in the days when Evelyn had been trying to train her in English ways, but shrugged and left the room. When she had gone, Evelyn laid the brush down, put her elbows on the dressing-table and propped her chin on her clasped hands.

'What on earth are you doing here?' she asked her reflection.

The pale, square-chinned face of which she had been so proud ever since John had told her that it was beautiful looked blankly back at her as she sorted through the immediately practical answers to her own question: because you are too young to join the nurses at the Front; because you begged your parents to let you go away, anywhere, just away from all the places you had known with John; because Cousin Natalia needed an English-speaking governess for

Dindin and Natalie; because . . . because you have to live somewhere until they find John and you can tear up his mother's letter.

Instinctively she touched the jewel box where she kept it. Even though she knew that she could not bear to read it again, she lifted the lid of the box and took out the creased sheet of thick writing paper. The words of the letter were burned into her mind just as deeply as those of the advertisement his mother still put in the English *Times* week after week:

> TEMPERLEY. Would any officer or man with any information about Captain John Temperley, who has been missing since Loos, write to his mother, the Hon. Mrs James Temperley . . .

When she had first read that advertisement, Evelyn had not been able to stop tears seeping into her eyes, but in the eleven months she had spent with her cousins in Russia she had learned some self-control and no longer embarrassed them with displays of misery. But she could never control her memory, and now it hit her again with a frighteningly vivid picture of the last day of John's last leave. With an effort that made her clench her teeth, she wrenched her mind away from the image of his face, and tried to concentrate on the question she had asked herself.

When the news of her fiancé's disappearance had reached Yorkshire, all Evelyn had wanted to do was get across the Channel to the Front and find him. Yet there she was, more than a year later, dressing for her cousins' Christmas Eve dinner in the immense luxury of the bedroom they had given her, almost as far away as she could possibly be from the realities of the war that was the most important as well as the most horrible thing that had touched her life.

For months she had been too homesick and too miserable even to recognise the irony of her predicament, but that evening, with her expensive new dress ready to put on and her hair half done, she acknowledged to herself that if she had not been so hysterical in her demands to leave Yorkshire and learn to be a nurse she would probably have been nearer her goal. She might even have been in some field hospital near the trenches, helping the men who had fought beside John; by then she might even have found him, confused by loss of memory, perhaps, or unrecognisable to anyone else because of wounds or bandages.

The pretty gilt clock above the fireplace chimed seven times and dragged her mind back from the nightmare pictures of the trenches that snaked all the way from the Belgian coast to Switzerland, the stinking mud and barricades of vicious wire, and the men who lived and died there. Evelyn shuddered at the memory of the things that John had told her.

She picked up the hairbrush again, determined not to give way to her fears and memories. When she had driven the last big tortoiseshell pin into the gleaming, dark-brown mass of piled hair, she rang the bell.

'Annoushka, thank you,' she said when her maid appeared. 'Please help me with the dress.'

She stood in front of the long pier glass while the maid lifted the heavy garnet-coloured silk and settled it over her mistress's shoulders, before carefully doing up the thirty-eight, satin-covered buttons at the back. Then she stood back and waited for instructions.

Evelyn looked critically at herself, wanting to look her best and to show no signs of mourning, because that would give weight to her unspeakable suspicion that Johnnie might be dead. She was glad that she had yielded to Natalia Petrovna's suggestion that she should have a new evening dress made in time for Christmas. The silk was far richer than anything she had brought with her from Yorkshire and, unlike her old dresses, its hem hung a fashionable two inches above her ankles. The gown's combination of luxury and fashion gave her increased standing in her own eyes and would, she thought, help her to be a better ambassador for England in front of the fifty Russians who were to be at dinner.

She might have got over the worst of her homesickness, but as she walked down the wide staircase towards the big salon, she could not help thinking of her parents, who must be spending a bleak Christmas in Yorkshire, alone except for her younger brother, Dick. As for Anthony, her beloved elder brother, she could hardly bear to think of him suffering in some cold, wet trench with his men. Her mother's latest letters had been full of Tony's triumphant promotion to captain and the gallantry for which he had been mentioned in despatches, but Evelyn could not think that even that honour would compensate for his absence.

'Thank God,' she murmured aloud, 'that Dick's asthma is going to keep him well out of the war.'

When she got downstairs and pushed open the heavy mahogany doors to the salon, she was relieved to find that the room was empty so that she would have a few minutes to compose herself. She had discovered long ago that any mention of the war to her father's cousin, Andrei Alexandrovitch Suvarov, or his wife was unwelcome and she had tried to learn to keep her fears to herself.

She wandered aimlessly around the great room looking at the pictures and admiring the massed flowers that had been sent all the way from Nice for the party. Their heavy scent seemed to fill the room and banish the slight mustiness to which she had become accustomed, but there was something about them that made her feel uncomfortable. As she passed one magnificent vase of lilies and tuberoses that had been placed on an ornamental gilded pillar, she touched one of the heavy white petals and was almost repelled by its cold waxy texture. It seemed so out of place in the flat snow-ridden city of Petrograd, surrounded by pines and birches. These exotically scented, flaunting flowers were all wrong. Suddenly they made her think of funeral wreaths.

Snatching her hand away, she went instead to inspect the massed photographs on one of the side tables. A square silver-framed print she had never noticed before caught her eye and she picked it up to look at it more closely. It was of a large white house, obviously very beautiful although the sepia colour of the photograph muddied its clarity, and it stood on a small rise above a broad, calm-looking river. She was just wondering where the house could be when she was startled by a deep, liquid Russian voice behind her.

'That is my home.'

She turned so quickly that she felt dizzy for a moment and was in danger of dropping the photograph. The young man who had spoken took it from her with gentle fingers and then introduced himself as Sergei Voroshilov. Evelyn managed to smile at him as she told him who she was and then, as she looked up into his face, she thought she could understand why Dina, the elder of her two pupils, had been so excited at the prospect of his arrival. He was the most glorious-looking man she had ever seen. As tall as John, he was far more graceful. Where Johnnie was fair and handsome in his traditional, strong-looking, very English way, this man was lithe and dark, and his lavishly gilded uniform made him look like some figure from a more glamorous past. Evelyn caught her breath for a second or two and then said:

'Ah yes, Dindin has spoken of you. May I wish you a happy Christmas, Sergei Ivanovitch.'

He put down the photograph and kissed her hand in a very foreign way. Then he led her to a sofa and made her sit down beside him. Her eyes softened as she noticed that behind the magnificence of his features he looked tired and somehow spent. Evelyn remembered that he was on leave from the Front and it occurred to her that he was the only person she had yet met in Russia with first-hand experience of the war. Something about his heavily lashed, dark-grey eyes reminded her of John's, although the two men looked so different. She forgot all her formal small talk in the face of that and said much more naturally than she usually could to strangers:

'I am so glad that you have come. When do you have to go back?'

As his full lips thinned suddenly, she was sorry that she had reminded him of what he must have left behind, but he answered easily enough.

'I have eight more days' leave.'

'What is it . . .?' She stopped, but then her desperate aching need to talk to someone who might have understood about John, pushed her on. 'Do you hate talking about it?' He shook his head and smiled down at her with kindness in his face. She was unaware that she was smiling back at him as she went on: 'Can you tell me something of what it is like?'

Sergei thought about the lice-ridden uniforms, the lack of ammunition, the hatred of his men, the inadequate food, the wet and cold and fear and pain and wondered what he could possibly tell this sad, beautiful girl. He looked down into her expectant eyes and smiled again, as he decided to compromise.

'It is terrible – like Hell, I think – but it has to be done; and we are winning.'

'Truly? That is wonderful to know. The others, everyone who comes to this house, say such awful things and don't seem to understand why it matters so much.'

'I know. But let's forget it for the moment. It is Christmas tomorrow; I am on leave; let's talk of something more cheerful.'

'I am not sure I know of anything cheerful nowadays,' she said, but she could understand why he wanted it. When he saw that she could not think of anything to say he helped her out in a way that neither of Dina's elder brothers – or their friends – would have bothered to do. It made her very grateful.

'How do you like Petrograd, Miss Markham? Has my aunt taken you to the ballet yet? And the opera?'

She smiled up at Sergei, feeling at home at last with someone who played the social game by the rules she had been taught in England.

'Yes, indeed. I have never seen anything so magnificent as the ballet. It's almost magical, isn't it? We saw Karsarvina last month, dancing in *Swan Lake*. I could hardly believe how she could change so beautifully from Odette to Odile; one so glitteringly evil, the other so soft, charming.'

'I have always found *Swan Lake* a rather depressing ballet. I prefer the lighter ones, *Petrushka* and *Coppélia*, that sort of thing.'

Evelyn was just beginning to say that she had thought *Petrushka* much sadder than *Swan Lake*, when they were interrupted by the arrival of Natalia Petrovna. She caught sight of Sergei and gave a little scream of welcome as she ran, ungainly as a Strasbourg goose, across the room to land in his arms. Evelyn was astonished to see her kiss her nephew on the mouth before patting his handsome face between her hands.

'Seriosha, welcome. Thank the good God that you are safe. Those terrible guns and the wicked Germans – I knew they could never touch you. You are here: it's wonderful. But, naughty boy, why did you come in here instead of up to my dressing-room? You should have known I would want to see you at once. How is my brother?'

Evelyn's Russian was not good enough to allow her to catch more than the general sense of her cousin's outpouring, and she withdrew slightly. The movement caught Sergei's eye, and he switched politely back to French.

'Ah, Natalia Petrovna, it's good to be here. My father is well, though he could not understand why I wanted to come to Petrograd for Christmas instead of staying at home. He sends you all kinds of messages and I have a parcel for you from him. What was your other question? Oh yes, I did not come up to your room because I found your charming English cousin alone here in the salon – how could I leave her?'

Evelyn blushed becomingly at the compliment and Natalia Petrovna smiled warmly at her.

'Yes, of course. Isn't she charming? And don't you think the gown becomes her? I chose it for her and it really suits her. It's a great success, Evelyn dear, though I still think you should have had the velvet. You will catch your death of cold. And you're far too thin. Don't you think so, Seriosha? Like an insect, almost. She never eats enough despite everything I do.'

Evelyn's face stiffened at the implied criticism, and her voice became a little clipped as she defended herself.

'You forget, Cousin, that I am accustomed to much cooler houses in England – and no one at home has the kind of meals you all have here in Russia. I think my mother would stare in surprise if she saw how much I eat nowadays.' Natalia Petrovna smiled mechanically, bored with the familiar topic of what was done in England, and turned back to her nephew.

7

She remembered Evelyn a little later as she wondered aloud what had happened to the rest of the household and asked her to run up to see what Dina and her Russian governess were doing. Resenting the errand, Evelyn nevertheless did as she was told, only to be greeted by the governess's saying, in French:

'I do not know why you felt it necessary to chase after Dina Andreievna, *Mademoiselle*; you knew that she was with me.' Evelyn sighed but she thought it would be beneath her dignity to excuse herself by saying that Natalia Petrovna had sent her. She turned and left Dindin's room, afraid that after all there would be no pleasure in the party. The new dress suddenly seemed an unwarrantable extravagance. She thought of going to her room and spending the evening there alone, writing to John. She never sent the letters she wrote him – she had nowhere to which they could be sent – but writing them helped her to believe that he was still alive. Only the thought of Sergei Voroshilov persuaded her to go back downstairs.

When she returned to the salon at last, she saw that he was the centre of a laughing, chattering, gesticulating group between the two long windows, his dark handsomeness magnificently framed by their heavy red velvet curtains. She had never seen a face quite like his: sometimes it looked harsh, but at other moments the flashing deep-grey eyes could soften and the full lips smile in a way that robbed his high well-defined cheekbones of their drama. Evelyn stood watching him for a while, admiring the way he hid his feelings about the war and rather pleased that he had just allowed her to glimpse them.

She did not think she could interrupt him and so she looked around the rapidly filling room for another familiar face. Andrei Alexandrovitch was standing before the fire, but she did not feel strong enough to talk to him and risk arousing his sarcastic temper. She sometimes thought how odd it was that he and her father could be so very different in character when their mothers had been sisters and the two of them had spent much of their early boyhood together in one country or the other. Just occasionally Andrei Alexandrovitch would use an expression or make a gesture that brought Andrew Markham vividly to mind, but for most of the time her Russian cousin's manner and appearance seemed quite alien.

At the opposite end of the room she caught sight of Dindin's twin brothers and made her way slowly towards them. Three years older than Dindin, and fluent English-speakers, they did not come under Evelyn's jurisdiction, but she had got to know them well in the year she had spent teaching their sisters. They really were impossibly alike, she thought yet again, with their long, slightly tilted dark eyes and finely drawn, almost delicate faces. To her astonishment and pleasure, they were also dressed alike for once; even Piotr, the rebel, was wearing impeccably correct evening dress. His hair was sleekly combed, and the smooth blackness of his tail-coat showed off his slim, elegant figure in a way that his normal, deliberately shabby, clothes never did. An involuntary smile opened her lips.

'Piotr Andreivitch!' she exclaimed. 'Happy Christmas.'

He correctly read the expression in her face and said with an unusually frivolous teasing note in his voice:

'I know, it is extraordinary to see me looking so tidy, isn't it?'

Evelyn, who hated teasing, was quite unable to answer him in kind, but she did manage a reply.

'I can't think why you don't always wear those clothes. They suit you so well.'

'I could hardly fail to know that, seeing Georgii in them every evening I dine at home, could I?'

At that Evelyn did manage to laugh, and turned to Georgii to say something nice to him too, but his face, so like Piotr's and yet somehow imprinted these days with an expression of resentment, stopped her. Instead, she looked back at Piotr.

'Why did you decide to honour us like this tonight?' she said. He smiled at her with the oddly sweet smile he rarely let her see, apparently pleased that she had found such lightness of tone.

'It's a sort of Christmas present for my mother. My father's been in such a bad temper with me that he's given her rather a bad time this last week or so.'

Evelyn had noticed nothing out of the ordinary in his father's cold, tyrannical behaviour and so she did not believe Piotr's ingenuous explanation and pressed him.

'But you seem much happier than before. What has happened?'

'Don't you know?'

'No. Have you fallen in love? Georgii, is Piotr going to get married?'

They both roared with laughter at that as though she had said something deliberately comic and she stiffened again. For some reason that made them laugh the more and when he could speak, Georgii said:

'That would hardly be cause for rejoicing. No, Rasputin's dead. Did you really not know?'

'Of course I knew. But what is there to be so happy about? He was murdered – horribly. Whatever you thought of his influence over the Tsarina, you cannot possibly be so delighted about that.'

'Oh, come on, Evelyn,' said Georgii in nearly as irritable a voice as his father used. 'Everyone in this city, with the possible exception of the Tsar and his immediate family, is pleased. Rasputin was a monster.'

'He really deserved to die, Evelyn,' said Piotr, not laughing at all any more. 'He caused untold misery and was dragging the whole of Russia down.'

Her instinctive revulsion made her think of something else that she wanted to say to him.

'Piotr, I have been speaking to Sergei Voroshilov and he said that they are beating the Germans – that's not what you told me last week.'

'Well he is exactly the kind of chivalrous fool who would tell lies to comfort a woman.'

Evelyn's eyes flashed and she was about to turn away when Piotr stopped her.

'All right, all right, I'm sorry, Evelyn. But that kind of irresponsibility always makes me angry. He . . .'

'He at least has been at the Front, fighting our enemy,' interrupted Evelyn, for once hotly angry. 'I prefer to take his word than that of a mere student who has no experience of what he is talking about and believes every word he is told by an ignorant, prejudiced, Conchie American.'

'That must be me,' said a familiar and unwelcome voice, 'since I'm the only American you know. But I don't much like the rest of your description of a hard-working, impartial newspaperman doing his best to report on the war for his editor back home.'

Evelyn blushed and felt even angrier with Piotr, whom she blamed unreasonably for putting her into such an embarrassing position. She turned to his friend, suppressed her surprise that he too was wearing conventional evening dress, and wished him a pleasant Christmas in her chilliest voice. His amused expression did nothing for her anger or her embarrassment.

'Well, Miss Markham, and how have I offended you *this* time?'

'I beg your pardon, Mr Adamson,' she said with icy correctness. 'I should not have said what I did, particularly when it was my cousin who had spoken so absurdly.'

'Against the war, was it? Or did he offend against English manners yet again?'

At that piece of familiar mockery Evelyn looked directly at the big American journalist who seemed such an unlikely friend for the twins and put all her dislike and contempt into her expression. He almost flinched, but then laughed again and she turned to go, tears of temper rising inexorably into her eyes. She blamed Robert Adamson for turning her cousins from their usual casual friendliness to the mockery she hated. When he was nowhere near, both of the twins talked to her as though she were an equal and even when they disagreed with her were reasonably polite about it. But Mr Adamson, ten years older than they, experienced, well-travelled, and with a kind of power that Evelyn recognised even though she loathed it, could always make them turn on her as they had done just then.

As she was walking away from them through the crowded salon, Sergei found her again. He was about to make a joke about his aunt's having sent her away from him, but just in time saw that she was troubled and instead took her hand and said in a low, almost conspiratorial voice:

'Miss Markham, what has happened? Please tell me. I hate to see you so unhappy.'

His voice was so kind and the pressure of his hand on hers so comforting that she looked up at him and her lips smiled despite herself.

'Tell me, please,' he urged. But it would have sounded so childish to say to this man who was facing horror and death every day that she had been brought to the brink of tears by a tiny piece of rude teasing; so instead she murmured:

'It's only the war. I can't forget it, however hard I try.'

'I too,' he said gently and pressed her hand again. 'But won't you try? Just to make one soldier's Christmas leave happy?'

Tall though she was, Evelyn had to look up into his face and what she thought she saw there made her say without considering her words at all:

'Of course, Sergei Ivanovitch, I shall do anything.'

'Then smile for me – a beautiful smile like the one you greeted me with. Yes, that's right. Now, come to the buffet with me and have some champagne.'

'Of course I'll come, since you wish it, but, Sergei Ivanovitch, I do not really like champagne.'

'What? That's almost heresy! Well, we shall find something that you do like. Come with me now.'

So she went, and in the knowledge that now, at last, she was doing something for someone who was involved in the fighting she began to relax. For that one evening she did not mind that it was her duty to smile and enjoy herself and behave frivolously.

He hardly left her side before dinner as they stood chatting, sipping their wine and choosing delicacy after delicacy from the heavy silver trays of *zakuski* that the servants were handing round. There was caviare served on warm *kalatches*; there were canapés of smoked reindeer tongue, pickled grapes, smoked fish of all kinds and *foie gras*. Evelyn ate sparingly, and when Sergei urged her to take more told him of the first large dinner she had attended in Petrograd when she had assumed that the *zakuski* constituted the entire meal and, smothering her astonishment that the Russians dined on their feet, she had eaten all she could, only to be faced with an entire dinner half an hour later. He laughed, but she felt that half his amusement at least was directed at the odder customs of his people and so she did not mind it.

'It must have been difficult, finding yourself in the middle of a society like the Suvarovs' when you were accustomed to something very different.' She looked up at him, silently blessing him for his understanding.

'Yes, Sergei Ivanovitch, it was very difficult. There were so many things I did not understand and could not ask.'

'But it is better now?'

'Much better,' she said with feeling. 'It's not only that I know a little of your language now and so I don't feel quite so helpless outside the house or with the servants here; it is partly that I understand so much more of the way my cousins live and why things are done as they are. Have you ever been in England?'

'No. My only contact with your country has been through Andrei Alexandrovitch.'

He noticed her involuntary shiver and asked: 'Are you afraid of him? Surely not?'

'It is ungrateful, I know,' she answered, 'but, yes, I am. You see I never know how he is going to react – some days he will listen to the twins ranting at each other and only smile; at other times Piotr has only to open his mouth and his father will shout at him and send him out of the room.' She looked speculatively at Sergei and decided to trust him. 'It is almost as though he were a tiger or something; one goes into his cage not knowing whether he will want to be stroked and purr peacefully or whether he will bite. It's very unsettling.'

By the time Evelyn reached the end of that little speech, Sergei was laughing again.

'But, my dear Miss Markham, I do not believe he would ever bite you. Why should you be frightened of what he may say – or do – to his sons?'

She looked up at him in surprise.

'It is not that I'm afraid exactly, but ... but ... Well, I

suppose it is just that I'm not used to it. Neither of my parents ever speaks like that. I mean, if my brothers or I did something wrong, they would just talk to us quietly and show us why we should never do it again.'

'And did you always obey?'

'Of course.'

'Well, that is charming. But I do not think that Andrei Suvarov would control those twins of his by such means. They . . .' For once Evelyn interrupted without thinking how rude she was being:

'But perhaps they would have done if they had not been accustomed to his temper. If he had practised some restraint himself, then perhaps they would have accepted his authority.'

'I doubt it,' he said, his voice dry. 'And now if you will forgive me for a moment, I must speak to my aunt.'

Evelyn watched him go, wondering why he should have slipped away, and whether she had insulted him by her criticism of Andrei Alexandrovitch, but Sergei soon returned.

'That's settled,' he said with a dazzling smile.

'But what have you done, Sergei Ivanovitch?'

'Don't look so worried, Miss . . . Oh, why should we be so formal when you are my aunt's niece by marriage? Will you let me call you Evelyn?'

The girl blushed again, and he thought how much the colour improved her rather severe beauty.

'Well?' he prompted.

'Of course, Sergei Ivanovitch, if that is what you want.'

'Good. Well, Evelyn, all I was doing was persuading my aunt to change the seating plan for tonight's dinner. Having discovered you, I do not want to be stuck miles away down the table talking to one of these dull Russian girls I have known all my life.'

A sort of glow rose within Evelyn and just for an instant, as she tucked her full lower lip under her white teeth and looked up at him through her eyelashes, there was an almost mischievous glint in her smile. Whether it was the romantic unconventionality of his action, or the compliment of his preferring her over those Russian girls, she was not sure. All she knew was that this dashing, heroic, handsome man had picked her out of the whole glittering company to sit beside him. She caught sight of Dindin and smiled at her in welcome. When the girl came up to her, Evelyn said warmly:

'You were quite right, Dindin, about your cousin.'

Dina laughed and kissed Sergei and, holding one of his hands against her rosy cheek, said:

'Yes, but, Evie, you must be careful. This wicked cousin of mine is a terrible breaker of hearts. Aren't you, Seriosha?'

He pulled his hand away from her clasp to tweak her dimpled chin.

'What a cheeky little cousin you are, Dina Andreievna. And how do you know about broken hearts? You should be in your schoolroom, you bad girl.' Dina laughed and turned her back on them, looking over her shoulder to fire her parting shot.

'Oh, cousin, I know all about your love affairs and the hearts you have played with. He's dangerous, Evie.'

Evelyn suddenly sobered and said in a voice so sad that it rebuked her flirtatious cousin:

'I am in no danger.'

She did not see the narrowing of Sergei's eyes, nor the unmistakable gesture of dismissal he sent to Dina, but she heard the change in his voice.

'Don't mistake Dindin's nonsense for unkindness, Evelyn.' At that she looked at him again.

'I don't. And there is no reason why my sorrow should blacken her happiness. How did you know?' she asked.

'I asked Natalia Petrovna – I hope you will forgive me: it was not just curiosity.' A gesture of her elegant hands brushed aside his apology, and he went on: 'There was something about your lovely eyes that looked so sad when I first saw you that I had to find out what had hurt you so much.'

'And she told you about Johnnie.' There was an indescribable relief in saying his name. She had not spoken it aloud since she had left England, but Sergei understood; he had shared John's ordeal and there was no danger in showing him her sorrow and fear. He could understand and would never mock her, she was sure. Sergei touched her thin, blue-veined wrist again and she knew that her trust had not been misplaced.

The footmen coming in at that moment with place cards for all the guests put an end to their moment of shared emotion. She discovered that Sergei had been placed on her left and so she turned correctly to the man on her right as the servants brought in the first course. She had met him several times before and when she had greeted him and enquired about his wife's health, she chatted politely until the plates were removed. Then she turned back to Sergei with a feeling of release, for the first time recognising an impatience with the conventions that ruled her life.

Later she could not remember what it was that they had spoken about, but she knew that at last in Russia she had found someone who understood what she was going through, and who shared her passionate desire for victory over the Prussians. It was not that they talked about the war, for they did not; it was just something in Sergei's eyes and the sympathy in his voice that told her he thought as she did.

The only reference either made to the fighting was after dinner when the expensive orchestra Natalia Petrovna had hired struck up 'The Blue Danube' and Sergei begged her to dance with him. She looked at him in reproach and said softly:

'Sergei Ivanovitch, I cannot dance while . . . while my brother and Johnnie . . .' Even to him, she discovered, she could not quite say everything she thought. But he brushed her protests away and took both her hands, bending his extraordinarily handsome face towards hers and saying almost under his breath:

'Even to give this poor soldier a taste of paradise before he goes back into Hell?'

How could she refuse such a request? As he straightened up and put out his arms, she walked into his embrace and allowed him to lead her on to the dance floor.

2

During the six days between Christmas Day and the end of Sergei's leave, Evelyn was happier than she had ever expected to be in Russia. It was partly that he was so attentive to her, of course. There was something in the way that he got up from his chair and turned to greet her whenever she entered a room, no matter whom he was with or what he was doing, that warmed her. He seemed to have a special smile for her, too, and one much kinder than those of the twins. Unlike them, he never turned from her in irritation, and he even allowed her to ask him questions about the war. He listened to her accounts of John, too, and tried to comfort her by talking about either the nobility of sacrifice or the number of men who had been wounded and lost their memories only to be restored to health months or even years later.

Such talk did comfort her, and fed her desperate need to be in some way involved with the great struggle. The twins had made it quite clear that they considered that the war had been imposed on Russia by the Allies and that, as Piotr had once said, 'The Allies are fighting to the last drop of Russian blood.' He and Georgii were only interested in what was to happen in Russia and when or how the Tsar could be persuaded to introduce some form of democratic government, and Evelyn was shocked at their selfish insularity. She could almost have clapped at dinner on Sergei's last evening, when Piotr had said something to that effect and Sergei had looked down the table, an expression of severity in his dramatically beautiful eyes, and said:

'Piotr Andreivitch, all such preoccupations must be set aside until the war is won.'

Piotr's thin face grew bleak and determined.

'Face facts, Sergei Ivanovitch, how can it be? You know, if you would only admit it, that without at least one gun to every man and adequate ammunition, there is no hope of winning. And the fight is bleeding Russia white. It has to stop.'

All the other conversations around the table stopped. Evelyn looked towards Andrei Suvarov, feeling sick and nervous as she wondered when he would stop the talk, and who would be the object of his wrath. But nothing happened; it was as though Sergei somehow defused all the quarrels and difficulties of the household. Natalia Petrovna and Dina adored him and perhaps it was for their sake that Andrei Alexandrovitch curbed his temper. Or perhaps it was because of the way in which Sergei smiled at Piotr and refused to be ruffled. Evelyn looked back across the table at Sergei, silently thanking him for bringing this new peace to the Suvarovs.

He caught her eye, and a tremulous smile broke across her face as she read the expression in his handsome face. He looked at her for a long moment. Then he turned back to his cousin.

'We'll never agree, Piotr Andreivitch,' he said at last. 'You see, you live here as a student, free, safe and comfortable, in Petrograd; how can you know the determination felt by everyone at the Front to thrash those d—— I beg your pardon, Natalia Petrovna, the Prussians?' Then, without waiting for the boy to answer, Sergei turned to his host and asked some question about the labour troubles he and every other manufacturer was facing. Evelyn sighed in relief and turned back to her interrupted conversation with Georgii, and dinner progressed on its way.

When the servants had cleared the last of the plates, Sergei said to his aunt:

'Don't you think Evelyn ought to hear the gypsies playing just once? She tells me she's never heard them.'

'Oh Seriosha, how can she? She cannot go to a public restaurant. Don't worry about it; one of our friends is bound to have them at a private party before long.'

'She could if you would come too, all of you.' He looked round the table, a tantalising smile playing around his lips. Dindin drew in a deep breath and, without waiting for either of her parents to speak, said excitedly:

'All of us? Oh Mamenka, please do let us. Papa, you would like to come, wouldn't you? I've never been to a restaurant, please, please, Papa. And one can never hear too much gypsy music, can one, Seriosha?'

Evelyn watched an indulgent expression creep into Andrei Suvarov's ice-blue eyes as he smiled at his pretty, impulsive daughter. Before Natalia Petrovna could say any more, he had given his permission, adding only:

'But if you will forgive me, Sergei Ivanovitch, I shall not come with you. I have some papers to deal with. You will take care of them, won't you?'

'Of course. Well, Aunt?'

'Very well, Seriosha. We shall come. Evelyn, Dindin, come on upstairs and fetch your cloaks.'

As they came down the broad red-carpeted staircase, Evelyn whispered to Dina:

'But what is so special about the gypsies, Dindin?'

'Wait till you hear them – it's the most exciting music in the world, Seriosha told me.'

'So, you haven't heard them either?'

'Well, no actually. It's usually only men who go to those places, and . . . well, you know the sort of women I mean. And I haven't been to the private dances where they have the gypsies yet. But I will next year, when I'm seventeen.'

With that introduction, Evelyn hardly knew what to expect when they arrived at the restaurant. She half suspected that the room would be filled with scantily clad satyrs and street walkers, and was agreeably surprised to be taken into a luxuriously decorated hall, with perfectly respectable-looking men and women in evening dress sitting at white-clothed tables. There were no signs of impropriety and indeed nothing to shock her at all. She relinquished her cloak to a waiter and followed Natalia Petrovna to a large table quite near the small orchestra.

At first she thought that the whole expedition must have

been a hoax for there were no obvious gypsies, only ordinary musicians going through the usual repertoire of fashionable waltzes. But just as the second bottle of champagne had been opened, the orchestra put down their instruments and made way for a gaily dressed troop.

'Now!' said Sergei, leaning back in his chair and turning to smile at Evelyn. 'Now you will hear them.'

'Don't expect too much, Evie,' said Piotr sardonically. 'You won't understand the words and the music is an acquired taste.'

'Don't listen to him, *chérie*,' said Natalia Petrovna, smiling.

But at first, it was Piotr who was proved right. Evelyn listened puzzled to the plaintive, wailing music and the incomprehensible words sung by a gaunt-eyed, swarthy woman with a red silk scarf bound about her dark hair. As the song ended, clapping broke out at all the tables around them, and Evelyn politely joined in. Then Sergei called something to the leading gypsy, who nodded and swayed forward as he drew his bow across the strings of his violin.

'What did you say?' Evelyn whispered to Sergei.

'I just asked for my favourite song. Listen, it is about a beautiful girl who is in love with an enemy of her father's. She will not admit to her feelings, even though he begs and pleads with her. Then her brothers, who object to him bothering her, go and kill him, and then she understands how she loved him. It is very sad. Listen.'

Obediently Evelyn leaned back in her chair and let the wild, passionately sad music wash over her. This time she did not even try to understand the words; she just listened and began to feel the music. As the song unwound itself in her mind, she became very conscious of Sergei sitting so close to her and his hand resting very near hers on the white table cloth. She knew she should move her hand, but a peculiar languor seemed to have invaded her and she allowed it to remain. Then, when the song was over and he looked into her eyes, she dropped her lashes and blushed.

He tried to catch her alone the next day before he had to leave for the railway station, but she was inaccessible in the schoolroom with Dindin and her little sister, Natalie, and he had to say goodbye to Evelyn at the same time as all the others. He kissed them all in the usual way and as he reached her said caressingly:

'Since you are nearly a cousin, Evelyn, will you let me kiss you too?'

She was too embarrassed to know how to answer that, and as he took her in his arms she looked up at his face a little worried. He bent his head and kissed her full on her beautiful lips and she was shocked to find herself responding to him and wanting to press herself closer. She knew that she was blushing again as he drew back, but she forced herself to say:

'Sergei Ivanovitch, goodbye – and good luck. I shall be thinking of you.'

'*Petite* Evelyn,' he said, smiling at her. 'It will help to remember that at night in the trenches.' He might have said more, but Dindin threw herself at him just then, crying and kissing him. Evelyn turned away, frighteningly reminded of the day John had left Beverley after that last leave. A kind of resentment seeped into the regret she was feeling. It seemed so unfair that these men should make her care for them so much and leave her to such terrible fear. She left the hall and walked wearily up to her room to re-read some of the letters she had written to John and to try to dismiss thoughts of what had happened during his last leave, or of the trenches and the bodies and the blood and the wire.

She was interrupted an hour later by Natalia Petrovna, who had come in search of some distraction from her own sadness. Her excuse was that it was nearly time for her baby, little Alexander, to leave his nursery and have some simple lessons with his two sisters. After all, Sasha was four years old now and it would be a pity to miss the opportunity for him to learn English.

Evelyn dragged her thoughts back from Flanders and tried to talk intelligently about how she would set about teaching so young a child and how to fit him into the lessons she gave his elder sisters. His mother was soon bored with the topic and tried to change it.

'Were you writing home, my dear?'

Evelyn almost scowled in her embarrassment and told the first deliberate lie of her life as she hastily pushed the letters back into the morocco blotting book.

'Yes, that's right. To Dick, my young brother. He wants to know all I can tell him of life here. I was just trying to describe the gypsies to him. And then I was going on to explain why the twins get so angry with each other when they talk politics together; I mean, explain about Georgii's Cadet Party and why Piotr thinks it is so worthless and approves of those Bolsheviki and why they think that only the workmen should form the government. But it is hard, since I still can't really understand them.' Evelyn knew that she was saying too much and almost at random, but having no experience in lying, she felt she had to add colour to her first bald statement.

'It's so tiresome,' was Natalia Petrovna's comment. 'Andrei Alexandrovitch gets so angry with them when they talk all their revolutionary nonsense; but I tell him that all young men think like that. And not only young men now-adays. Everywhere I go people are talking about how to increase the powers of the Duma and what is to be done about the war. I think it's since that dreadful Rasputin was killed. It seems less dangerous to speak out now.' Then her voice changed as she was forced to think of the dangers her beloved Piotr still faced. 'But I wish Peterkin would be more careful. These books he brings to the house; I know they're forbidden. The Okhrana are everywhere even now.'

'Okhrana?'

'The police – secret police. If he were caught . . . Well, it's no good talking about it. Promise you won't tell anyone what I said?'

'Of course,' answered Evelyn, not quite sure whether to take any of it seriously, or whether Natalia Petrovna shared her elder daughter's undoubted enjoyment of melodrama.

Not very long after that conversation Evelyn discovered how much substance there had been to her cousin's fears. Towards the middle of February there were riots in the city which grew daily worse and more widespread instead of petering out as usual. The government was frightened enough to have machine guns set up on top of strategically positioned buildings in the city centre and one morning they opened fire on the crowd.

In the schoolroom, Evelyn and the three children heard a sharp ratt-tatt-tatt bursting through the still air. At first Evelyn tried to tell herself and her pupils that it was thunder, or a motor backfiring. When the sound persisted, she ran to the window and tried to open it. But like all the others in the house it had been sealed for the winter and she was frustrated. Absurdly she felt as though she had never been allowed to breathe properly since she had arrived in Petrograd. Her long-standing anger at the unhealthy custom of sealing the windows nearly boiled over and her long fingers scraped and picked at the gluey material that kept out every trickle of fresh air.

'You mustn't open it, Evie,' called Dindin, shocked at what she saw. 'You will make us all ill.'

'Fresh air never hurt anyone, Dindin,' answered Evelyn. 'In fact a little cool air in this hothouse would benefit everyone.' But then she remembered the necessity of backing up their mother's rules and turned away from the window, saying: 'You're right, of course, Dindin. I keep forgetting how much colder it is out there than at home in England. Now I think we should forget the riots and turn back to the last paragraph. Natalie, will you read it out?'

The child, who was always gentle and obedient, started to read, but the sound of gunfire came again, unmistakable now, and she paled and put down the book.

'Evie, what is happening? Can't we find out?'

'I shall go downstairs and ask. You may read to yourselves, and I shall tell you whatever I can discover.'

Despite their protests, she left them and ran lightly down the stairs to the morning room, where to her surprise she found not only the twins but also Robert Adamson. None of them stood up as she came in or spoke to her but for once she did not notice the discourtesy.

'Is it guns? What is happening? Do you know?' It was Georgii who answered her.

'Yes, machine guns, being fired on the people.'

'They have no bread,' burst out Piotr. 'And Bloody Nikolai is shooting them for asking for just that.'

'Nonsense,' countered his brother. 'There's plenty of bread in the city. Our people have checked it out.'

'Oh, you Cadets are hardly better than the Tsar's ministers. You believe all the lies they tell you.'

'I heard that it all started when a workman started to beat his wife when he discovered she had no bread for his meal,' said Adamson, perhaps trying to defuse the twins' arguments. 'Their neighbours started to beat him for beating her and so it went on.'

'What does it matter how it started?' demanded Evelyn. 'All that matters is that people are being killed out there.'

Piotr looked at her with rare approval and said:

'I know. What kind of a government can do that to the starving? They used to call him "The Little Father" you know. It is sickening that he can be so cruel.'

'What will happen, Piotr Andreivitch?' she asked, her voice softened by her recognition of his real distress.

'I don't know, Evie. But I expect the people will disperse in the end; the Okhrana will hand out savage sentences to the men they grab; and it will all happen again and again.' His voice sounded hopeless.

The riots grew worse and the anxiously waiting citizens of Petrograd told each other that the Cossacks would soon be sent out against the demonstrators. Even outsiders like Evelyn knew that the Cossack regiments had always been notorious for the cruelty with which they carried out the Tsar's orders, and they all waited for news of a massacre.

As the strikes and riots infected more and more of the city, the Suvarov Timber Works, in common with many of the metal foundries and factories, had to be shut down. Andrei Alexandrovitch could do nothing to prevent it and was forced to wait out the strike at home. Acerbic and impatient, he increased the tensions in the house tenfold, and Evelyn wished that he would be summoned to the family's forests and estates in the northern province of Archangel, or even be ill so that he would be confined to his room. She knew it was ill-natured of her to entertain any such thoughts, but she thought it was just too much to have to face his anger indoors while such a storm was raging outside.

His unaccustomed presence at the breakfast table was really only a trivial matter, but it turned a once-pleasant meal into an ordeal for her, particularly before Dina arrived downstairs to draw his fire with her flirtatious smiles and chatter. They were sitting alone together in silence, sipping coffee, on the morning of the 27th when Piotr and Georgii came rushing into the room.

Evelyn, whose nerves had made her jumpy as she spent the last few days incarcerated in the house, almost dropped her half-empty cup. Piotr stopped dead just inside the door as he saw his father and then said:

'It's started. Bob just telephoned. It *is* the Revolution.'

Andrei Alexandrovitch touched his thin lips with a damask napkin.

'Must you burst in here as though this were some convocation of students? Sit down and behave in a civilised manner for once. Evelyn, would you pour me some more coffee?'

'Certainly,' she said automatically, and rose to take his cup to the coffee pots on the sideboard. Then, in spite of the older man's obvious dislike of the subject, she could not help saying to Piotr:

'But what about the Cossacks? My maid told me yesterday that they were being positioned across all the main roads to stop the marching people. What happened, Piotr Andreivitch?'

His face seemed to blaze and she saw that he was happy as well as excited.

'They joined the rioters. Can you believe it? The Cossacks actually drew their horses aside and let the march go past, and some of them even joined in.'

'Yes,' added Georgii, for once in a voice that carried no hint of complaint, 'and today the Volhinya regiment were ordered out into the streets and they mutinied. At last it's happened. Russia is free today!'

The triumph in the twins' faces and their friendliness were such that Evelyn found herself smiling back at them and, as she gave their father his refilled white and gold cup, she said:

'Andrei Alexandrovitch, isn't that wonderful? That Russia should be free, I mean?'

'If you believe that, you're as childish as my sons,' he said, flattening her instantly. But the boys looked at each other as though nothing on earth could dim their excitement.

'Everyone's going to the Taurida Palace to hear what the Duma has to say,' said Piotr. 'Are you coming, Evelyn? You're not due in the schoolroom until this afternoon. Do come. It's a historic day.'

'Oh may I go, Andrei Alexandrovitch?' asked Evelyn, suddenly longing to be out of the house for once.

'It is a matter of complete indifference to me,' he answered. 'If you have no duties in the house this morning, you may do as you wish. But all the *istvochiks* are on strike and I cannot allow any of our horses out on the streets today. You will have to walk.'

'Oh, what does that matter?' said Piotr. 'Come on, Evelyn.'

'Georgii, I trust you are not thinking of joining your brother.'

All three of them stopped at the door of the breakfast room and Evelyn sympathised with the expression of despairing resentment that distorted the elder twin's face. He turned back to his father and said in his old, familiar voice:

'But, Papa, the Works are shut today. What could I do? Why can't I go?'

'Stand up to him, for once in your life,' Piotr hissed at him.

'There is plenty of paper work in the study. I shall expect you in half an hour.'

Georgii took a deep breath.

'No. Today Liberty has been brought to Russia. I won't come.' And then as though to fend off his father's anger, his voice sounded pleading as he went on: 'Papa, truly, if there are papers to be dealt with, I could do them this evening.'

Piotr sighed, but his father said coldly:

'See that you do. And look after your cousin.'

They escaped and as soon as the door was closed behind them, Georgii burst out:

'Why is it always me? Why didn't he even try to stop you, Piotr? It's not fair.'

'It's only because you allow him to coerce you like that. But don't let's quarrel now. Evelyn, if you're coming, go and get your coat, and you'd better wear a shawl instead of a hat. You don't want to look too conspicuous this morning.'

Evelyn did not wait for anything else, but ran upstairs to change. The governess, Ekaterina Nikolaievna, was in charge of the children until luncheon, and so Evelyn would have plenty of time to go with the twins to find out what was happening. As she was searching through her bottom drawer for an old woollen shawl to wear, Dindin looked round the door.

'Where are you going?' she demanded.

'To the Duma with the twins. The riots are over, but something terribly important is happening.'

'Take me with you, please, Evie. The Kat is horrid today and she's told me to write out "I must not chatter during lessons" three hundred times.'

'Poor Dindin – but I don't think I can take you.'

'Please, please. If it's so important, can't I come?'

Despite the fact that Dindin had been cooped up in the stifling, airless house and must be restless as she was herself, Evelyn could not bring herself to help the girl into disobedience. With regret mixed into her decisiveness, she said:

'Dindin, I can't. I'm sorry. You really must do as Ekaterina Nikolaievna tells you. I can't wait. I'll see you this afternoon.'

'I hate you, Evelyn. You're so selfish. Why should you be allowed to go out with the twins while I have to stay here? You're only three years older than me. It's not fair. I hate you.'

'Try not to say things you will regret, Dina Andreievna. Go back to the schoolroom at once. I'll tell you everything about it when I get back. Go on. Do as you're told.'

Dindin flounced out of the room, disappointed out of her hero-worship for the first time since Evelyn had come to the house. Evelyn looked after her, dismissing the charge of selfishness, but wishing that her cousin had not said such things. Rather disturbed, she went slowly downstairs to meet the twins, who were waiting impatiently in the hall.

'Come on,' said Georgii crossly. 'We're missing it all and Piotr wants to pick up Adamson at his flat.'

As they linked arms and walked over the hard, rutted snow on the pavements, it occurred to Evelyn that she had hardly seen the American for weeks. For some reason she felt a kind of embarrassment at the thought of meeting him again and looked rather furtively at him when he came down from his flat in response to Piotr's loud knocking. But he seemed just as he always had, tall, untidy, eager, feeling in his breast pocket for his spectacles.

He balanced them as usual far down his bony nose and looked at her:

'And what are you doing on this expedition, Miss Markham? Surely young English ladies don't come to political meetings.'

At the mockery in his voice, Evelyn flushed, but Piotr defended her.

'Now, now, Bob. There's no need for that. Today is a great day; it's right that Evelyn should witness it.'

At that moment they all heard the crack of a rifle, and the blood drained out of Evelyn's face.

'Piotr, you said the guns had stopped. What was that? Isn't it safe?'

'All the machine guns have been silenced. That was just a *feu de joie*. The people are so excited that they are firing into the air. Don't you see? After so many years of cruel suppression, they have won their liberty at last. Everyone in this city is free today.'

Evelyn smiled shakily and wished that she had not betrayed her fear. As they turned into the Nevski Prospekt she saw that the broad street with its serenely spaced neo-classical buildings was full of people. There were commandeered motor cars packed with soldiers, their bayonets fixed and sticking up out of the crammed vehicles like unwieldy bunches of flowerless winter roses. The red flags on the bonnets flew bravely against the hard, greyish-white snow, and despite their weapons the men waved cheerfully and yelled exultant greetings to the people they passed, calling them *Tovarisch!* Comrade! Parties of students hurried along the street and groups of workmen talked together, gesticulating, shouting and slapping one another on the back. Almost everyone seemed good humoured and although every soldier carried guns and many of the civilians had naked swords for walking sticks, Evelyn saw no killing.

But, as they turned left into the Liteini Prospekt to walk the mile and a half down to the Taurida Palace, she became aware that among the thickening crowd there were some less comfortable sights. In between the happy students and excited soldiery there were grimmer parties, surrounding unarmed, white-faced men who were being herded down the street towards the palace.

'Police,' answered Bob Adamson to a question of Evelyn's. 'Mainly, I think, the men involved in the machine-gunning.' If that were true, she thought, they deserved their fate, and she tried to suppress the memory of the fear she had seen in their faces. Looking round for something to help her forget them, she saw smoke in the distance and the reddish-orange glow of fire. As they walked towards its source, she saw that the whole of the Palace of Justice was on fire and that there were rows of smaller bonfires in the snow outside it, being fed with heaps of papers by people who from that distance seemed to be dressed entirely in black and to be dancing like devils around the flames. She could hear the roar of the fire that fed off the great building, and even from a hundred yards away could feel its fierce heat. As they walked nearer and nearer to the building, the roaring crackle seemed to force itself in on her, and as sparks fountained up into the white sky, she felt an impulse to clutch Mr Adamson's arm for reassurance. She tore her glance away from the figures circling round and round the smaller fires in the road and watched the back of his head as he walked ahead beside Piotr.

Once they got within shouting distance of the fires, the spindly, cavorting creatures were transformed into perfectly ordinary-looking men and women wrapped in the familiar poor overcoats and mufflers of the Petrograd people, and Evelyn saw that all they were doing was walking round their bonfires, stoking them.

'What are they burning?' she asked.

'Secret police records,' Piotr answered cheerfully. 'Look at those piles of paper and files: all the spying and trickery of the past is being wiped out. They are ensuring that we can start again – free – as though the Okhrana had never been. All the exiles will be able to come back from Siberia and abroad. The political prisoners will be freed. There won't be any more imprisonment without trial, nor censorship or spying.'

Evelyn heard the ringing tone of hope in his voice, and with the free, cold air on her face, felt that she was breathing properly for the first time since she had come to Petrograd. Her stride loosened and her chin lifted. As the words 'start again – free' echoed again and again in her mind, for a few blessed moments she believed it might be possible for her too to wipe out everything that had happened in the unhappy and shameful past. She smiled at Piotr so openly and warmly that he was astonished.

But her exhilaration did not last. When they reached the magnificent, colonnaded Taurida Palace, the semi-circular courtyard in front was filled with lorries and motors, some with their engines running and pumping smelly exhaust into the freezing air, and streams of people were milling aimlessly around. Forcing their way through the crowds and up the steps into the packed building, the twins' only concern was to get a good enough place to hear what was going on. Evelyn, leaned on, her toes stepped on, buffeted in the back by burly workmen, began to wish strenuously that she had not come. The Suvarovs seemed quite unaware of what she was suffering, and pushed their way through beside Bob Adamson, using their elbows as aggressively as anyone. Together they forced a tiny space at the edge of the Ekaterina Hall and tried to listen to the impassioned speaker.

Evelyn's poor Russian meant that she could not understand what was being said, in spite of Georgii's whispered comments. She gave up trying after a while and looked around to get some understanding of the events that way. Her eye was caught by an immense gold frame that hung, empty, above the speaker. As soon as he stepped down to cheers and yells and stamping from the crowd, she asked her cousin about it.

'It used to hold a portrait of the Tsar; I don't know what happened to it.' He turned aside to speak in Russian to one of the men behind him, and then looked back to Evie. 'Some soldiers ripped it down with their bayonets only this morning.'

Evelyn looked thoughtfully at the blank framed space and said half to herself:

'But what will they put in its place?'

The man Georgii had consulted understood English, and it was he who explained in a heavy accent:

'This is Liberty, Comrade. Nothing and no one will hang in his place. Tyranny is dead. Long live Liberty.'

He was a large man, rather dirty, and he held a half-smoked cigarette in one hand and a rifle in the other, and Evelyn thought he looked dangerous. She gave him a small, cold smile of acknowledgment and turned away without speaking, but Adamson caught the expression of distaste that crossed her face. He shrugged: he too, found the empty frame an eloquent symbol, but to him it was one of hope.

A few minutes later there was a disturbance by the door and, with many of the other latecomers, Evelyn craned around to see what was happening. She saw a frightened old man being hauled through the crowd by two young soldiers. He must have been some sort of priest because he was dressed in a long black robe with a large gold cross on his chest. As he staggered, his terrified eyes looking this way and that as though desperate for some help or at least sympathy, Evelyn whispered to Georgii:

'Who is that poor man?'

'Don't waste your pity: that's the Metropolitan Pitirim – a creature of Rasputin.'

But Evelyn could not control her pity as the old man was dragged through the hall, obviously frightened for his life, taunted by the crowd.

'What are they saying, Georgii?' she asked and was surprised to see him blush.

'Oh, just insults. They are pretending that he was, well, intimate with the Tsarina and they're promising to send her to him. It's crude, but quite good humoured – and he deserves anything he gets, really he does.'

'But what will they do to him?'

'God knows. Shoot him probably. Evelyn, you must not look like that; he caused far more misery for years than he could possibly suffer now.'

But for her, at that moment, what he had done was not the point. All she could see was one man at the mercy of many hundreds. The slogans and the bonfires that had exhilarated her paled before the realisation of what 'starting again' and 'wiping out all the cruelty and tyranny' might actually mean to the people who had participated in the old regime.

The proximity of the armed and unwashed men pressing so closely all around suddenly made her feel faint. She started to breathe erratically, in great gasps, and her forehead was soon covered in sweat. She wanted to attract the twins' attention, but could not bring herself to speak. At last her hoarse panting alerted Georgii to the urgency of doing something to help her. Piotr and Bob Adamson were too wrapped up in the proceedings to have noticed, and when Georgii said caustically to them, 'Look here, Evelyn's fainting. Someone's got to take her home. I suppose it'll have to be me,' Piotr did not even reply; but Adamson looked around, and raised his eyes to heaven. How absolutely bloody typical of the silly girl, he thought. Insisting on forcing her way in on a day like today and then demanding to be taken home. Well, he was not going to miss this, the most important moment he had ever witnessed, just because a ridiculous British girl felt ill.

'Good idea,' he said. Quite apart from his own determination not to miss anything that happened on this day of days, his editor would have something to say if he did not telegraph at the first possible moment an eye-witness account of what was happening.

Georgii shrugged resentfully as he realised that yet again he was going to have to do the tedious work while his brother selfishly enjoyed himself, and then turned to push a way through the massed spectators behind them. With an arm round Evelyn's shoulders he helped her forward, murmuring encouraging words and apologies as they went.

As soon as they got outside, Evelyn began to breathe more normally.

'Thank you, Georgii. I shall be all right now. I am sorry. Do go back if you wish.' But he still did not like the look of her and dreaded to think what his father would have said if he had left her alone in amongst the rabble. He pushed all the loose snow from the top step and told her to sit down and put her head between her knees. A clumsily dressed man who was apparently standing guard with a cigarette in one hand and his rifle loosely held by the barrel in the other, slouched over to tell them to move on.

'Can't you see she's ill?' Georgii said angrily. The man shrugged, and jerked his unshaven chin at her.

'Well, be quick.'

Georgii waited until her face was pink again and her eyes looked much less wild; then he said:

'Can you walk? I think we'd better go.' Without looking again at the uncouth sentry, he shepherded Evelyn down the steps, across the littered, crowded courtyard and out into the street.

The long trudge home seemed endless, and the people they passed looked much grimmer than those they had walked among only an hour or so earlier. Evelyn knew that it was only her mood that had changed, but it did make everything look different. The fires at the Palace of Justice seemed to belch out far more smoke than before: it caught at their throats and made their eyes smart. Black smuts blew into their faces and dragged grey dirty lines across their skin.

Evelyn wiped a gloved hand across her cheeks to brush away the grime, but succeeded only in smearing it all over. She wondered sickly whether she would be able to walk all the way back to the Suvarov house and lowered her head to stare down at her feet and count her steps. In that way, she thought, she might forget how far there was to go and how much her legs ached and her feet burned.

33

She had lost count before she reached two thousand, but it was not long after that that they reached the house and found Natalia Petrovna waiting anxiously for them. As she saw them, she cried out:

'Evelyn, whatever has happened? You look terrible.'

Very tired after the long walk and the emotional tension of the morning, Evelyn found she could not answer.

'Come into the morning room.'

Evelyn followed her, expecting the reprimand she knew she deserved for staying out so long and missing the first hour of her afternoon lessons. When she had shut the door behind Natalia Petrovna, she tried to speak, but the elder woman forestalled her.

'The mail from England has arrived at last.'

Evelyn's drawn face lit up and she stretched out a hand towards Natalia Petrovna, who gave her two letters. She had a curious expression on her face that Evelyn had never seen before. In a trembling voice Natalia Petrovna said:

'Sit down here on the sofa while you read your letters.'

In that instant, Evelyn seemed to understand.

'Tony?' she whispered. Natalia Petrovna nodded. Evelyn wailed, 'No,' on a single high note, and to her cousin's consternation sank on to the sofa, bent almost double in pain.

'No,' the agonised protest came again and, really worried, Natalia Petrovna watched the girl put her head on her knees and, pulling off the shawl she had worn around her head, throw it on to the floor. Tortoiseshell pins were dragged out of her collapsing hair with the shawl, and her shoulders shook as she wept for her dead brother, for John, and for everything the war was taking from her.

'How did it happen?' she asked at last.

'Your father could not explain much in his letter to us. He only said that it happened when Captain Markham was leading his men across No Man's Land to the wire.'

Evelyn flinched and then said in a voice so composed that it sounded hard:

'I think if you will forgive me I shall go up to my room.'

That was the last any of the Suvarovs saw of Evelyn for four days. Natalia Petrovna sent up trays of the most delectable food she could think of that was still available; she sent oral messages by Anna, the maid; she sent Ekaterina Nikolaievna; she sent kindly phrased written notes; but Evelyn answered none of them. When she eventually emerged, she was pale and she looked thinner and more tired than ever, but her dark eyes were calm, her wide mouth looked resolute, and she was as perfectly dressed and tidy as she had ever been.

None of her cousins dared to speak to her of her brother and it was only Robert Adamson who thought that behind the hard coolness of her face lay a need to talk about Anthony. But Adamson's attempt to break through to her was clumsy, and she turned away from him, the pain in her face so severe that he was silenced. But for once he felt really sorry for her, and so he tried to touch her, in a gesture of comfort. She was as taut as a violin string and only looked at him angrily until he took his hand away from her arm.

He could not know that through her sorrow was beating the memory she had tried so hard to keep out of her mind. Now that Tony was dead, it was becoming almost impossible for her to believe that John could have survived. Ever since the news of his disappearance had reached her, she had told herself that while she hung on to her hope, she would be doing something to keep him alive. If she ever once allowed herself to doubt, to break the link that she still felt between them, she believed that the telegram confirming his death would come.

Now with the link begining to crack, Evelyn was unable to keep away the memory of John's handsome face as it had hung above her in the dimmed sunlight, distorted by the tears that shocked her so much, and of his hoarse, unfamiliar voice telling her about the horrors to which he must return. She had been unable to give him any comfort as she lay there on the floor of the old summer house in his parents' garden, looking up at him, aching and ashamed.

If she had not loved him so much she would never have been able to yield to his desperate pleas, she would never have gone with him to the summer house, and she would not have become indissolubly linked to him. For persuading her into that frightening surrender and then breaking up in front of her eyes when he had always been so strong and confident and right, she had almost hated him. Then had come the telegram, and her hate had seemed so cruel that she had tried to wipe the memory of it out of her mind and concentrate on the man he had always seemed to be.

Now she was beginning to find it difficult to forgive herself for concentrating so hard on John. There had been times when she had almost forgotten that Tony, too, was out there, fighting, being wounded and afraid, perhaps even as frightened as John had so astoundingly shown himself to be. Now Tony was dead.

All the happy nursery years she had spent with him were smirched in her mind, and she would never be able to think of them without pain. All his hopes and ambitions could never be achieved now. He was destroyed, dead, nothing.

Desperately trying to think of something – anything – else, she remembered Sergei Voroshilov. Why had she allowed herself even to like him? Was it not enough that she should torture herself with fear and misery about her brother and her lover? Must she also be afraid for Sergei? She did not think that she could bear to hear any more bad news of anyone for whom she cared at all.

3

For Evelyn the fact of the Revolution was entirely overtaken by her knowledge of Tony's death. When she thought of her morning in the Taurida Palace at all it was only to wonder how the Petrograd people could be so obsessed with their own affairs when an apocalyptic war was killing so many thousands of heroic men on both the Eastern and Western Fronts. What the revolutionaries might be doing to Russia scarcely troubled her as she thought of what must have happened to Tony.

All she knew for certain was that he had been killed leading his men to the wire and that word conjured up some of her most frightening nightmares. John had, in his one terrifying moment of weakness, told her that one of the things the men hated most at the Front was watching their friends spread-eagled on the barbed wire, not quite dead, and calling out to their comrades for help. She would never be able to forget the tone in which he had said, 'They always look as though they've been crucified.' Now in her dreams and waking nightmares it was always that picture she saw, and it was always Tony's voice she heard calling futilely across the mud and craters of No Man's Land.

Struggling to contain her terrors and not let her misery show, it did not once occur to her to escape the Revolution and go back to England. Sometimes she thought wistfully of her home, but always in connection with either Tony or John. She had no wish to go home to live in England without them, and she was too worn out to face the prospect of a renewed battle with her parents. If she could not follow Tony and John to the Front as a nurse she would prefer to stay in Russia.

She tried not to think of the trenches and the suffering Tony must have endured, but there were times when she could not help it. She tried not to wait for news of Sergei, but every letter that was brought to the house put her in a fever of guilt and fear. It seemed impossible to forget the war whatever else she tried to do. Her fears and memories so obsessed her that at times she could hardly answer rationally the simplest question any of her cousins put to her, and she never seemed to hear the conversations that swirled about the dinner table each evening.

It was some weeks before she began to understand what had actually happened in Russia. For a time she did not notice even the most obvious signs in her cousins' house: the disappearance of white bread from their table; or the growing surliness and unruly behaviour of the servants. The first thing that broke through her consciousness was the twins' increasingly heated anger. They had always quarrelled, but never before had she seen them looking as though they hated each other.

One morning in early July Evelyn actually listened to what they were saying and she could not believe what she heard. When Robert Adamson, who was sitting beside her on a sofa in the morning room, felt her jerk upright, he turned to see her staring white-faced at her cousins. When he asked her what the matter was she said:

'What has happened? Why did Georgii say that?'

'What?'

'That Piotr was a traitor who wanted the Germans to win the war.'

For the first time in weeks Bob Adamson really looked at her and noticed that her big eyes had no life left in them, her skin looked thick and heavy, and her mouth was slack with worry as she turned to him for an answer.

'Miss Markham, you must know what they are arguing about,' he protested. When he saw that she really did not, he reminded himself that she had lost both her brother and her fiancé in the war, as he gathered together the rags of his patience to try to explain. 'You know that after the Revolution a provisional government was set up?' Evelyn nodded. Relieved to get some rational reaction from her, he went on, trying to simplify the turmoils of the Revolution for her. 'Most of the members of the government are from the Cadet party.'

'Like Georgii?' she suggested, sounding puzzled.

'That's right. Most of the middle-class intelligentsia belonged to the Cadets, and they, like the Provisional Government, want to carry on with the war, because they believe that your country and France will help them if they do and abandon them if they do not. Piotr, like most of the opposition parties — the Bolsheviki and the Social-Revolutionaries and so on — believes that there is no hope for Russia's survival unless she is allowed to leave the fighting. He thinks — as I do — that the Provisional Government won't be able to hold on to their power much longer.'

A furious voice interrupted him:

'Only because of the machinations of your damned left-wing parties. If my dear brother and the cursed Bolsheviki would only put Russia before their insane desire for world revolution, we could all work together and save our country.'

'Georgii, please explain to me what is happening,' begged Evelyn, flinching from the anger in his voice.

'I'm surprised you're interested,' he was beginning, when Bob Adamson said through his teeth:

'There is no need to be so offensive, Suvarov. Don't you understand what your cousin has been going through?'

Evelyn's mind was in such a turmoil that she did not even notice his championship and just waited for Georgii's explanation.

'Well, Evelyn, if you really don't know, this is what has happened. After the Revolution, Prince Lvov formed a government, which has been recognised by all the other Allies. They are struggling to wring some kind of order out of the shambles left by the Tsar and his ministers and they are thwarted at every turn by the other parties and factions in the Duma, the worst of which are the Bolsheviki. They want to ensure that revolutions like ours break out in all the countries of Europe – and America. And they want the Germans to defeat us so that the country is smashed to nothing. Then they can pick their way about the ruins and force their damned tyranny on us.'

'I don't understand. What are they doing?'

Adamson opened his mouth to try to explain, but Georgii rushed in to speak first.

'They are inciting the men to desert from the Front. They are having it put about that great estates are being broken up all over Russia and that land will be handed over to any man who is there in his village to be given it. And they are encouraging the men to murder their officers.'

Piotr had listened in silence to his brother's wild indictment. When he was certain that it was over, he rubbed his thin hand across his eyes, pushing away his hair, and said quietly:

'Georgii, you know that's not true. Why do you help spread such lies?' He turned back to look at Evelyn and tried to explain: 'It is true that some of the most hated officers have been assassinated, but you can't blame those poor devils, who have spent the last two years being made to stand up there and be killed without even a rifle to defend themselves, if they do anything they can to stop the madness.'

Evelyn's head began to swim. She could not believe what she was hearing and she wondered how she had escaped the knowledge of what was happening. The thought of Sergei facing not only the Hun, but also his own murderous men horrified her. She looked from one twin to the other and then across the sofa to where the American was now standing.

'Mr Adamson, it is not true, is it?'

'Which bit? Officers certainly have been killed and there are many desertions.'

It was impossible to believe any of them, since each one had his own axe to grind. She badly wanted a disinterested intelligence to help her sort out truth from propaganda. The only person she could think of was Andrei Alexandrovitch. He had demonstrated often enough how much he disliked the factions that were snarling over the decaying body of the Autocracy, and his arrogance and severity no longer seemed a barrier. She believed that he would know what was really happening and she went in search of him.

It was not until she had looked for him in his smoking room and the library that it dawned on her that in the middle of a weekday morning he would be at the timber works. She heard the front door bang and ran into the hall desperately hoping that it might be he. But when she got there she could see no one except the one remaining footman. He told her rudely that the twins had just gone out. She was turning to climb the stairs to the schoolroom when Natalia Petrovna came clumsily down towards her, saying:

'Where are the boys? Where's Peterkin?'

'He's just gone out with Georgii and Mr Adamson,' said Evelyn, noticing that Natalia Petrovna looked almost as distraught as she felt. 'Has something happened? Has there been any news of Sergei?'

'Of course not,' snapped her cousin. 'But I need . . .' She stopped speaking and almost dragged Evelyn into the salon. 'I don't trust any of the servants,' she whispered. 'I've just heard that parties of the men they call Red Guards are visiting all the houses near here to steal all the food. I must have Andrei Alexandrovitch here and the telephone has been cut off again. The boys must go and fetch him.'

Something in her cousin's hysterical voice helped to calm Evelyn and she said almost coolly:

'There's no way of knowing where they've gone. I shall have to go to fetch your husband.'

'But you can't. A young girl alone out in the streets? I could never forgive myself if something happened. And how will you know the way? There are no cabs again because of the strike at Kronstadt.'

Evelyn felt suddenly ashamed that she had been so absorbed in her personal sadness that she had been unaware of what had really been taking place around her. She wanted to make some kind of amends to Natalia Petrovna for her selfishness.

'I could take a tram. I know that there are some that go to the Vyborg district and surely the driver or someone could tell me where to go.'

The desire for her husband's protection was stronger than Natalia Petrovna's convictions about the unsuitability of young girls walking alone through the streets of a notorious district, and she told herself that although there were demonstrations by the sailors who were stationed at Kronstadt, they would not affect the main parts of the city, and so she reluctantly accepted Evelyn's offer, adding:

'But you must take Dindin with you. Two girls together should be safe. I could not let you go alone. No,' she went on, seeing that Evelyn was about to argue, 'my mind is made up. Go and change your shoes and I'll fetch Dindin.' Evelyn obeyed, apprehensive but determined to do what she could. She was surprised to find that Dindin was excited when they met in the hall, and irritated to see that she was wearing a fashionable and expensive-looking hat.

'Oh, Dindin, really! Why are you dressed like that? Go up and change – and put a shawl round your head. You know we must look inconspicuous.'

'And look like a servant . . . or a Bolshevik? Certainly not. Evie, you know my father likes us all to be properly dressed; he's always criticising Piotr's clothes. He wouldn't . . .'

'It is just not safe nowadays to go out dressed like that. You'll only draw attention to us. Please change.'

The girl stamped her foot and her pretty face set in sulkily determined lines. For the first time, Evelyn realised how much Dindin would resemble her mother when she was older. She shrugged. There was no time to waste quarrelling.

'Well, it's your funeral. Come on. We can't waste any more time.' The first tram that passed their nearest stop in the Nevski Prospekt was so full that passengers were already clinging to the step in serious danger of being pushed off, and Evie refused to let Dindin even try to board it. But the next was slightly emptier and they managed to squeeze a space for themselves inside.

'Where to, Comrades?' asked the conductor, jamming one of her elbows in Evelyn's back and nearly winding her as she balanced herself against the swaying of the tram.

'Vyborg,' answered Evelyn in her obviously foreign accent, holding out a handful of small change.

'That's a big area, Comrade. Whereabouts?'

'We want the Suvarov Timber Works.'

'Going to the meeting then? I didn't know they'd let foreigners in,' said the woman taking some of Evelyn's money and handing two tickets in exchange. Evelyn could see that she was looking critically at Dindin and obviously wondering why so obvious a *bourguika* would be going to a factory soviet's meeting. Tucking the ends of her own worn grey shawl into the waistband of her shabby black skirt, Evelyn said briefly:

'The meeting. Yes. Thank you, er, Comrade. Can you tell me when we reach the right stop?'

'I haven't time to act as city guide, Comrade,' she answered, but then something in Evelyn's face or voice made her relent enough to say: 'Someone will tell you when we're over the river. Suvarov's is well enough known.' The heavy sarcasm in her voice made Evelyn wonder for the first time whether Piotr's well-known dislike of his father's business might have some basis other than his own absurdity, but she said nothing more. Dindin whispered to her in English:

'What did she mean?'

'I don't know. But don't let's talk about it now. What do you suppose is happening out there?' said Evelyn, peering out of the grimy windows to a large crowd gathered round a speaker.

'Oh, only some meeting. There seem to be meetings about everything these days.' But as she spoke so dismissively the unmistakable sound of shooting hit them both. They waited, tense, surrounded by apparently unconcerned Russians, but the sounds were not repeated. There had been no real trouble since March, but both girls remembered enough of what they had seen and heard about then to dread a repetition. Evelyn was just wondering how she would get them both home if the striking sailors were to infect the rest of Petrograd

43

and they found themselves in the middle of another demonstration when the swaying overcrowded tram jerked to a stop, the iron wheels screaming in the tramlines.

Thrown backwards almost into the lap of a large and unfriendly-looking woman with a basket on her knees, Dindin saved herself by twisting her body violently and putting one arm out to steady herself against the window.

'Evie, look!' she said urgently but softly and still in English. Together they watched a dark-green armoured car bustling importantly across the lines in front of their tram, twin red flags stiffly flying from the bonnet. It was followed by an open truck filled with young men in peaked caps and working clothes, each one carrying a rifle and most of them wearing great belts of bullets slung ropewise across their shoulders.

'What can be happening?' whispered Dindin.

'I don't know, but I don't think we should look too interested. We must be almost at the river. It can't be long now.'

Evelyn hoped that she was right. She felt as though all the other passengers on the bus were staring at Dindin's ridiculous hat, and all of them seemed hostile. They were clearly as bad as her cousin's servants: insolent and greedy. Suddenly she saw a man stand up and put both his hands on Dindin's shoulders. The girl flinched violently and Evelyn braced herself to intervene. But all he wanted was to make enough space to squeeze past her in order to get off the tram. Evelyn sighed in relief and wondered how much more she would be able to bear.

They saw the Neva embankment about five minutes later and knew that their ordeal was almost over. As soon as they reached the Suvarov Works, the two girls knew they would have nothing more to worry about. Evelyn leaned towards one of the least villainous-looking men and asked in her broken Russian whether he could tell her which stop they would need, and even smiled a little to herself as he said, 'Yes, Comrade', but she did not like the way he looked at her cousin. The man nodded his head towards a large building they were passing on the left, and as the light fell slantwise across his face, Evelyn saw how dirty and unshaven he was.

She felt a sickening mixture of disgust and fright, but all he said to them was:

'The fortress of Peter and Paul, Comrades, where the enemies of the Revolution are held. Old Suvarov should be one of 'em. It won't be long now to his infernal factory; just across that small bridge. Then when you get off you take the first left and then the second right.'

Enemies of the Revolution, thought Evelyn. Well, we are both that. Bitter enemies of the Revolution. Oh, why did that idiotic girl wear her stupid hat? And why didn't I make her change? How are we going to get out of this? She could feel panic closing in on her and gripped her purse between her hands to try to stop them shaking. She could not bear to look at Dindin, just silently begged her not to arouse the dislike of these people in whose power they now were.

Then Evelyn realised that she had not listened properly to the man's directions and she started to ask him to repeat them. But her voice came out like a croak and he did not understand. She coughed to clear her throat and managed to say reasonably clearly:

'The second right, did you say?'

'Da,' he said simply, nodding, and at that moment the tram drew up at its stop.

The two girls had to force their way off the tram and it took them so long to push through the crowd that the tram had begun to move before Evelyn could get off it. She had to jump off, but landed safely, and together the two girls turned off to follow the man's directions.

As they left the main road, they were both shocked to find that the side streets were not cobbled and that they had to pick their way through mud, made sticky by the last night's rain. There did not seem to be anyone about, and all they could see were the high blank factory walls that towered over them and the thick, blackish-grey smoke that unfolded itself out of tall brick chimneys. Everything seemed dirty and strange, a world away from the broad elegant streets they had left on the other side of the Troitski Bridge.

They could hear trains chugging by a few blocks away, and the clatter of machinery from somewhere closer; then a man's shout, suddenly harsh. Evelyn instinctively whipped round to see where it had come from. Turning, she slipped into the grey-brown mud, wrenching her left ankle back under her as she fell. Dindin had not realised what was happening and was hurrying onwards, her head down so that she should see and smell as little as possible of her surroundings. Evelyn tried to get up and, failing, called out:

'Dindin! Help me, please.' The girl stopped at last, about a hundred feet away, and turned in consternation. Just then a man, perhaps the one who had shouted, came running out of a narrow cavernous passage between two vast buildings, and grabbed at Dindin's purse. She pulled it back, saying haughtily, quite unaware of any danger:

'What do you think you are doing? Let go at once.'

Evelyn, trying to stand and get to her cousin, watched powerless as he put one large hand on her cousin's shoulder and the other on her wrist and jerked one of her arms high up behind her back. The agonised screams forced Evelyn to get to her feet and limp towards the man, who was now pushing Dindin against the grimy brick wall and grabbing at her pearl necklace. Evelyn was terrified of what he might do to Dindin and shouted loudly as she limped towards them, trying to ignore the pain that seemed to scream up from her ankle through her spine to her head every time she put her left foot to the ground. As she got closer, she saw that the hairy, dirty man had both his hands at her cousin's neck, fumbling among the lace trimmings of her bodice. A nightmare mixture of disgust and terror forced her on. As she reached him she grabbed at the greasy collar of his coat and pulled for all she was worth, screaming out:

'You beast, you beast! Leave her alone. You horrible man. Dindin run, run!'

She did not see him turn, but she felt a tremendous blow across the side of her face and she slipped back into the mud. A sharp pain exploded in her side as his heavy boot crunched into her ribs and she screamed. There was nothing she could do to stop him, but she hardly had time to feel the fear as she saw his hands coming to her throat. Just before she lost consciousness she thought he was killing her. In the split second of terror, she saw John's face, and she thought that he smiled at her in welcome.

When she came back to consciousness the first thing she saw was Dindin's white face hanging over her. The memory of what had happened returned in a rush. She tried to get up and said faintly:

'Dindin, are you all right?' A tear fell on her face and her cousin tried to wipe it away.

'Oh Evie, you shouldn't worry about me. You saved me. Papa is here.'

'Thank God,' she said and shut her eyes again. She heard his voice capably directing some men he had with him and soon felt herself lifted into his motor car. When she heard the door banged shut, she opened her eyes. To her astonishment he smiled down at her and his voice had lost its rasping edge.

'We shall get you home, Evelyn.'

That reminded her of her errand and she said:

'Natalia Petrovna . . . She sent us because she needed you.'

He patted her hand.

'Yes I know. Dindin told me when she came running to fetch me.'

'Fetched you?' repeated Evelyn, puzzled and wincing from the pain in her ribs as she drew in her breath too deeply.

'Yes, you let her escape from that pig and she came for me.'

'What happened to him?' Evelyn asked, shuddering.

'He ran off as we came round the corner. We couldn't catch him. One of those damned anarchists I imagine. He got your purses and Dindin's pearls. But none of that matters compared to your . . .' Uncharacteristically he stopped, and her imagination had to supply the rest of the sentence.

By the time they reached the Suvarov house the shock of what had happened began to reach Evelyn, and she started to shake. She caught her lower lip between her teeth and held on to her skirt with both hands to try to control herself, but the reaction was too strong, and she felt as though every muscle in her body was locked into a separate spasm. Andrei Alexandrovitch understood and called the chauffeur to come and carry her into the house. Then he followed, his arm round his chastened, tear-stained daughter.

Natalia Petrovna met them almost before they were through the front door, bursting with indignation that they had taken so long and raging at what she saw as the rape of her larders. But the hot fury in her husband's blue eyes, let alone the sight of Evelyn's terribly bruised face, silenced her almost as soon as she had begun her tirade. When both girls had been put to bed and the doctor had administered sedatives, Andrei turned his attention to his wife.

Much of the horror she had felt had been overtaken by what she had learned of the ordeal to which she had subjected her daughter – and Evelyn. But she had to reconstruct it to justify herself to her wrathful husband. She told him how the Red Guards had come to their house only half an hour after the girls had left, and how the leader was a young man of birth and education. In fact that had been almost the worst of it: he had called her Madame Suvarova in the old courteous way, and he might almost have been a friend of one of her sons coming to call if it had not been for the ugly, violent-looking men with him.

She had tried to explain to the young leader who was stealing her food that none of it was hoarded; the stores were no different from any she had kept before the Revolution; that any self-respecting mistress of any house would have cupboards full of dried, bottled, smoked or pickled meat, eggs, vegetables and fruit. But the raider, charming though he looked, had said:

'That is why we made the Revolution, Madame Suvarova. While you had your cupboards full of expensive delicacies, outside your warm, rich house people were starving. Now you must just scavenge like the rest of us.'

'And how am I expected to feed my family and my servants? I have nearly twenty people in the house, my good man, and someone must provide for them.'

'They are hardly "yours", Madame, and they must take their chance with the rest of the city,' he said, the courtesy seeming only to underline the brutalities of the world into which she had been plunged. She had had to stand beside

48

him, wondering desperately when Evelyn would bring Andrei home, as the rough workmen carried past her all the smoked hams and reindeer tongues, pressed caviare, bottled vegetables, sacks of flour and sugar and coffee. Whole cheeses were trundled out in their wooden cradles through the hall and down the front steps, and Natalia Petrovna had only just enough control not to order the men to use the tradesmen's entrance and not risk damaging the marble floor of her gracious hall.

When it was all done, the young man had smiled as though he had enjoyed the whole episode and bowed to her, thanking her for her contribution to the Revolution. Hating him for the sarcasm and for his treachery to their class, she had said nothing; but the instant he had left after his men, she had called imperiously for one of the servants to shut the door and when she thought she detected a reflection of the young man's smile on his face she rounded on him and berated him for his insolence.

He, in turn, had betrayed her by saying as angrily:

'I do not have to listen to this any more, Comrade. I am leaving.' And he had gone, just like that, taking his few miserable possessions with him and leaving her even more short-handed than ever. Having told her story to her husband, Natalia Petrovna finished up pathetically:

'And you left me here alone to face that, to watch those brutal men stealing all our children's food.'

He felt rage, hot and dangerous, surging up through him and he wanted to force into her stupidity some realisation of what was really happening outside her house and to what she had condemned the two girls, children almost, because of her absurd obsession with her larders and her servants. But he had long ago recognised that she had neither the will nor the capacity to tackle anything unpleasant and that his own life was slightly easier if he kept her serene, and so, ignoring the riots, the sounds of guns in the streets nearby, and what had happened to his daughter, all he said was:

'Did you not say they had guns, my love? There is little I could have done except die in defence of your larder.'

'Don't mock me, Andrei Alexandrovitch. You did not have

to suffer as I did, and you do not have to worry about the feeding of all these people. And the servants are leaving, more every day. You don't understand how difficult it is without a housekeeper. I have never had to worry about this kind of thing before and it is too difficult.'

'Well at least the servants' leaving means that there will be fewer mouths to feed. No, Natasha, I am not laughing at you. But you must face the fact that until order is restored, there is nothing we can do. Most of Petrograd is close to starving. You will just have to do what you can. Be thankful they have not requisitioned the house – yet. And that we at least can afford to buy what food there is.'

She closed her eyes at the thought of losing her house and of all the other things that might happen and said from the bottom of her heart:

'I wish to God that the Germans would arrive. They would soon stop all this nonsense.' She turned away from him and was distressed to see Evelyn standing in the doorway about five feet away. Her dark eyes were appalled and stared out of a face that was the colour of unbaked clay, disfigured by the huge bruise, already yellowing at the edges, and the cut lips, which were swollen and deep red. Natalia Petrovna hurried forward.

'Evelyn, my dear, you ought to be in bed. Come along, I'll take you back up and tell them to bring you some hot milk with sugar in it. Come.'

Evelyn resisted the kindly pressure of Natalia Petrovna's plump arm and said:

'Did you mean what you just said? You cannot have meant it.'

'Never mind about it now. Come back to bed.' As Evelyn still resisted, her cousin tried to explain: 'Evelyn, at least the Germans would know how to keep order. There would be proper arrangements for distributing the food and the streets would be safe enough even for young girls. I hate what happened to you and Dindin. I shall never be able to let you go out alone again – you will all be ill if you never take walks. But come along now. We won't talk about it until you're better.'

Evelyn gave up and went with her, to lie in bed pretending to sleep. Natalia Petrovna sat beside her until she was certain that the pretence had become reality and then went downstairs in search of her husband.

'Andrei Alexandrovitch, why can't we go away this year? If we could at least get out of Petrograd . . . I know we can't go to Finland any more, but even Archangel would be better than this. You know how I hate that house, but we can't stay here.'

'And how much of this house do you think we should find when we got back? This situation cannot possibly continue. Either the Provisional Government will pull itself together, discipline the Kronstadt sailors and institute some kind of order, or someone else will take over, and we shall be able to get back to normal.'

Natalia Petrovna shuddered to think what the revolutionaries might do to her house if it were left undefended. After all, they had walked in and seized all her food and no one had been able to stop them. She thought of her paintings and the ikons she had brought with her when she married, and the furniture she had selected so carefully over the years, and pictured them all splintered and desecrated.

'But what if it's worse? I mean, what if these people of Peterkin's, these Bolsheviki take over?' Her husband was able to laugh sardonically at that ludicrous possibility.

'I wish you wouldn't call him by that ridiculous name. You're not at all English, and even there it's never used outside the nursery. But you needn't worry about your son's irresponsible friends; they're the least powerful opposition faction in the Duma, despite their destructive influence on the factory workers and deserting troops. They could not possibly form any kind of government. As far as I can gather they can't agree about anything among themselves. Trotsky is said to be all for the war and the other one wants anything, defeat even, that will stop it. They're never going to be able to organise each other, let alone anyone else.'

4

It was weeks before Evelyn could forget what had happened to her in the Vyborg, and the prospect of leaving the house filled her with such dread that she could no longer take Natalie and Sasha out for their afternoon walks. What had happened to her was trivial in comparison with what her brother must have suffered and she despised herself for not being able to shake off her fears. Her dreams were filled with men who came at her with strong grabbing hands and cruel faces, and sleep no longer seemed to promise peace. She read for hours after she went to bed and wrote letter after letter, anything to put off the moment when she would have to turn out the lamp and remember everything that had happened and think about the things that might have happened if Dindin had not brought her father in time.

The cracked ribs had healed and the bruises on her face faded long before she had learned how to come to terms with her memories. But gradually the increasing affection the Suvarovs showed her had an effect and she learned to ignore what had been done to her in the Vyborg.

Her whole relationship with her cousins began to change. Andrei Alexandrovitch no longer seemed to her to be like some wild beast ready to spring, perhaps because the respect and gratitude he had felt for her when he realised what she had done for his daughter, and at what risk to herself, deepened during the summer into something approaching real affection; and the twins, to whom he confided the full story of what had happened, became much more open with their

English cousin. They no longer treated her as a kind of second-class sister, to be mocked when she said things they disliked or patronisingly admitted into their confidence when she behaved herself. Instead it was as though she had become a person to them. As for Dindin, her hero-worship and her resentment alike dissolved into trust.

By the week of Evelyn's twentieth birthday in early November she had almost overcome the whole Vyborg incident, and when Andrei Alexandrovitch told her that her birthday would be a celebration for them all she even felt a kind of anticipation. He did not tell her that it had been with the greatest difficulty that he had wrung from Piotr a promise to join the rest of the family. Andrei Alexandrovitch did not know what his second son was up to, but there was some trouble brewing, he felt sure. Still he was determined that his family should be united in their observance of Evelyn's birthday. Without her his daughter might have been killed – or worse – and so he had demanded Piotr's presence.

When Andrei Alexandrovitch and his wife asked Evelyn whether she would prefer to hear Chaliapin sing or see Karsarvina dance, she chose the opera and decided to wear the garnet silk she had had made for the previous Christmas. She had not worn it since then and so the evening before her birthday she rang the bell in her bedroom in order to give Anna, her maid, the necessary orders to hang the dress out and press it. To her dismay the girl to whom she had always tried to be kind looked insolently at her.

'No, *baryshnia*, I will not press out your gown, nor come to your room to dress you tomorrow.'

'Annoushka, you must not talk like that . . .' Evelyn was beginning, but the maid interrupted: 'Why not? We have Liberty now. No one can make me do anything now that I don't want.'

A feeling that was very like hate rushed through Evelyn in a hot tide. So, Anna had now joined the hordes of resentful, ungrateful people who had spawned the man who had beaten her and Dindin.

'You will do as you are told or I shall speak to Madame Suvarova at once,' she said.

'So what?' demanded the maid. 'She can't make me slave for you any more and she won't either, Miss Markham, because she knows that she will find no one else to wait in queues for her or cook her food or clean her house. Now that there are only four of us left, she knows how much she needs us.'

Remembering her dignity just in time to prevent her from slapping the girl's taunting face or shouting at her, Evelyn said quietly:

'I think you will regret what you have just said.' She then left the room without waiting for any response, and went straight to her cousin, whose reaction was just as Anna had foretold.

'Evelyn, please don't make me dismiss the girl. It is impossible to get any servants and if she goes too, the others will join her and I don't know what we should do. See what you can do to smooth things out, please.'

'You sound almost as though you want me to apologise to her,' said Evelyn, shocked and hurt.

'Oh, would you? That would be such a good thing. And I know that Dindin will help you to dress tomorrow. Please do not be angry, Evie.'

'Apologise to a servant! For asking her to do what she is paid to do? What can you be thinking of, Cousin Natasha? If the servants get out of hand, you know, nothing will ever be straight again.'

'But, Evelyn, be reasonable: we have had a revolution. Nothing is ever going to be the same again; and it will be so much worse if you – any of us – offend even the few women who are still prepared to work for us.'

'Cousin Andrei says that everything is simmering down well. He told me yesterday that everyone seems to agree that the Revolution has gone on long enough and it is time to start reorganising normal life. I was only trying to do my part.'

Her cousin looked doubtful, secured an undertaking that Evelyn would do nothing more to upset the remaining servants and went reluctantly down to the kitchens herself to listen to Anna's imprecations against the *Anglichanka*, and calm her down.

Evelyn left the room in such a rage that she could hardly think at all, and almost despised her good-naturedly selfish, indolent cousin. She slept very little and awoke the next morning feeling that something momentous and terrible was about to happen. As she sat brushing her own hair before the glass, she traced the sensation to the previous evening's quarrel and squashed it down as far as she could, determined to enjoy her birthday, and not to think at all about the servants or the Revolution.

It turned out to be not so difficult after all. Her cousins had been kidnapping all the letters and parcels that had arrived for her over the previous week, and, with their own presents, had made a great pile for her on one of the Boulle tables in the salon. She opened theirs first, although she longed for news of her real family, because it seemed only polite to show them that she was grateful for the trouble they were taking over her.

The youngest children had made her a little book in which they had written out their favourite English story. It was the one that she had first told them, and Natalie had put it down in her best handwriting while Sasha had decorated it with little pictures. As she turned its pages, four-year-old Sasha stood beside her chair, pointing out its glories and telling her which pictures he had drawn himself and to which Natalie had contributed. Evelyn could hardly believe that they should have taken so much trouble for her and felt silly tears at the corners of her eyes. To disguise them, she hugged Sasha and laid her head on his silky black straight hair for a second. Then she looked up at the two of them, who stood hand in hand in front of her, and said:

'It's lovely. The nicest present I have ever had. Thank you very much.'

They were pleased that she appreciated their efforts, but Natalie was a little embarrassed by the fervour of her thanks and quickly directed her attention to their parents' parcel.

'See what Mama has for you, Evie,' she said in French. 'It

is wonderful, truly.' Evelyn laughed kindly at her and said to her mother:

'You are all being much too kind to me. No one at home ever made so much fuss over my birthday.'

But when she had opened their huge parcel she could not speak at all. They had given her a quite magnificent fur coat: thick and glossy black sable, the most luxurious and expensive fur there was in all Russia. They watched her white hands helplessly stroking it, feeling the sumptuous texture. She lifted her head at last and said:

'Cousin Natasha, Cousin Andrei, I . . . I don't know any words. You should not give me something like this. It's far, far too much.'

'Silly child,' said her cousin. 'Andrei Alexandrovitch, tell her how silly she is.'

'Never that, Evelyn. But we are very grateful for what you have done for Dindin, and we knew that you needed a proper coat. Winter is coming, and it may be very bad this year,' he added, thinking silently: and I, at least, feel guilty that we have involved you in the terrible things that have been happening in Russia. And I wish to God that I could get you home and out of the trouble that may be coming.

'Try it on, Evie,' said Dindin, excited and very envious. The tension broke into laughter, and Evelyn stood up while Dindin helped her to put the coat on. It fell in glamorous folds around her, and she turned its great collar up round her pale face, and gently caressed her cheek against its softness. A long, slow smile – almost sensuous, thought Georgii – dragged at her lips, and her eyelids lowered until the black lashes brushed the yet darker fur.

'You look wonderful,' cried Dindin. 'Look!' And she turned her cousin round so that she could see her reflection in the tall gold-framed glass that hung above the inlaid table.

Piotr, coming deliberately late to the small celebration and deliberately ignoring his father's angry rebuke, could not help admiring the picture that he saw, although its reality disgusted him in a city that was supposed to have revolted against riches and privilege. She stood in front of the black and gold table, gilt wrapping paper strewn around her feet, framed in the ornate gilded carving of the pier glass, looking quite ravishing, more relaxed than he had ever seen her. Forgetting for a moment the myriad problems he had to sort out, he smiled and rather wished that Bob could have seen Evelyn like that. He might have changed his tune about her coldness if he could have seen the way she smiled then. Catching sight of his reflection in the glass, Evelyn turned from her own to hold out her hand and say, 'Piotr, it is days since I saw you.'

The conflict of feelings she had aroused in him made him feel a little of Bob's often vaunted antagonism and instead of shaking her hand, he put a small, plain-wrapped packet into it.

'Yes, Evie. I, too, have brought you a gift.' He half expected a reprimand for deliberately misunderstanding her gesture of welcome, or perhaps an angry blush and a tightening of those beautiful lips, but she only smiled at him. When she had undone the white paper and revealed a cheap copy of *Capital* by Karl Marx, her smile even widened.

'Oh, Piotr Andreivitch, you are trying to corrupt me.'

'No, Evelyn, to counteract the corruption of all this.' His thin hand swept out to embrace the richness of the room and the shameful extravagance of the fur. She slipped her shoulders out of the coat and laid it reverently on a chair.

'Well, I promise to read it, but I won't promise to believe any of it.'

At that he, too, laughed.

'If you even read one chapter you will have won my bet with Bob. You can tell him yourself tonight at the opera.'

'Is he coming with us then?' she asked, more coolly, disliking the fact that they had been betting on something to do with her, and not wanting her birthday evening to be spoiled with his sarcasm and too-obvious dislike.

'Not with us, no. But he has a ticket – and he especially likes *Boris Godunov*, or so he tells me.'

He smiled to himself as he remembered the conversation they had had the evening before when he and Georgii, their bitter quarrels submerged for once, had shared a frugal supper in Adamson's flat. It had been almost like the old days before the Revolution when their differences were only academic. They deliberately avoided talking politics and the conversation was frivolous as they laughed at each other and made all the old jokes. When Bob had poured them a glass from the last bottle of brandy he asked:

'So tell me – how is the *Anglichanka*? I haven't seen her in weeks. Has she got over it yet?'

'I think so. She seems all right, Bob,' answered Piotr judicially. 'I wish that it hadn't happened, and I feel desperately sorry for her, but it has had one good result. She seems more settled now – and we get far less of what they do in Yorkshire and how a lady is supposed to behave.'

'Well that's something. I've sometimes thought she can't be as stupid as she makes herself out to be, and when it mattered she was darned brave, wasn't she?'

'Do I detect a certain admiration for our English cousin?' asked Georgii, sipping his brandy. 'I thought you had foresworn women since your great disillusionment in Petrograd.'

'But Georgii, you must have noticed: he can hardly keep his hands off her,' said Piotr, laughing.

Georgii looked from one to the other, noticing Piotr's mischievous grin and Adamson's rueful smile.

'But, Bob, you can't bear her,' protested Georgii, who had noticed nothing of the kind. 'Didn't you tell me weeks ago that she is the symbol of everything you most dislike and mistrust about the idle kept women of the capitalist classes?'

Bob's self-mocking smile deepened and the corners of his wide mouth turned downwards.

'Unfortunately a guy's senses can play traitor to his reason. But don't look so shocked, Georgii Andreivitch, I know too much about women to give in to my baser instincts. I can't stand the girl.'

'I can't imagine desiring a woman I disliked,' said Piotr meditatively, but Georgii, swirling the last of the brandy round the bottom of his glass, murmured provocatively:

'Nina Rybakova?'

'Actresses are different,' said his brother more sharply, and then relaxed back into teasing their friend. 'But, Bob, I wonder how long you'll be able to resist that mixture of cool beauty, luxuriant glossy hair, slender bones, perfect lips, huge eyes . . .?'

'Stop, you tormenter,' he protested, laughing. 'She's a tiresome, stupid girl who happens to be packaged in a way that tickles my fancy. But unlike you two young boys, I'm too old a hand to be taken in by packaging.'

Piotr laughed again and then said irrelevantly:

'She told me the other day that her brother – the dead one, I mean – used to call her "Old Toffee-Apple Eyes" because that's what he thought they looked like.'

'That's a bit unfair,' said his brother. 'They're not the least protuberant – or sticky-looking.'

'No, but I know what he meant,' offered Bob, trying yet again to joke himself out of the unsettling emotions that had been aroused in him. 'They seem huge in that elegant face, and much glossier than you'd expect.'

'What is amusing you, Peterkin?' asked Natalia Petrovna, recalling him to the present.

'Nothing much, Mamenka. Just nicknames.' Then he turned to Evelyn and rephrased his answer to the question she had just asked: 'No, Bob is not actually coming with us, but he will be there and he said he'd come round to the box to offer his congratulations if you allow it.'

It was partly her determination to show Mr Adamson just what she thought of his careless dress and shocking manners, and partly a desire to appear a credit to her generous cousins, whose presents had been so much more lavish than her parents' slim garnet necklace and her brother Dick's *Golden Treasury*, that led Evelyn to take enormous care when she was dressing for the opera. She had pressed the dress herself, and cajoled Dindin into helping her with her hair. When she emerged from her room, with the new sables slung cloakwise from her white shoulders, she had every reason to feel satisfied with her appearance.

She had half expected to find the theatre full of the sort of people and atmosphere she and Dindin had encountered on the tram to the Vyborg, but to her delight the vast red-and-gold foyer was filled with ladies in low-cut gowns, displaying their finest jewels, and their escorts in perfect black-and-white dress clothes, with here and there an officer in the gorgeous uniform of one of the old fashionable regiments. It was almost as though the Revolution had never happened, and it helped Evelyn to see that her two forays into the new world of the workers were nightmares: horrible enough, but unlikely ever to be repeated. She began to believe Andrei Suvarov's view that the excesses of the last seven months were over and that even the revolutionaries themselves were anxious to get back some stability and internal peace so that they could rebuild their shattered country.

Suddenly very much happier, Evelyn smiled at Dindin, who was standing beside her almost shaking with the excitement of her first opera and her first 'grown-up' evening dress. Robert Adamson, strolling towards them through the crowd, saw the smile and recognised in it a kind of complicity with Dindin that he had never seen her show before. He was just starting to wonder whether he might have been wrong about her when all his self-protective instincts rose up and reminded him of everything he knew about beautiful women. His voice was as sardonic as ever as he greeted her:

'You're looking very lovely tonight, Miss Markham.' She heard the sarcasm and acknowledged the words with no more than a dignified inclination of her head. But Dindin answered:

'Oh, yes, isn't she? Isn't the necklace pretty? Her father asked Papa to find it for her birthday. Doesn't it suit her?'

'You must not get so excited, Dindin. Oh, listen. There's the bell, and your mother is beckoning. Come along. Good evening, Mr Adamson.'

He watched them go, cursing himself mildly for his instinctive admiration of her looks, and frowning horribly at Piotr, who was laughing openly at him.

'I give you six months at the most, Bob,' the boy whispered as he passed in the wake of his family.

'Never!' he answered in mock dramatic tone, his hand on his heart, and went alone to his seat in the stalls.

As the opera wound onwards to its dramatic end, he found himself looking up towards the Suvarovs' box and watching her face, wondering why he should find her quite so beautiful – and why he could not forget her. He had never suffered from such a violent mixture of emotions about any woman before, and he tried to tell himself that it was only because of her pretty face, oddly foreshortened now by the angle from which he looked up at her, and her exasperating attitudes. But as she sat, erect in her gilt chair, her head turned slightly away from him, looking down at the stage, he could not help looking more at her than at the singers, and wondering about what she was really like. It was hard to believe that the person she seemed to be would have risked so much for Dindin – or that Piotr could like someone as artificial and stupid as she made herself appear; and it was clear that Piotr did like her. But Bob was determined never again to allow his susceptibility to land him in the kind of mess he had tumbled into when he first came to Petrograd and fell in love with a beautiful woman who turned out to be shallow, selfish and obsessed with money. The memory of his misjudgment could still bring an unpleasant taste into his mouth whenever he thought of it, and the episode had cured him for all time of mistaking physical desire for anything else.

For her part, Evelyn was quite unaware of him, absorbed as she was with the scenes played out on the stage. She had never been taken to the opera in England, and she found much of the posturing absurd, and often thought that the unnecessary elaboration of a simple narrative was typical of the over-rich stuffiness of the life she had discovered in Petrograd, but when Chaliapin himself was singing she was transported.

The great voice seemed to vibrate through her body, and the power and majesty of it held her in complete subjection. When he was not singing she studied his stocky figure in the incongruously gorgeous costumes and wondered how such an ordinary-looking man could produce sounds of such magnificence, but when he sang she could only listen.

When it was over and the astounding voice had died into silence for the last time before the elaborate swagged and fringed velvet curtains swung down and hid the stage, Evelyn felt a piercing regret. She wanted to sit quietly for a while and think about what she had just heard, but Natalia Petrovna seemed anxious to get home and hurried her out of the box. Evelyn left, looking regretfully back into the opera house.

'Come,' said Andrei Alexandrovitch offering her his arm. She took it and allowed him to lead her down the grand staircase to the foyer, where he sent Piotr for the ladies' coats and Georgii to alert the chauffeur. As soon as the car was at the door, he handed the ladies in and announced that he and the boys would be following on foot.

Sitting comfortably in her own motor, a pleasant and conventional evening behind her and the streets around them apparently peaceful, Natalia Petrovna shared Evelyn's satisfaction with the end of the upsets brought by the Revolution. She had had no more visits from Red Guards, and her husband had used his many contacts to ensure that her larders were as full as ever. On the few occasions when she thought about what had happened to her daughter and Evelyn in July she felt all the old horror, and so she never did think of it if she could help it. She lay back against the soft pale-grey upholstery of the motor car and watched the two girls.

Dindin was chattering excitedly about what she had seen, and repeating all the compliments she had been paid, and so Evelyn's silence was hardly noticeable. But at last it became apparent even to Natalia Petrovna and during a pause in her daughter's prattle she said:

'Did you dislike this evening's performance, Evelyn?'

The English girl smiled slowly, almost falteringly, and said:

'How could I have disliked it, Cousin Natasha? It was wonderful, of course, but there was more to it than I had expected. I can't really explain it, but listening to that voice seemed to tell me that there is much more in life than I had thought about.'

'Such as?' asked Dindin, interested enough to forget her own success for a moment.

'I don't know: it just seemed to tell me . . . I can't explain. I'm sorry.'

'Don't be, Evie. It's what Piotr used to say about you — that there were whole worlds you knew nothing about.'

'Don't be childish, Dindin, and don't repeat things other people have said to you,' snapped Evelyn, her elation spoiled and collapsing. 'It was silly of me to try and tell you.'

She felt so angry that she would have gone straight upstairs when they got home had not Natalia Petrovna said:

'Ring for the *samovar*, would you, Evelyn? I think we all need some tea after that chilly drive.' Always obedient, she pulled the bell and when one of the last remaining servants appeared, she gave the necessary orders. Then she walked slowly round the room as Dindin sat beside her mother and asked questions about some of the notable people who had been pointed out to her in the boxes near the Suvarovs' own. Evelyn felt restless as well as angry, about she knew not what, except that she longed for someone to talk to who would have understood, or at least tried to understand what she was trying to talk about, and who would not sneer or laugh at her even when she was silly. For once she did not think of any of the young men who had been filling her mind. She had never talked to any of them in the way she wanted to talk now.

'Evelyn, come and sit down and have a glass of tea. You are making me quite tired prowling around like that.' Reluctantly she turned.

'I beg your pardon, Cousin Natasha. Thank you.' She accepted the long glass in its silver holder, and sat straight-backed on a low chair by the white-and-gold porcelain stove. She had just taken her first sip of the strong, aromatic tea when they all heard urgent voices in the hall outside. She and Natalia Petrovna exchanged surprised looks as the door was slammed back against the crimson damask wall.

Andrei Suvarov stood there, his hat in his hand and his astrakhan coat flung open. He said, appalled and angry:

'Adamson has just told us that the Prime Minister has fled and the Bolsheviki have seized power. The Bolsheviki!'

The satisfactions of the evening were smashed beyond repair. Evelyn said without waiting for anyone else to speak:

'I don't believe it. You told me that that could never happen. All that was finished, done with. After the July Days they were stopped, exiled again. You told me yourself that it was all over.'

'I thought it was. Like others, I have been misled. Oh, for heaven's sake, Dindin, don't cry like a fool.'

It was the first time any of them had heard him speak to his daughter in such tones and Natalia Petrovna, who had put a plump arm around her daughter's shaking shoulders, said:

'How could you be so thoughtless? Announcing such news in so brutal a way. You know Dindin hates loud voices. And after we had all had such a pleasant evening, too.'

Her husband looked at her as though she were a complete stranger, and said:

'God knows how long they will be able to keep this supremacy. But while it lasts you will all have to be extremely careful.' He came into the room and put his hat on a small side table. 'Come in, Adamson.'

Evelyn watched the tall broad-shouldered American as he strolled towards her, and could not help the words that rushed out of her.

'I suppose you are pleased with this news.'

The hate in her voice stopped him dead, about four yards away from her. He looked down at her, his mouth twisting into a smile that seemed to be half a grimace of pain, and his hands stuffed nonchalantly into his pockets.

'Yes,' he said. 'I think it is the only way forward. You must know that the Provisional Government was losing what little support it had ever had, and was quite incapable of saving this country.'

Evelyn did not speak but the scorn in her face was too much, and he turned his back on her to rejoin Piotr, who alone shared his ideals.

'Piotr, I must get back to the Smolny Institute and find out what is happening so that I can telegraph first thing in the morning. Are you coming?'

Evelyn wanted to protest, but Andrei Suvarov did it for her.

'Certainly not, Adamson. I am grateful for the intelligence you brought us, but neither of my sons will be present at a Bolshevik conspiracy to subvert my country from her allies. My son will stay here.'

Piotr looked at his father and wondered why he had ever been afraid of him, and why he had not just walked out of the house months and months ago. The Revolution had shown him at long last that no one could exercise power over you unless you submitted. All it took to free yourself was resolution and a determination not to be frightened by the loneliness of freedom. Trying to keep the sound of triumph out of his voice, he said with great formality:

'No, Andrei Alexandrovitch Suvarov, I shall not stay.' Piotr could feel the whole family suddenly still and he recognised an intoxicating feeling of power. 'You have no right to give me orders. And I shall go with Bob to the Smolny Institute. Georgii?' His eyes seemed to narrow as he looked at his brother.

Georgii looked away and found himself face to face with his father. Evelyn could see no change in Andrei Alexandrovitch's expression but Georgii flushed and clumsily nodded as though in submission. Piotr saw the gesture, too, and, remembering the warmth and friendship they had regained that one evening in Adamson's flat, he walked towards his twin. Ignoring their father, he put a hand on Georgii's shoulder.

'Georgii, he is only a man. The state will take over the works now, and make him and you and me equal with the rest of them. You do not have to submit to him ever again. Be strong for once, and do what you believe in.'

Georgii moved sharply and pushed his brother's hand away. His face looked closed in and bitter once more. Their moment of easy friendship might never have happened. There was venom in his voice as he said:

'Yes, you would enjoy taking me with you, wouldn't you? You hate the family now and would do anything to spite them. It would be like extra sugar in your *pashka* to prove that you could get me away from them. You don't believe in the Bolsheviki at all: you are just doing what you know will hurt our father most. It is only revenge.'

'For God's sake!' cried Evelyn, burying her face in her hands. As though she had touched some switch and released the others, they all started to talk at once. Dindin ran to

Georgii and put her arms round him, begging him not to leave her and telling him she loved him.

Andrei Suvarov stood his ground and said to his second son:

'You have one chance to undo the harm you have started. Will you stay and apologise?'

Piotr did not even answer. His expression of disdain said everything. His father threw back his head and in the tones of a judge passing sentence, said:

'Then you are no longer my son. No house of mine will ever give you shelter. And I never want to see you again.'

After a long, tense moment, Piotr shrugged and said:

'So be it.'

He turned away.

Natalia Petrovna heaved herself up from the sofa and ran to her favourite child, crying:

'Petrushka, where are you going? Please stay here; it must be dangerous out there tonight. Petrushka, please stay.'

He looked down at her plump, wrinkled, tearstained face for a moment, as though he still had a decision to make. Then with a determined expression that hid his sudden doubts, he put her away from him, detached her clinging hands and walked away.

In the unhappy days that followed, Natalia Petrovna would say to Georgii whenever she saw him:

'Where is your brother? Where's my Peterkin?' All Georgii could say was:

'Mama, I have told you often: I do not know where my twin brother is, or what he is doing. He joined the Bolsheviki even before he went to university: you knew that; and you know what they want to do – how they want to drag us all down to the levels of our own servants.'

'My Peterkin? You must be mad. He would never do anything like that.' Then her voice hardened. 'You always were jealous of him, weren't you? And now you are trying to turn me against him.'

His eyes closed and he gripped the bridge of his nose for a moment. Then he looked at his mother, who had always ignored him when his twin was in the house.

'Jealous! No, Mama, I was not and am not jealous. I think he is a dangerous fool, and if I could stop him, I would for his own sake. But he spends all his days at the Smolny Institute, and I can't get near him. They know that I'm a Cadet and they hate us because we know what they are trying to do. Unlike these deluded workers and "Red Guards", we know that they care nothing for Russia. They only want their precious Revolution to break out all over Europe and they will lay my country to waste to do it. Then they will leave for Europe and someone else will have to clean up after them.'

Evelyn listened to such exchanges day after day, becoming more and more worried that no one would be strong enough to stop the Bolsheviki and save Russia. The only thing that gave her any hope as the snow began to fall and winter started in earnest on 15 November was a report she heard that Lev Davidovitch Trotsky, People's Commissar for War, had said:

'Either the Revolution will create a revolutionary movement in Europe, or the European powers will crush the Revolution.'

Evelyn waited for that day.

5

Evelyn waited, too, for news of Sergei Voroshilov, as she had waited for almost a year. Soon after her birthday, it occurred to her that Sergei's face was far clearer in her mind than either her brother's or John's, and that worried her. She had known Sergei for only a week or so and he meant nothing to her compared with the others, and yet it was his flashing dark eyes and high cheekbones that she saw when she closed her eyes. Having slowly learned to accept that Tony was dead, Evelyn still fought to believe that Johnnie was alive, and to keep the link firm between them.

But sometimes it was hard to concentrate on her good memories of him, his kindness, his loyalty and protectiveness, the gaiety of his approach to life before the war. In the frightening disintegration she could see all around her Johnnie had no place. He could know nothing of the Revolution and its consequences, and just sometimes Evelyn wondered how she would ever be able to explain it all to him when they found each other again. Sergei, of course, would know at once what she meant from the slightest reference to the bread riots or the Taurida Palace or the July Days. It was a curiously upsetting admission to have to make, even to herself, and it renewed her determination to hold John in her mind, whatever else she had to think about.

Then on 29 November came the news that Evelyn at least had half expected. Sergei was missing. There was no proof that he had been killed by his own men, but so many officers had died that way that it seemed horribly likely.

The news almost broke Evelyn and she waited only until she could control her voice and be certain that she would not cry before going to Andrei Alexandrovitch.

'Cousin Andrei, I . . . Can I go home? I know I'm not supposed to until the war is over, but . . .'

Mercifully he interrupted and saved her from trying to put her multifarious reasons into words.

'Evelyn, I wish that I could get you home. It's been in my mind for weeks now. But our present masters are not giving exit permits to any English at the moment.'

'What?' she demanded and then, remembering her manners, said more quietly: 'I beg your pardon, but I don't understand. Do you mean that they can force us to stay here?'

'Yes. Just that. Without a permit you would be stopped at the frontier and probably arrested.'

'But why should they do such a thing? They hate us; there isn't enough food in the city anyway for its real inhabitants. Why should they want to keep us foreigners here?'

'As a way of trying to force your government to allow two of their leading revolutionaries out of England. They've been in prison there and your government is refusing to let them out.'

For the first time Evelyn felt the Revolution actually touch *her*: she was no longer a bystander. The man who had beaten her might have been its product, but he was not a deliberate part of it, and when he had assaulted her it had only been because she had been there. His victim could have been any defenceless woman. Whereas this, this virtual imprisonment, was different. It felt as though it were aimed specifically at her. Now she could no longer feel herself a neutral observer, albeit sympathetic to the Suvarovs in their increasingly unpleasant plight. She, too, was a victim, hated as they were hated, and a target for the Bolshevik malice. Knowing that Piotr was a member of the Bolshevik party, she found herself blaming him for it, and yet it was hard for her to believe that the boy who had teased her, skated with her, sat beside her at dinners, concerts and ballets, could belong to a group of men who would do such a thing to her.

'But how long . . .?' she said, and then: 'I'm sorry Andrei Alexandrovitch, I know you couldn't possibly know the answer to that.'

'No, I don't. But I can promise you that as soon as there is a way to get you out, whatever it takes, I shall do it.' He looked at her, admiring the coolness with which she was struggling with her obvious fear and so he did his best.

'If conditions get worse here, and I am afraid they may, I shall take you all up to Archangel.'

Her dark brows straightened to meet across the bridge of her nose as she frowned.

'But that's up in the Arctic. Surely no one can live up there. I know you go sometimes to visit your forests there, but you can't live in it, can you?'

At that shocked protest, he even laughed. 'Not quite in the Arctic, my dear, and many people live there. My family has always had a summer home in a town called Shenkursk, which is only about five hundred miles north of here; we don't use it now, because Natalia Petrovna dislikes it and has always insisted on our going to Finland for the summer, but it is a perfectly comfortable house. I think we might all be safer out of the way up there, and it would be easier to get to Archangel itself from there if necessary.' She looked at him in puzzled surprise and he went on:

'Don't talk about this to anyone else, but as it's a port from which there has always been a lot of traffic to England it might be much easier to get you out from there – on an English ship, perhaps. My manager up there is English and he will know the best way of doing it. I can't find out any-thing from here, because of course all our letters are read by those swine; but he's a competent man and he's worked for your father in the past.'

Evelyn's face relaxed a little. If there were an Englishman, a former employee of her father's side of the business, in Russia ready to help her get home, things would look a lot brighter. As a way of thanking her cousin for the reassurance; Evelyn said:

'Andrei Alexandrovitch, I am so sorry about Piotr . . .' She got no further. He looked murderously angry, and she was vividly reminded of the fear she had felt in her first weeks in his house.

'That is not a name I wish to hear spoken. Do you understand me, Evelyn?'

'I beg your pardon,' she said, asking herself how any parent could behave so to his son. Was it pride that made him so tyrannical, or was there some kind of fear in him that made it impossible for him to allow his sons the freedom to think and say what they wanted? For the first time, it dawned on Evelyn that until his father had driven him into outright rebellion, Piotr had done nothing that any young man might not have done too. What hidden weakness could there be in Andrei Suvarov that could not allow him to trust his sons and let them be their own men? Unaware of the way her face had hardened, she left him and went back to the schoolroom, determined to do her best to keep the household as normal as possible for the sake of Natalie and Sasha, who missed Piotr so much and talked about him in a way that told Evelyn more about his gentler side than anything he himself had ever done or said.

That determination was badly shaken only the following day when another party of Red Guards stormed into the house in search of hoarded food. Evelyn had been sitting with Natalia Petrovna in the morning room when they arrived and so she saw at first hand what happened. This time the leader of the raiding party was no gentleman and the roughness with which he spoke to Natalia Petrovna really frightened Evelyn.

She stood, powerless and trembling with anger and terror, as the men loaded their cart with the contents of all the larders and store cupboards. Then, adding the last touch to Natalia Petrovna's torment, the leader of the Red Guards turned to Anna and the one other remaining servant and said:

'And what are you doing here in this rat hole of the bourgeoisie, Comrades? Come and join us. Leave these vermin to their own filth.'

Anna, whose insolence had grown with every new piece of evidence that people like the Suvarovs were losing their influence, threw off her apron.

'Yes, you're right. Why should I slave like this and take orders as if I was some kind of animal? I'm as good as them.'

Evelyn, whose hatred of the maid had become almost an obsession, said through clenched teeth:

'And how do you think you will live, Annoushka?' The usually affectionate diminutive was spoken with such suppressed rage that the girl flushed. 'Who fed you, housed you, clothed you, taught you civilised behaviour?'

'And made me sleep on the floor and all that. You can take a turn at it now, Miss. You can sweat down here in summer and freeze in winter cooking, and you can break your back lugging trays upstairs, and cans of hot water. You can find out what it's like to be so tired at the end of the day that even the floor seems a comfortable place to sleep, and be told to be thankful for scraps and hand-me-down frocks. And may you rot!' She scrambled up and followed the laden Red Guards out of the door with the other maid.

Natalia Petrovna sat down at the sticky, dirty kitchen table, put her head on her arms and wept. Evelyn looked at her and saw how thinly the grey hair had had to be distributed over the horsehair pads that supported it around her head and felt great pity – and anger. She could understand the hopelessness Natalia Petrovna must feel, and the desperation at being faced with feeding and clothing the household without servants, but she could not understand her giving way. Natalia Petrovna was in charge; it was her responsibility. Evelyn said in as neutral a tone as possible:

'Cousin Natasha, come along upstairs. The *samovar* is already in the morning room; come and have a glass of tea while I do something about this unspeakable filth.' She looked round the squalid, greasy kitchen and wondered how she would be able to touch anything in it without being sick. Then, to cheer them both up, she added: 'And if there is no food in the shops, we can always ask that English journalist Mr Adamson told us about to fish in the river for us too.'

Natalia Petrovna was beyond understanding a joke, but at least she lifted her head. Evelyn saw that little bits of old food from the table were clinging to her cousin's hair, and waited to hear what she would say.

'But I can't abide freshwater fish. Oh, Evelyn, what will we do? If only Peterkin were here.'

'Well! There's nothing he would do, beastly Bolshevik that he is. Try not to worry, Cousin Natasha, I shall get this cleaned up and find something we can eat for luncheon.'

'But how can you? You know nothing more about cleaning and cooking than I.' Evelyn, her irritation rising, forebore to say that she knew considerably more since in Yorkshire they at least oversaw their servants' work and inspected the kitchens and servants' quarters every day to ensure that everything in the house was properly cleaned and hygienic. Instead she said:

'I'll do my best; and I expect Ekaterina Nikolaievna will help me, and perhaps Dindin and the children, too. Now you come along and rest.' Evelyn made her cousin get up, and shepherded her out of the room and upstairs, thinking that at least if she were out of the way and not having to be comforted, it might be possible to do what had to be done. Then she went up to the schoolroom, where she found the governess and all three children.

Dindin greeted her ecstatically, showing too obviously how bored her lessons made her, but the Russian governess tightened her thin lips and said instantly:

'Pray have the goodness, *Mademoiselle*, not to interrupt my classes. You have done enough to damage this family. Dina Andreievna will come to you for English conversation after luncheon; until then, please do not interfere.'

Holding on to her temper with difficulty, Evelyn said in French:

'There will be no luncheon, *Mademoiselle*, unless I have some help from you and Dindin. The last of the servants have disappeared and the Red Guards have stripped the larders again. Someone must go to fetch today's bread ration, and since I do not expect you would be prepared to scrub the kitchen floor, you had better go for the bread.'

'I? With my chest? Stand out there in the snow in a bread queue? You must be out of your mind. I am employed to teach these children and that is what I was endeavouring to do when you came bursting into my room. Please leave.'

'Don't you understand?' began Evelyn, but then the closed obstinacy of the thin grey face stopped her. 'Well, Dindin, will you at least make a start with the kitchen while I go for the bread?' She knew that she could never ask Dindin to go out in the street after what had almost happened to her in the Vyborg during the July Days, but the girl said:

'Of course I will, Evie, but couldn't Georgii go for the bread? I know he is up in his room.'

'Is he? Thank God. Well, will you go down and start to wash the cups and things from breakfast – they're all in the sink – while I go and tell him?'

'Can I help, Evie?' The shrill voice stopped Evelyn as she was turning to go, and she looked down at little Alexander. His face was eager and his eyes were shining.

'Yes, Sasha, my little dove: of course you may. Go with Dindin, and I'll come down in a moment.'

'Mademoiselle Markham, I must protest. No, Natalie, stay where you are.' Evelyn spun round as the little girl smothered her disappointment and obeyed. The clear fury in Evelyn's eyes made the Russian woman shrink back in her chair.

'If you won't help, the least you can do is to stay out of the way, you frightful . . .' She gasped and bit back the last three words she had been going to say. Without waiting for any response, she left the room and walked down the passage to Georgii's private little study. She was in too much of a hurry to knock and so she marched straight in to find him kneeling at his fireplace in his shirtsleeves, feeding the fire with sheets from a pile of papers. She shut the door behind her and at the sound he looked round. The fear in his face shocked her.

'What on earth are you doing, Georgii?'

'None of your business, Cousin. Please forget what you have seen, and go away.'

'I can't. I need your help.' He had already turned back to his task and so she repeated the plea. 'I need you, Georgii Andreivitch.'

'I'm sorry, Evelyn, I can't stop. Try someone else.'

'There is no one else. All the servants have gone. The food has been taken again. Your mother is in such a state that I've sent her to put her feet up in the morning room. Your father is not here. Ekaterina Nikolaievna is worse than useless. Dindin mustn't go out alone. I would, but if I do, they'll never get the kitchen in a state in which we can prepare food.'

Without stopping his careful burning, Georgii said to her:

'It can't be me. I must get all these destroyed.' Then, deciding that he must make her understand: 'We have heard that the Bolsheviki are going to outlaw the Cadets, and my delightful brother will no doubt have told them about my place in the party. If they come here and find all these . . . Well, they must not, that's all.'

'What are they?' she asked, coming closer.

'Better that you don't know.' He looked up at her, and saw from the shock in her brown eyes that she understood.

'As soon as I have finished, I'll come down.' She turned to go, understanding that she would get no help except from the children until either Georgii or his father could spare her some of the time they felt they had to spend on their far more important work. Resenting them, afraid that she would not be able to do what had to be done, she went heavily downstairs.

She averted her eyes from the sight of Dindin standing on an upturned bucket at the sink, her sleeves already soaked with dishwater above the elbows, and searched for any food that might have escaped the raiders' keen eyes. All she could find was a little of the coarse black bread the servants had always eaten and a small bag of potatoes. Well, they would just have to do, she decided, and then undid the ten small buttons of each cuff and rolled the sleeves well up her arms, before tying an old sack around her waist as an apron and making a start on her self-imposed task.

By the time she had swept the floor, scrubbed the table and refilled two buckets with clean water to start the floor-scrubbing, her back was aching, and so were her arms and the backs of her legs. She had broken two fingernails and she could feel herself sweating unpleasantly all over. She plumped down on to her knees on the floor, dipped the big scrubbing brush in water, rubbed it on a cake of hard yellow soap and bent forwards. As she put the brush down, the shadows in the corner nearest to it began to move. Faint with disgust, she put her hand to her forehead and then she saw that the shadows were in reality black beetles, cockroaches, that scuttled out of their hiding place and ran past her. Suppressing a childish desire to scream, she sat back on her heels for a moment to recover. Then she heard Sasha's voice:

'Dindin, Dindin, who's that at the back door?'

Before Evelyn could stop the girl, she had run to the door to open it. Evelyn just leaned forward to her scrubbing brush, not wanting to see whatever was going to happen next, but then she heard Dindin say: 'Mr Adamson, isn't it terrible? We have nothing to eat for luncheon and all the servants have gone and we are having to do all their work.'

'So, you have come to jeer, have you?' said Evelyn in a biting voice.

'No,' he said, his voice almost gentle as he took in her tiredness and her dishevelled hair and dress. 'To help. Georgii called to say you needed help.'

'Not from a Bolshevik,' she said and turned away to scrub hard at the floor.

'Don't be silly,' he said almost reverting to his old tone of voice. Before she could say anything else, Dindin intervened.

'We do, we do, Mr Adamson. We need someone to collect the bread ration; and to find us some food. They took it all!' There was outrage in her voice. Evelyn, scrubbing away, sitting back on her heels to rinse the brush and swinging forward to scrub again, wondered at the lack of fear in it. Dindin did not seem to understand how desperate their situation was becoming.

'OK,' came his voice. 'I'll see what I can do. So long then, Miss Markham.'

Evelyn did not answer. She was determined to have finished scrubbing and to be tidy and in control when he came back. She hated the idea that he should have seen her so degraded.

Dindin, who had finished the washing up, came to give Evelyn a hand, and little Sasha brought cans of fresh water whenever they were needed, although Evelyn would not let him even try to lift one of the big galvanised iron buckets.

'But I can, Evie, honestly. Look. They're not heavy, really,' he said, his small face already red with the effort. She smiled at him and ruffled his dark hair with her dirty hand and said:

'No, no, little one. Put it down. I'll carry them.' She pushed herself up off her aching knees and straightened her back agonisingly before picking up the heavy buckets. When some of the evil dirty water slopped over the edge she felt ready to swear, but Sasha quickly mopped it up with a cloth he had found, and his sympathy turned her anger into an almost tearful laugh. She hauled the buckets up to the old stone sink one at a time and watched the filthy, scummy water slosh round and slowly seep down the drain, leaving a rim of greasy muck round the sink.

They had just finished and were all three standing tired but triumphant surveying their achievement when Robert Adamson reappeared. He dumped a couple of packages on the table.

'I am sorry, but I couldn't get much. There's a mass of *halva* here that I found in a shop off the Liteini, and more potatoes. I wish I could have done better for you. Now I'll peel these spuds for you.'

'The what, Mr Adamson?' asked Sasha, interested in the unfamiliar word.

'Potatoes, Sasha. They need scrubbing and then peeling.'

'Oh, no, not more scrubbing,' said Evelyn involuntarily. He looked down at her, and smiled in a way that she had never seen him smile before.

'Don't worry, Miss Markham, not that kind of scrubbing. Sasha and I'll just hold them under the faucet and rub the mud off. I must say you have made a great job of this floor. You sit down. Now, Dina Andreievna, can you find something to cook them in? No, not a skillet – a pan. I think that one.' He pointed to a large black pan beside the range, and Evelyn knew that she ought to insist that it was scoured. She even opened her mouth to say something, but he took off the lid and rinsed it himself.

'Oh, well, it's clean enough, I suppose,' he said before filling it with water. 'Now, Dindin, put it on the range. Yes, that's right.'

Evelyn sat down at the table abruptly and pushed the heavy dark hair away from her forehead. She wondered vaguely how he knew what to do and assumed that in spite of his education he must come from a very poor family in America where he had had to learn that sort of thing. She was trying to think of an inoffensive way to ask whether she was right when he said:

'Where's Andrei Alexandrovitch?'

'At the works, I suppose. He usually is.'

'I don't think so. They've been taken over by the State.'

When Evelyn did not answer, he turned from his potato-peeling at the sink and, seeing that her face had closed in once more, said:

'Now what's up?'

'I suppose I should have realised that you had come here just to spy.'

At that he dropped potato and knife into the water, splashing Sasha and the newly bright floor, and came over to where she was sitting. She turned her face abruptly away. But he put one of his strong, wet hands under her chin, forcing her head round to face him again.

'Miss Markham, will you stop it? I came because Georgii told me that you needed help, and I had time. The telegraph office is shut and so I can't do any work. I am not a Bolshevik agent. I am not a Bolshevik. I am a foreign correspondent watching the affairs of this country for a paper in my own.'

Evelyn looked him full in the eyes, and he was distracted for a moment by how magnificent she looked, her cheeks for once flushed with exercise and anger, her eyes wide open and her usually silkily perfect hair falling all about her face. But she said:

'Then you are even worse than I had thought. You took my cousin's hospitality while you tried to suborn one of his sons to a destructive, cruel political creed to which you do not even subscribe. What kind of person can you be? You have destroyed this family and now you say it was just for your newspaper.' Suddenly everything that had happened to her and to the Suvarovs in the past terrible year seemed to be his fault and she wanted to hurt him, to make him angry.

'You are despicable, a parasite and worse. You deliberately set out to damage something that may not have been perfect, but was a great deal better than what you put in its place. You are a destroyer, Mr Adamson.'

His hand dropped away from her chin.

'I guess there's no point talking with you if you're set on believing that,' he said, but he found that he could not leave the subject alone. He wanted to make her understand.

'You know nothing about this place, or the way that people without money have had to live . . . and die. Far too few people know and I'm trying in my telegrams to explain it.'

'That may be true,' said Evelyn coldly, 'but even if it is, it does not excuse the way you . . . you made Piotr behave so that he had to leave this house.'

As though he understood at last that her rage was fuelled by her regret for what had happened to Piotr, Adamson forced himself to smile at her. Then he took a deep, steady breath and tried to make her understand.

'Miss Markham, it was not I who took Piotr to the Bolsheviki, but they who introduced me to him. He had to teach me what they want, and how they have suffered to get it. Jesus, I did not bring revolution to this family. Why, even his uncle was exiled for sedition after 1905.'

'His uncle?' she repeated, surprised out of her anger.

'Yes, you knew surely? Andrei Alexandrovitch's twin brother. He was sent to Siberia after the 1905 revolution and only got back last May. You must have heard about him. He's living in Archangel now, at the Suvarov house in Shenkursk.'

'Why not here?'

'Piotr thinks it's because after Siberia he can't face the upheavals of political life. He has done his bit. No doubt he will be useful when it comes to organising the North. But first they must sort out the cities.'

'Ow!' A cry from the sink brought the antagonists back to the present. Dindin had cut her knuckle as she inexpertly sliced the skin off a large squashy potato.

Evelyn held the bleeding finger under a spout of cold water, trying not to see how the mud from the potato skins mingled with Dindin's blood, while Bob Adamson searched his pockets in vain for a clean handkerchief to use for a bandage. In the end Evelyn had to use her own, a pretty lace-edged square of delicate Irish linen that John had once given her. She watched Dindin's blood soaking through it with regret, but she thought that John would prefer it to be used for so practical a purpose than to be left in a drawer smelling of stale lavender and sad memory. Then she wondered. He had changed so much on that last day; how could she be certain any longer of what he might think or say or do? She shivered. Bob Adamson touched her cold, wet hand for a moment.

'Don't fret. It's not such a bad cut,' he said. Evelyn smiled briefly and nodded, grateful for the warmth of his hand in her sudden moment of solitude.

It was a small incident, but in some way it healed the hostility between Bob and Evelyn, and cemented the relationship between the four of them, as though they were a party of conspirators plotting against the rest of the world upstairs. When Georgii arrived, having succeeded in destroying all the incriminating documents in the house, each of them felt the contempt soldiers feel for those comfortable civilians they are dying to defend. But they allowed him to load a tray with plates and cutlery and to search for the salt, and even, once the potatoes were cooked, to carry the heavy tray upstairs to the dining room.

The difference between the two factions was even more marked when the others saw what constituted their luncheon. To Evelyn and her helpers, the boiled potatoes and sickly *halva* constituted a triumph; to the rest, a privation hardly to be endured.

Andrei Alexandrovitch arrived just in time to stop Ekaterina Nikolaievna from taking the last potato, and both she and his wife burst into explanations and excuses while Sasha and Evelyn exchanged happily amused glances. Sasha's father was more surprised to see Evelyn's uncharacteristically impish expression than the unconventional luncheon table, and so it was she whom he asked for the story. She gave him a colourless account, but Sasha and Dindin filled in the parts she had glossed over.

As he listened and watched their faces, Andrei Suvarov began to believe that the Russia into which he had been born had gone for ever. It had been becoming clear to him that the theft – or 'nationalisation' – of his giant timber works was no temporary aberration, and that even if the Bolsheviki were crushed as he fervently hoped, it could be many months before Petrograd returned even to the spurious peace of the last weeks of the Provisional Government. He thought once more of the letters he had received from his brother, begging him to bring his family up to live in Shenkursk until the troubles were over.

According to Nikolai Alexandrovitch, the Archangel Soviets were peaceful and conciliatory; there had been no burning of land or looting of the big houses; and life continued much as he remembered it from the years before his exile. Were it not for the knowledge that he would irrevocably lose the Petrograd house and much else if he left the city, Andrei would have accepted his brother's suggestion at once. As it was, he allowed himself to say:

'If this gets any worse we shall go and live in Archangel.'

'In winter? Andrei Alexandrovitch, you must be mad. No one lives there who can help it, even in summer. You know quite well that winter temperatures are as bad as minus fifty degrees. We should all die.'

'Nikki seems happy enough, and he has survived so far, Natasha.'

'But, Papa, he has had all those years' practice in Siberia,' offered Georgii, equally perturbed at the prospect of being dragged away from Petrograd, where he might actually be able to help the Cadets' cause, to Archangel, which was too far away to have any importance. Andrei Alexandrovitch left the subject then, but he was certain that it could not be long before they had to leave.

In fact, it was Christmas Eve when it became clear even to Natalia Petrovna that Arctic temperatures would be preferable to what was happening in Petrograd. At about three in the afternoon, when it was already beginning to get dark, a party of secret policemen smashed their way into the house and ransacked it in search of the papers Georgii had so prudently destroyed. The men, all of whom had once been employed by the Tsar's Okhrana, rampaged through the house, kicking down any door or cupboard that was locked without even asking for a key, removed a whole cartful of books and left the entire house looking as though it had been sacked by some barbarian army.

The men had hardly been gone for more than fifteen minutes when Piotr arrived at the house for the first time since his party had seized power in the city. He stood in the doorway of his mother's salon, looking sadly at his distraught family surrounded by the wreckage of their home. His mother's treasured Boulle cabinets had been kicked open and some of the doors wrenched off; pictures had been slashed and delicate china ornaments swept disastrously to the floor. His mother and Dindin were in tears, his twin brother was arguing violently with their father, while Evelyn was clearly trying to wrest some kind of order from the books and papers that were strewn about the great room. None of them noticed him standing there, regret written all over his face, until Sasha looked up.

'Look Evie, there's Piotr.'

At the sound of that shrill voice, Georgii stopped shouting at his father and jerked his head round to stare at his twin in contemptuous accusation. Piotr's face hardened as he saw the message in his brother's eyes. He might have said something then, if his mother had not stopped weeping and run clumsily across the room, crying:

'Peterkin, my darling. Peterkin. Thank God you are all right.'

Georgii snorted and then said:

'Mama, for God's sake! It's my dear brother's friends who have just been here to smash up your house and you're concerned for him. When will you learn? You're besotted.'

His twin put a restraining hand on their mother's arm and said:

'I came, brother, to warn you that the Cadet party is to be outlawed.'

The bitterness in Georgii's laugh shocked all of them

except Evelyn, who shared most of his feelings. Looking at the two of them, so alike, she understood a little of the anguish each must feel as his convictions cut him off from the other. She herself could not hate Piotr although she hated what he had done. She looked at the two pale, chiselled faces, mirror-images of each other even to the lines that the recent months had driven into their thin cheeks. As she watched, Piotr's face seemed to soften. Georgii's was as stony as ever.

'Oh, yes?' he said. 'Well, your family loyalty and devotion are quite mesmerising, brother. We've already had a visit from your friends in the Cheka. Did it give you satisfaction to put them on to your own family? When we made the Revolution it was to do away with the injustices like secret police and censorship and imprisonment without trial and the death penalty for political offences. For six months Russia was free – and whatever else will be forgiven you, there can be no mercy when you are brought to trial for the crime of reversing all that. You and your friends are as bad as Bloody Nikolai.'

'Georgii, that is your brother you are talking to,' said his mother, shocked into some sort of rationality. 'You must not talk to him like that.'

'Why not? It's true, Mother. He and the Bolsheviki are breaking Russia a little more every day and soon there will be nothing left except miserable workers scraping a bare living and men like him lording it over them and keeping them under a tyranny as cruel as anything the Romanovs achieved. Just wait.'

Piotr put his mother away from him and stood alone in the doorway, his plain, shabby, black breeches, blouse and damp boots in severe contrast to the ruined luxury of her salon and the formality of his brother's clothes.

'We are fighting for our lives and for the lives of all Russians. We have to stop counter-revolution in any way that we can to preserve the Revolution for the people of this country.'

'Ha!' The single, derisive sound from Georgii seemed to galvanise their father into life. He had been silent throughout the quarrel between his sons, but now he said:

'Stop, both of you. There is madness in Russia now and until it is cured we must do everything we can to stop it invading this family. Twelve years ago my brother and I quarrelled as you two are quarrelling now and it got us nothing. He has been brought to his senses by Siberia; I, by what has happened here in Petrograd. He has been begging me to take you all north to Shenkursk to wait for sanity to return and now I understand. We shall leave as soon as possible. And you two must make peace, for the family at least must not be broken.'

His eldest son listened with a kind of pitying tolerance and said:

'Papa, I am ready to make peace any time he renounces his Bolshevism and admits what he has been trying to do to Russia.'

Piotr did not even answer. Instead he addressed his father.

'There can be no peace and no family until the Revolution is safe. I will do all I can to ensure that you get away from here safely, but that must be the end. I am committed. I stay in Petrograd.'

'Piotr Andreivitch,' said his father formally but with some coldness, 'I know I said that you would never be welcome here again, but think, boy: you will not be safe either. These men are savages. When they turn on you, as they will in time, you will have no one to help you – and there will be no hope for you.' Piotr realised with amazement that his father was coming as close to pleading with him as his pride would allow. He was surprised to find himself able to feel pity for the man he had feared and loathed for so many years. He said, with no anger in his voice:

'I am one of them. But you are wrong about us: we are desperate, not savage. If you must go, then go as quickly as you can and as unobtrusively. You will have to take minimal luggage. Goodbye.'

He put out his hand, and then he let it drop as his father made no move towards him. He turned away from them, then, and heard his mother cry out.

'Peterkin, come back. Come back.'

When he did not answer, only straightening his shoulders

and lengthening his stride as he walked towards the front door, she screamed:

'You must come with us. You will be killed if you stay. Or else you will starve.' Georgii grabbed her wrist as she started to run after his brother.

'Stop it, Mama. Let him go. He's got what he wanted, and you will never make him change his mind. Good God, he's been waiting for this day for years.'

Natalia Petrovna looked at him with hatred and wrenched her hand out of his grasp. But before she could leave the salon, her husband said in his coldest voice:

'Natasha, we have no time to waste. As he said, we won't be able to take much luggage and you must sort out now what you don't want to leave behind. Remember that what is left won't be here when we come back.'

'What does that matter? What does anything matter now that you have driven my son away. You always hated him because you knew how much he meant to me.' Her husband closed his eyes for a moment as though praying for strength, and Evelyn said quickly:

'Don't worry, Cousin Andrei, I shall help, and Ekaterina Nikolaievna will give me a hand, won't you, *Mademoiselle*?' She looked round at the upright sofa, where the Russian governess was sitting, and was hard put to it not to laugh at what she saw in spite of the tragedy she had just witnessed.

The woman was half lying against the hard back of the sofa, her head lolling and the tight collar of her blouse unbuttoned, while Natalie, her most faithful pupil, was fanning her with a large handkerchief.

'Oh, pull yourself together, for heaven's sake,' said Evelyn, trying to keep the amusement out of her voice, 'you are a grown woman and you are needed. Come on.'

'You are a spiteful, jealous snake,' came the answer, in a surprisingly vigorous voice. 'You do not understand how we suffer, Natalia Petrovna and I.' Her employer looked round at the sound of her name.

'I beg your pardon, Katisha, did you say something?' she asked.

85

'No, Natalia Petrovna, of course not. I was merely telling Mademoiselle Markham . . .'

'Oh, be quiet,' ordered Andrei Alexandrovitch. 'Ekaterina Nikolaievna, go at once and help my wife to select whatever she and the girls will need for Archangel. We'll leave the day after tomorrow, please God, and anything not ready by then will be left behind for the Bolsheviki. Hurry.'

'Archangel,' the governess repeated, at last understanding what he wanted of her. 'I am not going to Archangel. I could not survive in all that cold.'

'Well then, you will just have to stay for the Bolsheviki too,' said Georgii viciously, 'and I hope you enjoy what they do to you – except I don't suppose even those degenerates would want you.'

Evelyn gaped at him in astonishment, unaware until that moment how much he had hated his erstwhile governess. Much as she disliked the woman, the crudity and violence of what he had said made her almost sympathise when Ekaterina Nikolaievna said:

'You always were a hateful, cruel boy. But don't you think I'm at your mercy. I shall go home to Rostov, to dear Natalia Petrovna's family. They will know how to treat one of their family, even if you do not.'

'By Christ, you bitch!' said Georgii, forgetting the last vestige of his manners in the strain of that moment. 'You have battened on to my mother all these years and now when you could really be of some use to her you're leaving. Well go, you old bag of bones. She doesn't need you. And nor do any of the rest of us. We shall all be glad to be rid of you.'

She gasped at his violence and looked for support to his father, but Andrei Alexandrovitch appeared unmoved. With as much dignity as she could find, she rebuttoned her blouse, turned to Natalie, who was standing shocked and frightened beside her, and said:

'Darling, you see how I am treated. When I have gone, you must try to remember me, as I shall never forget you.' Then she walked out of the room, giving Evelyn a look of searing hatred as she passed.

Shaken by the whole horrible, violent scene, Evelyn looked at the girl who was in tears, tightened her lips, and said with as much control as she could muster:

'Right, that's that, then. Now all we have to do is sort out our possessions. How much shall we be able to take, Cousin Andrei?'

'I don't know any better than you, Evelyn. Pack all your jewels, of course, in some inaccessible place, preferably sewn into your stays. Then sort out your warmest clothes to wear on the journey: I'm told that the trains are unheated now. Try to get everything into one case that you can carry yourself. I can't imagine that there will be any porters.'

He was half afraid that she would protest so that he would be left without any sensible adult female, but she did not.

'Come along, children. And you, too, Dindin. We must do our own things first, and then you can help me with your mama's.'

'Can I take my ikon, Papa?' asked Sasha in a robust voice that betrayed no fear. 'You know, the one my godfather gave me?'

'Of course,' said his father, trying not to show the irritation he felt at such an irrelevance, because he was determined that with this son he would not make the same mistakes. 'You are going to be a great help to us, Sasha, and your ikon will remind us of everything we have to fight for.'

6

Only the thought that she was on the first leg of her journey towards home and England kept Evelyn from despairing as she sat with Sasha on her knee, squashed between Natalia Petrovna and her daughters in a filthy, stinking, third-class carriage on the train to Vologda. She knew that they were lucky to have won even that much space, but the sight of four shabbily dressed, armed men sitting on the hard bench opposite her was making her shake with fear. If only Andrei Alexandrovitch and Georgii had been able to sit with them, she would have felt safer. But there was no protection – and the men looked exactly like the one who had assaulted her in the Vyborg.

Remembering how she had been taught as a very young child that to show fear towards animals was the very thing that would make them attack, she tried desperately to hide her feelings, but when one of the men spoke to her, reaching a grubby hand across the narrow gangway, she nearly screamed.

'Food, Comrade. Give us food. I know you've got some.'

Evelyn hugged Sasha tightly against her breasts, trying to reassure both him and herself. Then, refusing to look at the rifles each man had across his knees, she found enough Russian words to say:

'Comrades, we have very little, but of course we'll share with you. I do not grudge you *my* food, but please leave enough for this child.' She felt in her bag and fished out a small packet of bread and four hard-boiled eggs. The man opposite grabbed it from her hand. Her voice shaking, Evelyn said: 'Please leave some. We have nothing else with us,' hoping that neither Natalie nor Dindin would betray their knowledge of the rest of the food that had been carefully wrapped up and hidden among their bags. 'The boy is delicate enough as it is; please leave him a little.'

One of the men hawked and spat at her feet and with the fingers he had used for scratching his no-doubt lousy head, he broke off a small piece of bread and handed it to Sasha who smiled in unfeigned pleasure.

'Thank you, *Tovarisch*,' he said and took the offering. Evie was horrified by the dirt and likely germs, but she could do nothing about them – and at least the child was being fed, however inadequately. The soldier grinned back and asked Sasha a question about their journey. He answered, displaying none of the fear and disgust his sisters had such trouble hiding. Evelyn watched the man talking to Sasha in an almost jovial, kind way, and obviously taking pleasure from the perky answers. She had just begun to relax, thinking that perhaps Piotr had been right when he had tried to make her believe that there was no important difference between different kinds of people when one of the other men spat a mouthful of sunflower seeds out on to the carriage floor and scratched his groin openly and luxuriously. When Natalie shrank back against her sister and tried to push some of the seeds and spittle that had landed on her foot away with the other shoe, the man leaned forward.

'Have you never seen one, then?'

The little girl looked at him in obvious fear and incomprehension, recoiling even further from his foul breath. He roared with crude laughter and unbuttoned his trousers.

'See, that's what it's like. Take a good look.'

Natalie pressed her face into her mother's shoulder and it was Evelyn who cried out.

She put her hand over Sasha's interested face as she thought Animal!

So this is the sort of creature Piotr and Mr Adamson think

should take over this country and lord it over people like us. I knew they were mad.

All three soldiers joined in the laughter at Evelyn's reaction. Her terror was almost overtaken at that moment by the feeling that the whole world mocked and despised her. She felt she could bear no more and put her hands over her ears to shut out the cruel laughter and screamed at the top of her voice:

'John. Oh John, for God's sake.'

The carriage door was flung back and Georgii came in.

'What's happened? Mama, are you all right?' Then he saw Evelyn and, glancing across at the rough-looking men, gradually guessed at the reason for her screams. He hissed something in Russian that Evelyn did not understand and put both hands on the man's shoulders and shook him back and forth.

It must have been a full minute before the man's two friends got over their surprise and stood up to pull Georgii Suvarov away. Then one of them held his arms, while the other gave him a heavy backhanded blow across his face. His head snapped back, and they all saw the blood on his lips. At that, even Natalia Petrovna screamed. Evelyn could do nothing except hold on to Sasha and feel guilty for her part in turning an unpleasant if hardly dangerous scene into this horrible violence. She prayed that something would intervene.

Her silent pleas were answered as the train screeched to a halt and a voice called out:

'Vologda. Vologda. Everybody out.'

The armed peasants dropped their victim, picked up their rifles and grubby bundles and with a final foul insult pushed their way out and off the train. Evelyn ran to Georgii and made him sit down, examining the darkening bruise on his right cheek.

'Are you all right?' she asked urgently.

'Yes. Dazed for a moment, that's all. Don't worry.'

'Thank God,' she said devoutly, grateful at least that she had not been responsible for some dreadful injury to him. 'Where's your father?'

'He went further up the train at that last halt to see if he couldn't find seats for us nearer the engine, but . . . No, there he is . . . Look.' He waved out of the window, over the heads of all the milling passengers to attract his father's attention.

'Good. He's all right, then,' said Evelyn. 'Let's wait for a bit to let him catch up. Dindin, Natalie, will you get the bags down from that rack? Come on – it was horrid, but it could have been much worse.' The least she could do in reparation was to take charge of the children and, telling herself that at least the men had not touched any of them, she got them all off the train with their baggage, and then persuaded Georgii to find out about their new train.

Diligent enquiries revealed that the next train for Archangel would not be leaving until three the next morning. Georgii asked the only station official he could find whether they could at least board the train, but he refused permission, pointing to the crowded, filthy platform and saying:

'Wait there, with the rest.'

Realising that their only hope of escaping disaster lay in dumb acceptance, Evelyn led the way over to a relatively empty spot at the back of the platform by the station building, only to discover that it had been used as a latrine. Wrinkling her nose and trying hard not to breathe in, she turned her back on it and searched until she found them enough space to sit down.

There they stayed throughout the night, violently hungry, increasingly cold – and frightened. Evelyn leaned back against the piled baggage and felt Sasha fall asleep in her arms. Taking comfort from the soft regularity of his breathing, she endured the long hours.

Despite all the much more dramatic things that had happened, the thought that obsessed her as she waited throughout that cold horrible night was that she had had to leave her dressing-case behind. Rationally she knew that she had had no option. It was far too heavy for her to carry and it would have held almost nothing compared to the soft canvas bag she had brought. But it had been the most generous present her parents had ever given her, and she now understood as she had not at the time that it had been a way for them to

91

express the real sympathy they had felt for her when they heard of John's disappearance.

At the time she had thought that they could not understand how she felt, and the only words either of them had been able to find had been stiff and had sounded unsympathetic. But they had gone out and ordered for her the most luxurious possible dressing-case, with her initials engraved on all the silver tops to the bottles and the backs of the brushes. Understanding at last the feelings that must have prompted them, she wished that she had not had to leave the case for the Bolshevik and anarchist thieves who were probably ransacking the house at that very moment.

As the night passed and her back and legs grew stiffer and more painful, she thought more and more of her home and parents and wondered why she was stuck in such a frightful situation, trying to take care of these cousins of her father. They had no real claim on her, yet she felt herself to be responsible for them. The beginnings of resentful anger seemed to be forming in the depths of her mind when Sasha stirred in his sleep and put out a hand which fell on one of Evelyn's. The slightly damp fingers drifted across the back of her hand, feeling almost like grapes as they touched her skin. She tightened her arms round him and felt him turn a little against her breast. Dropping her head until her cheek lay on his hair, she thought that perhaps this was why she had unthinkingly accepted both the situation and the responsibility. Sasha might not have been born to her, but he seemed to be her own child as she held him. He trusted her, needed her, and was warm in her arms. In that security, so different from anything she had known in the midst of her own family in the bleakness of their Yorkshire life, she even slept.

It was not until dawn that the doors of the train were opened and by then the Suvarovs were all so cramped and cold that they could not move with the speed necessary to secure seats on the train. As they forced their way into the clogged corridor, eight-year-old Natalie made an effort to raise their spirits and said, croaking a little:

'Well, at least we're together now, and there are no soldiers near us.'

'Well done,' whispered Evelyn, pleased to see that the little girl who had always hidden in Ekaterina Nikolaievna's skirts was doing her best. 'Could you hold Sasha for a few minutes, while I see to your Mama?'

'Of course, Evie.'

Evelyn then squeezed herself between her cousins and the partition and knelt down in front of Natalia Petrovna, whose plump white face seemed to have shrunk against her cheekbones, and whose eyes were blank and dazed.

'Cousin Natasha, it should not be too long now.'

The elder woman looked at her vaguely, but she said nothing, and so Evelyn tried again.

'Are you hungry, Cousin? We have some potato cakes. Could you eat one?'

'Yes, thank you, Evelyn. I should like that,' she said, apparently in control of herself. Evelyn pushed her way back to her own place, opened her bag with difficulty and, fumbling in the folds of her precious sable coat, found a limp, parchment-wrapped packet. She untied the string and taking one soft potato cake for herself, passed the rest along the line. She heard Natalia Petrovna thank Dindin and, taking the last cake, say:

'But there isn't one for Piotr. What will he eat?'

Evelyn put her head back against the cold glass of the train window behind her, unable to bear the thought that her cousin was pretending that nothing very bad had happened and that life would soon return to normal. Her eldest son patted her carefully on the shoulder, and said as calmly as he could:

'Now, now, Mama. You know quite well that Piotr stayed behind in Petrograd. He will have plenty to eat in that restaurant at the Smolny Institute.'

'Oh, yes,' she said, smiling at Georgii. 'When will he come back to us? My little Peterkin, he must be in such terrible danger all alone in Petrograd. Who will see that he wears enough clothes and eats properly? He is always bad at looking after himself. I am so worried about him.'

'Well!' hissed Natalie into Evelyn's right ear. 'Isn't she worried about the rest of us? She jolly well should be. Look at Sasha: he's only four, but is she anxious about him? No – only for that pig traitor.'

'Hush, Tallie,' said Evelyn, using her cousin's nursery nickname for the first time. 'She can't help it. Try to get some sleep.'

But none of them managed to sleep much, and it was a full fourteen hours before the train even moved out of Vologda Station. They tried to keep each other amused with guessing games and the retelling of old favourite stories, but by the time the train actually started, they were all argumentative with exhaustion. Andrei Alexandrovitch uncharacteristically allowed them each three sips from his flask of brandy, and Evelyn sanctioned a round of hard-boiled eggs for their one meal.

It took three days for their train to limp its way four hundred miles up the track towards Archangel. For Evelyn and her charges, they were days of strain and vile discomfort. There were no sanitary arrangements on the train and the only possibilities for washing or getting hot water for tea came whenever the train stopped at small country stations. Evelyn told herself that the journey would end in time and that she had no option but to wait. But there were times when she longed to beat her fists on the steamed-up windows or fling open the train door and get out, even though she knew that the single railway track was crossing a waste of frozen marsh, forest and lake in which she would have no chance of survival.

During their last day on the train a peasant family vacated a whole carriage and Evelyn was quick to commandeer it for the Suvarovs. Sitting down at last, even on a hard, splintery bench, with the prospect of release from its purgatory within the next twenty-four hours, the whole family cheered up. The children began to pester their father for stories of the house they had never seen, and what he had done there when he was their age. He obliged, dredging his mind for long-forgotten memories. After a while he turned to his eldest son, and said:

'You're very quiet. What's bothering you?'

'Apart from worrying about our future, our houses, our lands and our business, Father?' He laughed bitterly. 'I've been trying to decide what to do. There's no point in my wasting time at Shenkursk. I'll go on up to Archangel and find out what's happening.'

'You certainly won't,' said his father. 'I need you to help my brother get your mother and the girls to Shenkursk. I have to go up to Archangel to talk to Baines and discover whether there is anything left of the company and if he's managing to get any timber out of Murmansk; and there's no point two of us going. No,' he added as his son started to protest. 'I don't want you to get involved in anything dangerous at the moment.' He did not specify what he meant and Evelyn wondered, feeling sick, what the danger was that would have threatened Georgii in Archangel.

But the young man understood exactly what his father meant, and felt all the old resentment that Piotr should have so easily escaped from their father's tyranny. In spite of Piotr's example, Georgii was still too much afraid of his father to do more than say petulantly:

'And what if Uncle Nikki is not at the station? He can hardly have any idea when this God-forsaken train is likely to arrive, even if he did get your message that we would be on it. If he is not there, will you still go on?'

'We'll meet that when we come to it. No, Georgii, I won't have it. Leave it alone.'

After that exchange, no one dared to expect Nikolai Alexandrovitch, but to their delight when the train at last drew into Nyandoma station, Andrei Suvarov, who had been peering through the misted windows, called:

'He is there! Nikolasha!' He banged on the window with a gloved fist, and called again, 'Nikolasha!' Then he turned back into the carriage. 'He is there. All is well. Take all your bags, all of you. Georgii, help your mother.'

'Of course, Papa, but I must tell you that I am going on to Archangel.'

Cold fury flashed once more in Andrei Alexandrovitch's blue eyes as he said bitterly:

'Going the way of your treacherous brother?'

'No, Papa, of course not. But somebody must do something to . . .'

'Then you will help Nikki look after your mother and sisters. Ah, Evelyn, can you manage?'

'Yes, thank you, Cousin Andrei,' she answered, feeling her way out into the darkened corridor, holding her bag in one hand, and Sasha's in the other, as he scampered on ahead of her. At the door of the train she was met by a bearded man, who seemed enormous in his sheepskin *shuba* and hat. He smiled at Evelyn without speaking, lifted his young nephew down and then turned back to help her. Together they pulled down the baggage that Georgii brought to the door and then waited for the rest of the Suvarovs. Natalia Petrovna could hardly bear to let her husband go on without her, and he had to speak quite brutally to her and forcibly push her away from him. Then, on the dark and icy platform he stood and faced the brother he had not seen for thirteen years. Evelyn thought there could hardly have been so great a contrast between any two men. Andrei, despite the last horrible days, looked suave and almost dapper beside the bearded giant in his woolly *shuba* and huge, black boots. As she watched, they flung their arms around each other and, to her astonishment, actually kissed each other, twice. Then Andrei said:

'Take care of them, Nikolasha.' She thought she saw something glinting in the corner of his eyes in the dim lantern light. 'Thank God you survived it. The first good thing that's happened as a result of this Revolution.'

'Don't worry, Andrushka,' came the deep voice of his brother. 'And come back soon. Archangel is a poxy town. We'll be waiting for you.' With a last hug, they drew apart, and Andrei Alexandrovitch remounted the train and slammed the door shut.

'Come along then. It's a long, cold drive,' said Nikolai, leading the way out of the station to where two sleighs were waiting.

Somehow he packed them all in with their gear and, taking the reins of one team of horses, he called to the middle-aged man in charge of the other, who was dressed in boots and sheepskins identical with his own:

'Forward, Mischa.'

A lantern swung from the front of each sleigh and, with the light of the waxing moon, served to show the way. The swift, smooth running of the sleighs and the comfort of the thick sheepskin rugs were wonderful after the train, and for the first time since they had left Petrograd, Evelyn felt able to relax. She was no longer responsible. Nikolai Alexandrovitch was in charge. She pulled the rug up round her face and dragged her hat down almost to meet it and lay back, looking up at the clear northern sky and the myriad stars that looked astonishingly close and brilliant in the sharp air. Her eyes closed, fluttered open and then closed again. She slept.

Although she woke later as the sleigh drew up alongside a large building with broad, shallow steps leading up to the open front door, she was too dazed with sleep to notice much. A motherly woman seemed to welcome her, and someone told her not to worry as she looked round, asking:

'Where is Sasha? I ought to put him to bed.'

She was taken by the hand and led, stumbling, upstairs to a warm room, with a huge, inviting-looking bed. The kind woman helped her to undress, put her into a nightgown that had been warming near the stove, and led her to the bed, piling brightly coloured quilts on top, and firmly tucking her in. Evelyn tried sleepily to remember her Russian, but fell back on French to murmur:

'*Merci, Madame. Merci bien.*'

She was asleep before she heard the answer.

Waking about fifteen hours later, she was afraid to open her eyes in case the delectable warmth and softness she felt all around her should turn out to be part of a cruel and tantalising dream. She lay, savouring them, putting off the moment of discovery for as long as she could, a small smile twitching at her lips. A familiar and well-loved voice broke through her happy, dream-fuddled brain:

'See, Tallie. She is awake. I told you she was just pretending.'

'Sasha?' she said slowly, still not opening her eyes. She felt his fingers on her face.

'Yes, Evie, it's me. Wake up! Wake up! There's warm rolls for breakfast, freshly made, and coffee and eggs and jam. If you don't wake up, you'll miss them. Come on.'

At last she allowed her eyes to open, and she saw Sasha's face, bright and rosy, just beside hers.

'Good morning, Little Dove,' she said, smiling back at him.

Then she felt the fineness of the linen sheet that covered her and the softness of the big pillow behind her head.

'So it is really true. We are here.'

'Yes, yes,' answered Tallie, impatiently. 'Get up, Evie.'

'All right, all right, but take Sasha away while I dress.'

'Why?'

'Don't be silly, Tallie. Take him away.' She laughed. 'I'll be as quick as I can, I promise.'

'Uncle Nikki's housekeeper, Karla, has put clothes out for all of us. They're quite strange, but she says we'll be warmer and more comfortable than in our city dresses,' said Natalie. 'She's Mischa's wife, you know.' Evelyn, who could not for the moment remember who Mischa was, noticed that her cousin was wearing a thick black skirt embroidered in vivid colours around the hem, which hung several inches above her ankles, and a peculiar arrangement of blouse, overblouse and waistcoat.

'She says it's like what they wear in Siberia and it's better for the climate. It doesn't matter that they don't really fit properly. Only the boots. And she says that if they're wrong, there's a bootmaker in the village who can make more. Oh, yes, and you don't need stays with them, Dindin says.'

'Hush, Tallie. Sasha's still here.'

'So what? He knows all about stays, don't you Sashenka?'

'Well he should not. Go away, both of you, while I dress.'

Evelyn was embarrassed by the shortness of the skirt that she found laid over a wooden clothes-rack near the big stove, but she put it on obediently together with the brightly coloured blouse, and had to admit to herself that it was all much easier to wear than her fashionable dresses. And the comfort of not wearing any corsets was wonderful, if disgraceful.

When she walked downstairs towards an opened door through which she could hear talk and clinking crockery, she felt very conscious of the embarrassing way her unconfined body moved independently within the clothes. She resisted the temptation to pull at her skirt or cross her arms over her chest as she stood in the doorway, shyly murmuring, 'Good morning' in Russian.

Nikolai Alexandrovitch turned at the sound of her voice and, putting down his cup, got up from the table and came to her side.

'Good morning, my new English cousin. Did you sleep?'

Evelyn looked up at him, thinking irrelevantly how kind his eyes looked, and said with feeling:

'Marvellously. I couldn't really believe it when I woke up this morning.' As she spoke, she looked at the windows and then at the number of lamps lit all round the room.

'But is it morning? My watch has stopped, and it looks dark outside.'

Nikolai gave a great laugh, and put a rough, calloused hand on her shoulder.

'It is dark almost all day in winter up here. But we make up for it in summer. Then it's lighter even than in Petrograd.'

'Of course, how silly of me,' said Evelyn, for once not minding that she had made a fool of herself. 'Forgive me, I must still be half asleep.'

'Come and sit down. Have you brought your watch down with you?'

For answer she held out her delicate wrist, and the Russian proceeded to take the watch off in order to put it right and wind it up for her. The feeling of his rough fingers on her skin was peculiar, but not at all disagreeable, and she smiled. Dindin and her elder brother, who were already tucking into their breakfast, exchanged astonished glances; despite the thaw in Evelyn, which they had all welcomed, they had never seen her so soft or confiding or immediately trusting as she was with their uncle.

'Uncle Nikki?' came Sasha's voice, imperiously demanding attention.

'Yes my boy. What is the matter?' he asked as he came back to the table again, Evelyn's little gold watch in his big hands.

'Why are you taking Evie's watch?'

'Taking? What is all this? She said it had stopped and I'm winding it on for her. Come along, Evelyn, and have some breakfast.'

'Thank you, Uncle Nikki,' she said, taking her cue from Sasha, and sat down.

On the beautifully laundered white cloth was an array of food such as she had sometimes despaired of ever seeing again. There was none of the horrible coarse black bread that in Petrograd had been all they could buy. Instead there was a basket of soft-looking white rolls, their golden tops gleaming in the lamplight. The sight of a pottery dish of butter standing near the basket, and a bowl of boiled eggs, made saliva spurt humiliatingly into her mouth. She swallowed.

'How . . . how is it that you can have so much food?' she asked, and then in case she might have been misunderstood, quickly added:

'I don't mean that you should not have. God forbid! It is just such a wonderful sight.'

'It is more than that,' said Georgii robustly, handing her the eggs. 'Come on, get started. It's not just for looking at, you know.'

They all laughed and Evelyn helped herself to a large brown egg, amused now to see that her hand was even shaking a little in her eagerness. Someone else passed her the bread and the butter, and Nikolai himself filled her coffee cup.

'Where is Natalia Petrovna?' she asked, as she broke the top off the egg.

'Mischa's wife has taken her up a tray. She ought to stay in bed for a few days, I think. She seems to be exhausted.'

'Yes, she was very tired by the journey, and having to leave Piotr, and . . .'

'I know,' he answered, 'but we'll talk about it later. What we must do now is decide who will do what.' He looked round at their puzzled faces and explained himself. 'With so many extra people in the house, Mischa's wife won't be able to manage all the work, and I shall need help with the animals and the wood for the stoves and so on.' There was a moment of stunned silence among the refugee Suvarovs, who had been lulled by the comfort and food and security into believing that they had returned to normal life. Then Georgii spoke:

'But, sir, I mean . . . what about the servants?'

'Servants, my boy?' repeated Nikolai, pretending to be shocked and not to have understood the consternation in all their faces. 'There are no servants. We have had a Revolution in Russia.'

Dindin began to cry quietly into her starched linen napkin, but it was Sasha who put the general feeling into words.

'But Uncle Nikki, we have all been working at home. Dindin and Evie and I were always scrubbing the kitchen and peeling potatoes and things. We thought it would stop now.'

'Sashenka, work does not stop until we are dead. If we don't work, we don't eat,' he answered, his voice gentle, but his meaning implacable.

'Is that what you learned in Siberia, Uncle?' asked Georgii and even Natalie could hear the sneer in his voice. She stopped sniffing into her handkerchief and looked up, interested to see what would happen next, but their uncle did not rise to the bait. All he said was:

'That and much else, Georgii Andreivitch. One day we can talk about it, but there's no time now. Finish up, all of you, and we'll share out the tasks.'

7

They fell awkwardly into their new routine, and it was many days before the girls could become accustomed to rising at half-past six in the morning to see to the stoves and the lamps and begin to prepare breakfast. After breakfast Evelyn would take them and Sasha for English history and conversation, while the two men sawed up logs for the stoves and mended and made whatever was necessary in the house. Then, for two hours, Nikolai Alexandrovitch taught the children mathematics and Russian history, Evelyn joined his housekeeper in the kitchen to help prepare luncheon, and Georgii had two hours to himself.

Evelyn's hours off did not come until the late afternoon, by which time she and the girls had washed up the dishes and pots and pans from luncheon, used the few hours of dusk-like daylight to clean the rooms, or tackle the huge pile of laundry. Dinner was usually early, about half-past six, and for an hour or two after it, struggling with sleepiness, she would sit at the big round table in the hall, cleared of its dishes and dirty cloth, and listen to the talk between Georgii and his uncle.

It was less acrimonious than the discussions she had heard in Petrograd, although its subject was often the same and, as she listened, she came more and more to admire Nikolai. From him, at last, she began to understand why a revolution had had to come to Russia, and she could almost accept that a period of privation and fear was a small price to pay for the freedom and tolerance that were to come. Sometimes she would interrupt them to ask a question or two, and always Nikolai would answer directly, with none of the implied comment she had been used to from Piotr and his American friend. Nikolai's answers always seemed to make sense, and to be imbued with the tolerance of human inadequacy that seemed so basic a part of his character.

She trusted him. And she began to think that he might have some of the answers for which she yearned. If she had ever seen him alone, she would have spoken to him of John, who seemed to be in danger of fading from her memory. To talk to someone like Nikolai about John might help to fix him in her mind as the strong, gentle man who had first told her that he loved her, instead of the distraught, unhappy victim of their last day together.

In the early days of their romance John had been full of a charming kind of authority, and she had believed everything he had told her. When he had said that she was beautiful she had been able to smile and believe him; when he had first said that they would love each other for ever, she had known that he was right and never suspected that one day she would have such difficulty remembering how it had felt.

She longed to tell Nikolai all of it, to describe John's mixture of seriousness and gaiety, his thick blond hair, his superb seat on a horse, the courage that had so frighteningly deserted him at the moment when he had most needed it, and so bring them all back to her. Then she might be able to ask Nikolai about some of the other things that worried her still, and perhaps banish the unhappy memories. But the only time Nikolai appeared to sit down was after dinner, and Georgii was always there, and usually Dindin as well, even though Sasha and Natalie had been sent to bed after an early supper in the kitchen.

When Evelyn herself went to bed, she was so tired that the effort involved in collecting her can of hot water from the huge kettle in the kitchen, taking it upstairs to her room, and washing herself was almost more than she could manage. In spite of her labours in Petrograd, it was a revelation to her how tiring regular housework and cookery could be. Her muscles would sometimes ache so much that she thought she would never be able to lift another bucket. At other times it would be her hands that worried her: chapped and raw, they hurt even when she was lying in bed; plunging them into cold water was agony and using them to grip a rag and polish a table almost unbearable.

But there were curious, unlooked-for satisfactions too. Her exhausting days left her little time to think, and when she lay in bed she did not dream. Although she still hurt all over whenever she thought of her brother's unbearable death, she came to dwell less and less on the mud and blood and bodies of the battlefields in Flanders, in France and all along the Russian front, and gradually learned to enjoy the way her world had shrunk until it was circumscribed by the grey wooden walls of the old house in Shenkursk. There was an extraordinary luxury in not having to worry about anything except whether the floor for which you were responsible was properly clean, or the sheets unmarred by wrinkles, or the food laboriously brought in by the men nicely cooked so that it could be enjoyed. The fact that she was living what was really a servant's existence no longer worried her, and if she ever thought about the future, it was with a certain peaceful faith.

One evening Georgii, who had wrenched his back inexpertly splitting logs, had retired to bed early so that when Dindin went upstairs, Evelyn was alone with Nikolai. She said something to him about her new content and the pleasure of sleeping soundly through whole nights. Her sense of ease with him was such that she could look at him as she spoke and so she saw the reminiscent smile that spread slowly across his face as he quoted:

> '"Never sees horrid night, that child of hell,
> But, like a lackey, from the rise to set
> Sweats in the eye of Phoebus, and all night
> Sleeps in Elysium . . ."'

'That's right,' she said enthusiastically. 'Who said it? "Child of hell" is just what a sleepless night becomes.'

'Shakespeare, in *Henry V*. Don't you know it?' Evelyn blushed faintly, which amused him.

'No. My governess did not believe in Shakespeare,' she said. 'I overheard my mother asking her once why she would not read the plays with me, and I remember her answer very well. She said, "Mrs Markham, William Shakespeare may be a famous dramatist, but he was a man of the utmost crudity, and his work is not suitable for a young girl."'

'And didn't that make you rush to your father's bookshelves for a copy?' asked Nikolai with a smile.

'No. I was such a goody-goody. It never occurred to me to break any rule or court any kind of trouble. Isn't that stupid? What I must have missed! I think I always did what I was told.' Her face changed and in place of the warm confiding expression came a pinched, pale look that Robert Adamson would have recognised. But Nikolai had never seen it before.

'What is the matter, child?' he asked.

Evelyn almost wept at the kindness in his voice as he called her 'child'. She felt as though no one had ever called her that before, that she had never been allowed to be a child. It took a minute or two before she could control the quivering in her voice, but she said at last:

'I would like to tell you all about it, but somehow I don't think I can. It is just that I once did something I was asked to do, and it had the most . . .' Her voice became wholly suspended and she put up one arm to cover her eyes. He put a large hand out to her across the table and took her clenched fist in it, and gently bore it down on to the table top. At first she tried to resist, but then as she allowed him to overbear her, a deep relaxation seemed to flood through her. She lifted her head at last and looked at him again. 'Thank you, Uncle Nikki. You are very good to me. One day, perhaps, I shall be able to tell you about it. It was just something that turned out badly and might have had terrible consequences.'

'Evelyn, out of the things I have done and those that have been done to me I have learned one thing above all others,' he said, still holding her hand. 'Blaming yourself for things that you have done is the most sterile exercise a human being can perform. It leads only to self-hatred, which cuts a person off from the rest of humanity. All you can do when you acknowledge that an action of yours – or words – has caused trouble or pain for someone else is to try to heal that pain and to learn how to avoid doing the same thing again.'

'And if you cannot heal the pain, if the opportunity is taken from you?' she asked, the tears outlining her huge, dark eyes, but not falling.

'Then it is you who will feel the pain. But, dear Evelyn, somehow you must try to make that hurt take you closer to other people, not divide you from them. That is the only way in which it will be eased.'

He thought for a moment that she might be going to tell him what it was that troubled her so, but all she said was:

'Uncle Nikki, why do you take such trouble with me?'

'It is not trouble, child. I am interested in you. And I like you.'

At that the welling tears fell, flooding down her face and making her eyes larger than ever. He let go her hand at last and got up off his chair to come round the table. He made her stand up and then took her in his arms. There was nothing in his embrace that reminded her of John or even of Sergei. The sensations that filled her were of comfort and safety. She leaned against him and could feel his heart beating steadily and slow. After a moment of peace, she drew back from him.

'Thank you, Uncle Nikki. Thank you.'

He patted her head and smiled a smile of such tender amusement that something in her answered it. She brushed the last tears away with the back of her left hand and said:

'You have done something for me tonight . . . I don't quite know what . . . but I think you have made me very happy. I ought to go to bed now.'

'Yes, I think you probably should. We all have an early start. I am glad we were alone tonight.'

'I too,' she answered and left him.

Their evening confidences were not repeated, and neither of them referred to what they had talked about, but everywhere Evelyn went, whatever she did, she heard his voice saying 'And I like you.' She did not believe that she had ever been truly liked before. She had been loved, perhaps, but that was different: difficult, laying burdens and responsibilities on her and carrying with it possibilities of infinite pain. Few of her so-called friends had really liked her, she now understood, just as she had liked few of them; her governess had seemed to detest her, and even her parents, who she was sure felt about her as parents should, never seemed to welcome her company or want to listen to her. She rarely saw her father except at the stilted, formal meals they had three times a day, and her mother had always been too busy telling her what she should do and how she should behave and dress to spend time talking with her.

Tony was very like a friend to her, but once he had gone away to school he seemed to have left her behind. Occasionally when he came back from school or his one term at university they managed to retrieve the old relationship, but his life had become so different from hers that sometimes it was difficult. She had hoped that John might take his place – his old, real place – when they became engaged, but there had not been time for that.

The rest of the household did not particularly notice any change in Evelyn, but Andrei Suvarov saw it at once when he arrived from Archangel and she greeted him with a great beaming smile and a plate of hot, highly flavoured stew. He tucked into the food with the pleasure of extreme hunger, and answered the questions they all flung at him as best he could.

During the first pause in the conversation he turned to Evelyn to say:

'I am sorry to say that I've no real news for you, Evelyn. Baines, my manager, could tell me nothing and so I went to see the British Consul, but he told me he has no instructions from his government about the English subjects at present in Archangel. There are fourteen hundred in Archangel town itself and no one knows how many more in the province, making their way up there. The ice won't break up until May at the earliest, but even then it is not certain that there will be British ships to take so many people off, and the Soviet's not likely to provide transport.' He was surprised to see her shrug. Then she smiled and said:

'Cousin Andrei, I seem to have been on a roundabout journey home ever since I left in 1916. I know I'll get there in the end. And Shenkursk is not Petrograd.'

'No,' he agreed, looking round at their rosy, bright-eyed faces. 'You all look very much better than on that day when I left you at Nyandoma station. You've done them well, Niko-lasha.'

He smiled across the table at Evelyn.

'I couldn't have done it without our *Anglichanka*. She has been invaluable.'

Neither of the men noticed the scowl that crossed Georgii's face, but Evelyn saw it, and later in the day found an op-portunity to say:

'Georgii, what made you so angry this morning?'

'Oh, I don't know,' he began and then as his resentment boiled up all over again, he burst out: 'It's just that no one ever notices that I do just as much work as you do.'

'But, Georgii,' she protested, smiling, 'of course they do. It was only that Uncle Nikki said . . .'

'I know what he said, and I know I'm being stupid, but it's so unfair. It's just like everything that's ever happened. Just like them letting Piotr go off and do whatever he wanted while I had to work for Papa. No university for me, and I'm just as clever as Piotr ever was.'

Evelyn could not hide her smiles at his childishness and after a moment's petulance, he joined in.

'I know, I know. I'm behaving badly. It's just that my father always makes me angry and I can't ever show it to him without seeming foolish. And now, you see, he seems to be exempt from Uncle Nikki's rules that anyone who doesn't work doesn't eat.'

'Come on, Georgii, he's only just arrived. You can't really expect him to be out there in the vegetable patch already.'

'But he won't be tomorrow, either. He's going to write a report for Uncle Nikki about his thirteen years' stewardship of the Suvarov Works. It's quite absurdly unnecessary now they've been stolen by the Bolshevik rabble.'

Evelyn shared Georgii's view that his father's report was a ludicrous exercise, but at least it kept him quiet over the next few days. Whenever he was not writing it or sitting with his wife, he tried to get Nikolai to sit down with him so that he could tell his brother of the guilt and anxiety he had suffered when Nikolai had been sent to Siberia. Evelyn would never have believed that the man who had always seemed so overbearing could have become so cowed. One evening she heard him say:

'Nikolasha, I know that what I suffered was nothing compared to what must have happened to you in Siberia.' He paused there, as though waiting for his brother to deny it. But Nikolai just sat with his back to the stove, a pipe between his lips and his face impassive, waiting.

'But I felt so guilty always. And I tried to do everything you would have done at the works and then with my sons.'

At that Georgii got up and left the hall, as though he could not bear to listen to any more, and Evelyn looked speculatively at Nikolai, knowing that Georgii had already told his uncle much of what he had always called his father's 'tyranny'. Still Nikolai sat without apparent judgment, waiting until his brother had rid himself of the accumulated feelings of thirteen years.

'When Piotr started to attend those meetings and bring his revolutionary friends to the house, I tried to explain to him what he was risking, what had been done to you. He wouldn't listen, Nikolasha. He just said that Russia was worth risking everything for. And I lived in terror of what would happen. After that I did everything I could to stop him – short of reporting him to the Okhrana myself.'

At last Nikolai spoke, relieving a tension that was becoming unbearable to Evelyn at least.

'Andrushka, you had no reason for guilt. You did not send me into exile. You were no provocateur or informer. I was arrested during a demonstration which you had refused to attend. What happened to me was not your doing.'

But his brother did not seem to want to be comforted, and Evelyn saw for the first time how self-indulgent the guilty can be, and she began to understand why Nikolai had called guilt a sterile exercise. As such conversations continued evening after evening, she wondered if Andrei Alexandrovitch were not trying to elicit from his brother a blanket absolution for the way he had bullied his two elder sons and perhaps for all the other things he might have done with which he was not satisfied. She watched him feeding off Nikolai's strength as he tried to excuse himself for the regrets that made him uncomfortable and she began to sympathise much more with the absent Piotr and with Georgii, whose slowly increasing courage to rebel seemed to grow in parallel with his father's abasement.

One afternoon Georgii was sitting in the dark warmth of the kitchen while Evelyn was putting dried beans into a large wooden bowl of water to soak for the next day's dinner. He had forgiven her for Nikolai's championship; after all, as he had once told her kindly, it wasn't her fault and she did work fantastically hard around the house. The atmosphere between them was peaceful, and the scent of stewing pork mingled with those of the drying clothes hanging on a line across one end of the big kitchen and the bread that Mischa's wife had left to prove at the side of the big black range.

Georgii watched his English cousin and suddenly said:

'Did you realise how weak my father was when we were all in Petrograd?'

Evelyn, concentrating on her tasks, did not at once understand what he was asking, but after he had repeated the question, she put down the spoon she had used to stir the simmering stew and said thoughtfully:

'I don't think it is weakness. I think he is behaving like this because for all those years he was in charge and so he blames himself for letting the timber works be stolen by the Bolsheviki. Now he is back with his brother, he sees a chance to share some of his guilt and lessen his self-hatred.'

'You're too charitable; but then you never suffered as I did. He never tried to bully you and choose your friends and forbid you this and that.'

Trying quite strenuously not to see a parallel between Georgii's petulance and his father's exculpation, or between Piotr's rebellion and Nikolai's strength, Evelyn decided it was time to end the conversation.

'It must have been horrid for you, Georgii.'

As she stopped speaking, they heard a light knock on the back door. Wiping her wet hands on the voluminous white apron she wore over her peasant skirt, she went to open it. There, silhouetted against the dingy twilight, stood the figure of a dirty, unkempt, exhausted man. For a moment she did not recognise him. But then he spoke her name. She could not believe what her ears told her. Before Georgii could speak, she whispered, 'Sergei Ivanovitch?', holding both hands out across the threshold.

'Yes, Evelyn. It is I.' He took her hands in a clumsy clasp and almost pushed her back into the kitchen.

'Georgii! What are you doing here?' he demanded, his tired, white face severe.

'What do you expect? Waiting on my father and my uncle.'

'That's absurd at a time like this. We're fighting for our very survival. We need all able-bodied men.' Then he turned away from his young cousin, almost as though he had dismissed him as a nonentity or a coward, stripped off his gloves and took Evelyn's hands again, raising first one and then the other to his lips. 'My dear, I rejoice to find you here, safely out of Petrograd.'

'But what have you been doing? Where have you been? We thought you were . . . had been killed. Are you really all right? Sergei, tell me everything.'

'All right. But will you let me sit? I am really very tired.'

'And hungry, too, I expect,' she said, full of compunction. 'Here, take this chair and I will find you some food. There is not quite so much as I thought there would be when I saw our first meal here, but it is far better than we had in Petrograd. Is pork all right for you? It's a stew of pork and dried beans. The first fresh vegetables won't be ready for a few more weeks Uncle Nikki says.'

She knew she was babbling like a fool, but she was quite unable to control the force that sent words gushing out of her. She noticed that Georgii was sitting the other side of the table in resentful silence, smarting under the reprimand that was so unjust – he would have done anything to escape from Shenkursk and fight for his country instead of working like a peasant. Evelyn felt sorry for him, in spite of her earlier irritation, but his problems seemed so trivial in comparison with Sergei's reappearance that she ignored him completely.

Sergei's return was in itself miraculous, but there was more to her upwelling happiness than a recognition of that. In his survival she had instantly seen John's. If this man could live despite not only the Germans and the horrors of trenches, but also the treacherous assaults of his own men, then perhaps John too might really be alive. Tony was dead and she would ache forever with the loss, but if Sergei Voroshilov could turn up months and months after he had been posted 'Missing believed killed', then John might do the same, might even have returned to Yorkshire already. No letters had got through to Shenkursk since she had arrived. Perhaps there was one waiting somewhere with the news of John's escape. Her sense of hope renewed brought a light into her face and a smile to her lips.

As she bustled about the spotless kitchen finding a spoon and a bowl and ladling the thick stew into it, she was happy, unaware for the moment that Sergei was disgusted that she should be doing such things, appalled to see that she had given up the battle with her hair and had bundled it back in a simple plait and that she was wearing peasant dress. If he had not been almost dropping with exhaustion he would have been lecturing both Georgii and herself on the importance of keeping up the old standards and not compromising for one second with the levelling ambitions of the Bolsheviki.

When she put the wooden bowl of stew in front of him at the kitchen table, he ate ravenously and asked her for more. Evelyn would have done anything for him then and hurried to refill the bowl, asking anxiously when he had last eaten and then without waiting for his answer, begging him to tell them how he had escaped the murderous deserters and where he had been and what his plans were.

His hand gripped the spoon as though it was a weapon and an expression of near cruelty distorted his handsome face. For an instant Evelyn was afraid of him and wished she had not asked. Then he put the spoon down, looked at her and Georgii with narrowed eyes and an expression of suspicion, and at last said:

'I got out just in time and went to England.'

Despite her delight in his survival, Evelyn was filled with a sudden, violent resentment that dismayed her. If she, English and a bystander in this country, were trapped in it, why should he have been able to get out? She managed to say nothing more than:

'But how?'

'You ought not to ask things like that. It's not safe.'

'I'm sorry,' she said, gulping a little. Before she could say anything else, he turned to Georgii.

'Who else is here in this house? I know that Piotr has joined them, and is – thank God – out of the way. But who is here?'

'Uncle Nikki, of course, and Mischa and his wife. My parents, and then Dindin and the children.'

'And Nikolai Alexandrovitch? Will he let me stay here, or is he still in favour of the Revolution?'

Evelyn could not let that pass. More angrily than she had ever spoken to Sergei, she said:

'As far as I know he is in favour of Russia and peace and the betterment of everyone who lives here. I am sure he will let you stay.'

'And not betray me to the Soviet?'

'He would never betray anyone.'

'You sound very sure, Evelyn. How can you know?'

'If I ever had to trust one person in this world, I think it would be him. He would never willingly hurt anyone and he would never betray a confidence.'

'Well I'll have to believe you for I need a base in the town, and it's easier to rely on family than strangers, although with traitors like your brother, Georgii, it pays to tread warily. Who comes to this house and whom do you all visit?'

Evelyn looked very surprised, but it was Georgii who answered the question.

'No one, of course. There are other respectable families here from Petrograd and some from Moscow, but we are all too busy to visit or receive any of them here.'

'It's that damned idealist, Nikolai Alexandrovitch, isn't it? Well, don't worry, Evelyn, things are going to change around here now. It need be no secret that some of your countrymen are in Murmansk already and if we can start to rouse the countryside, we can rely on their help. Georgii, whatever you've been doing until today, you must join us now. It's no time for idealistic pacifists. You are either with us or a Bolshevik.'

Evelyn's face drained of colour as she understood at last why he had come.

'But that means civil war, Sergei. There has been no trouble here. The Soviets leave us alone. What are you going to do?'

'Everything I can to restore my country and protect its people from those fiends.'

She looked sideways at Georgii and was amazed to see him smiling. He realised that here at last was someone who would get him out of his uncle's house.

'Of course, Seriosha,' he said. 'I have been wanting to help, but Father . . . I'll do whatever I can. You can count on me.'

His cousin stood up. 'I do, Georgii Andreivitch. I must sleep now, but wake me in three hours' time and you can brief me about the town. Evelyn, will you show me where I can sleep?'

'Well, Sergei, of course. But . . . I mean, I shall have to ask Uncle Nikki first. It is his house.'

'Then Sergei will have to wait until tonight,' commented Georgii. 'Don't you remember? He's out all today.'

'Oh, dear, yes. Of course. Well, you've obviously got to sleep. Come on upstairs, then. We'll talk to Nikolai Alexandrovitch tonight.'

As he watched her fill a can with water from the kettle and fetch linen for his bed, Sergei burned inside with rage at what had been done to the immaculate elegant Evelyn he had known before the world broke up.

8

During the afternoon Evelyn crept into Sergei's room several times to make sure that he was all right. He had been so tired that when she showed him the room he had almost collapsed on to the bed in all his clothes and had barely been able to thank her before he fell asleep. He looked very fragile as he lay on top of the bedclothes, one hand curled up under his cheek and his usually faultless hair tumbled about on the pillow. She wanted to stroke the untidy hair back from his face and smooth away the dark purple bruises from under his eyes and her hand had even moved towards him before she realised what she was doing and controlled herself. The brief moment of resentment that had flamed in the kitchen had died out completely. Now all she felt for him was protectiveness. When Georgii tried to wake him after the stipulated three hours, she refused even to let him through the door.

'He's far too exhausted, Georgii. Let him sleep. There's nothing he can do now. Give him until tomorrow morning. Look at him.' She stood aside. Georgii looked obediently into the room and said:

'All right. But if he's angry when he wakes . . .'

Evelyn looked very straight at Georgii and said in a clearly contemptuous tone:

'Don't worry, Georgii. I shall take the blame if he is cross.'

The young man blushed.

'You don't know him. He can be violently angry. We were all afraid of him as children. Just because he's taken a fancy to you doesn't mean that he'll treat the rest of us any more kindly. He has a frightful temper.'

Evelyn shrugged and went back to her tasks, waiting for Nikolai. When he came back at last, she made herself wait until he had taken off his *shuba* and hat and lit a pipe before saying:

'Uncle Nikki?' He looked up in surprise at the almost wheedling tone she used.

'Yes, Evelyn. Is there something you want?'

'Not really me. I mean . . .' She found it very hard to phrase her request. 'Look, Natalia Petrovna's nephew, Sergei Voroshilov, did survive after all. He's been all over the place, and he arrived here this morning in a state of terrible exhaustion. I'm not quite sure how he got here, but he did and I've put him to sleep in one of the empty rooms upstairs. Will you let him stay? Uncle Nikki, please?'

Finding it hard to meet his eyes, Evelyn felt extraordinarily uneasy and waited tensely for his answer. When it came it surprised her.

'Why do you think I would not?' At that she did look at him, her eyebrows raised.

'Well, because he's on the other side. He'd reverse the Revolution if he could. And you . . .'

'So long as he does not try to do any such thing in Shenkursk, he's welcome to stay.'

Her eyelids dropped over her eyes again and she discovered that she could not repeat what Sergei had said to Georgii. She did not see Nikolai's expression of understanding, but she did hear the comfort in his voice as he said:

'Evelyn, it is not something you need to worry about. I shall talk to the young man myself and find out his plans. You can forget about it.' At that she shot him a small, grateful, apologetic smile and went away to the kitchen.

Evelyn never discovered exactly what the two men said to each other, but Sasha and Natalie had overheard the conversation, and reported most of it at the end of their lesson with Evelyn. She knew that she ought to stop them repeating things they should not have overheard, but she cared too much about Sergei's future to do it. Sasha started it.

'Sergei Ivanovitch is going to stay with us now. Did you know that, Evie? Tallie and me were doing our sums for Uncle Nikki when Sergei Ivanovitch came to talk to him.'

'What happened, Sashenka? What did they say?'

'I didn't understand it all, but Uncle Nikki was quite cold and sounded nearly cross when he was talking. He said, "Sergei Ivanovitch, you are welcome to shelter here if you will give me your word that you are here for shelter only."'

'And then Sergei said, "Oh yes, Nikolai Alexandrovitch, I can promise you that. I'd not have come to a revolutionary household if I could have been sure of any other,"' contributed Natalie. 'And Uncle Nikki was very cross. He is always so gentle but then he was more angry even than Father.'

'But what did he say?'

The young girl flushed as she gave Evelyn a verbatim report.

'He said he was damned if he was going to take something like that from a young puppy. And then before he could say anything else, Sergei said: "Do you know what the swine have done on the Don?" And Uncle Nikki stopped shouting and sounded like he always does. "I'd heard a bit, and if it's happened to your home, I'm sorry. But, please give me your word."'

'Then Sergei said quite crossly that he already had and Uncle Nikki said he would have to trust him. There. So now there will be someone else to help chop up the logs and silly old Georgii won't have to hurt his back again,' ended Sasha triumphantly.

Evelyn smiled even as she delivered a gentle reproof for speaking so cheekily about his elder brother, and then sent both children off for a walk in the fresh air with Dindin and herself went in search of Sergei.

She could not find him in any of the downstairs rooms and so she went rather timidly to knock on the door of his bedroom. His voice, sounding rather harsh, called:

'Yes, who is it?'

'Evelyn.'

She heard footsteps and then he opened the door, smiling charmingly at her and said:

'Come in, Evelyn. Here, sit down and tell me what I can do for you.'

'Thank you, Sergei Ivanovitch, but I don't want anything. And I don't want to disturb you.'

'You could never do that, my dear. It is always the greatest pleasure to see you. Now, tell me.'

She could not help smiling back at him, but when she spoke there was no pleasure in her voice.

'Sergei, what happened to your home?' She was distressed to see his face transformed by a grimace in which she thought she could see pain and cruelty horribly married.

'I didn't want you to have to know anything about it, Evelyn. Our war is not fit for you.'

'Please tell me. I hate to think that something has happened to that lovely house you told me about. Sergei, tell me.'

He looked down at her and in a voice whose very coolness seemed dramatic he told her.

'The Bolsheviki threw back the Cossacks who were trying to restore order to the province and in their advance they came to my home. They burned the house and shot my father. And then they raped my mother and Ekaterina Nikolaievna, one after another until every man there had had a turn. My mother died. Ekaterina Nikolaievna lived, but she was terribly mutilated. She is being cared for by the Red Cross now.'

Evelyn sat silent, feeling sick and cold. There was nothing at all she could say. No words of sympathy or horror could possibly have expressed her feelings and, she felt, could only have insulted him by their inadequacy. She could not even look at him.

At last she felt his hand on her shoulder and heard his voice, quiet and nearly gentle again:

'Evelyn, perhaps I ought not to have told you, but I care for you so much that I could not keep something like that hidden from you, and I want you to understand why I have to do what I have to do.'

Trying to keep her voice from shaking, she asked:

'What is it that you must do, Sergei?'

'Ah, that's better, Evelyn. I love you looking up at me like that. I have to do everything I can to help your countrymen at Murmansk. If they move south into the country, as I hope they will, I shall be here to co-ordinate the local forces.'

'But Sergei,' she protested, 'the children told me that you had promised Nikolai that you would do nothing like that.'

'No, I gave him my word that I had only come to his house for shelter. And that is true. I have no home now.'

After what she had heard, she could not bring herself to protest any further, although she knew that Nikolai would be furious to hear of Sergei's plans. All she could do was to hope that he had guessed.

The next time he saw her, he looked at her with careful eyes and said:

'Child, what's the matter?'

She took a deep breath and said:

'Did Sergei tell you what the Bolsheviki did at his home – to his mother, I mean, and to Ekaterina Nikolaievna?'

'Yes, but I wish he had not told you. You must not think about it, Evelyn. It . . .'

'How could I not think about it? Something like that. How could any human being do something like that? Uncle Nikki, why do people do such horrible things? Isn't there enough horror at the Front without that?'

'Yes, child. Far too much. But there had been provocation.'

'By Sergei's parents and that pathetic spinster cousin of theirs? Surely not.'

'No, not them specifically. But the Cossacks had behaved as badly and as cruelly when they were winning.' When he saw her face beginning to close up against him, he went on: 'Neither side in this struggle has a monopoly on cruelty – or on justification. Try not to think about it, Evelyn.'

But she could not help it. Her mind returned to it again and again and even the pictures of Tony's body on the wire, or John's gassed or blown up or buried in a shell hole, began to give way to those created by what Sergei had told her. It was too easy to build up her memories of the man in the Vyborg and the louts in the train to Vologda into a scene that reflected what Sergei had told her.

He never referred to it again, but she could see the wounds

it had made in his mind, and she could only admire the courage with which he joined in the ordinary life of Nikolai's house. Accepting his share of the tasks that had to be done, he nevertheless brought to them all a new lightness, almost an air of frivolity. Instead of a quick walk for fresh air whenever the weather was bearable, he made Evelyn and the children wrap up warmly and go skating with him on the river, or made Mischa harness the one tired pony to the sleigh and take his cousins for a drive over the icy roads out of the town. Life seemed to move faster when Sergei was a part of it, and the slow, tiring, somehow gentle days turned into something more exciting.

There was one early afternoon in April when he decreed that they should all go skating. When Evelyn protested, he overrode her and urged her into sharing his pleasure in the day. The few hours of daylight were real light by then and the sky was a glorious, blazing blue, against which the leafless birches really looked as though they were made out of silver. The snow had not yet begun to thaw and made a pristine background for the little churches with their bulbous domes and painted walls. Evelyn had hardly noticed Shenkursk itself until that afternoon, but looking about her as they walked down to the river, carrying their skate blades, she thought how pretty it was and how sad that for six or seven months of every year there should be so little light by which to see it.

Sergei must have read some of the regret in her expression, for just then he moved closer and said:

'Don't be sad, Evelyn. Now that we have lost so much, it is our duty to enjoy every moment that we can wrest from fate for our pleasure.'

'You're so brave, Sergei Ivanovitch.'

'Not brave, my dear, but perhaps determined. Yes, determined. Look, there's Madame Avinkova with her daughters. Have you met them yet?'

'Avinkova? No. I'm sorry, Sergei, I don't know who they are.'

'Never mind, I'll introduce you. Charming family, from Moscow actually, but they've always come up here for the summer. Come along.'

Evelyn went obediently and was relieved to find that she had not forgotten how to behave in society during her months of domestic work. She found herself taking some pleasure in the trivial courtesies of chatting to the unknown Russian woman and her rather plain daughters, and when they all got to the river and buckled on their skates, she set off across the ice with a lighter heart than she had felt for months and months.

As soon as she had seen that the Suvarov children were happy and safely skating near the bank, she accepted Sergei's challenge and skimmed off with him down the river, feeling the strength of his hand as he pulled away from her only to swing back beside her and carry her with him in exhilarating loops and arcs across the river. She felt almost as though she were flying, and shivered at the excitement tingling all through her.

When at last her conscience drove her back to her charges, she was greeted with admiring comments from the Avinkov girls on her skill. Sasha immediately said:

'Evie's a wonderful skater. In Petrograd, she was the best too.'

'My champion,' said Evelyn, pleased with the effect the exercise had had on him and his sisters. Their faces were alive again, and their eyes sparkled.

'Yes, indeed,' agreed Madame Avinkova. 'How pleasant for you to have such admiring pupils, Miss Markham. I cannot think why we have not met you all until now. Do you think that your aunt would receive me if I were to call on her?'

Evelyn felt a little doubtful; Natalia Petrovna's reactions could never be relied upon, and she took great care to avoid any kind of obligation. But Sergei said instantly:

'She would be delighted, Madame Avinkova. She is so dull here in Shenkursk with none of her friends to visit, and all the life she knew left behind in Petrograd.'

'Of course. And she always went to Finland, didn't she? We used to look at that lovely house – much the nicest in Shenkursk, we used to think – and wish that it was occupied. Never mind, I shall call tomorrow. And I look forward to seeing all you pretty girls again. We must have a party, too. Sergei Ivanovitch, may I have a word with you?'

'Of course, Madame Avinkova. Evelyn, do you want to take the others back now? I'll follow you in a moment.'

Evelyn and the others obediently made their way home, chattering about their expedition and making plans for what they would do the next day. But when they pushed their way happily into the old house, Evelyn caught sight of Nikolai with both hands pressed to the small of his back, stretching as though to ease his aching muscles, and she felt wickedly torn between the things she wanted to do for him and the pleasures that Sergei seemed to hold out for her.

Ever since Sergei had shown his disgust at the way she was dressed and what she had to do in the kitchen she had lost her sense of rightness and content in the way Nikolai ordered his household. She felt that she had been living in a kind of limbo in which her real self had been forgotten. It was only when Sergei had told her that she was less than she had once been that she began to feel degraded by the way in which she was living. Now she could not forget it, and she began to think that she had seen surprise in the glances the Avinkovs had directed at her strange clothes.

As soon as she had made certain that Nikolai did not need her for anything she went upstairs to her room and looked in the wardrobe at the few clothes she had brought with her from Petrograd. They were all draggled and those she had worn on the train looked filthy and, to her shame, smelled unpleasant. She took them out to lay them on the bed and then she picked up all the washable clothes and carried them in a bundle down to the kitchen to add to the laundry pile.

Apologising to Mischa's Siberian wife for her lateness, Evelyn then went to the dresser to collect the dishes and cutlery so that she could go and lay the table for dinner.

It was when she was kneeling on the floor, leaning over the laundry tub with her sleeves rolled up high above her elbows, scrubbing at her stays and camisoles and blouses that Sergei found her. She could have sworn in vexation at being found yet again doing a servant's work rather than when she was teaching the children, or even mending sheets, but all she said as she continued her laborious scrubbing was, 'It seems strange to see you in a kitchen like this, Sergei Ivanovitch.'

'Evelyn, I have to talk to you.'

'Yes?'

'Oh, take your arms out of that damned washtub and come and sit down.'

Startled and becoming more than a little angry at his odd abruptness, she nevertheless obeyed and, wiping her soapy arms on her apron, went to a chair by the stove and sat down.

'Well?' she prompted.

'Evelyn, you probably know that I am going to have to leave this house.'

'Have they come?' she asked, her face lighting in eagerness.

'Not yet, but it can't be long now according to my sources, and I won't compromise Nikolai Alexandrovitch by working for them from his house. He's been too good to me – and to you, Evelyn – for me to take advantage of him.'

Evelyn's eyes seemed to glow as she took in the fact that Sergei, too, seemed to care for Nikolai in spite of their political differences.

'Madame Avinkova has invited me to lodge in her house and so I shall be moving there tomorrow. Will you visit me, Evelyn?'

'Of course, Sergei Ivanovitch. How can you ask?'

'And come to the parties she is planning? It seems so sad that you and I have never danced together since that first Christmas Eve, or – Evelyn . . .'

'Yes, what is it, Sergei?'

'Well, now that the Bolsheviki have made peace with Germany and . . .'

'Peace, when? How?' she interrupted, shocked out of the warm content his words had given her.

'Didn't Nikolai Alexandrovitch tell you?'

'No. We have never talked about the war.'

'Last month Trotsky and Lenin signed a peace treaty at Brest-Litovsk, ceding to the Germans nearly one-third of the

Russian empire. The whole of the Ukraine has gone and Poland, Lithuania, Finland, Latvia and Estonia. There are Germans in Petrograd now, and the rest of the Allies have to fight on alone, with nothing to divert the Prussians from the Western Front.'

All Evelyn's old terrors came rushing back in an overwhelming tide. She felt as though she had been a traitor to her country, seduced from her allegiance by the emotional comfort of Nikolai's unreal world. In her shame she looked up to Sergei and said:

'I did not know. I am so sorry. I wish I could help in some way.'

'You can,' he said, gazing down at her with an intensity that made her a little afraid.

'Tell me what I can do.'

He put both hands on her shoulders, very close to her neck and rubbed his thumbs gently under her chin. For a moment she was oddly reminded of the day in Petrograd when Robert Adamson had come to help her in the kitchen and had touched her in almost the same way. A little worry showed in her eyes, and Sergei frowned. Then he said:

'I am alone now, Evelyn, and I have nothing to offer you, no estates, no wealth, not even a house. But I love you, as I have loved you since that first evening in Petrograd when I came back from the Front and found you alone in Natalia Petrovna's drawing-room, so beautiful and so understanding. I think you were the only person in that whole house who had any idea of what the war was like and how we suffered for our country. I want you, Evelyn, and I need you . . .' Her sudden pallor stopped him in the middle of his proposal and he said in quite a different voice: 'What is the matter? Are you ill?'

She shook her head and her eyelids dropped, hiding her thoughts from him. Her sudden, instinctive response to his words appalled her in its disloyalty to John. Never had he seemed so far away, so lost to her. But she could not allow herself to let him go, and knew that she had to find some kind of convincing explanation for Sergei that would stop him from tempting her with promises of love. Making a supreme effort to control her voice, she said as gently as she could:

'Sergei Ivanovitch, you do me too much honour. But I cannot ever return such a love. I did not know that you felt like that and if I had, I would have tried to explain to you . . .' She stopped, unable to find the right words to say what she had to say.

'What must you explain?'

'That I love John.' Sergei opened his mouth as though to protest, but she stopped him with a look and carried on: 'I expect you are going to tell me that he must be dead and that I ought to forget him, but it is not so. I would know if he were – I am sure of it – and even if he is I could never love anyone else like that again.' Even as she said it, she wondered whether it could possibly be true. But she had promised Johnnie on that last dreadful day that she would wait for him, and she could not break her word. In giving herself to him then, she had given herself to him for ever. She could not just go on to some other man now, whatever might have happened to John, whatever her treacherous feelings might be urging her to do.

Sergei's hands moved gently over her face and she made herself stand and let him touch her as he wished. Her stillness irritated him. Women he touched always shivered with desire.

'Evelyn, you are like a stone. You were not like this in Petrograd when I went back after Christmas. I could feel you under my hands, my lips. You were moved then. What has happened since? Why are you so cold?'

'Oh Sergei, so much has happened. Far too much to explain. Please, please try to understand. I cannot love you, however much I might . . . might wish to.'

At the quiver in her voice as she said those last three words his aquiline face seemed to lighten. He took his hands from her face and raised one of her hands to kiss it. Then he said:

'I think I do understand, *duschinka*, and I will try to behave as you wish. But will you promise me something?'

'What?' she asked baldly, desperately trying to hold on to her detachment.

'That if you need anything you will tell me. If you ever hear . . . I mean if there is bad news from the Front you will tell me. That you will call for me if things are different – ever.'

She nodded, quite unable to speak.

He said no more, only smiled with great brilliance as he left the kitchen. When he had gone she turned again to her washing and scrubbed with vigour, almost as though she could wash away her troubled thoughts.

No one else came to disturb her and she finished her task without interruption, hanging the clean garments on a line near the kitchen stove and hoping that if the Avinkovs really invited her to dine or dance, she would not reek of wood-smoke and stewing pork.

The note came two weeks later, addressed to Natalia Petrovna and inviting her, her eldest daughter and her cousin to a small reception in ten days' time. Despite Nikolai Alexandrovitch's obvious if unexpressed disapproval, Dindin took the letter to her mother. As usual Natalia Petrovna was in bed, this time with apparently crippling pains in her legs. The fiction that she was unwell was carefully maintained by the whole household, not least because no one could spare the energy to listen to her complaints and persuade her to ignore her hypochondria. But when Dindin held out the beautifully written invitation, her mother's eyes brightened and as she took it she said:

'What is this, Dindin? An invitation? How charming. Madame Avinkova – I am not sure that I remember her. Ah,' she went on, 'she has dear Sergei Ivanovitch staying with her. Well that explains it all. Well, my dears, shall we go?'

Very surprised to hear her mother talking so cheerfully, Dindin said:

'Oh, Mama, could we? I should so much enjoy a party again. It seems far too long since I dressed up or saw anyone outside this house. Evelyn, you would like it too, wouldn't you?'

Equally surprised by her cousin's enthusiasm and very pleased, Evelyn found herself able to say yes without the slightest doubt or reservation, and entered into the subsequent plans for what each of them should wear with all the lightheartedness that Sergei would have wished.

All three of them decided that the clothes they had brought with them just would not do, and Natalia Petrovna summoned the inarticulate Siberian housekeeper to ask what there might be in the house that could be used to make new dresses.

Karla took a while to understand the question, but when she had, she proved extremely helpful. She led Dindin off to one of the attic boxrooms and showed her a large, brown-leather trunk. Dusty and covered with cobwebs, it looked anything but promising, but the girl obediently knelt down and opened it. The lid lifted to reveal a welter of bolts of brightly coloured silks, reels of thread, papers of pins and beads and sequins. There were hanks of seed pearls and crystal beads: everything that could possibly be needed to create dresses for the entire company at a costume ball.

Closer inspection proved that not all the silk and gauze was in good condition. Some pieces were damaged or coming apart where they had been folded for so long, others were not as clean as they might have been, but by the time they reached the bottom of the treasure trove, Dindin and Evelyn had discovered at least enough sound pieces to make gowns for all three of them.

The mystery of the trunk was unravelled by Andrei Alexandrovitch, who laughed when he saw them staggering downstairs under their burdens of gaudy stuffs.

'I see you have found my mother's fancy-dress trunk. Goodness, I had forgotten all about it. She loved dressing up and masquerades. Well it makes a nice change from the winter's dreariness. What are you going to make with them?'

'We have been invited to a reception, Papa. Mama and Evelyn and me. For the week after next. We may say yes, mayn't we? Mama wants to come – and she says that she is well enough, really she does.'

Evelyn thought that Andrei Suvarov looked as though he were going to forbid it for a moment, but Dindin rubbed her cheek against his arm and whispered appealingly:

'Papa, please. You're always so nice to me – and you like me to be pretty and happy, don't you? Dear Papa . . . please.'

He allowed his stiff lips to relax and his bright blue eyes to soften as he said kindly:

'Yes, of course you may go, Dindin. You have all been working so hard you deserve a bit of a treat. And I would certainly like to see you in a pretty dress once again. Do you think Madame Avinkova would allow me to come as well?'

9

The invitation was accepted and Dindin and Evelyn, with Natalia Petrovna's help, started to cut out and sew new dresses for themselves during their few hours of free time. Nikolai said nothing to try to persuade them not to go to the party but Evelyn felt sure that he was ashamed of her. One evening as she sat sewing the last seed pearls round the hem of her frock of old-rose silk he complimented her on the creation, and she searched his face for signs of sarcasm.

'Are you very angry with me, Uncle Nikki?' she asked.

'Angry? No, of course not. Why should I be angry?'

'Well, but . . . because you do not approve of parties and things, and because there's so much to do here.'

'My dear Evelyn, I have no such prejudices,' he said, nearly laughing. 'My only determination is that no one living in my house should ever depend on a servant to do for them tasks that they believe themselves too good to do. Provided that you don't idle away your days while others work, I do not mind what you do in the evenings. In any case, it is for you to decide; you are a grown woman.'

Nikolai's permission removed the last of Evelyn's anxieties and she started to look forward to the reception with unshadowed pleasure. At first she had thought that there might be some awkwardness with Sergei, but she had seen him in the town once or twice since he left the house, and he had behaved with all the friendliness that she could have wanted. He made no references to marriage or love and so she relaxed and simply looked forward to seeing him again. The spring thaw had made it impossible to skate any longer and the melting snow had turned all the roads into morasses of unwalkable mud and so there was no obvious way for them to meet except at organised social occasions.

Because of the mud, Nikolai had asked Mischa to drive his sister-in-law and the girls to the Avinkovs' house, and as she stepped into the carriage, dressed in silk, with her hair elaborately arranged for the first time in months and long gloves covering her work-ruined hands, Evelyn could almost imagine that the Revolution had been a nightmare and that she had woken up to find herself back in the old life.

When they arrived they found the Avinkovs' pleasant brick house spilling over with light. There seemed to be almost a hundredweight of candles burning in sconces and candelabra all over the three rooms that had been flung open for the party. The sound of violins and a piano enticed them into the biggest of the rooms and Dindin took a deep, happy breath as she watched gaily dressed girls in the arms of handsome young men whirling around the dance floor to the lilting sound of a Strauss waltz. Evelyn stood at her side, hoping that Sergei was not going to embarrass her, and wondering whether she would embarrass herself when she saw him again.

Madame Avinkova came to greet them as soon as she caught sight of them and took Natalia Petrovna off to introduce her to the other Shenkursk ladies, leaving the girls to Sergei, who appeared in front of them, as attentive and polite as he had always been. He quickly introduced Dindin to another young man and swept Evelyn off into the middle of the dance floor. The music was irresistibly light-hearted and almost in spite of herself she leaned towards him and allowed him to lead her into the seductive steps of the waltz. They did not speak, but she felt as though his smiles were telling her that he had understood and accepted what she had said to him and would never again press her to forswear her love for John. That certainty allowed her to give herself up to the pleasure of dancing with him, feeling the strength of his arms as they held her and looking up into his handsome face.

Sergei looked down into her happy, ingenuous eyes as he danced and thought that it would not be long before he could persuade her to forget the lover who had quite certainly died in the trenches. He relinquished her with regret at the end of the waltz to an importunate young man who had obviously been struck by her luminous beauty, and went off to talk to his host, who understood exactly what he had been sent to do in Shenkursk and wanted to help.

Evelyn went from one partner to the next, never suffering the indignity of having to retreat to Natalia Petrovna's side, although there were fewer men than girls at the party, and only slowly began to wonder why she was not enjoying herself more. She had not expected the old, unthinking delight that she had always felt dancing with Johnnie at the Yorkshire hunt balls before the war. That innocent happiness was gone for ever. But to think, in the middle of a waltz, that she would actually prefer to be darning sheets and talking to Nikolai, or even reading stories to Sasha and Tallie was a surprise.

The music was charming, she was back in the old life, complimented, sought after, danced with, and yet something was missing. Her partners talked of places they had visited 'in the past', although none was crass enough to say 'before the Revolution', and of people they knew, the ballet, the Moscow Arts Theatre, the weather, the new arrivals in Shenkursk and the talents of the small orchestra that was playing in an alcove at one end of the elegant room. It was all just as it ought to have been and yet it seemed hollow. Evelyn wanted to forget what she had seen and suffered in Petrograd just as much as anyone there, but to pretend that none of it had happened began to seem absurd.

One of her partners took her into dinner and asked her about the differences between life in England and Russia and she so far forgot herself as to mention her last months in Petrograd. His shocked expression reminded her of her social duty and she toned down the rest of her answer to make sure that nothing unpleasant could be read into it. In her turn, once she had run out of things to tell him, she asked about his home, and he described to her the glories of his family's

131

estates in the Crimea, which she assumed must have been broken up and distributed among the peasants like all the others there. But she said nothing to hint at this and nor did he.

He danced with her again after dinner and paid her extravagant compliments while she tried to find him amusing, delightful, charming, but by the end of the party she found herself wondering how they could all be so blinkered. It was absurd to carry on like that once the whole world had changed.

When Sergei Ivanovitch said goodnight to her as he saw her and Dindin and his aunt to their carriage and asked her if she had enjoyed herself, she smiled as well as she could and said:

'Oh, yes, it was good to spend time frivolously once again.' Then she thought even that was not enough to satisfy him and so she turned to her cousin. 'Wasn't it, Dindin?'

Dindin, snuggling into the fur collar of her evening cloak, looked up towards the black, starry sky and said voluptuously:

'It was the most wonderful evening I have ever spent. I felt alive again.'

Sergei appeared to be satisfied and assured Dindin as he kissed her that he would see that she was invited to every party that was planned in the town. They all thanked him and he watched as they drove away, congratulating himself on bringing Evelyn out into the world again, certain that she would not be able to resist him for long.

The three women hardly spoke on the drive back, but as they drew up outside the pillared portico of the Suvarov house, Evelyn said in a tone of surprise:

'Who can be up still? It is after one and there are still lights in the hall.'

'Well of course there are, Evelyn,' said Natalia Petrovna, 'they will have been left on for us.'

'Not so many, surely. One lamp and our candles would have been enough. Uncle Nikki is never extravagant with the lamps.'

'What are you worrying about?' asked Dindin, laughing at her and still floating in her state of delight.

'I am not sure, but we must go in and see what has happened.'

She almost ran up the shallow steps and pushed angrily at the door when it refused to yield. After another try she managed to open it and almost burst into the hall to see Nikolai and his brother standing by the empty stove talking to another man who had his back to her.

Natalia Petrovna and Dina were not interested in anything except the splendid time they had just spent and went upstairs to bed, calling 'Goodnight' to the men as they went, but Evelyn walked curiously to the other side of the hall. Nikolai Alexandrovitch had turned to smile at his niece, and as the other men moved aside, Evelyn was amazed to recognise Robert Adamson.

He looked even more untidy than he had in the old Petrograd days, and very tired. As he felt in his breast pocket for his eccentric spectacles, Evelyn noticed some other change in him, but she could not define it. He seemed somehow softer and, without thinking, she went in at once to attack him.

'What on earth are you doing here?'

He laughed ruefully and answered unhelpfully:

'That's a poor welcome for an old friend after the kind of journey I've had from Moscow. Piotr sends his regards, by the way.'

Evelyn stepped back at that, and her lips thinned and her nostrils flared in a parody of disgust.

'I never want to hear anything of him again. Don't you know what his Bolsheviki are doing to Russia?' As he put up his hands in a gesture of surrender, she said furiously: 'It's not funny. Do you know what they did to Sergei Ivanovitch's parents and poor Ekaterina Nikolaievna?'

His big, bony face sobered at once and the lips that had twisted into the familiar half-mocking smile straightened again.

'Yes, Georgii told me right after I got here. Look here, Miss Markham, I am as disgusted as you must be and as Piotr would be if he knew. We both hate brutality. But you can't judge all the Bolsheviki by the actions of the criminal element – just as I don't judge all the "Whites" by the atrocities some of them have committed.'

Evelyn was about to challenge him when she felt Nikolai's hand on her wrist and heard his familiar, deep voice.

'Child, don't. Mr Adamson is our guest here. His paper has sent him up to the North to write articles about what is happening here and I have invited him to stay with us for a while.'

She turned away, disappointed in Nikolai for the first time.

'I'm sorry, Uncle Nikki. I just can't bear to think about the Bolsheviki he admires so much and the things they do. Andrei Alexandrovitch, can you allow this man who took Piotr away from you to live here?'

Her tone brought a small flush into her cousin's pale cheeks and a harsh glitter to his eyes. He looked at her so angrily that she expected him to speak in his old manner.

'Andrushka.' There was no sound of command in Nikolai's voice, but his brother shrugged. Then he turned back to Evelyn.

'I have told you before that I do not wish to hear that name spoken,' he said with uncharacteristic calm, and then he walked away.

'Evelyn, you're tired,' said Nikolai quickly, seeing that she was about to protest. 'Come, up to bed. We can talk about all this in the morning.' He walked with her up the stairs, as though to make certain that she did not join battle with Adamson again, asking questions about the party.

'It was all right. Sergei sent his respects. What did Georgii think about Mr Adamson's arrival?'

'Much the same as you, my dear, and I am afraid he flung out of the house to join Voroshilov. He'll come back, though.'

'I wouldn't be too sure of that. He's been restless and angry for ages, and when Sergei told him he ought to be fighting he said he'd do anything to get out of here.' She looked sideways and then in a rush of compunction said: 'I'm sorry, Uncle Nikki. I shouldn't have said that.'

'He's a fool, but I can't stop him if that's what he wants to do. Now, forget all about this, dream of your dancing partners and sleep well.'

She tried to smile for him and left him at the door of her bedroom. But it was some time before she slept as she worked over what she would like to have said to Adamson if she had been allowed to speak her mind, and what she would have done to Piotr if he had appeared, and how very much she wanted to be out of Russia and back in England where people behaved as they should and were polite and honest and straightforward.

During the days that followed, she often looked up to see Nikolai watching her with his eyebrows raised as she rushed into angry quarrels with Bob Adamson, but he annoyed her so much that she could not accept Nikolai's unspoken rebukes.

Almost everything Adamson said jarred on her and she could not understand why Nikolai allowed him in the house and – worse – seemed to like him. With Sergei and Georgii both gone, Evelyn had looked forward to a few evenings alone with Nikolai, but now, whenever she had finished clearing away the dinner and tried to talk to him, there would be the American talking, playing chess, monopolising Nikolai. It was too bad; Evelyn felt an unaccustomed and distasteful jealousy that made it still harder for her to behave to Adamson with even the barest civility.

It was only the recognition of his usefulness that eventually made her accept his presence. He turned out to be enormously capable and seemed to have set himself to outwork his host, digging up vegetables, feeding the pigs and chickens, splitting logs for the stoves, climbing ladders to mend roofs that had been discovered to be damaged once the thaw sent streams of water through every crack and gap in the shingles.

Evelyn watched him. Much as she admired his industry and apparent talent for the work, she decided that he must have been bred to it, and had perhaps fought his way up in his career. In a way that excused his peculiar manners and the sarcasm she had come to expect from him, and it made it easier for her to ignore him at all but the most superficial level. They spoke to each other at meals, or when he brought a bucket of potatoes into the kitchen when she was working there, but that was all.

Adamson was annoyed to find how much he minded her attitude. He had thought about her often in his increasingly bleak months in Petrograd and later in Moscow as the chaos of the Revolution made life more and more difficult – and as the growing realities of power bit into the Bolshevik leaders. He had welcomed his editor's demand that he find out what was happening in North Russia not least because it would get him away from witnessing the undeniable changes in the men who had transformed the Revolution. Even Piotr had seemed to harden as the painful months dragged on. They quarrelled often about what could or could not be justified in the name of preserving the Revolution, and once kept apart for nearly a month because they had hurt each other so badly. Then, when Bob got his editor's orders, he went to see Piotr to try to rescue their friendship before it was too late.

Piotr greeted him stiffly, obviously still smarting and angry, but Bob made himself hold out his hand and say:

'Piotr Andreivitch, I guess that many things I have said have offended you very much, but now that I have to leave Moscow, won't you forgive me?'

Piotr's thin, tired face broke into something like his old smile and he used the Russian diminutive he had once bestowed on his friend:

'Romochka, we have been like two children. You're right to try to put things together again.' He took Bob's hand in both of his and held it in a warm clasp for a moment. Then he asked where Bob was going and, on hearing that he had been sent North, insisted there and then on writing to his uncle. As he handed the single sheet to Bob, he said:

'Do go to Nikolai Alexandrovitch. He's a good man. You'll see Evelyn when you get there: will you tell her I often think of her?'

Taken aback that at this emotional moment of reconciliation Piotr should be worrying about his tiresome English cousin, Bob said coldly:

'If you like.'

Piotr stood up from the rickety table where he wrote his letters and gripped Bob firmly by the shoulders.

'Don't be misled by her ridiculous attitudes and conversation, Romochka . . .' Then he took his hands away and there was a hint of exasperation in his tone: 'Why do you insist on seeing only the political opinions of the people you know? There's much more to them than the way they believe the world should be organised.'

After that he had talked of other things, leaving Adamson surprised to have been so taken to task by a boy ten years his junior. After he had left the shabby room, Piotr's letter to his uncle in his pocket, Bob allowed himself a minute or two to examine the charge, but he had no difficulty in dismissing it. Anyone who could show Evelyn's cold disregard for all people who did not fit into the classes and nations she admired, had to be dismissed: intolerant, insensitive, selfish, arrogant – she could never be trusted, any more than his own family could be trusted.

Even so, there was the unfortunate fact that he could never quite banish the thought of her from his mind, and during the tedious and difficult journey up to Shenkursk he had toyed with the thought of what it would be like if he found her changed: as beautiful and alluring as ever, but with her mind and character transformed.

And then her greeting had hit him like a blow in the face. During the first days in Shenkursk he came to detest the accusation in her fine eyes as much as the superiority of her manner. He was surprised to see how much she obviously liked Nikolai Alexandrovitch and how easily she talked to him, but she was not the woman he had imagined he might one day discover. He tried to laugh at himself for his fantasies and for his inevitable disillusion, but somehow he could not.

One evening in June, when she and Dina had gone to yet another party, he and Nikolai were playing chess, and he was trying to stop thinking about her. He had no idea of the time, and the light streaming in through the windows made him feel that it must still be early. Both men were dressed in loose peasant blouses and thin breeches, for the weather was sultry, and they looked almost like brothers: tall, rangy men with determined faces and clear eyes. Nikolai's full beard and greater bulk singled him out as much as his twenty years' seniority, but there was something akin about them.

Bob had just escaped checkmate by the skin of his teeth for the third time in their fifth game, when he said out of the blue:

'Why does she carry on like that, Nick?'

The elder man picked up his queen and sat turning it slowly round and round in his big, calloused hands. Although they had not spoken of Evelyn all evening, he knew just what Bob meant. There had been an unpleasant scene as Evelyn, already dressed for her party, brought in the dinner for those who were not going out and Bob had tried to compliment her on her appearance.

'She is unhappy, Bob; deeply unhappy. You must make allowances.'

'But she makes none.'

'How can she? Think, my boy: her lover was probably killed at Loos and she doesn't know any longer what she really feels about him. She is homesick; she is stuck here, in danger and anxiety and – for her – privation, in a revolution that has nothing to do with her. She does not know when or if she will get home; she has done her best for the family and she gets little enough in return except from Sasha. Do you wonder that she is edgy?'

'I give you all that, Nick. But it's not just the circumstances. She is better – just – than she used to be, but that darned condescension of hers – how can you bear it?'

'I say it again, Bob: think! What defence does she have against this world she's been catapulted into? She was getting better here, with plenty of work to do and no outside interference, when that damned nephew of Natalia Petrovna's must ruin everything by whisking her into this ridiculous "season" in the town. She hates going to their parties, have you noticed? But she can't not do it. It's the only thing she's been educated for, and she thinks that it is the real world. When you or I seem to mock it, of course she condescends.'

'I suppose so. You're a tolerant man, though.'

Nikolai put his queen down again on the chequered board, said, 'Checkmate,' and then after a small pause, 'But I am not in love with her.'

Bob looked at the carved limewood chessmen and then up at his friendly adversary. He took off his spectacles and rubbed both lean hands across his wide, high forehead.

'Can you seriously believe that I . . .?'

Nikolai did not try to hide his smile of amusement as he started to pack away the chessmen in their long box, and Bob Adamson saw it, but before he could speak, Nikolai said:

'Every time you look at her, or are standing near her, it shows. The anger is only hiding it from you. When you take a plate or a glass from her your hands move towards her as though you want to touch her; when you're talking and she stands beside you you lose the thread of what you're saying as your mind locks into wanting her; you . . .'

'All right, all right, I surrender,' said Bob, putting up both hands and laughing.

'Yes, but, perhaps I ought not to say this . . .'

'Come on, Uncle Nikki,' answered his friend, using the children's name for him, 'out with it.'

'I was just going to say that you must be careful with her. She has no energy to spare at the moment; I don't think she could bear to have to deal with your feelings now – or her own.'

Adamson's strong, wind-tanned face was lit by a smile of some sweetness, but his voice was sardonic as he said:

'Don't tell me what she feels or I may have to do something about it. You can put your mind at rest, though, I won't. Apart from the fact that I can't stand talking to her, it'd be impossible to deal with the consequences in a place like this.'

Nikolai concealed his instinctive anger at the American's disparagement of Evelyn and was about to speak when they both heard voices outside the window. Then the door opened and in came Natalia Petrovna and her daughter, followed by both Evelyn and Sergei. Her face was brightly alive in a way the two waiting men had rarely seen, and her eyes were alight. She almost danced up to Nikolai as she said breathlessly:

'Uncle Nikki, have you heard? Oh, I know Sergei shouldn't be here, but you will forgive me for bringing him, won't you? I thought you would want to know, and you would have had no reason to believe me. But he will tell you. They were all talking about it tonight. Oh, go on, Sergei Ivanovitch, tell him.'

The outburst convinced Bob that his first suspicion was wrong. His heart stopped thumping in his chest. Like Nikolai, he turned to the Russian officer and waited.

Sergei apologised formally for his presence in the house and then said far more quietly than Evelyn had spoken, but with almost equal triumph:

'They are here, Nikolai Alexandrovitch. In Archangel. They landed at Murmansk some time ago, but now they have taken Archangel and the Bolsheviki have fled.'

'Who', said Nikolai in a voice that sounded as sharp and cold as ice, 'are they?'

'Us,' said Evelyn incoherently but with the happiest of smiles on her beautiful lips. 'The English. Oh, and some Americans too, Mr Adamson. Under Admiral Kemp and General Poole. Everything is going to be all right now. They're here. Isn't it wonderful?'

'They didn't do it all themselves, you know, Evie,' said Sergei in a tone of amused indulgence. 'Captain Chaplin played his part.'

'Oh I know, Sergei Ivanovitch,' she said, the basic generosity of her character displaying itself for once. 'I know that if the Russian officers had not organised the coup the landing could not have been made so easily, but isn't it wonderful?'

Robert Adamson did not stop to analyse the anger that caught at his throat as he saw her turn so confidingly – almost lovingly – to the Russian, whom he had always considered to be a self-important, dangerous, melodramatic fool; he just said in a biting voice:

'"Landing" seems an over-friendly word for what sounds to me like an invasion. How many people did they kill?'

The joy died slowly out of Evelyn's face, leaving it pale and pinched. Her voice was a little hoarse, too, as she repeated, 'Kill? Why should they have killed anyone?'

Disregarding Nikolai's restraining hand on his shoulder,

Bob moved right up to her and, looking down into her up-turned face, he said:

'People get killed in invasions, Miss Markham. How did they do it? By shelling the town from the sea?'

She shrank back against Sergei, who immediately put a protective arm around her waist and smiled tauntingly at the American, whom he considered to be dangerously unsound, almost a Bolshevik himself.

'Really, Adamson. There is no need to be so unpleasant.'

'Very well, I shan't interrogate Miss Markham, since she obviously knows nothing, but you tell me: shelling?'

'A little, I gather, just to silence the batteries of guns at the mouth of the Dvina. There were no casualties.'

Seeing that Bob was about to burst into intemperate speech, Nikolai intervened.

'Evelyn, will you please take Dindin up to bed? It is very late, and you will all be exhausted with the excitement. I am happy for you that your countrymen are here; you must be feeling very relieved.'

She turned to him in gratitude and moved out of Sergei's embrace. 'Thank you, Uncle Nikki,' was all she said, but she looked no happier as she went upstairs with Natalia Petrovna and Dindin, who had been chatting to one another about the dance, hardly listening to the angry talk that swirled about them.

Quite soon everyone in the town seemed to know that there had been no casualties up in Archangel and as soon as she came to accept that, Evelyn quickly regained her delight in the arrival of the Allied army. She began to feel that she was dancing away the time until the advance reached Shenkursk. Sergei was sometimes busy on some secret business of his own, but she had become acquainted with enough of the other young men to rely on partners at the endless dances or escorts to picnics. She took up riding again and after she had rushed through her share of the housework and given Tallie and Sasha their lesson, she would often join small parties on forays out into the surrounding countryside, visiting tiny picturesque monasteries or particularly beautiful views.

It was a country of forests interspersed with marshes, lakes and rivers and she became quite accustomed to standing on the edge of some vast, silvery-blue sheet of water at nine or ten at night in full daylight, watching the duck fly past in strict formation, or listening to the sound of the myriad birds that seemed to inhabit the fringes of the great forests.

It was on one such evening that Sergei renewed his serious pursuit of Evelyn. She had almost forgotten his importunate proposals and was entirely relaxed in his company. That evening she was standing peacefully beside him, looking up at the birds flying across the low sun, when he took her arm. She thought he was directing her attention to some special sight, and turned eagerly to find out what he wanted. At the sight of her face, lovelier than he had ever seen it in the soft, white light, he seized her other arm and with a quite frightening intensity said:

'Evelyn, how long are you going to keep me on a string like this? You know how much I love you, and you let me touch you, be with you, see you every day, and yet you keep me away as though you had a barbed-wire fence around you.'

His choice of words was the most unfortunate he could have produced if he had thought for weeks, and memories of her brother and John, and all the horrors of the war that was still being waged so far away came tumbling back into her conscious mind. The rosy colour faded into a pale greyish pink and deep lines appeared between her nose and chin.

'How could you, Sergei Ivanovitch? I told you I could never love you and I trusted you. You have been a soldier, too. How could you so betray a man who is risking his life for freedom?' The words of the last sentence were ones that she had often used to herself as she battled not to care for Sergei, and her voice was full of the accusation she wanted to direct against herself.

His eyes were dangerous and his mouth suddenly looked cruel. For a moment Evelyn was physically frightened of him and in a flash of memory thought of Georgii's description of his cousin's temper. But Sergei took visible control of himself and after a pause in which she could hear him breathing through his teeth, he said:

'I do not forget. But it is far too long for anyone to remain missing. You must know perfectly well that he is dead. But it is convenient, isn't it? It means that you can flirt to your heart's content, drive a man to the very brink and then leave him hanging. If I did not love you so deeply, I could play that game with you. I could probably be far nicer to you. But it is eating into me, Evelyn. I can't wait like this for you to wake up to reality.'

The angry tone of his voice helped Evelyn to hang on to her promise to Johnnie and forget all the things that Sergei made her feel. She understood, as she had not in the last few weeks of dancing and picnicking, how unfair she had been to enjoy his company and his admiration. A tiny part of her mind, of which she was thoroughly ashamed, enjoyed the violence of Sergei's protestation and thrilled to his suggestion that she was making him mad with desire and love. But most of her was sorry for it, and she stepped a little way away from him to say:

'Sergei, I never meant to flirt – I didn't understand. I thought that since you knew everything about my situation and still wanted to take me to dances and riding and picnics, it could not be unfair of me to accept. But I see that it was and I will stop it now. I am sorry.' He came to her at once and taking her hands in an almost painful grip tried to make his peace:

'Yes. You did tell me. I just didn't quite believe it. And', he added, looking into her face, 'I'm not certain that I believe it now. No, don't say anything else. Let's go back. I'll just have to try to make you see sense.'

He was turning to untether their horses just then and so he did not see the thinned lips and angry eyes of his love. She had apologised and he ought to have done so too; not suggested that he could break down her constancy to John. She was quite silent on the ride back into Shenkursk, and made herself refuse to see Sergei for at least the next week, until he forced himself to apologise and promise faithfully never to mention marriage again.

Then she forgave him, and let him dance and ride with her once more as she waited for the arrival of her countrymen, who might, perhaps, bring letters. She still told herself that she believed that one day the letter would come to tell her that John had survived.

10

It was not until halfway through September that any of the invading force actually reached Shenkursk. By then winter had begun to close in once again. The nights were dark, and the days were becoming shorter and shorter. The pretty sleighs that had been put away for the summer were taken out again to be polished up ready for the first snows, when the wheeled carriages would have to be stored under canvas covers in the stables behind Shenkursk's richer houses. Evelyn and the other ladies unpacked their sables from the protective linen bags in which they had been kept during the hot weather and set about reorganising their wardrobes for the cold.

Andrei Alexandrovitch's mother's fancy-dress trunk was raided yet again, but this time for velvets, fur trimmings and heavy silks. Bob watched Evelyn making the clothes in which she went out evening after evening and tried to mock himself out of his resentment. He would remind himself that he disliked talking to her, that her opinions exasperated him, that he did not enjoy her company; but he could not help wishing that she spent more time with him. One evening Sasha came into Bob's room when he was struggling with an article on the background to the Allies' intervention in North Russia. He looked up at the sound of the door opening, hoping against all expectation that Evelyn might have come to talk, and be sensible and feeling and warm. At the sight of Sasha's small dark head peeping round the door, he said kindly enough in Russian:

'Well, Sashenka, what's the trouble?'

'I'm so bored, Uncle Bob. It's horrid now Evie is always out or busy sewing. She never plays with Tallie and me now.'

Adamson smiled and ruffled the boy's hair.

'I know, Sashenka, but she always reads to you when she puts you to bed, doesn't she?'

'Yes, but it's not the same. Tallie and me used to help her cook and when she was doing laundry or mending she told us stories and helped us with our drawings – things like that. She never has time now. And she forgot to take my picture to her room. I'd done it specially for her.'

'I guess you should tell her, Sasha. Maybe she hasn't noticed how much she's changed,' suggested Bob.

By chance he overheard the result of his advice as he passed the children's bedroom that evening. He caught only the end of Sasha's protest, but he heard the whole of Evelyn's answer.

'Oh Sasha,' she said, and he thought there was a note of sadness in her voice. 'I wish I knew what to do.'

'Well I'll tell you, Evie: stay here with us and stop going to all those horrid parties,' came the quick, bright reply. Adamson heard her laugh ruefully.

'It's not that easy, Little Dove. You see, Sergei and Georgii are my friends – most of the time – and they think as I do about the English army that is fighting to keep the Bolsheviki from helping the Germans. It helps me to be with them instead of always here with Mr Adamson and even Uncle Nikki, who both think that my people ought not to be in Russia.' Then, as though she had suddenly remembered that it was a five-year-old child to whom she was talking, she went on: 'But you must not worry about the soldiers or the Bolsheviki. Promise me, Sasha?'

'Oh yes, Evie, of course. When do you think they'll get here?'

'Who?'

'Your soldiers, of course. I know they will beat the Bolsheviki and the Germans.'

There was silence and then Evelyn's voice came through

the door muffled as though she were speaking very close to the boy:

'I hope you're right, Sasha.'

'And what will happen then? Will they go on to Petrograd and put everything back like it was before?'

'I don't know. Sergei thinks they will. But we mustn't think about all these kind of things now. It's much too late at night for that. Which book would you like tonight?'

'It can't be very late, because you're going out, aren't you?' For the first time there was a hint of panic in the child's voice and Adamson waited, a little ashamed of eavesdropping but badly wanting to know what she would say. There was quite a long pause. Then in a voice of soft, warm kindness that he only dimly recognised, she said:

'I don't have to go, Sasha. Not if you want me to stay.'

'Yes, I want you to stay with me, Evie.'

Evelyn came self-consciously to the dinner table that night, wearing her ordinary house-clothes. She was grateful to Nikolai for making no comment on her sudden decision to stay away from the evening's party and when Andrei Alexandrovitch said, 'Well, I had not expected to see you here this evening, Evelyn,' she almost snapped at him:

'You all seem to think that I am addicted to pleasure. I can enjoy a quiet, rational evening sometimes, you know.'

'Now, now. Please don't misunderstand me. I meant only that tonight is sure to be a celebration that you would have enjoyed. After all, the first Allied troops arrived here this afternoon.'

Her expression of astonishment told them all that this was the first she had heard of the matter, and Adamson took it on himself to give her the details.

'Two hundred US troops started by river from Berezhnik yesterday and they "took" the town today. Did you hear nothing?'

'No,' she said as though dazed. 'There were no shots, were there?'

He shook his head.

'Thank God for that. No, I knew nothing about it. What does it mean?'

His voice was dry as he said:

'That the attentions of the increasingly efficient Red Army will be directed at this town and there will be a series of pitched battles and people will be killed.'

'Adamson!' came a sharp protest from across the table. The American looked up as he said:

'Andrei Alexandrovitch, you cannot deny that the whole intervention is an act of gross stupidity – and provocation. Such a pitiful number of Allied troops is going to be an irresistible invitation to Trotsky's army. Your celebration in the town is likely to be cut short.'

At just that moment there was a series of explosions. Evelyn jumped up from the table, her face whitening under their eyes.

'Oh, God, what is that?'

Nikolai put a large, comforting arm around her shoulders and drew her to the windows. He wiped a patch so that she could see out and pointed to the myriad colours splattering up against the black sky.

'Fireworks, my dear child, at the party you cut.'

She covered her face with her hands and they could see that her whole body was shaking. Muffled, her voice was hard to hear, but Adamson at least understood:

'I am sorry. What must you think of me? I am sorry.'

'Evie, my child, don't,' said Nikolai. He gently pulled her hands away from her eyes and was relieved to see that there were no tears. He was about to say something to comfort her when she said:

'It's all so difficult. I don't know what to think. I don't know what's right any more. I hate it. I wish to God I was at home.'

The big Russian took her back to the table and made her sit down again. With his hands gently resting on her shoulders she had no option but to sit still. She looked down at the tablecloth and tried to regain her self-command. At last she looked up again, apologised for making a scene and picked up her spoon.

It was not until winter had truly arrived near the middle

of November that she found any kind of resolution of her incessant thoughts. In the interval she had attended some parties and allowed Sergei to take her for exhilarating dashing drives in the Avinkovs' luxurious sleigh, which, unlike Nikolai's workaday version, was drawn by four ponies. Each time she returned from such an expedition, Bob Adamson would notice that her cheeks were flushed and her eyes bright and wonder whether it was just the effect of the sharp chill or whether the colour and light had been instilled in her by the Russian officer's caresses. Once, when she looked particularly happy and almost sleek, he was driven to say:

'Do you know what that man's job is here in Shenkursk?' She looked at him, puzzled.

'Sergei? Is he doing a job?'

'Of course he is,' answered Bob as irritated as he had ever been. 'How else do you suppose he got here or is supported here? He is conscripting local men for the White Russian forces.'

'Conscription,' she repeated, dazed both by the American's tone and by what he was telling her. He wanted to shake her, but Nikolai's warnings made him try to be reasonable.

'Yes, hadn't you heard? The only reason why they are here in Shenkursk is so that they can net more peasants for this civil war.' He saw that she had put on her haughty, disbelieving expression that hid her like a mask, and so he said almost viciously: 'If you don't believe me, ask him.'

'I shall. He will be at the dance tomorrow night. I can ask him then.'

But she did not, because by then the most astonishing, wonderful news had come down to Shenkursk by field telephone to the commanding officer of the Allied forces in the city, and from him to all the inhabitants who were interested. The Hun had surrendered. The war was over.

Everyone, even Nikolai and Robert Adamson, was able to share Evelyn's joy that the four years' blood and sacrifice and waste and cruelty and stupidity were over. Joy could not be unalloyed, of course. Those years had taken her brother and hidden John from her in a waste of fear and danger. Millions had died, but the world was safe again from the scourge of Prussian militarism. Peace would return; the Bolsheviki, however cruel they might be to their own country and its people, no longer constituted an enemy of her own. The Allies would be able to leave Russia and she, too, would be able to go home at last.

It was with a light step and a happy heart that she put Sasha and Tallie to bed that night and promised to show them her new dress before she went to the evening's dance. She had been a little afraid that Sasha might repeat his earlier demand that she stay with him, but her happiness had spilled over into him and he showed no fear or reluctance to let her out of his sight, and when she peeped into his bedroom an hour later to show off her sea-green gown, he flung his arms around her neck as she bent over him in the half-light cast by his candle, and said:

'Evie, you look beautiful. I wish I could come to the party with you.'

She laughed and kissed him.

'I wish you could, too, darling, but it's not for children. But now all this war is over, when I go home you must come for a visit and I'll have a special party for you in Beverley.'

'Promise?'

'Of course. Now I must go. Sergei will be waiting, and you must sleep. Good night, happy dreams.'

She watched him snuggle down under the quilts and she felt as though her whole being was flooded with love for him. She almost floated down the stairs and smiled at Dindin, who was waiting with her cousin at the door. Sergei bent his dark head to kiss her hand and then said:

'You are dazzling tonight, Evelyn. The perfect embodiment of England's triumph.'

'What a nice thing to say, Sergei Ivanovitch!' she said and did not even hear the snort of derision from Bob Adamson, who, Cinderella-like, was staying behind.

The party that night was like a draught of the very best French champagne for Evelyn. She had no reservations this time, danced with anyone who asked her, accepted their compliments on behalf of her country, and talked happily about the possibilities of peace and of England. Near midnight Sergei came up to her as she came off the floor with Georgii and said:

'She's mine now. Surrender her to your senior officer.'

'Must I? Oh, very well, but it's cruel of you to use your military rank to monopolise the most beautiful girl in all North Russia.'

Too busy smiling in happy deprecation of her cousin's exaggeration and in acceptance of Sergei's masterful intervention, Evelyn did not think about the significance of all the jokes of military seniority or remember Adamson's information. She merely looked up at Sergei in delight as he put one arm around her waist and took her hand. He swept her with him into the middle of the dance and looked down at her with an expression that was almost possessive as she put her head back and gave herself up to the music and the dance.

'The boy's right, you know,' he whispered into her ear. 'You are the most beautiful woman in all Archangel – if not Russia. When will you let go of your memories and let me love you as I ache to do?'

'Don't, Seriosha,' she answered as softly. 'I'm too happy tonight to behave as I ought and I feel as though I were in love with the whole world.'

'Then I am jealous of the whole world, Evelyn. I mean it. I don't think you understand how desperately I love you. You are mine, you know. You were meant to be mine, born to be mine. And on such a night as this I long to hear you admit it.'

Smiling, not taking him seriously, she moved a little closer into his embrace as they turned. She thought suddenly that all her times with Sergei seemed to involve speed and movement. Perhaps that was why being with him seemed so different from her happiest hours with Nikolai, which were all spent in still, deep peace.

Before Sergei could speak again the music stopped, and in the sudden silence before conversation swelled to take its place, Evelyn heard dull booms and crashes. Puzzled, she asked:

'Is someone else giving a ball tonight? I thought everyone was here.'

'Another ball? No, I am sure there isn't. What made you ask that?' he demanded, annoyed that she seemed hardly to have heard his carefully rehearsed words.

'Aren't those fireworks? Those explosions. You can't hear them now, but when everyone was quieter just then, I heard them distinctly.'

'Oh, that. That's just the guns at Tulgas. You can only hear them when the wind's blowing from the east.'

'What do you mean "guns"? There's an armistice.'

'In Europe, yes. But what bearing has that on our war with the Bolsheviki?

'But ... I thought ... Mr Adamson told me that the reason for our troops coming here was that there were supposed to be huge stores of war *matériel* that the English owned, which were lying on the docks at Archangel. And now that Germany has surrendered, none of that could be used against us, so there's no reason for the British to be fighting anyone in this country. We're not at war with Russia, are we?'

'With Russia? No, of course not. But with that devil Trotsky and his master? Yes, of course, as any sane men would be. The *matériel* was the excuse, not the reason for the intervention.'

Her shocked expression irritated him and when he spoke he seemed to have forgotten some of his passionate devotion to her.

'Evelyn, you are being naïve – or perhaps just silly – but no stable government of a once-allied country could sit back and watch what has been happening in Russia without trying to put things right. Surely even you must remember that what the Bolsheviki really want is revolution in all the developed nations in the western world. Your government understands that and is making a push to cut the Revolution off.'

She flushed and, assuming that she was ashamed of making him angry, he pulled her towards him and said kindly:

'I should not have spoken so roughly. There's no reason why you should understand such dull things as politics, my angel. Your lovely innocence is one of the reasons why I love you so much.'

Evelyn looked up at him and there was such scorn in her eyes that his arm dropped away from her waist before he could think or say anything else.

'Really, Sergei,' was all she said before turning away and going to make her excuses to her hostess and try to persuade Dindin and Natalia Petrovna that it was time to go home.

During the short drive the others were surprised by Evelyn's silence, which was in marked contrast to her excitement earlier in the evening, but she was too busy turning her thoughts over and over in her mind to notice them. She remembered shamingly that she had wanted, even expected, her country to come to the aid of the old Russia and to crush the Revolution. But since then something had happened to change her. The armistice should have ended all the fighting, she was sure. And Lenin and his *confrères* could no longer be seen as Prussian agents, destabilising Russia only in order to help Germany win their war with the Allies. She still hated them for what they had done to people like her cousins; the violence of the Cheka's search of the Suvarov house in Petrograd – quite apart from what had happened to Sergei's parents – would shock her whenever she thought of it. But somehow . . . She could not decide what she thought and she wanted to talk to Nikolai – or even Bob Adamson – so that she could sort it all out.

But when they reached the house, the only light to be seen was the small lamp waiting for them by the front door. Clearly the men had gone to bed. Frustrated, Evelyn went up to spend half the remaining night arguing with herself, recalling things she had said and that other people had said to her. Foremost among them was Bob Adamson's remark – 'They have to let Russia settle her own future; and they must let her out of the war: she has no resources or energy to go on fighting it for them.'

Nikolai realised that something had happened to Evelyn the moment he saw her face across the breakfast table, but he waited until the meal was over and he caught her just as she was about to pick up the heavy wooden tray of dirty crockery.

'Evelyn, wait a moment would you?' he said softly.

'Of course, Uncle Nikki,' she answered, putting the tray down again. 'Has something happened?' He waited until everyone else was out of earshot. Then he said:

'I think something has, but I am not sure what. You have lost all your happiness. Did something frighten you at the dance last night? Did that ass Sergei upset you?'

She shook her head, but he was pleased to see some of the eagerness come back into her dark eyes.

'I wanted to ask you about it, but you'd gone to bed last night, and I thought I should wait until this evening when everything had been done.'

'There's plenty of time now,' he said, pulling out a chair for her. She sat down gratefully, but seemed to find it difficult to begin, and so he prompted her.

'Sergei?'

'Only indirectly. He will go on pressing me to marry him, but that doesn't really matter. I've said no often enough. It's not my fault that he doesn't listen or believe me. No, Uncle Nikki, it was when he said that there's still fighting at Tulgas.' She looked up, the distress in her face impossible to ignore.

'And at Ust-Padenga twenty miles to the south and at Plesetskaya seventy miles to the north – between us and Archangel. I assumed that you knew. I'm not surprised you are frightened, but there isn't anything we can do.' She shook her head vehemently.

'It's not that, really. Oh, I suppose I am afraid, but I can't understand it: the war is supposed to be over. Yesterday, when we heard about the German surrender, I mean, I thought that meant the army would leave Archangel.' Her voice dropped, 'And that I might go with them.'

He put out a hand to touch hers and said:

'Evelyn, there are only two things that can happen: either your soldiers will push the Red Army right back to Moscow, which looks exceedingly unlikely; or the Allies will be forced to withdraw. When that happens I will make sure that you go with them. The colonel is a decent man; he wouldn't refuse something like that.'

154

'I didn't know you knew him,' she began. 'But never mind that. If he takes his troops away, what will happen to all of you – and the conscripts? I saw what the Bolsheviki did to Cousin Andrei's house on nothing more than suspicion; what would they do to people who had actually fought against them?'

'Probably what the Whites are doing all over Russia to the people in territories they capture from the Red Army,' he said drily and she was afraid to ask him what that was. He might have told her anyway, if Mischa had not come into the hall, stamping the snow off his boots by the door.

'May I have a word, Nikolai Alexandrovitch?'

'Of course, Mischa, old friend. Come and sit down.'

Evelyn got up and picked up the big tray to carry it out to the kitchen. As she was clumsily shutting the door behind her, she heard the kindly peasant say:

'They've called me up. Can I do anything about it? I don't want to fight my own people, Nikolai Alexandrovitch.'

'By God, I would like to thrash that man Voroshilov!' came Nikolai's voice, more angry than Evelyn had ever heard it. Not wanting to hear anything else, she pulled the door to and walked heavily to the kitchen. As she washed up the dishes and pans that had been used to prepare breakfast, she grew steadily angrier until, finished at last, she went up to the little room that had been set aside for lessons and said to the assembled Suvarov children:

'I am sorry, all of you, but something has happened that means I have to go out. We can have our English conversation later, at luncheon, perhaps, but now I want you all to write me a composition – in English – on . . . on . . . oh, what you would most like to do if you were to visit England. And I will read them all when I get back. Yes, Sasha, you can try too.'

She did not wait for any answer or protest, but shut the door smartly and hurried to her room to change her boots and put on a respectable hat and coat to cover her peasant house-dress. Then she walked out of the house, down the slippery steps and into the snow-packed street. She had never walked about the town on her own before, but obviously she could not demand Mischa to drive her this time. No one seemed surprised to see a young woman walking alone, which was a relief, but she did detect some curious glances as she neared the barracks, where, she now knew, Sergei had his headquarters.

The sentry at the gate, a young man from Michigan, was much taken with her appearance and, before going to telephone from his guard hut, tried to engage her in conversation in simple Russian. She was too involved in her thoughts to catch more than the last, interrogative, '. . . *baryshnia?*'

'Don't be ridiculous,' she said, at her most stiffly English. 'My name is Miss Markham. Please do whatever it is you have to so that I can go in and speak to my cousin.'

'You're English?' said the man in surprise. 'Hey, Johnnie, there's an English girl here.' At the sound of that name, Evelyn's face flushed and she moved forward towards the hut, before the impossibility occurred to her. Ashamed of herself, irritated with the young American's obtuseness and delay, she said:

'Oh, for goodness sake hurry up. I have no time to waste here.'

Shrugging, the man did as she wanted and after a short colloquy on the field telephone, he came out again.

'You're to go in. You'll find the conscription office upstairs on the left as you get to the second floor.'

She left him without a word and walked so quickly up the stairs that she was quite out of breath as she reached the door of Sergei's office. But for once dignity was forgotten and she went straight in without knocking and started to speak before she was even through the door.

'Sergei Ivanovitch, how could you? Do you hate Nikolai so much that you have to take Mischa? It's none of his business this wretched battle of yours; he doesn't agree with you. Why couldn't you leave us alone?'

'Us?' queried Sergei with something very like a sneer. 'I never thought to hear you identify yourself with a peasant like that one. You'll give Lieutenant Oldridge a very strange idea of yourself if you talk like that.'

Evelyn had not noticed the young English officer standing,

rather embarrassed, near Sergei's desk with a bundle of papers in his hands.

'I beg your pardon, I had not realised that you were engaged. Forgive me, Lieutenant. But Sergei, this won't wait. Will you release Mischa? What do I have to do to make you?'

'My dear Evelyn, what can you mean? There is nothing you can do to alter military necessity. There have been a great many casualties in the last week or so and we need more men.'

'I don't believe you,' she said, her eyes narrowing into angry slits and all the warmth she had ever felt for him freezing out of her. 'I think you have done this to hurt us because of what I said last night, because I wouldn't . . .' She remembered the Englishman and stopped just in time. Regaining her self-control, she went on, 'Please, Sergei Ivanovitch, will you do something? Mischa is much more than Nikolai Alexandrovitch's servant; they are old friends. Please let him off.'

'Evelyn, this is not something for discussion. Come, I shall take you back to Suvarov's house now. You know, you really ought not to walk unchaperoned into a barracks,' said Sergei, reverting to his old, caressing tone. But this time it sickened her, and she suddenly wondered how she had ever responded to him or thought him cast in the same mould as John and her brother. John had never seemed more lost to her; her need to believe in his survival had never been greater.

Without a word she turned to go, but she was halted at the door by the Englishman's voice.

'Miss Markham, he is right; a barracks is hardly a suitable place for a young lady like yourself. Won't you allow him to escort you back to the gate at least?' She turned back and smiled politely at the young man.

'You're right, of course. Thank you, Sergei.'

Sergei got up from his desk and came round to fetch his heavy coat from a rack by the door. Lieutenant Oldridge opened the door for Evelyn and she smiled up at him, thinking how young he looked and untouched. As she moved towards the door, he said with some hesitation:

'It's quite a surprise to find an English lady in Shenkursk, Miss Markham. If it's not impertinent to ask this, I wonder whether you would consider visiting some of our chaps in the hospital? They get very low, you know, so far from home and even the rest of the army. Some of them begin to wonder why on earth they're here, and they don't recover from the wounds as the doctors say they ought. I can't help thinking that if, I mean . . .' She saved him from more embarrassment by saying emphatically:

'Of course I will. I had not even realised that there was a military hospital in Shenkursk. I have been wanting to do something to help ever since you all arrived, but I did not know what, or how to go about it. I shall be honoured. When . . .?'

'Certainly not, Evelyn. It would not be suitable for you,' interrupted Sergei, buttoning his coat and putting on a fur hat. 'Oldridge, I'm surprised at you. I'll take Miss Markham home now, and we can continue our meeting this afternoon.'

The arrogance of it took Evelyn's breath away and she could not even look at the lieutenant for embarrassment. But when they had passed through the barrack gate, she rounded on Sergei. He listened to her furious outburst and then said coolly:

'Of course it is my business, Evelyn, what you do and how you behave. I love you and one day you will be my wife.'

At his assumption of ownership, her slowly seething anger reached boiling point and for perhaps the first time in her life she allowed herself to say just what she was thinking.

'You are the most selfish, arrogant man I have ever met. I have told you time and again that I shall never marry you. You are so insensitive and cruel that you continually tell me that John must be dead. You order me around. You try to insult and hurt everyone and everything you know I care for. I cannot imagine how I ever, for one single second, thought I could like you or why I have spent so much time with you. I feel quite sick that I allowed you to come so close to me.'

To her surprise, his expression of condescending amusement did not change, but his grip on her wrist tightened and he said:

'You are being rather silly to talk like that. I have considerable power in this town, you know. Not only can I take Mischa, but I can have Nikolai Suvarov's house requisitioned, his carts and carriages and the horses, too. And I will do it if you do not . . .'

Rage seemed to have given Evelyn a command of words she had never suspected in herself and taken away the last vestige of inhibition.

'You are a coward and bully, Sergei Ivanovitch. And if you are typical of the Whites then I am not surprised that Piotr turned to the Bolsheviki. You are quite despicable, and if you do any of those things you've threatened I shall go at once to the Colonel and explain your spite. I do not think that you will then last very long in this *powerful* position. And now leave me alone. I do not want ever to see you again, or speak to you, or hear your name. Let me go.'

She did not wait to hear how he would answer or whether he would find something else to intimidate her with, but pulled hard to free herself and walked quickly away. He did not follow, and she had no way of knowing whether he tried to put any of his threats into practice. But when she got back to the house she went at once to Nikolai to tell him what had happened. Some time later he told her that he had spoken to the colonel and had Mischa released from military service on the grounds of his age and poor health. She wondered what else they had discussed, for Sergei soon departed for another post further south. He took Georgii with him as a parting gesture. Evelyn was sorry about Georgii and felt ashamed every time she watched his father's bleak face in the days just after they left Shenkursk, but she could only feel relieved that she would not have to face Sergei again.

His departure seemed to have given her a kind of freedom. For the first time since he had introduced her to the social life of Shenkursk, it dawned on her that she really did not have to carry on going to parties she did not enjoy and pretending to be interested in the inane compliments of the blinkered men who danced with her. Dindin and Natalia Petrovna were amazed by her defection, but eventually accepted her explanation that she could not face dancing while her countrymen and their allies were risking death in battles so close to the town.

She also took up Lieutenant Oldridge's suggestion and as soon as she had some time to herself, she went to the hospital. There, her new feelings of freedom and relief were shaken by what she saw and heard. For the first time she discovered what bullets, shrapnel and even frostbite can do to the living human body.

At first everything was as she had expected: she was introduced to a young officer who had been sent in to have a small flesh wound in his upper arm dressed, and they chatted to each other as courteously and ordinarily as any two well-bred English people. But later she was taken into a ward full of much more seriously ill patients, some of them officers, others enlisted men. There she saw evidence of real pain and it horrified her.

In every suffering man she saw John and she felt closer to him than she had for months. She knew that she had to do something to help the men, something more than talking soothingly to them of England and America or their courage and sacrifice, and promising to write letters to mothers and wives at their dictation. She went in search of the Medical Officer and begged him to let her come and work in the wards.

He looked carefully at her, as though weighing up her capabilities and character. Then, after a pause during which she expected to be snubbed, he said:

'There is a great deal that a voluntary nursing aide could do, if you are really prepared to do it. We are severely short of nurses and need help. But it is unpleasant work, and I am not sure if . . . '

'I have become accustomed to hard work this last year, Major.'

'That isn't really what I meant. I expect you are too young in any case. You know, surely, that the rule is that no lady under twenty-one shall nurse in the battle zone?'

'But I am already here, in it. Helping you in the hospital won't make me any more vulnerable than I should be if I remained in my cousin's house.'

'No,' he agreed, still unconvinced. 'Perhaps I should have

a word with your cousin, if he is in *loco parentis*, and ask his permission.'

Evelyn gave a short, slightly bitter, laugh. 'Very well. But I expect he will say, "She is a grown woman; it is her decision."'

II

At first Evelyn was allowed to do little more in the wards than refill hotwater bottles, brew tea and take cups to the men, and check that the new arrivals were warm. She felt frustrated. Having taken her resolution to do what had to be done despite the vileness of the wounds and the upsetting groans of pain, it was annoying to find that no resolution was needed and that the only feeling against which she had to struggle was boredom mixed with guilt that she was leaving all her household tasks to her cousins. About a week after she had started work for him, she mentioned her feelings to the Medical Officer and asked if she could not do some 'real nursing'.

'Miss Markham, I haven't time to go into the innumerable reasons why you have been assigned these particular duties. I will mention only two: you are entirely untrained and have a very great deal to learn; and cold and frostbite are two of the most dangerous conditions these men have to face. They are brought here on stretchers from the temporary dressing stations through temperatures that you know perfectly well reach minus fifty degrees. It is absolutely vital that the wounded are warmed once they get here. Do you understand, or would you rather give up your work now?'

His tone and his ultimatum jolted her out of her resentment and a blush stained her pale cheeks as she whispered:

'I am sorry, Major. I had not understood.'

He did not wait to reassure her, but stalked off, far too busy, with few drugs and fewer trained people to treat the

162

patients in his care as they should be treated. Evelyn looked after him filled with a determination never again to complain or to fall short of his standards.

Of course she did fall short, more than once, but somewhat to her surprise the MO did not dismiss her even when she fainted the first time she was ordered to help change the dressing on a suppurating wound. Slowly she became accustomed to assisting doctors perform the vilest duties on the wards. She learned how to control the retching nausea and the dizziness that assailed her when she had to deal with the pus that drained from great wounds torn into the flesh of the men, just as she learned that when changing dressings or cleaning wounds, firm, decisive movements were both less painful and more useful than the featherlight touch she had tried to use at the beginning.

But she could not alter her feelings, and every time she had to touch one of the men she felt revolted. After a week or two she could deal with their wounds, but the smell of their bodies made her feel sick, and their hairiness disgusted her. Taking them bottles and bedpans, let alone dealing with the results, took more resolution than cleaning the beastliest, bloodiest wound, and she dreaded the day when she would first have to give one of them a blanket bath.

When it came, she knew she could not refuse the order. This was a man wounded in the service of his country, who had risked his life for the defence of all the things in which she believed. She reminded herself as she collected warm water, flannels, soap and towels that he deserved all the help and care she could give, but the idea of putting her hands under his bedclothes, touching him, filled her with horror.

Gritting her teeth, she set about her task, taking care never to look at the man she was washing. Her embarrassment seemed infectious and he flinched whenever she touched him. Doggedly, with closed eyes and tightened lips, she completed her task. Then, trying to subdue the nausea she felt, she carried the bowl of dirty water to the sluice room, where she was thoroughly sick.

One of the younger doctors passed by and saw her. He said kindly enough:

'Are you all right, Nurse?'

Wiping her mouth with the back of her hand, Evelyn nodded. A smile of understanding rather than mockery flashed across his preoccupied face for a moment.

'You'll get used to it. We're all human, you know. The difference between them and you is not very significant. It's all skin and muscle, nerves and blood – just like yours.'

'Please go,' she said, covering her eyes with her other hand.

Much as she hated nearly everything she had to do in the hospital, Evelyn steeled herself to go on duty every day. But, once home again, she could not bear questions about her work at the hospital and so, tired though she was by the end of every shift, she would change as soon as she arrived home and go straight to the kitchen to help with the dinner.

One evening Nikolai found her there, leaning for a moment on the edge of the range almost swaying with exhaustion. He put an arm round her shoulders and drew her to the table.

'Evelyn, my child, you ought not to work so hard. I don't think you should do all this after a full day at the hospital.'

She leaned gratefully against his strong shoulder, feeling the vast solace of his kindness, and she said without complaint:

'Uncle Nikki, I have to. There are so many things I can't do now – even the English lessons – that the least I can do to contribute to the housekeeping is help with dinner.'

'Not if it's going to make you ill, child. Besides, there are enough of us now to manage without you. Dindin can stay away from some of the parties if necessary . . .'

'Oh poor Dindin. She enjoys them so, you see, Uncle Nikki. I can't think why, but she does.'

He noticed that for the first time she had admitted her own dissatisfaction with the social round, but all he said was:

'Nevertheless, she does not need to go to one every night. I'll explain to her; she is a good-natured girl; she'll understand. Come, what else is to be done tonight? You sit there and I'll see what I can do. Just tell me.'

For a second or two she could think of nothing except the fact that in moving away to help, he had withdrawn from her. But she took herself to task and forced her tired brain into order.

'It's only the cabbage now, I think. Yes, only the cabbage. It's in that big black pot. It just needs putting on the range and testing in about twenty minutes. The stew is in the oven and the potatoes are on the left-hand plate. They might be done. Could you test them – with a fork? There's one here.' She picked it up and held it out to him.

He took it from her and as she watched him clumsily but conscientiously doing what he was told, she felt a sense of peace. She felt that she was back inside the warm circle of Nikolai's approval and no longer had to pretend or fight with herself about what she wanted.

When they took the food into the hall the only person already there was Bob Adamson. He had spent the day at the barracks, interviewing as many of the men and officers as he could find in order to write an analysis of the recent events for his editor. The interviews had been easy enough, but writing them up was proving unexpectedly difficult.

It was not the first time he had had to struggle to work since his arrival in Shenkursk, and he could not understand what had gone wrong. The short, factual telegrams he sent off whenever he could persuade the army to despatch them, presented no problem. It was the longer, more considered articles that he seemed unable to make himself write. This piece was to be a full description of the events he had so baldly reported, weighing up the evidence for and against the actions of all the factions involved, but when he sat down to write up his notes he found himself almost paralysed. He knew that he had the elements of an important story, with all the facts that he needed, but for some reason he could not weld them together. His first attempt was wordy, full of statistics and flat. Reading it over, he tried to work out where the problem was and could not.

Here in Russia, five weeks after the Allies had signed an armistice with Germany, ending the greatest war the world had ever known, an army of British, American and Canadian troops was fighting a series of battles with one of its erstwhile allies. There had been no declaration of war; consuls and ministers of most of the invading countries were still at work in Russia negotiating with the Bolshevik leaders, even though the Allied governments had not formally recognised those leaders.

The Americans, he had been told that morning, had been sent to Russia with explicit instructions from the President to do no fighting: they were there only to assist in the evacuation of any White Russians who were fleeing persecution by the Bolsheviki. Yet the British command had somehow turned the young, untrained, unpractised American soldiers into fighting units. They bitterly resented the British officers, some of whom they claimed had been deliberately overpromoted to ensure that they were senior to any American in charge.

The British were resentful too. Time and again when he was talking to British officers and private soldiers, they had apologised to him for discourtesy but explained to him that his fellow Americans were causing the 'usual trouble', some of them even refusing to fight; others fighting but making a mess of whatever they attempted. The Canadians now were a different matter, Adamson was told more than once. They seemed to know how to fight from blockhouses buried deep in snow in the middle of dense forests; they always managed to keep their guns firing, despite the murderous temperatures and the probability of getting frostbitten fingers if one took off one's gloves to clear or clean a gun. And somehow they never burned themselves on the viciously hot metal of their weapons as everyone else had done at the beginning. They were good chaps, those Canadians. They kept morale high despite the depressing perpetual twilight and boredom in which they all had to live.

All the ingredients for a rousing, indignant story were there, but Bob Adamson could not put it together. At the end of two hours of frustrating rewriting, surrounded by crumpled balls of waste paper, he was forced to think that he had somehow, somewhere, lost his anger, and with it his stock in trade. It was that anger which had driven him out of his own country and as far from his family and their money as he could get; driven him to demand a foreign posting from his editor in the first place and then kept him going during the first lonely months of his assignment in Petrograd.

Now all he could see were the reasons behind the actions and prejudices of every group of players in the Russian melodrama. That did not mean that he liked any of them, but he could not prefer any one player over the rest. Ever since he had had his first short article published he had never lacked a cause to champion or an enemy to vilify. Now, they were all doing things he hated for reasons he could understand, and he felt lost. It was as though he had no point of reference any more. He felt he no longer knew anyone, least of all himself.

The words Piotr had used in Moscow just before he left came back to him. Had he really ignored truths and facts and things to admire in people just because he thought they were on the wrong side of some line he had drawn between right and wrong? Could he even have drawn some of those lines in the wrong places? He tried to jerk himself out of this paralysing sense of doubt and failure, telling himself that however much he might have come to admire the tolerance that Nikolai Alexandrovitch had always shown, it was not something a campaigning journalist could afford to catch. He put his head in his hands and asked himself despairingly how, if he could not even make a convincing article out of such components, he would ever be able to write again.

The sounds of voices and an opening door put paid to his introspection and he lifted his head to see Evelyn and Nikolai at the door of the hall, bearing trays of cutlery, plates and food. Bob quickly got up from the table to go and take Evelyn's tray. Too tired to be surprised by so uncharacteristic a gesture, Evelyn did notice the downturned mouth and the hopelessness in his hazel eyes that usually looked so challengingly out at the world.

'What's happened, Mr Adamson? You look so tired.'

Nikolai watched the pair of them and in his heart rejoiced that at last she had seen the man and not the enemy in Bob. It might come right even now, he thought, as he went as slowly as he dared to round up the rest of the household for their dinner.

When he came back at the head of his little family he saw that they were sitting side by side at the table. They were not talking but he could feel from the atmosphere in the dimly lit room that they were at ease, and the way that they were both sitting – relaxed against the chair backs, their hands still and their faces calm – told him that all was well with them for the moment.

Evelyn looked up at him as he came to the table and her smile found an answering one in his own eyes. He could not say anything to her then with all the others present and in any case he was not sure that she knew what had happened to her, but as he sat down on her other side he touched her warm cheek for a second.

The next morning Evelyn woke with none of the dragging tiredness that seemed to have been her constant companion for months. She discovered that she had slept on her back in the same position all night, like someone recovering from a serious operation, instead of turning back and forward and winding the sheet round her in an angry tangle as usual.

She dressed in her grey uniform frock, putting a clean apron and veil in her bag ready to take to the hospital and went down to breakfast, not even wondering at the transformation, so grateful was she for the peace she had been given.

Dindin and Natalie were laying the table when she got downstairs while Sasha was talking earnestly to his father and Nikolai, and Bob Adamson was scribbling on a big pad of white lined paper by the stove. Karla brought in the eggs and coffee just then and they all sat down at the old round gate-legged table. It was an ordinary morning, yet Evelyn found it even harder than usual to make herself leave them all when it was time to go to the hospital and stood at the front door looking back wistfully until Nikolai said:

'Good luck today, my child. We shall have dinner ready when you get back tonight.'

She laughed and said:

'Uncle Nikki, I think you are spoiling me by being so nice to me. Goodbye.'

Then she left, but the warmth stayed with her all morning, even through the operation to remove two gangrenous fingers from a gunner, who had not noticed they were frostbitten until it was too late. As she stood beside the Surgeon Major, holding the chipped enamel kidney bowl to receive the stinking, ruined fingers, she was filled with sympathy for the gunner, but there was none of the sick revulsion she normally felt during such operations. For the first time, she could see the blood and the mutilation for the healing measures that they were, and feel admiration for the quick deftness of the doctor instead of disgust at what he was doing to the unconscious body on the table.

When it was over she stripped off her theatre gown and gloves, deeply thankful that it was her turn to sit with the patient until he regained consciousness instead of forcing herself through the disgusting routines of cleaning the operating table, emptying the blood and swabs and sterilising the instruments. He groaned and cried as he came up out of the anaesthetic, and swore at her for the pain in his hand as she restrained his automatic movement to pull off the bandages.

'Leave me alone, you bitch,' he said. 'It fucking hurts.'

'I know it hurts, Corporal Jones. You have had an operation,' she said, trying to keep calm and telling herself that most post-operative patients said such things before they knew fully where they were. But she was unable to help thinking: are all men such beasts underneath the surface? She kept one cool hand on his undamaged arm, speaking to him as gently as she could until the fog in his mind dissipated. When it was safe to leave him, she got up from the hard chair at his bedside and went about the rest of her duties, returning every twenty minutes or so to make sure that he was still sleeping normally and that there was no blood seeping through the bandages.

Towards the middle of the afternoon he woke clear-headed and as she stared down at him she saw him blush. Then he said, in as rough an accent as she had ever heard:

'Was it you I was swearing at, Miss?'

'Yes, Corporal Jones, it was. But you mustn't mind; a lot of patients do talk like that before they are properly conscious. They can't help it.'

'Well, I'm f——, very sorry, Miss.'

'That's all right, Corporal. Now, would you like something to drink? You're probably rather thirsty after the ether.'

Jones ran his tongue round the inside of his mouth and found it was as dry as the bottom of a parrot's cage. But his mind had returned to him, and she was a lady, and so he just said:

'That'd be nice, Miss. I could do with a cuppa.'

She smiled and went away, her ugly grey skirts swirling and her flat shoes squeaking on the polished floor. He wondered how she came to be there, an English lady like that, so kind and pretty, in the middle of this benighted arctic country in which he had found himself fighting. Jones had missed the main war, being classified C 3 because of his miserable physique and poor lungs – he had seen so many of the chaps from his town march off in their pals' brigade to fight and die gloriously for their country. He had always felt bad about that; it wasn't right somehow. And so when he'd heard they were recruiting for another bit of the war when your physical state didn't matter, he'd gone straight off and joined up. It hadn't been much fun, of course, but then it wasn't the proper war and being stuck in a blockhouse in the middle of a forest all winter would be boring. He'd fired a few shots, and he'd heard the Bolo guns, but he'd never seen one of them and none of his comrades had been wounded. This frostbite was just stupid, and it'd be tough getting a job with only one usable hand. But he'd done his bit for England like the other boys, and he was proud of that.

When the nurse came back with his tea, she had to help him drink it, but he felt better after it. She took the cup away when it was empty and then she sat down again on the old wooden chair by his bed and he could see how tired she was.

'Can I do anything else for you, Corporal Jones?' she asked in her quiet voice.

He was still ashamed to have sworn at her like he had, and

he didn't want to make her do anything else for him. Anyway, it wasn't right for a lady like her to be waiting on someone like him. But he thought it would do her good to sit for a bit, and so he said:

'Would you . . . I mean would you mind reading to me a bit?'

She looked quickly round the ward, as though checking that there was no one who needed anything more urgent, and then, full of relief that he wanted nothing that would make her touch him, she said:

'Of course I will, Corporal; though if the doctor calls for me, I'll have to stop. What would you like?'

'I've a book of poetry in my kit, Miss. There's a letter marking the one I like best. Would you read that one?'

She found the book from his pack and opened it, putting the letter carefully away in the outside pocket, and she started to read. He shut his eyes as the stirring words flowed over him, but as her voice faltered a bit he opened them again to look at her. Then he saw that she wasn't reading at all; she was speaking from memory and there were tears in her brown eyes.

'The sand of the desert is sodden red –
Red with the wreck of a square that broke; –
The Gatling's jammed and the Colonel dead,
And the regiment blind with dust and smoke,
The river of death has brimmed his banks,
And England's far, and Honour a name,
But the voice of the schoolboy rallies the ranks:
"Play up! play up! and play the game!"'

Jones put out his good hand to take the stained, tattered edition of Henry Newbolt's poems from her.

'I'm sorry, Miss. I didn't mean to make you cry.'

Evelyn shook her head and brushed the tears out of her eyes with the back of a hand that trembled.

'That's all right, Corporal,' she said, betraying none of the emotion that was boiling beneath her calm demeanour. 'But I'll have to go now. There's the night nurse arriving. She'll look after you. She doesn't speak much English, but I'll explain to her about your hand and you'll probably be able to show her anything you need. If not, call one of the doctors if you have to.'

'All right, Miss. G'night. And thanks ever so.'

She left him, flinging her bloody, soiled apron into the laundry room as she walked past it. Then she made her report to the doctor in charge, briefed the night nurse in her slow Russian and walked briskly home, the anger beginning to show in her face now that she did not have to keep it hidden from the patients.

Bob Adamson seemed to be waiting for her when she shut the big front door, and he made her sit down by the stove before she went to change.

'Nick says you're not to dream of going to the kitchen tonight. He wants you to rest, then change and eat your dinner in peace.'

She acknowledged the instruction with a rueful relaxation of her angry eyes and sat gratefully down on the cushioned chair in the warmth. Bob pulled up another chair and sat opposite, looking at her bleak face in concern.

'What's up? This is more than just exhaustion. Did something happen at the hospital?'

She nodded and then, taking a deep breath, astonished him by saying:

'Mr Adamson, do you remember that day in Petrograd when you asked me about Johnnie, about what he was like, I mean?'

Remembering with humiliating vividness the sarcasm with which he had said, 'So, tell me, Miss Markham, what was he like, this hero of yours?' and bitterly ashamed of the cruelty that had made him sneer when she had answered, 'He was prepared to die for his country. What more could you possibly need to know?', he said:

'I'm sorry to say that I do.'

'But you shouldn't be sorry, truly. It's I who . . . I've only just realised what I was doing then.' She lifted her face and looked at him with an earnestness that he had never seen in her before.

'You see, I believed it all then. The idea that he was wounded, gassed perhaps, with his memory gone or even his mind, was terrible. Of course it was. It still is. But then I didn't know. You see I thought it was all true.' She stopped, unable to pick words from the seething cauldron that seemed to have replaced her brain.

'What was true?' asked Bob, wanting to take her hands, but not daring to make any move that might make her retreat into the freezing superiority she had used so often for protection. And then in an instant he saw it and as gently as possible said: '"*Dulce et decorum est, pro patria mori*"?'

'Yes. Just that. I don't know how I could have been so, so stupid.' Her head had drooped again and her eyes gazed at the floor. Once again, but with what different emotions pounding through him, Bob Adamson put his hand under her chin and forced her to look at him.

'What happened to you today, Evelyn? I wish you didn't have to deal with those wounds and operations . . .'

She instinctively moved away from the touch of his hands and said urgently:

'No, no it wasn't that. It wasn't anything medical. It was a corporal, a pathetic, deluded man who has lost two fingers from gangrenous frostbite. He wanted to be a hero, and he thinks it's a good thing to be. He asked me to read *Vitaï Lampada* to him.' Her voice dropped and he had to listen hard to hear her words. 'I'd learned it with my brothers in the schoolroom at home, and I used to thrill to it, too. I didn't know till now what wicked, wicked words they are to teach the ignorant.'

He was at a loss; he didn't know what she was talking about. He repeated, '*Vitaï Lampada*?'

'Don't you know it? You should, for it shows that the things you used to say to me are right. I don't know why I didn't understand before.'

'Tell me.' And so she recited the whole rhythmic, dangerous poem to him.

At some of it he was hard put not to laugh, for the risible childishness of it was astonishingly funny. But the things she had seen were not remotely amusing, and the agony she was feeling was real. He watched her as she fought her way through all its verses. Then to his dismay she said:

'And Johnnie and all the others were brought up to believe it and so they went into that murderous hell to die for a false ideal. Oh, dear God, Johnnie.'

His hand went out towards her, but when he saw her lean away from it and press herself into the chair back, he knew she would not be able to accept the comfort he suddenly ached to give her. He went as quietly and quickly as he could to find Nikolai for her.

12

The trickle of wounded that had been bad enough began to swell by the time they were halfway through January. For a while the significance of the daily increasing number of patients escaped Evelyn, but by 21 January she understood. After a harrowing day during which she had had to sit by a young American boy dying from a head wound, she walked home watching the flashes of the guns to the west and listening to the roar and crash of explosions that seemed very near in the still, cold air.

'You always know what's happening: where is the battle?' she asked Bob as soon as she saw him.

Looking at her thin, anxious face, which seemed somehow stripped these days, he was tempted for the first time in his life to lie and protect her from the truth. But his impulse died in the face of her searching eyes.

'Ust-Padenga, yesterday. But they've evacuated the village, and fallen back on Matveevskaya today.'

'Ten, no, eleven miles away? Three or four hours march from here?'

'That's right,' he said shortly, wondering what she would say next and how he could deal with her if she fainted or wept. She surprised him by laughing, but there was no joy in the sound.

'Three years ago – it seems a lifetime – I fought my parents to make them allow me to go to Flanders because I wanted to be in on the war. I wanted to find Johnnie and share what he and Tony were having to put up with. It wasn't safe or suitable, they said, and they sent me to Russia. I suppose I deserve whatever comes tomorrow.'

'Listen, Evelyn: whatever I've said about your countrymen, and I know I've said a lot that hurt you, I know that they won't just leave this place to be wiped out.'

'What can they do? You've said yourself that there are absurdly few of them here, and there are thousands and thousands of Bolos. Some of the men in the hospital were saying that Trotsky himself is somewhere around here, egging them on.'

Again he was surprised to find that he wanted to lie to her, but before he could open his mouth she said, in a very different voice:

'Mr Adamson . . .'

'Evelyn, must you? At such a time, couldn't you call me Bob – or even Robert?'

She looked surprised, but obediently rephrased the question she wanted to ask him:

'Robert, if they go, what will happen to people like Uncle Nikki?'

His face contracted as though he was in pain, and he forgot that he wanted to protect her.

'I know,' he said meaninglessly. 'I asked him when the attack on Ust-Padenga forced the retreat whether he would join an evacuation from here.'

'And he said that he was a Russian,' came the deep, slow, beautiful voice that Evelyn loved. She turned and although she stood still, he felt almost as though she had run towards him.

'Uncle Nikki, you will come,' she burst out. 'You must.'

He shook his big, shaggy head and said again:

'Evelyn my child, I am a Russian. This is my country. To leave with an invading army on the retreat? How could I?'

In that moment she understood why Natalia Petrovna had taken refuge in the fantasy of illness when Piotr had torn himself out of her family. She wished that she could do the same, or even succumb to the dizzying faintness that hovered somewhere at the edges of her mind, but with Nikolai's steady dark eyes on her own she had to face the truth. She was going to lose him. Whatever happened in the next few days, he was going to stay to face the wrath of the Bolsheviki when they eventually threw her people out of their country. They would not know that Nikolai had done nothing to help the invaders; but they would find out that he had sheltered English and Americans and fugitives from Petrograd in his house. His agony in Siberia might not save him. The injustice of it, the cruelty of fate, held her speechless.

Nikolai came towards her and said slowly, calmly:

'Child, it may not happen like that. But even if it does, it will be better for me than perpetual exile. I have spent long enough barred from my home.'

'But will they understand that you have been on their side? It's not your fault that the English came to your home. Can you trust them?'

His smile cut through her as she saw in it all the knowledge and pity that had made him.

'No one can be trusted who is pushed to the limits of endurance.'

Evelyn turned away. She had too much respect for him to beg and plead and try to persuade him with threats of what might come. Whatever he decided would be the product of his past and his reason. She could never change that; and for one, short, comforting moment she knew that she would not want to.

But the knowledge of what she would be losing when she lost Nikolai made it almost impossible for her to leave his side the following morning to go to the hospital. She felt as though in tearing herself from him, she would leave part of the tissue of her own self indissolubly glued to him. It seemed that he understood that, as he had understood everything about her, and said as she got up from the breakfast table:

'Evelyn, I have to talk to the colonel this morning; I'll walk with you to the hospital. Bob, will you look after things till I get back?'

'Of course, Nick. But can't I go to the barracks for you? The colonel will be besieged with people of all kinds; you may have to wait God knows how long before he'll be able to see you. Let me go.'

Evelyn was beyond understanding anything except that she might lose some precious time with Nikolai, and she looked angrily at the American. He did not notice, but Nikolai shook his head.

'Thank you, Bob, but I have to go myself. I must sort some things out with him.'

There was so much Evelyn wanted to say to him as they walked down the embankment, past the great convent towards the hospital and the barracks, that she did not know how to start, and they had almost reached the nurses' entrance before she managed to say:

'Nikolai Alexandrovitch, you have given me so much since we got to Shenkursk that if I were to live in your house for the rest of my life I should not be able to repay you. And now we have only a few days left.'

'Dear Evelyn, I have done nothing except to try to show you a little of yourself. All I want from you is your promise . . .' He paused, his very articulateness getting in the way of the simplicity he needed.

'Yes, Uncle Nikki? I would promise you anything.'

He stopped and stood before her, his familiar figure silhouetted against the ornamented whiteness of the convent.

'Child, I am afraid for you. You are a long way down the road, but there is further yet to go before you reach safety. And as you go you will find that you will meet many people who have not set off on their own journeys, who will recognise what you have done and try to batten on to you. When that happens it will be hard for you to keep on.' He looked at her as she stood with her back to the faint lightening in the east and said with a smile that robbed his words of some of their vague menace: 'You don't know what I'm talking about, do you?'

Evelyn shook her head, but she said with the confidence of utter certainty:

'But I won't forget the words; and when whatever it is happens, I will try to stand firm for you, Nikolai Alexandrovitch.'

He bent to kiss her cheek, oblivious of the interested passers-by, and sent her off to her day's work.

It was heavier than it had ever been, and with the hugely increased numbers of casualties, the doctors and few trained nurses and orderlies were unable to do everything that had to be done. And so Evelyn found herself allocated tasks infinitely beyond the menial things that she had done so far. Not only did she have to stand by watching the cleaning and dressing of serious wounds, ready to finish the exterior bandaging and clear up the mess; now she had to do the actual dressing herself, and she was terrified of making a mistake, hurting the men beyond bearing, doing something that might stop their dreadful wounds from healing. And she still had to take them their bedpans and wash them and stop herself from showing by word or look how horrible she found all that. There was no time to stop for luncheon, or even to sit down for a few moments, and by the evening she was tired to a pitch she had never yet experienced.

The sound of the guns had come closer and closer as the day dragged on, and by five o'clock, just as Evelyn started to think she could not go on, the sharpness of the bangs and the cries of wounded told her that the enemy shelling had reached the town. She had her hands full of bandages and she was supposed to go to a boy whose right arm had been blown off when the realisation of what might be happening hit her with all the force of high explosive. Now it was not only unknown soldiers who were in danger of mutilation and death – Sasha even was at risk.

Her hands tightening on the bandages until it seemed as though the knuckles might burst through the reddened, rough skin, she worked to control her desperate, overmastering impulse to run back to Nikolai's to help protect them all – or at least be with them when the shells ripped into the house.

'Nurse! *Nurse!*' The exasperated voice of one of the medical officers eventually reached her. She turned, the sterile bandages slipping disastrously on to the dirty floor. Tears spurted into her eyes at her clumsiness, but they would do no good and she went to him at once, saying:

'I beg your pardon, Sir.'

'Nurse, there is no time to stand and dream.'

'I know that, Sir. Tell me what you want me to do.'

'There's a man – a civilian – just been brought in with both legs broken. He was hit by some madman's sleigh and driven over. The legs are in a mess and he needs sedation before we can deal with them. Fetch the morphine.'

Evelyn hurried to do as she had been told, her mind mercifully empty of everything but the list of things she would need: syringe, swabs, alcohol, the morphine itself, and perhaps a tourniquet. She collected the equipment, found one of the hospital's few trays, loaded everything on to it and went as quickly as she dared to the doctor's side.

He was bending over the patient and did not hear her arrive.

'Doctor, the morphine's here.'

'Excellent, Nurse. I'll put it in the right arm.' Evelyn moved round the bed to clean the inside of the man's right elbow, and as she heard the doctor say, 'We'll soon have you more comfortable,' she saw that the man was Robert.

It took superhuman control not to drop the bottle of alcohol; only his obvious anguish and what she could see of the multiple injuries to his legs held her firm. It wasn't until the drug had been injected into his vein and had reached his brain that he looked at her with recognition. Just before unconsciousness released him from the pain, his lips relaxed into an infinitesimal smile and he said:

'Thank God you're here, Eve.'

The medical officer was working too quickly to talk; the supplies of morphine were limited now, and he had little enough time to clean the deep cuts in which were embedded gravel and detritus of all sorts before he could begin to splint the broken bones. But when it was all done, and the legs were weighted to stop them from mending short, he stood upright at last and said quietly:

'I hadn't realised he was a friend of yours, Miss Markham. I would have got someone else if I'd known.'

He went away before she could say anything, and in any case, she herself had to go to fetch more sterile bandages and join the other doctor at the bedside of the armless soldier.

It was not until well after eleven that the wards and theatre had become quiet enough for the doctors to allow her to go off duty and by then she felt as though she might have to crawl home. Even so, she told herself that she had to speak to poor Robert before she left.

He was awake and greeted her with a difficult, painful smile. She put both hands inside the bib of her apron and said:

'Robert, I have to go now. I won't ask how you are, because I know. But they are good doctors here, and they will get you right. If the pain gets more than you can cope with, call one of them. Do you promise me that you won't try to ride it out on your own? You need all your strength to heal, not to fight that sort of thing. Do you promise?'

Her face was almost severe, and bleached by tiredness. He said:

'I promise, Eve.' She nodded stiffly, wished him goodnight, and left him.

Nikolai was waiting for her, almost as though he had known the state she would be in, and as she leaned against the front door, trying to find the strength to turn the big, heavy iron handle, he opened it from the inside, and caught her as she almost fell in towards the warm, lighted room.

He picked her up in his strong arms, kicking the door to behind him, and carried her upstairs to her bed. As he put her down and she felt the softness, she thought with relief that she could sleep at last, and just as her eyes were closing, she said:

'You're all right, Nick; how are the others? My Sasha, they haven't hurt him?'

'No, child, they haven't,' he answered as he untied the laces of her stiff, black boots and pulled them off. Then he came to the head of the bed and gently untied the veil, whose strings seemed to have caught in the short hairs at the back of her neck. She winced as he untangled them, and said:

''S'all right, Uncle Nikki. I can sleep in my clothes. Save time in the morning.'

But he paid no attention; and methodically undressed her. She was asleep before he started to take off the ugly uniform dress, and she did not wake even when he levered her into the nightdress he found under the pillow. Before he left her, he stood looking down at her and hoping passionately for her survival in the days and weeks to come. He had never had a daughter and until he had met Evelyn had never felt the lack. He was very proud of her; and he was terrified for her.

They had two more days before the colonel took the inevitable decision to retreat. By then the town appeared to be surrounded and it was only when some Russian scouts discovered that there was one rough, hardly-used logging trail through the forest that the Bolshevik pickets seemed to have overlooked that he knew how he could get his people out.

Evelyn heard the news when the youngest of the medical officers called to her just after she had wheeled a patient back to his bed after a short operation. She wondered why he had called her by her name instead of the impersonal and formal 'Nurse'.

'Yes, Doctor?'

'We're off tonight. It's to be done in absolute silence and with no warning to the enemy. They are all round the town and it is vital that they do not discover that we've gone. You have half an hour now to go and pack your essential belongings. Bring them back here, and then you will start to prepare the patients.'

The little colour left in her face drained away and the harassed doctor was mentally cursing her if she were to faint. But she said:

'You can't mean that we are going to leave them here for the Bolos.'

'Of course not, Nurse. Don't be silly and don't waste time. There's too much to be done for that. They'll all have to be carried on sleighs and so we've got to find some way to protect them from frostbite. Get back here as quickly as you can.'

She nodded and tried to run all the way back to Nikolai's house; but with a stitch in her side, and her lungs and heart pounding, she had to drop to a walk before she had even passed the convent. When she pushed her way through the door she could hardly speak. But the sight of bags and clothes and equipment strewn around the hall floor put everything out of her mind except deep, triumphant joy. Her face was transfigured as she ran to Nikolai.

'You're coming then. Thank God, Nick. Thank God.'

As gently as possible, he put one arm across her shoulders and said:

'No, child. I stay. And my brother and Natalia Petrovna. But we're sending the children.' He looked down at her head, drooping now to try to hide her rebellious feelings. 'They'll travel with Madame Avinkova, but they'd be much happier if they knew you would follow. Will you look after them when you get to Archangel, Evie, and help them get to your father in the end? It will be months before the sea ice breaks up and you'll be able to get away to England. Can I leave them to your care?'

'Of course, Nick. How can you ask?'

'I was sure of you, Evelyn.'

'I've only half an hour to pack, and then I've got to get back. And I'd better do Robert's stuff as well.'

'Off you go, child.'

Evelyn went as swiftly as she could up the branching wooden staircase to fling her few possessions into the canvas bag she had brought from Petrograd. The sable coat seemed a ludicrous possession for a refugee nurse; but at least it would be warm, and with the temperature falling every hour, she would need all the warmth she could get.

She took one last glance around the room where she had discovered how to be happy and knew that she would never forget it. Then she wasted no more time in sentiment, but walked into Robert Adamson's room to collect his clothes and the notebooks she knew would matter far more to him.

It gave her a curious sensation to be feeling among his clothes and possessions, but she had no time to worry about it. As soon as she had stuffed the last shirt into his bag and wrestled with its zip, she put on the fur coat and struggled downstairs, one bag in each hand.

The whole family was in the hall as she came down and she knew a moment's sharp misery that she would have to say goodbye to Nikolai in front of them all. But as he saw her coming down the stairs, he came to meet her, took the bags out of her hands and said:

'Come in here a moment, Evie.'

She followed him into the study and stood, waiting for him to take her in his arms. As he pulled her gently to him, she said:

'Nikolasha, I don't know how I can bear it.'

'Hush, child, hush.' She leant against him, feeling all the warmth and love he had to give her. At last the knowledge that she ought already to have been back at work pulled her away from him.

'I have to go. I'll look after the children, I promise you. And when we get back to England, they will be part of the family. If . . . when . . . I mean, they will be looked after as though they were my own and when you send for them or come to us, they will be ready.'

She looked up at him then and saw that there were tears in his eyes too.

'Evelyn, I shall never forget you.' His voice changed a little. 'Now, I want you to have this. It was my mother's and she gave it to me as she was dying. It's right it should go back to England.' He handed her a small scuffed leather box, bent his head and kissed her forehead. She ignored the box, put up her hands and held his face to her own for a long, sad moment. Then, without speaking again, she took his gift, turned and went back into the hall to say farewell to Andrei Alexandrovitch and Natalia Petrovna.

They kissed her too, and then Andrei handed her a heavy money-belt.

'There's gold here, Evelyn, as much as I could realise in time, and letters to my manager in Archangel and your consul. When you get there go straight to Baines's house and he will find somewhere for you to lodge. Dindin and the others will make their way to Baines's as soon as they get to Archangel, and meet you there.'

'Thank you, Andrei Alexandrovitch. I'll do everything I can to take care of them all. God bless you both.' With the tears streaming down her face, her heart twisting as she thought of what they might have to face, she walked out of the house and back to her work.

13

Evelyn was almost grateful for the amount of work involved in preparing her patients for the evacuation, for it made it impossible even to think about the Suvarovs. As she drove herself to renew dressings and bandages, gave injections, handed out drugs and began the almost impossible task of wrapping up the badly wounded men so that there should be no danger of frostbite, her mind was mercifully blank. But at about half-past ten, as she was taking her syringe and a phial of the precious morphine to an eighteen-year-old amputee, who cried for his mother as his mind wandered painfully away from the unbearable present, she looked across the ward to Robert Adamson's bed and all the thoughts she wanted to avoid rushed back into the front of her mind.

Leaning over him was Nikolai, come to the hospital to say goodbye. Evelyn stood by the boy's bed, a white enamel kidney bowl in her hands, looking across the long rows of beds at the two men. Nikolai, as though aware of her gaze, turned for a moment from Bob.

Evelyn and Nikolai had said what could be said; they knew that they were unlikely ever to meet again; one or both might be killed in the coming battles. There was no point in trying to put the inexpressible into words. They looked at each other for a full minute, and then each turned away.

Bob watched Evelyn standing there, her hair quite hidden by the white linen veil, her eyes huge in her tense face; the cross on her breast was the colour of blood, and in her dark eyes was such pain that he winced. As Nikolai turned back to him, Bob said:

'I'll look after her, Nick. You can depend on that.'

'I know you will, my boy.'

'Nick, God knows what's going to happen, but if there is ever a chance that I can help at all, go to the nearest US consulate or embassy and send for me.'

He put his hand out of the bedclothes and gripped the Russian's.

'Russia will survive, my friend, find its way out of this mess in the end, and so will all of us.'

'I know. Goodbye.'

'Goodbye, Nikolai Alexandrovitch.'

By 1.30 am enough transport had been commandeered for the patients, but the doctors and orderlies would have to march. Evelyn was the only nurse going to Archangel and it was clear that even if they kitted her out with the heavy felt Shackleton boots the men wore, she could not possibly last the march. It was fixed, then, that she should share a sleigh with Adamson, and once she had checked that all her patients were settled under their rugs and blankets, scarves around their faces, she slid in beside him, as careful as she could be not to touch him.

The soldiers who were to guard the hospital column formed up beside the ninety sleighs, the cloudy moonlight glinting sometimes on the bayonets each man had fixed to his unloaded rifle. The sleigh ponies' bits and harness had all been silenced with pieces of rag tied round the joints, and the three unconscious, delirious men who might groan aloud had been gagged as humanely as possible. The column would have to pass within less than a mile of Bolshevik outposts and the command were determined that no noise of any kind should alert their enemy. If anyone challenged them, he was to be killed silently and efficiently with a bayonet.

A signal gestured to the first of the drivers to move off, and, sliding on their iron runners, the sleighs began to move. It seemed an eerie sight to Evelyn as she watched the familiar buildings of Shenkursk drift silently away behind her in the inadequate moonlight. The Avinkovs' house, the convent, the shop where she had so often gone to buy tiny amounts of sugar, the jetty from which she and Sergei had gone skating on the Vaga, the place where she had stopped and faced him on the day he threatened her and she saw how she had misjudged him. She knew that in a few seconds they would be passing Nikolai's house and she resisted the temptation to look once more at it. But as they passed, she could almost feel its presence, and it brought stupid, irrational, dangerous tears into her eyes. She turned her head away from the man at her side, and surreptitiously tried to wipe them away. For some reason it seemed very important not to let him know that she was crying, but as she wiped her face with her gloved hand, terrified at some level of her mind that the tears would freeze and start the insidious action of frostbite on her skin, she felt him move.

He pulled his right arm out from under the rugs that covered them both and pulled her head down on to his shoulder. She resisted the pressure of his hand until she remembered that they must make no sound, and muffled her tears in the fur collar of a big coat Nikolai had given him.

Bob wished that he could speak to her. Some of her deep reserve seemed to have been broken by what had happened and for the first time he felt that if he could have used words he might have been able to reach her. But he could not. He could only hold her as cramp latched its teeth in his shoulder, and hope that something of what he felt got through to her.

She drew back at last, and in the poor light he looked into her eyes. For an instant he thought he saw anger there – or hate. He painfully withdrew his arm and pushed his hands back under the rugs.

They were being driven down a narrow trail between wedges of impenetrable pine forest. The soldiers plodding either side of the sleighs kept slipping in their clumsy felt boots and falling into the rutted snow. Evelyn was ashamed that she should be riding in the warmth, but knew that she was neither strong enough nor properly equipped to march.

The moonlight picked out odd features in the weird landscape, and made the fallen branches that poked up out of the snow look like dead limbs pushing up out of their dirty shrouds. Everything she looked at reminded her of death and decay. She ached for Nikolai and once more for John. Only the thought that there might be letters for her at Archangel, letters that might have news of him, kept her fading courage from disappearing altogether.

So they travelled for five hours until the head of the hospital column reached a junction with a real road at the village of Kitsa, well ahead of even the most advanced of the Bolshevik outposts. The need for silence was gone now, and they listened to shouted orders and watched the brave Canadian artillery wheel their great guns round and position them at the junction, ready to blast any Bolshevik pursuit to pieces.

By the end of 25 January, they had reached Bereznik, a village on the main road to Archangel, but it was not until 2 February that they marched wearily into the town itself. By then, Evelyn had more than once given up her place in the sleigh beside Bob to dangerously exhausted soldiers, checked every patient in her particular group for signs of frostbite, handed out rations, helped to brew hot drinks on pathetic fires lit by the roadside, and carried out myriad instructions from all the doctors in turn.

On 29 January they had heard sounds of rifle fire, and Evelyn had stopped in the middle of renewing a dressing to listen, appalled to think that her cousins might even at this late stage be involved in a battle with the Bolsheviki. Dull, thunderous crashes succeeded the sharp rifle cracks, and the man on whose wincing body she was working said in his strong Detroit accent:

'That's the Canadians, lady. That's why they were left there. They'll see to it. Don't you worry.'

'No. Thank you, Sergeant,' she said, looking at the stripes on the torn, bloodstained tunic. 'There, I hope that's a bit less uncomfortable.'

'I'll do fine. On your way now. There's no need to stay.'

She hid her relief in as bright a smile as she could summon up and plodded back through the icy hard snow to the sleigh. Adamson welcomed her back with a searching look and a curt instruction:

'Get in and sleep. You'll drop if you go on like this.'

She was too tired to answer, but she obeyed, taking care to lean against the side of the sleigh so that she might not slip over in her sleep and find herself lying against him.

Adamson understood what she was doing and wished that he could hug her – comfort her in the only way he could think of – but he could not find enough energy to try to batter down her resistance. He was so tired.

Trying to think of something other than the pain in his legs, he looked sideways at Evelyn. Something about the way her dark head drooped against the back of the sleigh made him think of the last scene with his mother before he left New York for ever. He had never written to her and had thrown her letters away without reading them, telling himself that he wanted to cut every feeling for her and the rest of them right out of his mind. What they had done still shocked him, but his own self-righteousness now tasted a lot less satisfactory than it had done.

He looked back at his younger self and if he had not been so weary would have laughed at the poor fool: so idealistic that he had exiled himself from home and family because all they seemed to care about was making themselves a second, quite unnecessary, fortune; and so ignorant that he had believed he could find people, somewhere in the world, who were governed not by the desire for wealth, but only by a love of humanity. An insidious idea suggested itself to him and he began to imagine the letter he might write to his mother.

Then he took himself to task and chided himself for his ludicrous sentimentality. That part of his life was over. He would never go back if he could help it. What he ought to be doing was sorting out in his mind what he would write in his next major article about the reconstruction of this country.

But that was no better; what was the point of pretending that Russia would soon be normal again and that the revolutionaries whom he had idealised would turn out to be the men he had always thought them? Stories of terrible cruelty perpetrated both by Whites and Reds came back to him and reports of unpleasant punishments invented by the Bolshevik leaders, which he could not ignore. The one that most horrified him had been imposed on Maria Spiridonova, a leader of the Left Social Revolutionary movement. She had paid terribly for her belief in the Revolution, suffering multiple rape by the Tsar's Cossacks who arrested her in 1906 and then sentenced her to penal servitude for life. She had been released by the first revolution and used her freedom to argue passionately for the rights of the peasants, whom, she believed, Lenin hated. Her opposition to the Bolsheviki had led first to imprisonment in the Kremlin and now, Bob had heard just before his accident, to forcible incarceration in a home for neurasthenics. That the leaders of the Revolution could not accept criticism or verbal opposition from people who were essentially of the same mind as themselves shocked him; that they could so severely and unnecessarily punish people for those criticisms reminded him sickeningly of the Tsar and Rasputin and all the most-hated figures of the past.

He had believed implicitly in the Revolution, convinced that its chief aim was the alleviation of human misery. Not until he had seen for himself what happens when idealists get their hands not so much in the till as on the executioner's rifle had he understood that human suffering did not concern any of them very much. He hated the way he had been forced to face the consequences of Marx's tenet that ends justify means, and he despised himself for ignoring them until he had been so forced. The only glimmer of light in the darkness he had pulled over himself was the memory of what Nikolai Alexandrovitch had said just before he left the hospital:

'My boy, if you truly want to make people happier, safer, even better fed, than they are, then you must set about it yourself – directly. Any mass movement, organised politically, will by its very nature create more misery than it can possibly cure.'

Half lying in the sleigh on his way to a town on the edge of the Arctic Circle, fleeing from a civil war that was becoming more vicious month by month, surrounded by danger and death, Bob tried to force himself to concentrate on that article of Nikolai's faith. But he could not, and in his depression and pain his mother's face and words as she said goodbye to him came back to him in the extra vividness of dream. He had always persuaded himself that she at least was untouched by the desire for money and then more money, but she had not tried to make him stay. 'My dearest boy', she had said sadly, 'I think I can understand why you want to get away from us, but please be careful – and come back to me.' Her beautiful dark head had drooped and her voice had been very low, the pain in it unmistakable.

A sound from the sleeping girl at his side interrupted his thoughts and he said, relieved:

'Yes, Eve, what is it?'

'Oh, it's you. I was half asleep. Sorry.'

'Yes, I'm here,' he said, and then added under his breath: 'I'll always be here when you want me.'

On arrival in Archangel they were separated. The military authorities categorically refused to treat a civilian, even an American one, in the military hospital and the senior doctor from Shenkursk was reprimanded for having included Adamson in the convoy of wounded soldiers. An ambulance was summoned and he was transferred to the Russian hospital in the town, while Evelyn had to stay with her other patients and see to their disposal around the tented army hospital. As he was taken away he looked at her anxious face for a few moments and then said:

'Don't worry about me, Eve. As soon as I can stand, I'll be out of there, and I'll come and find you.'

'Take care, Robert. Don't let them . . .' She let the sentence hang unfinished, and stood and watched him taken away, worried for him, but still more concerned about her cousins, who with the rest of the Shenkursk refugees had still not arrived in the town.

When she was allowed to go off duty she refused a billet with the other nurses and went at once to Andrei Suvarov's manager, Michael Baines, who lived in a middle-sized house on the Troitski Prospekt, about a mile and a half from the hospital. To her relief she found that the trams were not only working, but were also quite modern and efficient. She boarded the first one that came.

She was hit by an overpowering and unpleasant smell inside as the doors closed behind her, but she was too tired by then to care or even speculate on its origin. Leaning against the side of the vehicle, for there were no seats left, she peered out through the windows trying to catch a glimpse of the numbers on the houses in the gloomy dark of the Arctic afternoon. The conductor took her money and told her politely that he would tell her when to get off and she smiled in surprised gratitude at his courtesy.

It was the last encouraging thing that happened to her that day. When she found Baines's house and introduced herself to him, he greeted her sourly. Taken aback and freezing into a caricature of her old self, she handed him the letter Andrei Alexandrovitch had given her.

Baines read the thin sheets of crackling paper perfunctorily and handed them back to her, saying:

'It's all very well for old Suvarov to demand that I put you all up, but the house is full to bursting already. The only rooms I've got that aren't already too full of people are up in the attic. Three rooms, there are, but one's no more than a broom cupboard. You can have 'em if you like, but you'll have to get your own food. The kitchen can't cope as it is. I expect I can get you a stove and some fuel, though that's getting scarce too.'

'Fuel,' repeated Evelyn. 'Scarce in a country full of forests?'

'You'd be surprised at what this lot can turn into a scarcity,' he said with his first glimpse of humour. 'Come on up then.'

Evelyn went with him and found the three rooms relatively clean: each had a window, which pleased her even though there was no light to come through them, and if Baines could be persuaded to produce some furniture and a stove or two, they would be adequate. She turned to him with decision and said:

'Fine, we'll take them. Now, we'll need something for beds, five of them. Just mattresses will do if you really can't provide bedsteads. And we'll need some kind of chairs, at least one table, cutlery, crockery, saucepans and something to cook on.'

He ignored the end of her list of requirements and said:

'Five? Suvarov said you and three of his brats.'

Too tired and disheartened to rebuke the fat, red-faced man for his vulgar rudeness, Evelyn just said:

'Yes, but there's an American at present in hospital; he'll have to come here as soon as they discharge him.'

'I won't have any Americans 'ere. Suvarovs and you, Miss Markham, if I can and if I 'ave to. But no Americans.'

'You have no choice, Mr Baines. He counts as part of the Suvarov family too and Andrei Alexandrovitch would never forgive either of us if he were not allowed to come here.' She did not stop to think how odd it was that she was so determined to look after the man who, only a few short weeks earlier, she had thought she hated. She just knew that she had to do it.

Baines gave up the argument. He had too much to do, and he was too worried about his own future and that of his Russian wife and half-Russian children to pursue any argument with this girl. He shrugged, told her he'd see what he could do about basic furniture and left her.

When he had gone she sank down in a corner of the room and let her head droop down on to her knees. Tired out, worried, cold and hungry, she slept.

She woke about one and a half hours later to the noise of wood bumping against wood. There was a digging ache in the small of her back and her mouth felt as though she had just chewed a large ball of cotton wool. Shaking her head to try to get rid of the effects of deep daytime sleep, she pushed herself up off the floor and went out on to the landing. There in the dim light of an oil lamp on the landing below she saw Baines and three Russian men, all with long unkempt beards, struggling to push and heave furniture up the narrow, twisting stairs.

There was clearly nothing she could do to help until they got to the top of the stairs and so she waited, holding open the door of the largest room until the men stopped beside her, sweating and red-faced.

'Where d'you want the beds, Miss Markham?' asked Baines.

Evelyn had been giving some thought to the problem as she waited and said with a decisiveness that slightly appeased him:

'The American will have the broom cupboard to himself; the three Suvarovs can share the middle-sized room. We'll use the large room for daytime and meals and things, and I'll sleep in the little alcove off it.'

It was not ideal that Sasha should sleep with his sisters, but it was the most practical arrangement she could think of and the one that observed the most proprieties.

At last the man left and, feeling alone and bereft of everything that had made life even tolerable, Evelyn fumbled in her luggage for the box Nikolai had given her. There had been no time to look at it until now and in the inadequate light of the smelly oil lamp, she opened the small, shabby, brown-leather box. Lying inside on a faded red-velvet cushion was an old-fashioned oval gold locket, about an inch and a half at its widest point. There was an unreadable monogram on the front. Rather puzzled, a little disappointed, she tried to open it. Her thumbnail broke as she wrestled with the tiny catch, but at last it yielded and, removing a small scrap of stiff, folded paper, she saw two miniatures delicately painted on ivory. For a dizzy half-second she thought Nikolai must have commissioned someone to observe her in Shenkursk and paint her portrait beside one of him. Then she realised that the style of the lady's hair and dress was as old-fashioned as the locket itself. She turned it over and traced the convoluted, embellished letters of the monogram and eventually worked it out: the lady in the portrait must have been her great-aunt, who had come out to Russia to marry Nikolai's father. The man must be he, although he looked exactly like Nikolai, even down to the irresistible smile she missed so much.

She unfolded the paper and read: 'Evelyn, this was my mother's. She always wore it until she was dying; then she gave it to me. Now I want you to have it. N.'

With the gold locket clasped in her hand, Evelyn lay down on one of the beds, fully dressed. She pulled a threadbare, musty blanket over herself and with the tears oozing out of her eyes as she thought of what might happen to Nikolai, slept again in exhaustion and loneliness.

It was still dark when she woke the next morning, of course, and she had to grope blindly on the floor by her bed for her watch. Peering closely at it to see anything in the dimness, to her dismay she saw that it was already eight. She was going to be late on duty; and a quick look down at her uniform skirts showed her that they were filthy and irreparably crumpled.

Vaguely wishing that she could curse in the way some of her Shenkursk patients had done when pain or frustration got the better of their discretion, she pulled off the dress and flung it on the rumpled bed. Then she stumbled over towards the place where she had dumped her canvas bag to find another one. But she tripped over a stool and fell, grazing her knee on the rough, splintered wooden floor.

'I can't blunder about in the dark like this,' she muttered to herself and felt her way carefully to the table, where Mr Baines had left a lamp and some matches. After several false starts and burning her fingers on at least four of the matches she struck, she succeeded in lighting the lamp. She sucked the burned fingers and then put the glass chimney back over the burning wick and looked around for her bag.

There was a neatly folded dress at the top and she put it on before turning to the dirty one to unpick the studs from the collar and cuffs. But in her clumsiness, she must have pulled one out as she ripped the dress off and it had rolled out of sight. Evelyn took deep breaths to try to regain her patience and then got down on her hands and knees to search for the stud.

By the time she had found it, attached the tiresome, impractical stiff collar and cuffs and brushed the dust from her skirt, she had wasted nearly half an hour. There was no time to tidy up the squalid little room. 'Never mind,' she said to herself out loud, 'if Dindin and the children get here before I get back, she'll manage to do something about it.' Making certain that she had a clean veil in her handbag, she blew out the lamp and went out, carefully shutting the door behind her.

She saw no one on her way out of the house and felt more alone than she had done even in her first few days in Petrograd. Now there was no one to turn to if things became more than she could bear. She huddled the collar of her sable coat up round her face as the full force of the cold hit her when she stepped into the murky street and wondered desperately how long she would be forced to stay in this dark, icy, primitive town.

Setting her teeth, she turned into the wind and started off towards the hospital. Taking the tram might be quicker, but there was none in sight and so she walked, breaking into a half-run whenever she could. As far as she could see in the lamplight that streamed out from one or two of the bigger houses, the raised pavement was a kind of duck-board and in some places where the snow had been dug away, she could just see that the inferior wood was broken and splintered in many places. Terrified of tripping and breaking an ankle, Evelyn kept her eyes firmly looking at the ground. If she fell and broke her leg there would be no one to pick her up, no one to look after her, no one to help Dindin with the Suvarov children.

14

So certain was Evelyn that she was going to be reprimanded, that she hardly heard the ward sister saying:

'I think you deserve a little latitude on the first day after a retreat like that one, Nurse.' What she did hear was the final command: 'But don't let it happen again.'

'No, Sister. I'm sorry, Sister,' she said and waited for her orders.

At first she was sent to take temperatures and that was easy enough, but as the day wore on the tasks became more and more unpleasant and there was none of the informality of the little hospital in Shenkursk to help. In Archangel it seemed that none of the doctors spoke to the nurses except to give orders and there was an atmosphere of coldly official bustle. With no experience of any hospital except Shenkursk's makeshift version, Evelyn thought it all daunting and even more horrible, and as the hours ground on so slowly she would touch Nikolai's locket, which lay under her uniform dress, as though for protection.

By the end of the shift her every bone and muscle seemed to ache and she longed for a hot bath. But she knew there was no such thing in Archangel. There was no mains water supply, Baines had told her, and every drop of water used in his house had to be brought from holes cut in the thick ice that covered the river. He had recommended the public steam baths in the middle of the town, but when he told her that there were no separate facilities for men and women, Evelyn resolved never to use them. As she was washing her hands in the sluice room beside another nurse who was going off duty, Evelyn asked if there were anywhere in the hospital where she could bath. The other girl shook her head.

Miserable, discouraged and resentful, Evelyn dried her hands on a coarse huckaback towel and picked up her bag to leave. As she was standing at the tram stop, waiting in the grim, cold four o'clock twilight, she suddenly thought of Robert Adamson, alone in the Russian hospital, and knew that she could not go straight back to Baines's house. There was no way of knowing what the hospital was like, whether Adamson was being properly treated or if he needed anything. At that moment a tram bell sounded and she looked up to see the lights of the vehicle only about two hundred yards away. Her tired, aching body screamed at her to go home, but her mind knew that she could not. Squaring her shoulders, she left the tram queue and walked down a side street towards the Russian hospital.

There was no difficulty in finding Adamson's bed: everyone in the hospital seemed to have heard of the American civilian with the broken legs and Evelyn was escorted to him by a horde of interested ambulant patients. They stood about four yards back as she greeted Bob, too curious to disappear and too courteous to press forward to hear what was to be said.

He seemed to be asleep and she looked down at him, trying professionally to assess his condition. There was a whiteness about his mouth that suggested that he was still in severe pain and a deep crease between his thick brows that confirmed it. She was about to turn to go, not wanting to rouse him if he really was asleep, when his bruised eyelids opened. His hazel eyes focused at once and his lips twisted into a kind of smile.

'Good of you, Eve, to visit the sick.'

'Not at all, Robert. I had to come to make certain that you had everything you needed. Have you?'

'No. But I've everything anyone in this benighted town could provide.'

There was something in his tone that discouraged her. He

should have been grateful to her for coming, should have known how drained she felt and what it had cost her not to go straight back to her bed. He might have helped the conversation along. He had been so much friendlier in the last few days in Shenkursk and on the retreat. Now he sounded just as he always had, dismissive, sarcastic and bored.

'Well, if there's nothing I can do, I'll leave you to sleep.'

His eyes narrowed as he looked up at her from his dingy pillow. Then he smiled a real, warm smile and even stretched a hand out from under the bedclothes.

'I'm sorry, Eve. It just hurts damnably. I'm not much good at socialising just now.'

Very briefly she touched his outstretched hand, smiled in her crispest nursing manner and reassured him.

'Please don't apologise. Of course you're not. And I only came to see that you were all right. I'll look in again tomorrow.'

'Thanks. Oh, have the others got here yet?'

'No. At least not when I left this morning, but they may be at Baines's now. I hope so. Good night. Sleep well.'

'Night.'

Well, that didn't do anyone any good, thought Evelyn crossly as she made her way out of the hospital and back to the tram stop. There was no one queueing there any longer and so she must have just missed the tram. It wasn't fair; she had tried to do her best and here she was being punished for it.

By the time the next tram did appear, nearly half an hour later, she was bitterly cold as well as angry. The man who took her money returned her hard, furious stare in kind and glared at her rich furs resentfully. She shrank back and hoped that the Suvarovs might have arrived at last so that when she got herself up those steep curving stairs at Baines's house, she would find the little flat warm and lit, perhaps with some food waiting. It would be good, too, to have some company. Dindin's frivolous chatter would be almost as welcome as Sasha's affectionate pleas for bedtime stories and little Tallie's gentleness. As the smelly tram swayed down the Troitski Prospekt, Evelyn thought herself into a happier mood and was even smiling when she got carefully down from the high step on to the hard-packed snow outside Baines's. She tilted her head back to see if there was any light coming out of the attic windows, but the projecting wooden parapet below the top floor cut off her view.

Shrugging, she let herself into the hall and, seeing the master of the house, said in some excitement:

'Have they come, Baines? My cousins?'

'Yes, Miss Markham. Got in about four o'clock. They're all up there now.'

'Oh, good. Thank you, Baines, and good evening.'

He nodded in surly acknowledgment and Evelyn set off up the stairs, forgetting a good part of her tiredness. Her face was eager as she pushed open the door of the biggest room and even before she had walked in she was saying:

'Thank God you're all here. Dindin . . .'

Before she could finish she took in the tableau that was presented to her. All three Suvarovs were sitting in their coats on her bed, which had been pushed into a little alcove opposite the small window. Their bags were on the floor in front of them. Otherwise the frowsty, untidy room was just as she had left it that morning.

'I'm glad to see you managed to light the lamp at least,' she said and the sarcasm in her voice brought tears into Tallie's black eyes. Sasha, who was deaf to such subtleties, said gaily:

'Oh, no, Mr Baines lit that, Evie. Aren't you pleased to see us?'

Evelyn smiled, a small tight smile.

'Yes, of course. But why on earth are you all sitting like this? Dindin, why haven't you unpacked? And done something about supper?'

'How could I?' she asked, her eyes wide and ingenuous. 'I don't know where we're supposed to sleep and there isn't any food here. You're horrid.'

Bitterness surged through Evelyn at the sudden realisation of what her blithe promise to Nikolai was going to entail. Of course she could not have allowed Dindin and the children to live anywhere else, but she had not bargained for Dindin being so helpless. How was she going to be able to do what had to be done at the hospital every day if she had to nurse-maid them all as well? She felt her self-control snap and for the first time lost her temper with her cousin.

'For God's sake, Dindin, grow up. You're not a child. You're quite old enough to look after the others and they are your responsibility. Now that you're on your own, you'll have to take your mother's place. Good heavens girl, you're seventeen. Why didn't you ask Baines where the shops were and go out and buy some food? I've been working like a slave all day in the hospital and you've just been sitting here doing nothing – expecting me to wait on you when I get back, I suppose.'

It was only the whiteness of Dindin's stricken face that brought Evelyn back to her senses. She sat down at the table and put both elbows on it so that she could support her heavy head in her hands. After a moment or two, she felt a hand on her knee and looked up again.

'Sasha.'

'Evie, don't be horrid. We didn't know what to do. The girls were afraid of Mr Baines. And it's so dark and cold.'

She let one of her hands drop on to his silky black head and ruffled his hair.

'I'm sorry, Sashenka.' Then she looked over his head. 'There's no need to cry, Dindin. Tallie, dry your eyes. I'm sorry I shouted, but it was too bad of you. Life is going to be difficult enough here in any case until we can get away, and I just won't be able to do everything for you as well as going to the hospital every day.'

'But you don't have to go, do you?'

'Well, really!' she exploded, all her determination to be fair and kind shattering. 'Of all the selfishness. Those men who have been wounded trying to fight the Bolsheviki for you deserve all the care they can have.' She stopped there. What was the point? 'Dindin, since we've no food at all, you'd better go down and find Baines and ask him for some-thing.'

'No, Evie, I couldn't . . . he scares me. Don't make me do it. Don't make me.'

Recognising the sound of rising hysteria, Evelyn pushed herself painfully up from the hard chair and said in a voice that chilled her cousins:

'I'll do it then. You might at least unpack while I'm gone. Or is even that quite beyond your capabilities?'

She hated herself for that scene, as she hated herself for every snap and cross word that was forced out of her during the next few weeks. Although Dindin gradually accepted the idea that she should look after her brother and sister and prepare food for them during the day and even keep the little flat relatively clean and tidy, Evelyn could never make her think. She needed instructions for everything and if some problem arose during the day, she would wait for Evelyn to see to it and decide what had to be done. And she would ask the same questions day after day. One evening she unpacked the heavy bag of shopping Evelyn had bought on her way back from work and said:

'These beans again – how long should I cook them for?'

Mentally turning her eyes up to heaven, Evelyn said in a voice of exaggerated patience:

'Thirty minutes once the pot has come to the boil.' Then, to her astonishment and fury, Dindin said petulantly:

'You always say that and it's never enough. They're hardly cooked at all after half an hour.'

Evelyn found herself looking at Dindin as though she were a creature from a completely unknown species and wondering how she could communicate with it. At last she said:

'Words fail me, Dindin. I sometimes wonder if you ever listen to what you're saying. I know that you think I should do all the cooking and cleaning and washing in this place and that you should sit at your ease, but there is no need for you to pretend to be an idiot. If my timing for your bloody beans is wrong, then you should decide how long you want to cook them for.'

Dindin burst into tears again and Tallie came slowly towards the table to help Evelyn unpack the uninspiring contents of her shopping bag.

'Don't be too cross with Dindin, Evie,' she whispered. 'She never learned to cook.'

'Nor did I, Tallie. We're all learning at the same time,' answered Evelyn, more gently.

But her language deteriorated day by day as she caught the expressions used by some of her patients, and her temper became shorter and shorter. At last Robert Adamson decided to take a hand in a situation that was clearly becoming intolerable. He waited nervously for Evelyn to arrive on her daily visit and as soon as she had sat down, sighing unconsciously as she took the weight off her feet at last, he said:

'Dindin came to see me today.' The unspoken undercurrent passed by Evelyn and she said only:

'At last. She's the most selfish girl I've ever met. She has almost nothing to do and she's let you lie here alone day after day.'

'Evelyn, don't be too hard on her.'

'It's damned unfair, Robert. She has no conception of how tired I am after a day in the hospital and she's quite capable of doing anything that is needed to keep us all alive and fed, but she won't do anything unless I have worked it all out for her and practically written her a list of things to do and say. I wish Nikolai Alexandrovitch were here; he'd be able to show her why she just can't go on as she does.'

'As he once said to me about someone else, Evelyn, think: Dindin has had to leave her parents behind in Shenkursk, which we all know must have been taken by the Bolsheviki by now, and she has no idea what will have happened to them. Both her brothers are fighting – and on opposite sides. She is facing life in a foreign country, not just for a year or two as you did, but probably for ever. She is lonely and afraid.'

There was a long silence. At last Bob looked at her and saw that she was blushing almost painfully, the smooth skin mottled and puckering around her mouth.

'You're right, of course,' she said slowly. 'And I was too selfish to think. Oh God, what do I do now?'

Seeing the first breach in her defences, he said as gently as he could:

'Why not leave the hospital?'

'So that I can wait on Dindin?' she demanded as furious as ever.

'Why are you fixated on this business of waiting and servants?' he asked, suddenly as angry as she. 'There you are, every day forcing yourself to do work you hate for men you despise while your own family is living in misery that you could easily dispel. In Shenkursk there was a serious shortage of nurses, but here, with all these refugees and innumerable English women, it can't be the same. You're a volunteer anyway. You don't have to go on.'

'How did you know I hate it?'

He laughed at that and the sound was so unexpected in that gloomy hospital ward that it dragged an unwilling smile from Evelyn. Then he decided to answer more seriously:

'Eve, listen: you come here every evening so tense it's as though you'd been wired up. It takes a good half hour before you even begin to relax. The way you wince as a nurse takes a bedpan past here or an orderly carries out a bucket of blood tells me just how hard it must be for you to do any such things in your own hospital. You sure hate it.'

'Yes, that's true. I hate it more than I can say. But it's all I can do to . . .' She could not say any more.

'To help your country?' he suggested doubtfully.

'Nothing so noble. No, it's just . . . you see, Johnnie may be in a hospital somewhere. It's the only way I can do anything to keep . . . But I suppose you're right, it doesn't help him at all.'

'Eve, what would Nick say? Wouldn't he tell you that looking after your cousins, helping them to be less afraid and a bit happier was worth more than making yourself ill and tired doing work that fills you with horror?'

Put like that, there was only one answer and she did not even have to put it into words.

'I wish he were here,' was all she did say and Bob answered:

'I promised him I'd do my best to look after you for him, but stuck here like this in the dark there's not much I can do. If you could look on me as a second-in-command and let me help . . .'

'Thank you, Robert. It is good of you to try. And you have helped, truly. Now, how are the legs?'

'Oh, getting better – slowly. I guess I'll be out of here in about a week now, but not very mobile. I'll find an apartment then and . . .'

'You'll do no such thing. We have a room for you at Baines's. It's all ready for when you're discharged. The legs are going to hurt for a lot longer than a week and you'll need help. Besides, Sasha keeps asking me when you're "coming home" as he calls it. And I'll try to be more patient with Dindin, I promise.'

'Good girl,' he said without thinking and then watched her stiffen at what she took to be condescension.

She left him then, grateful for what he had tried to do, but cross with the tone he had taken at the end. However severe Nikolai had had to be with her at times, he had never patronised her like that. Wretched man, she thought as she plodded through the everlasting dark towards the tram stop. If only there could be some daylight, she said to herself, I might manage to be cheerful and more patient.

Pushing open the door to the biggest of the three rooms when she eventually got back to Baines's, Evelyn watched her cousins look up from their books with expressions of such anxiety that she began to understand what her fretfulness must have done to them. In that moment, she saw, too, that they were not the parasites they had seemed, feeding off her strength. If she had not had them with her in Archangel, her solitary life might have been less tiring, but it would have been yet more miserable.

'Oh, my dears,' she said, the contrition dissolving the rasp in her voice at last. 'I am sorry I've been such a beast. But things are going to be different now, I promise you. Robert says I should leave the hospital; and if we're all together all day and I'm not so tired with work and getting there and back every day I won't be nearly so horrid. I'm sorry, Dindin.'

The girl smiled, with none of the self-satisfied triumph that she might have felt, and said almost humbly:

'I've made a sort of stew, Evie. It's on the stove; but it may not be very nice. The meat looked rather odd.'

'Well, if it didn't smell bad, it doesn't really matter what it looked like. Thank you, Dindin, and I'm sorry I kept snapping at you.'

'You've said that three times now, Evie,' said Sasha, coming to stand beside her and lean against her thigh. 'Are you really going to stop going to the hospital?'

'Yes. And we can have some English lessons again, and go for walks and things. You will have to show me all the places you have found, because you probably know the town much better than I do now.'

'But it's always so dark; there's nothing to see,' he answered. Something, not quite a whine, in his voice made Evelyn look carefully at him.

'Sashenka, are you all right?' For the first time she noticed how his once-cheerful face had set into an expression of endurance.

'I just wish it would get light again. I hate it like this. The girls don't seem to mind it, but I hate it, Evie. When will it get light?' Evelyn, her heart twisting, hugged him and whispered:

'I hate it too, but the spring must come soon and then it'll get lighter and lighter until it never gets dark at all, Sasha. And it'll be warmer and we'll be able to bathe in the river, Baines says. Then you'll feel better.'

The Suvarovs looked at each other, plainly wondering whether this change in their cousin would last or whether she would revert to the tense, bitter organiser she had become in Archangel. But as the weary, dingy days before Adamson's release dragged on, they discovered that she had meant what she said.

She told the authorities at the hospital that she was too badly needed at home to continue her voluntary work and a little to her surprise they accepted the excuse and thanked her for what she had done. In fact, once the influx of wounded from Shenkursk had been discharged, there was no great crisis at the hospital and the permanent staff were adequate for the numbers they had to treat.

Feeling suddenly free and happier than at any time since she had left Nikolai's protection, Evelyn hardly noticed the hateful daytime darkness as she went away to visit Bob Adamson. His expression as he welcomed her told her that the change in her was visible as well, and for once she did not mind his knowing smile.

'So, they've let you go,' he said as she sat down beside him.

'Yes, and though I knew I hated it, I didn't know quite how much. It feels wonderful. And they didn't seem to be angry either.'

'Good. And I'm to be set free, too.'

'I'm glad! When?'

'Tomorrow if all goes well. They took the weights off yesterday and I got to practise walking this morning.'

'How did it go?'

'It was – rough,' he admitted. 'And I can't hobble far, but I can at least stand and . . . Never mind. The plaster can't come off for another few weeks, but if you'll really have me at Baines's, I can leave.' Evelyn wondered vaguely what it was he had not been able to say, but something inside her resisted the idea of finding out more about him and so she just said:

'Nikolai Alexandrovitch would never forgive me if I let you go anywhere else in that condition. And the children will be so glad to have you close. You'll be able to help me with Sasha. He seems very depressed by the darkness and I just don't know what to do to help him. I know he'll be happier once you're there to cheer him up.'

'And you, Eve?' he asked. She looked down at him, quick to suspect that he was getting at her in some way, but his hazel eyes were clear and his whole expression free of mockery for once. Even so, her voice was stiff and formal.

'Of course, Robert. But I'm not sure how we're going to be able to get you back there.'

'No, don't worry about that. They've offered me the services of the ambulance.'

'Excellent. We shall come and collect you tomorrow then. Goodbye, Robert.'

'You don't have to do that . . .' he was beginning, but a new quality in her expression stopped his protests and when she left him he wondered whether he was beginning to break through her apparently impenetrable armour to the woman he was increasingly sure lay there hidden from pre-dators.

When she came back the following morning with little Sasha, Bob was relieved to see that although the child looked drawn and pale, he happily held Evelyn's hand and chattered confid-ingly to her as he had always done. From Dindin's description of the way her cousin had ordered them all around and shouted at them, Bob had pictured the younger children as cowed and terrorised. Obviously the old love of drama had not deserted Dindin. Bob started to think he had been too hard on Evelyn. He searched her face for signs of resentment, but she looked untroubled. She was brisk too and very ef-ficient as she called for a nurse to get him out of bed and dressed. Then she helped the nurse to arrange screens around his bed and patiently waited until he was ready.

Dressing with both legs in plaster was a difficult business and required all his concentration, which stopped him wor-rying about whether he had jeopardised the slowly flowering friendship by taking Dindin's complaints too literally. When he was ready there were all the farewells to make to his nurses and fellow patients. At last the little procession, led by Sasha, turning all the time to talk to Bob, made its way down the long ward and out into the street. Although there was no light, the air felt clean and fresh on his face and he turned it up towards the deep indigo-coloured sky, taking deep breaths as he stood there on the top step.

'What a superb smell,' he said.

'But Uncle Bob, it doesn't smell of anything,' protested Sasha. 'It's just beastly dark as usual.'

'I know, little one. That's what I mean. If you'd spent all those weeks breathing in ether, formaldehyde, antiseptic and the other patients, smelling nothing would smell to you like all the perfumes of Arabia.'

'You are funny. Evie, isn't he funny?'

'Yes, Sashenka, but I know what he means. Bob, I hope you're not going to be suffocated in the flat. There are certain difficulties about keeping things as clean as they should be in this town.'

'Don't apologise. I know. The nurses have all told me, there's hardly any water.'

'Isn't it weird? The last thing I'd have thought about the Arctic Circle. With all this frozen water about. It's so frustrating.'

'It's like that poem, isn't it? We could add a new line, so that it would go:

> Water, water everywhere,
> And all the boards did shrink,
> Water, water everywhere,
> But all the people stink.'

He laughed and to his amazement, Evelyn managed to smile with him.

15

Evelyn sometimes thought that if light had not started to come back to the town a few days after they had brought Bob Adamson to the flat she might not have been able to carry on. In some ways his presence made life easier: he was much better company than Dindin, and in the evenings after Sasha and Tallie had been sent to bed, Evelyn could talk to Bob instead of having to listen to Dindin's complaints about the unfairness of life and the way she would have been spending the spring in Petrograd if it had not been for the Revolution. But there were constraints, too, and he needed a lot of looking after. Even after his plaster had been taken off and he could take care of himself again, he was still weak and could not walk far. She longed for the day when he would be strong and mobile enough to be of real help to her.

He, too, longed for it, not least because he had been afraid during the long solitary days in hospital that he would never be able to walk again. Although that terror had been to a certain extent dispelled by his first tentative attempts at walking on crutches, and later, once the plaster had been removed, with two sticks and after a couple of weeks with only one, he was still afraid that he would not regain his full fitness. To someone as active as he had always been that was a torturing thought. There were many times during their increasingly peaceful evening talks when he almost told Evelyn about his fears, but much as he wanted her understanding, he could not bear the thought of her pity. And since she had never evinced the slightest desire to know anything about him or his life before she had met him, he could not force his confidences on her.

The mixture of feelings she had always aroused in him seemed intensified by the closeness in which they had to live and there were many times when it drove him into something approaching his old sarcastic mockery. Always, as soon as the words had been spoken, he would regret them as he saw Evelyn flinch and touch something she wore just under her collar. But he could not stop himself.

Whenever it happened, Evelyn would remind herself that despite the occasional warmth Adamson had shown to her, he must dislike her thoroughly. Then she would retreat into formality and envy Dindin, who chattered and flirted as she always had. She obviously enjoyed having masculine company and once confided to Evelyn that since there were no eligible Russian men left for her to marry, she rather thought Bob Adamson might do. Evelyn, who thought he treated Dindin with commendable patience, said, carefully controlling her irritation:

'He is a little old for you, I think, Dindin, and not at all suitable. And as soon as we get out of Archangel there will be plenty of eligible men for you to meet. You really ought not to be thinking of such things – it is rather unsuitable, you know.'

'Oh, stop being like a governess! If I'm old enough to cook and clean and look after the children, I'm old enough to think of men as possible husbands. You're so prissy, Evelyn, just like any other spinster. I deserve some fun.'

Evelyn, smarting from the insult, which had landed inexorably on some of her deepest-hidden fears, suppressed the 'why?' that rose to her lips and turned the subject. But she could not talk to Dindin about the one that worried her most, or to Adamson. For some time, it had been becoming clear that the money that Andrei Alexandrovitch had given her to keep them all until they could get to England was not going to last until the ice melted. Food was so scarce in Archangel that it had become terribly expensive, and with five people to feed, she had been spending much too much, in spite of being as economical as she could have been. As she counted the few miserable coins and Intervention rouble notes in her purse, she had an impulse to tell Adamson and wait for him to do something about the problem. But she knew she could not. It was she who was responsible for them all, she to whom Nikolai had given the charge. And, besides, there was nothing Adamson could do that she could not.

He was often in pain, she knew, and still virtually immobile. There did not seem to be any way in which his paper could get any salary to him, and she was certain that he had no money of his own, even if he had somehow been able to draw on it in Archangel. There could be no help from him. This, too, was a burden she must carry alone. She had heard that other refugees were selling their furs and jewels to raise enough money to feed themselves and their children, but they were in such desperate straits that they had to sell for tiny fractions of what the stones and furs were worth. It had disgusted Evelyn when she found out that even officers, British officers, were taking advantage of the plight of the desperate Russians and buying up sables and gold and diamonds for no more than the price of a few meals or even with tins of cigarettes. She was determined not to allow that to happen to the Suvarovs' last resources and even if her life depended on it, she did not think she could have brought herself to sell the locket Nikolai had given her. It was all she had left of him, and the affection it symbolised was the only source of strength left to her in her dreary, enervating life.

Her first thought of a source of financial help was Baines, but it soon became clear that he was in almost as bad a way as the Suvarovs, and Evelyn was forced to recognise that she would have to beg from the British army. Hateful though that thought was, she knew that she had no choice, and the following morning when she had seen that Dindin was cleaning up the kitchen area of the living-room and Bob was giving lessons to the other two, she put on her gloves and a shawl and said:

'I have to go out now. I'll fetch the water on my way back, Dindin.'

'Sure, Evie,' said Dindin, having picked up the word from

Bob Adamson. 'See you later. Oh, aren't you taking a coat? Won't you freeze to death?'

'No, the sun's shining. I'll be all right in a shawl,' she answered, not wanting to explain that if one was going to beg for money to buy food it would be ridiculous to do so clad in the thickest, most luxurious sables anyone could have imagined.

As she walked out into the snowy street, the sight of the sun, pale and shrouded in piled clouds though it was, lifted her spirits a little and made her forget for a blessed moment what she had to do. She could feel its slight warmth on her face and thought that the thaw could not be much longer in coming and that as soon as the sea ice broke up it might be possible at last to get away from Russia. A group of soldiers, other ranks she noticed as she looked at their sleeves, passed her and stopped a few feet further on.

Evelyn hardly looked at them as she caught up with them, but one of the men said:

'Speak English, *baryshnia*?'

Thinking that perhaps they were lost or something, she stopped and turned to smile politely at them.

'Yes, what can I do for you?'

A raucous laugh greeted that, and the man who had first spoken said:

'Well, we'll 'ave to talk about that won't we, but in private don't you think?'

'I beg your pardon?' she said, as stiffly as she had ever spoken. Her accent did not appear to have registered on the men, who seemed from their rollicking voices to be drunk.

''Ow much, then, *baryshnia*? I 'ad a countess last week – at least she said she were a countess – and she was only three roubles the go.'

Feeling quite sick, Evelyn at last understood what the man was talking about. The foulness of it was underlined by the fact that she needed money, probably as desperately as the unfortunate countess they had mocked – and probably for the same reason.

'You disgust me,' she said in cold anger. 'And the fact that you are English makes me ashamed of my country and the army that fought and died in France and Flanders. I am on my way to General Ironside's headquarters now, and you should be grateful that I am not asking your names and numbers to report you to him.'

Long before she had reached the end of her speech, it had dawned on the men that this was not some Russian bint with a remarkably good knowledge of English. The man who had accosted her tried to shrink to the back of the little group. One of his mates, braver than the rest, said:

'We didn't know as 'ow you was English, Miss. We're awfully sorry. Chalky 'ere, 'e wouldn't have said that if 'e'd known. Honest, Miss. We're sorry.'

Evelyn thought she recognised genuine distress in the man, but she couldn't bear to speak to any of them, and turned sharply round to walk as quickly as possible away from them. She was half-afraid that they would follow, but that was the last thing they had in mind and even backed away from her retreating figure.

The unpleasant little episode did not make her any more eager to do what she had to do, but at least the anger it had given her carried her through the preliminaries. Then, faced with a young officer, she tried to bury every feeling that she had and forced herself to beg from him. She could not look at him as she said the words.

'There is no money left. My cousin's manager, in whose house we are lodging, would have helped us, I am sure, but all his money was in Tsarist roubles and he has been ruined by the Intervention. We have to eat, and I need money.'

The young man was quite as embarrassed as Evelyn, but his duty was perfectly clear.

'Miss Markham, please do not distress yourself. If you are in such desperate straits, you must go to the Acting Consul; he has a certain amount of discretion in such cases. You are a British subject, and I expect that there are funds that can be drawn on to help. But I am sorry to say that I don't think they can be used to help three Russians and an American. I regret this very much, but there is nothing any of us can do to help. Do you know how many refugees there are in Archangel now?'

'No, but it doesn't matter. I understand.' Then the whole idea of dutiful resignation stuck in her throat and she said for once what she really felt.

'Some men, British men, stopped me on my way here and offered me money to . . . to . . .' She found that she could not use any of the words she had learned in Archangel, but she saw from the poppy-coloured blush on the young man's downy cheeks that he understood. 'Perhaps I ought to have accepted in order to feed those children.'

'My dear Miss Markham, please,' he protested. 'Please go to the Consul. He will be able to help.' A thought seemed to occur to him and he looked more directly at her. 'Unless perhaps you have a bank account. Many of the shopkeepers here will take cheques drawn on London.'

'A bank account? Of course I haven't got a bank account.'

'No, no I suppose ladies don't. Well, there it is. Nothing I can do. Try the Consul. He'll help. Or the Americans, perhaps.'

Burning with humiliation she made her way to the Consul, who proved to be more helpful. He handed her a small sum in Intervention roubles for her own immediate needs, and suggested that he try to contact her father by telegraph so that he could arrange with the War Office to get some funds to her through the army. He was touched at the way her face lit up, and he warned her that it might take some time to arrange.

She did not realise that she was muttering to herself as she walked back along the Troitski Prospekt until a loud American voice called out to her:

'Hey, Lady, you can talk to me if you need to talk.'

Her face on fire with embarrassment all over again, Evelyn shook her head and kept her eyes firmly directed at the road in front of her. There were so many things that she wanted to say angrily to so many people that she must have been mouthing them furiously as they formed in her mind. Now she kept her lips tightly together and tried not even to think what she would have liked to explain to the officer, to the party of English other ranks, and everyone else with whom she had come into contact in Archangel.

When another male voice broke into her thoughts, she did not even look round, not wanting to know who had hailed her or what this one wanted. She thought that she knew. Then the voice came again:

'Evelyn? For God's sake, Evelyn! Come back. It's Dick. Evelyn!'

Eventually the sense of the shouting reached her and she stopped suddenly, her booted feet sliding on the hard snow. Turning to look at the running man behind her, she recognised her young brother and felt weak with astonishment:

'It can't be! Dick? What are you doing here? It is too absurd: people keep popping up in the most extraordinary way. How did you get to Archangel?'

He caught up with her at last and, panting, kissed her cheek. She stood back a little to look at him. When she had left England he had been a thin, rather sickly schoolboy; now here he was, planted in Archangel in his khaki uniform, looking taller and broader than she would have believed possible. As she inspected him approvingly from the top of his glossily polished brown boots to his sleekly brushed short dark hair, she became aware that he was looking at her, too, but with quite different feelings nakedly displayed on his face.

'Evelyn, what on earth has happened to you?'

'What do you mean?'

'Well, but . . . your hair, and those awful clothes. You . . . I mean, oh hang it; you look frightful. What happened?'

Belatedly understanding one of the reasons why Adamson had been so angry with her in the old days, Evelyn said drily:

'A revolution and a civil war, actually, Dick. It's rather hard, don't you know, to keep up appearances under such conditions.'

Her tone, if not the words she had used, brought blood into her brother's fresh face. He took both her hands in his.

'Evie, I'm sorry. I didn't mean what that sounded like. It was just the shock. Thank God I've found you. I'll do what I can for you now. You don't have to worry any longer. I'm here now, Evie.'

'But what do you mean, Dickie? Found me. Didn't Mother get my letters? You must have known that I was in Archangel.' She looked at him more searchingly, and then said: 'But you're in uniform. What about the asthma, Dick? Come on, don't just stand there. Tell me.'

'I will as soon as you stop talking.'

'Sorry, Dick,' she said, laughing a little at his pompousness. 'I'll be quiet.'

'Where are you going? Can I come with you?'

'Yes, of course. I'm just going back to the flat, to our cousins. I've three of them here with me, Dindin, Natalie and poor little Sasha. But you must tell me why you are here.'

'All right. You know that I couldn't get a commission because of the asthma.' He waited for her to nod, which she duly did. 'Right, then. After Tony died and when we heard what was happening in Russia and that you were stuck here, I couldn't bear it that I was sitting safe at home ...' He stopped and Evelyn was touched at the humble way he looked at her.

'I was never in any real danger, Dickie; just frustrated not to be able to get home, and very sad for our cousins as we watched everything they had lived for smashed up and thrown away.'

'Yes, well,' he said, clearly not very interested in the Suvarovs. 'So when I discovered that they were recruiting for an expedition to North Russia, and that it didn't matter if one was physically not in the pink, I had to come. We've been stuck in Murmansk all winter, but if I'd known that you were actually in this town I'd have wangled a job here sooner.'

'But how did you hear in the end? I assume this isn't just coincidence.'

'No, of course it isn't. But you got a letter to Mother from this place Shenkursk and so she wrote to me as soon as she got it and told me to get to Shenkursk and find you. But, of course, by then Shenkursk had fallen to the Bolos. I made what enquiries I could and discovered that Cousin Andrew Suvarov had stayed. I was pretty desperate when I thought that you might have stayed with them and came straight over here as soon as I could join a relief unit. And here I am.'

Evelyn stopped once again and put both hands on his shoulders and took a huge, deep breath.

'And, oh, Dickie. It is wonderful that you are. I have missed . . . But there's no sense in talking about it. I am so glad that you've come. Have you got any letters for me from home? I had one little note from Mother that got through to Shenkursk ages ago, but nothing since. If you get letters from her, why don't I?'

'Well she knew where I was and anyway our letters come through the War Office. I think it's different with civilians. I mean, after all we're at war with Russia now.'

'Are we?' she asked in a tone he had never heard from her in his life. 'There's been no declaration of war.'

'But of course we are,' he said as though to a rather backward child or a foreigner, wondering whether the Revolution had affected her mind as well as her quite dreadful appearance. He noticed in disgust that her skirt was actually dirty and her boots cracked where the upper joined the sole. 'Don't you realise what might happen if revolution got to England? It's bad enough already. I know that you won't spread this around the town, but some of those wicked trades unions are striking in protest at what we're trying to do to their Russian comrades. The miners, you know. And some of the dockers refused to load any more ships headed for Murmansk, trying to force the government to pull out of Russia. You don't know what it's like in England now. The lower classes are in a dreadfully dangerous state, Father says. It's absolutely vital that we nip all that sort of thing in the bud.'

Evelyn found herself laughing at his portentousness and again recognising some of her old self in the way he was carrying on. No wonder Piotr had laughed at her; no wonder Robert Adamson had been so sarcastic. Not until she had been presented with the young brother she had cherished in her mind all this time had she realised how much she had changed. Here he was fresh from England lecturing her, someone who had lived through the Revolution, on its significance, with all the ignorance and prejudice of their class.

'Dear Dickie, I'm sorry to laugh. But it is too absurd. Do you really think that a few units of highly reluctant Allied troops can really smother something like the Bolshevik Revolution in a country this size?'

'It's not just us, you know,' he said, lowering his voice even though there was no one anywhere near them. 'There are forces making their way up through the Ukraine, and others from Siberia. We're all going to meet in the middle and restore proper government here.'

'Look, we were only as far south as Shenkursk and had to retreat. That was only two hundred miles from here. Don't delude yourself, Dick. Now, to a more realistic subject. *Did* you bring any letters for me?'

'Yes,' he said and then stopped, his pink face now the very picture of guilt and distress.

'What's the matter, Dick? Nothing's happened to Mother – or Father – has it?' Then when he still did not speak, she understood and with her face beginning to freeze, she said: 'It's Johnnie, isn't it?'

'Yes, Evelyn; it seems that he *was* killed. At Loos.' He was profoundly embarrassed to see that tears were oozing out of her eyes in a public street and said hastily:

'I'd better get you home. Where are you staying?'

'Number two hundred and twenty, but we're nearly there. What happened, Dick? Tell me.'

'We don't know very much, Evelyn, but they think it happened during the attack on Hill 70. It seems that a lot of bodies were never found or identified, but one of his friends who was dreadfully wounded there was beside him when it happened. He, the friend, I mean, was invalided out of the army and spent two years in hospitals of one sort or another – he took some shrapnel in the spine, you see.'

'But couldn't he at least have got word to us about Johnnie? It's been three years. All those years when I thought he could be still alive,' she protested through the tears that she could not stop, however often she brushed her big, dark eyes.

'He didn't know, until he got out of hospital and came to Beverley, that no one knew what had happened.'

Listening carefully to his voice, Evelyn understood that there was something more to this story than simply the truth she had dreaded since the telegram had arrived.

'Now Dick, stop here in the street and tell me the whole thing. Why did this friend come to Beverley? What is it that you are hiding?'

He was appalled.

'Evelyn, I'm not hiding anything. I am trying to tell you so that you understand. He brought a letter for you. Johnnie gave it to him at dawn before they attacked and asked him to get it to you if he could. That's why he came. And it was a tremendous effort: he's paralysed, you see – in a wheelchair.'

His sister was clinging to his arm now, and he could feel her whole body shaking with the sobs that were forcing themselves out of her.

'Well give it to me. For the love of God, Dickie, give it to me.'

'Evelyn, try to keep calm. I came to give it to you, but it's in my kit. I haven't got it with me. I was going to the Consul to try to find out your address so that I could find you and give it to you. It was chance I met you out here in the street.'

'Never mind any of that now. Go straight back and get it, Richard, and bring it at once to the flat. Number 220. Come as quickly as you can. It's right at the top of the stairs. The front door's never locked in the daytime. Hurry. I must know what he wrote.'

'All right, all right, Evelyn. Try to keep calm. I understand. Don't think I don't, but you must be calm. I'll come back as quickly as I can.'

16

Evelyn tried hard to remove the traces of tears from her face as she hauled herself up the steep stairs to Baines's attic, but she saw from the expressions on the faces of all three of her cousins that she had not succeeded. Dindin, with the tact she was just beginning to learn after the long weeks of enforced intimacy, turned back to her cooking, but nine-year-old Natalie said:

'What's the matter, Evie? Are you all right?'

'Oh, I'm perfectly all right, Tallie. Have you finished your lesson?' answered Evelyn in a dreary voice that worried Bob Adamson even more than the stains of grief on her pale face. He intervened.

'I expect Evelyn's tired, children. Lunch in half an hour, didn't you say, Dindin?'

'That's right, Bob. What there is of it.'

He laughed, and then said:

'OK. You three stay here and get everything ready, while Evelyn has a little rest on one of your beds. Come on, Eve.'

He knew that she would never agree to sit with him in his little bedroom and so he led her to the room where all three Suvarovs slept. Then he made her sit beside him on Dindin's bed and said:

'What has happened, Eve?'

She turned her head sideways so that he could not see her face and said with no pretence of dignity:

'Johnnie's dead. He's been dead for three years – ever

221

since the telegram. He was blown up in the attack on Hill 70 at Loos.'

He wanted to hold her close to him and tell her everything that he felt for her and kiss her until she could smile again, but since he could not, he had to think of some words that might comfort her. All he could find to say was:

'Evelyn, I am so sorry. How did you hear?'

She turned her head a little. 'My brother's here with the army. I met him just now, and he told me. But, Bob, you knew John was dead, didn't you? Like Sergei. But you didn't say.'

'I thought he must be.'

'But you never said.'

'There seemed to be no point. If my silence has made the hurt worse, then I'm sorry for it. But I didn't see how it would help to tell you what I thought.'

At that she pulled herself together.

'Bob, I didn't mean that. I am grateful that you never said anything. If that sounds mad, I'm sorry. But Sergei used to tell me that he must be dead every time he tried to make me say I'd marry him. He was using my love for Johnnie . . . And he's dead. I suppose I knew it too, but I made myself hope. I'd promised him that I'd wait for him: I thought that if I never admitted that he might be dead, if I really believed I would see him again, it would somehow keep him alive. Stupid, wasn't it?'

'No, not stupid. Very natural. Look at me, Eve.'

She obeyed, but with such an expression of horror in her face that he quite forgot what he had been going to say.

'What did I say?'

'That name. No wonder you call me that. It was all sup-posed to be her fault, wasn't it?' He heard the beginning of hysteria in her voice and spoke sharply to her.

'Evelyn, stop it. Now. And tell me, quietly, what I have done. What name?'

'You call me Eve. No one else ever does.'

He forebore to say that was why he had chosen it. It had been the only way he had been able to find to single himself out in connection with her. It had seemed important to call her by a name that was used by him alone. He waited for more. She sat up straight again and took a ragged, greyish handkerchief from her sleeve to wipe away the tears.

Then, apparently quite composed, she told him of the horrible conviction that must have been at the root of her self-enforced loneliness for years but that she had only articulated to herself when she had heard the confirmation of John's death:

'I must have done it, you see. You do understand that, don't you? It's like Tony. Something terrible happens to everybody that I love, and I think it must be my fault.'

Adamson dropped his head into his clasped hands. He didn't feel capable of dealing with the neurosis she had revealed. His legs hurt abominably that day; he had faced a crisis of conscience that seemed to have made all the work of his adult life a mockery; he was unable to work any longer; he was tormented by what might be happening to his friends both White and Red all over Russia; he was in love with the woman beside him and living in almost unmanageable frustration so close to her yet unable to touch her. Now she had revealed a torment that had to be assuaged, and he did not know how. He wanted to seize her and make love to her, and show her that love had nothing whatever to do with death, that it was the only true manifestation of the reality of living. And he knew he could not. His only hope of reaching her was with words, and words, the one thing that had never failed him until Shenkursk, were now more difficult to manage than anything else. He was too tired. But he had to try.

'Evelyn, listen.'

'I'm listening, Bob,' she said as she watched him prop his elbows on his knees and move his big, muscular hands over his face. Then he sat up straight and looked full at her.

'Evelyn, I don't know what first put that thought into your head, but it is ridiculous. No,' he protested, grabbing hold of both her hands as she recoiled from him. 'You will listen to this. Do you know how many men were killed on the Western Front? I don't, but I can make some kind of guess. I know that 70,000 men died in the defence of Ypres in

1915, Loos cost 60,000, on the Somme 30,000 men fell dead or wounded in the first half-hour alone – that is one thousand every minute.'

Evelyn flinched at each statistic, as though they were bullets he was firing at her. But he could not – and would not if he could – hide the facts from her, and his voice was cold and sounded angry as he said:

'And those died in just three battles on the Western Front in the first two years. What about the rest? In Russia, in Turkey, on every front for four whole years thousands died. And every one was probably loved by a woman. Can you really think that it was the love of all those women that pushed wave after wave of inadequately armed men in front of superior weapons to die for stupidity and ignorance and vanity? What makes you so special that your two died for you and not for that? For Christ's sake, Evelyn, with the whole world torn and bloody around you, you have built yourself a nice little shelter, haven't you, a dug-out with all home comforts to keep you from understanding the truth. What if it is a little painful? A peck of painful guilt is a small price to pay for a sack of protection from the truth.'

He dropped her hands and went out of the room, cursing himself for his clumsiness, recognising that he had probably lost for ever any chance he might once have had of getting close enough to love her. He walked slowly straight past the door of the main room to his own curtained-off cupboard and lay face down on his bed, feeling the ache in his legs increase with the weight he was putting on them, but hardly caring. This was the end. The one thing he thought he might have salvaged for himself from the wreckage of his life had been thrown away. He lay there, trying to keep out of his mind everything he had ever said to her, but nearly every word came rushing back: all the sarcasm, the sneers, the clumsy attempts at compliments and, later, comfort. How could he ever have expected her to love him when he had never shown her anything but dislike or ridiculously inept gestures of friendship? As he came to that conclusion, another truth dawned on him: he had dug his own protective trench, too.

Piotr had been right about him. If Evelyn had stopped herself from seeing the true horror that the world had unleashed on itself by concentrating on her own imagined guilt, then he had protected himself from feeling ordinary human emotions by the anger he had built up and his insistence on seeing every person as a symbol of the political belief they espoused.

Adamson turned over and lay staring up at the boarded roof over his head, and began to listen to the sounds that had only vaguely reached him before. Angry voices, getting louder and louder, someone banging a fist on a table, a girl crying. He was just levering himself painfully up off his bed to go to find out what was happening when Sasha put his head round the edge of the curtain and said:

'Uncle Bob, Uncle Bob, please come! Evie's brother is here and he's saying dreadful things to her and making her terribly cross. Tallie's crying and Dindin's nearly fainting and I can't make them stop.'

'I'm coming, Sasha, give me a hand.'

The child came over to the bed and helped Adamson push himself up off the bed. Then he swung his still-stiff legs round and put them gingerly to the floor.

'There. We'll get there now. Don't worry, Sasha. We'll sort it out together.'

They walked into the main room together just as Evelyn was saying through clenched teeth:

'You are filthy, Richard. How could you say such things? And what damned business is it of yours anyway? Give me my letter.'

The boy in khaki had his hands behind his back; his determined chin was thrown forward, and his eyes, large and dark as his sister's, were as full of rage and disgust as hers.

'The fact that you can swear like that shows just how far you have been degraded by the life you are living. What do you think it feels like to be greeted with the information from a brother officer that my sister – my own sister – is the mistress of some nameless American scribbler? No wonder you look so frightful now. How could you? What will our

225

parents say? And it's not as though he's the sort of man you could possibly marry. God knows what will be done with you. You'll have to live abroad or something . . .'

'Will you be quiet?' said Evelyn, clearly entirely oblivious to her surroundings and the fact that the Suvarov children were listening. Never had Bob seen her lose her temper, but now he could see that she was almost drunk on her rage.

'You might have bothered to ask me before charging in here accusing me of being a prostitute. Yes, brother, dear, I know the words now. I have learned them because of what I have seen in your glorious army. As it happens I have not had sexual intercourse with the American and – unlike some of your men – he has never suggested it. And why the fact that I am living under the same roof as he should make me – what did you call it? – unfit to read the sacred last letter of one of the fallen . . . You make me quite sick. Your sainted soldier hero is the one who seduced me. Yes, dear brother, I am not a virgin. Does the fact that John deflowered me make me too impure to read his last words to me?'

'Oh, God': the protest, or exclamation, or whatever it was, came from Adamson, and pulled Evelyn back from the uncontrollable fury that was enveloping her. Her face was suffused with deep carmine shame as she saw him standing by the door with Sasha.

'I am sorry all of you. I forgot what I was saying. Look Dick, I think you had better just give me my letter and then get out of here. When I've recovered my temper, I'll find you. Goodbye.'

She held out a hand, which did not even tremble, and he was so shocked by what she had said and the way she had said it that he backed away.

'Give it to her, Markham,' said Bob from the door, and the authority in his quiet, deep voice could not be ignored. The boy handed over a crumpled, dirty envelope and left them, his face now pale with anger and distress.

Evelyn put it in the pocket of her dress and then, in a voice of nearly unbearable self-control, said:

'I beg your pardon, Dindin. Let's settle down and have luncheon before it spoils.'

'Eve,' said Bob quietly over the heads of the children. 'I must talk to you.'

'Not now, Bob,' she said, but her voice had taken on a little warmth. 'I'm not fit to talk about anything that matters yet. Let's eat and then I'll go out and walk it off. We can talk later.'

Appalled by the things that he had said to her, and what his presence in her flat had provoked her brother into saying, he could only acquiesce.

The five of them hardly spoke during the austere and uncomfortable meal and as soon as it was over, Evelyn picked up her coat from the bed and went out. Without really planning where to go, she found herself walking towards the river, immobile in the thick ice that still showed no signs of breaking up.

The sun was high and the sky for once a bright, clean blue, with hardly any of the thick, white clouds that usually hovered over the town, but Evelyn did not notice. All her thoughts were fixed on the letter she could feel in her pocket. She was afraid to open it. For so long she had lived with the thought of John and how he must have spent the days and nights after he had left her the last time, that the thought of confronting the real man again – even if it were only his words on a piece of crumpled dirty paper – frightened her. This letter was the answer to all the notes she had written and hidden in the top of her dressing-case. She was ashamed to find that she did not really want to know what the answer was.

She walked on along the bank of the Dvina until she came to an old, disused, wooden landing stage. There was no one in sight and Evelyn sat carefully down on the sturdy bollard where someone had once tied up his barges of timber or food from the interior. Looking across the mile-wide river to the further bank and catching a distant waft of the clean smell of the pine forest there, she sat quietly and tried to prepare herself for the letter.

At last she took it out of the pocket in her fur coat and looked down at the familiar handwriting of her name, blurred and stained as it was. She slid her fingers under the seal and ripped it open.

My darling Evelyn,

I expect that this is the last time I shall ever call you that. From the first moment I knew that I ought never to have told you I loved you: it was not fair. You were still a child and I, I was on my way to this. The things that I have seen and done here have unfitted me to be any kind of husband to you. I do not imagine that I shall survive it but even if I do, I can't come back to you.

We are not supposed to show any fear in case we increase the men's reluctance to march forward together to stop bullets and bayonets with the flesh of their bodies, but I don't know anyone, officer or private soldier, who is not afraid. There isn't any option, of course, we have to go forward, just as we have to kill the poor devils who march on our guns, and do things like ordering our men to be tied, spreadeagled, to the wheels of the guns as Field Punishment Number One if they commit any of the increasingly irrelevant infringements of rules made up by men who never faced anything like this in their lives.

We shot some Hun today in the town. They'd surrendered, but after yesterday and what they had done to our fellows, taking them prisoner didn't seem possible and so as they turned their backs to march as we ordered, we shot them in the back.

I'm not trying to give you a list of all the horrors of this war. I could not. There isn't enough paper in all the trenches to write them down. But I am trying to show you why I can never come back to you, never lie in your arms again.

Oh, Evelyn my only love, try to understand: how could I come back to you with all this blood on my hands and in my mind? What I have done to you seems worse, far worse than even this, but I can only plead that I loved you. You are still free, my darling, free of the knowledge of what man can do to man, of the terror and the hatred and the rage and the bloodlust. We can't meet again in this world, because our worlds have been torn asunder, but I shall never forget you.

You can never have known the man that I have discovered I really am, but for the love that you gave so generously and openly to the man you thought I was, I shall always be grateful.

Evelyn, forgive me for loving you.

Johnnie

Holding the thin sheets of paper on her knee, Evelyn looked up again, across the mile of four-foot-thick ice to the dark forest beyond, and deliberately opened up her mind to her letter. The agony of fear and shame that must have driven him to write it had been the last thing that he would have felt before the shell burst his body and brain into fragments.

He could never have known that whatever instinct had brought them together had been surer than he had guessed. He could never have known that the pretty empty girl he had loved had now seen the hatred, the bloodlust, the violence and the bodies, had felt the fear and the hate too. The injustice of it all and the pity of it were driven deep into her mind. They could have loved each other if they had been allowed to come back alive from their wars, and loved as whole people, not just the untouched, unaware children that they had been.

Now, at last, she understood what he had been feeling when he took her just before he went back. She saw and acknowledged what her ignorance must have done to him and how her lack of understanding then had driven him to write his last letter. She knew now that Bob was right: her love had not killed Johnnie. But her inability to love him as he had needed had sent him to his death in misery and she did not know whether she could find a way to forgive herself for that.

Tears, which had helped so many sorrows, could not touch this one. Every part of her body hurt with regret and the love she could have given to the man who had died. But she would not hide from it. She let it flow through her and made herself feel every bit of it.

Robert Adamson, who had been more surprised than he could now understand by the discovery that Evelyn had made love with John, stood watching her. He was not spying on her, but he was afraid for her and wanted to make certain that if anything happened to her he would be there.

After nearly half an hour of anxiety and trying to ignore the cold pain in his legs, he saw her stand up and stretch a little, as though sitting on the bollard had made her stiff. She carefully folded her letter and slid it back into its envelope. Then she turned towards him. He was too far away to see the expression on her face and was not sure whether to back away out of her sight or go to meet her. Dithering with indecision, he waited too long and she called out to him in surprise:

'Bob! Are you waiting for me?'

'Just to make sure you're O K, Eve.'

'Thank you. But I am all right – as much as I'll ever be now.' She stopped. There were so many things she wanted to say to him now that she did not know how to start. Then she thought that unless he knew something of the real John, whom only now was she beginning to know, he would never understand and so she took his letter out of her pocket.

'Will you read it, Bob?'

He stepped back a pace.

'But it's yours, Eve. It's kind of intimate, isn't it?'

'I'd like you to read it. Then you'll know what he was really like. Will you? Please?'

'If that's what you want.'

17

Evelyn left Bob by the Dvina while she went to find her brother. She tracked him down eventually in a small café much patronised by the younger British officers. The air was thick with the smoke of their cigarettes and the small room seemed to echo with their loud, commanding voices and braying laughter. There was a freak moment of quiet as she entered the café and she felt as though they were all breaking off their conversations to look at her as she inched past their tables and for the first time imagined them saying to one another things like: Oh, yes, that's Markham's sister – living with an American. Can you imagine? Of course she's been through a lot, but it's not right, is it? Just shows, women are all the same given half a chance.

Even though no one said any such thing, by the time Evelyn reached her brother's table she was angry and humiliated and in consequence her voice sounded hard when she said:

'Dick, I am so sorry I swore at you.'

He was ready with stern words of qualified forgiveness and orders for her future conduct, but she stopped him before he was halfway through his little speech and said, with calmness but absolute determination:

'No, Richard, don't do that. I was wrong to talk to you as I did, but you were wrong too. Even if I had been living with Robert Adamson in the sense in which you accused me, that would have been none of your business – and no justification for withholding Johnnie's letter. I know now that he would have understood that.'

'Evelyn, you're a lady, you don't understand these things as a man does. You simply cannot sacrifice your reputation like this. I must believe, because you have said it, that you are not . . . not that man's mistress, but other people may not believe it. And you will ruin all your chances. You probably don't understand that no decent man will ever willingly take second-hand goods.'

He was taken aback to see an indulgent smile cross his sister's pale, elegant face, once so familiar yet now so hard to read.

'Oh dear, yes, I once thought like that; to my shame it was one of the reasons why I was so desperate when I thought John might have been killed. You see, I thought of myself as you do – as a fallen woman. But it is so irrelevant to the real things.'

She saw that he was blushing and she felt sorry for him that he still had to learn so much and go through so much before he would even be able to see what he needed to learn.

'Evelyn, if – I mean if you're going to keep that man in your lodgings, what is the position? As I said this morning, you couldn't possibly marry him, even if he were to ask you. And that doesn't seem very likely.'

'The position, Dick? That's easy. We are friends; nothing more. He has been a tremendous help to me in looking after our cousins, and there has never been the slightest impropriety between us. There couldn't be – we don't like each other like that.' She saw his expression melt into one of mulish determination and changed the subject.

'Dick, do you have a bank account? A London bank account, I mean.'

'Of course I have. But what's that got to do with it?'

'Well, we are nearly starving. Until the Consul manages to get Father to pass some money through the War Office for me, I have nothing to live on.'

'I don't understand.'

'I'm sure you don't. When we fled from Shenkursk, Andrei Alexandrovitch gave me all the gold he could get hold of in time to use to keep his children – and myself – here until we could get away to England. But there are shortages of so many things that prices are terrible, and we have spent almost all of it. Baines can't help, because he has been ruined by the way the army has changed the currency. I will not sell the Suvarovs' jewels and furs at the sort of prices your colleagues are paying, but we have to eat. The only thing left that we could afford to pay for is vodka and that is no use to us.'

'Evelyn, this . . . I . . . Why didn't you say all that this morning?'

'There was too much else to talk about. But you have a bank account. One of the officers told me that shopkeepers are accepting cheques drawn on London, and if you could let me have some money I should be very grateful. There isn't another word for it.'

'Evie, I'm so sorry. I just didn't understand. Of course you can have a cheque. As many as you need. And I'm sure I can get some food for you. What have you been living on?'

'Dried beans and potatoes mainly.'

'No wonder you looked so mockingly when I told you that England is in a dangerous state now. Everyone has enough to eat there.'

'Do they, Dick? Everyone?' Her voice was drily amused.

'Well everyone like us, anyway. Is there a shop near here? Why don't we go now and get whatever you need. If he'll take a cheque I can buy everything, Evie. Anything you want.'

'Let's go. To be able to give those children a real meal tonight would be wonderful. They are so good and they must be so frightened. Do you realise, they have left their parents, two brothers and all their family behind, perhaps to be killed? They are living here in these dreadful conditions with Bob and me, not knowing when we'll get them out to England or what kind of life they will have when they get there.'

'Evie, don't say any more. I didn't understand. Can I meet them properly – I promise you I won't misbehave?'

'Of course, come and share the banquet tonight.'

As they walked back towards Baines's house, laden with packages of food, Dick suddenly said:

'You know, Evelyn, you have changed.'

'Yes, I do know. But the things I have seen and done and felt would have changed a dinosaur.' He wondered how she could sound so happy when they were stuck at the ends of the earth, surrounded by filth, disease, Bolos and ice, with John dead and the quarrel that they had just had still echoing horribly in his brain.

'Come on, I can't wait to feed the children.'

When she pushed open the door of the main room, she saw that Dindin was putting the last few beans into a pan on the small stove. Evelyn stood in the doorway, taking in the poverty and squalor of the room that had been her home for so many weeks, and began to wonder how the old Miss Markham would have coped with it. There was an odd little smile of amused acceptance on her lips. Then she said:

'We don't have to eat those things tonight, Dindin. Dickie has bought us meat, eggs, bread and butter – even sugar. We're going to have a feast tonight.'

Dindin looked anxiously at her cousin as though to make sure that this was not some kind of cruel joke and then flung back her head and laughed and laughed.

'A feast? Truly? Oh, Evie, how wonderful! Cousin Dick, I love you.'

Although Richard was looking suitably embarrassed at Dindin's exclamation, Evelyn thought suddenly that he would be much more suitable for Dindin than Adamson. And if she switched her attention to Dick, she might stop her increasingly embarrassing attempts to be left alone with the American and her rather more than sisterly strokings of his arm or shoulder or knee. Oddly relieved by the prospect, Evelyn smiled at Dindin and watched Tallie rather shyly take Dick's hand and tow him to the table.

'Sit down here, Cousin Dick, and tell us about England. Sasha and I want to know all about it. Evie has told us what she knows but it isn't enough.'

He thought her a pretty child with her delicate, pointed chin and the black curls falling around her pale forehead, and so he smiled at her and started to tell her and her brother of the life they might find in Yorkshire, while Evelyn and Dindin set about unpacking the food. Evelyn was absorbed in her task until she felt Dindin's hand on her wrist.

'What's the matter, Dindin?'

'Here's Bob, Evie.'

She looked up to see him standing in the doorway with John's letter in his hand and in his face something that made her put down the bowl and spoon she was holding. He started to speak, but then shut his mouth as he caught sight of Richard Markham sitting at the table with an expression of frowning inquiry on his face. Evelyn walked towards Bob and he held out her letter. As she took it from him, his fingers shook slightly and she looked up at him, wondering what it was that made his hazel eyes look so dark.

'I understand, Eve,' was all he said.

'Thank you,' she answered simply, pulling up her apron so that she could slip the letter into the pocket of her skirt. She ignored the interested looks of all her cousins and went back to her cookery.

Throughout the meal Richard Markham kept an eye on his sister and her unlikely companion, trying to discover just what had been going on between them. By the time Dindin got up to make tea Richard was satisfied that his sister had told the truth and was as innocent as she had claimed to be. But to his eyes it was obvious that the American had designs on her, and it was his clear duty as her brother, embarrassing though it would be, to tackle the man and show him that now Evelyn was no longer unprotected, he would have to give up any improper ideas he had.

To that end, Richard invited Mr Adamson to walk part of the way back to his billet with him. Rather surprised, and a little amused, Bob nodded casually, saying to Evelyn:

'All right with you, Eve, or do you need help here?'

'No, we'll do fine. You go off for a walk – as long as you can manage it.'

The two men left, pulling on their gloves and hats as they went slowly down the twisting staircase, but it was some time before Markham had summoned up what he felt were appropriate words. Then he began.

'I say, Adamson?'

'Yes?'

'My sister was a little hysterical this morning and said many things that she did not mean. One of them – we won't go into any details of course – might have given you a false idea of her. I can rely on you, I am sure, neither to repeat it to anyone in this frightful town nor to take any kind of advantage of it.'

When he got no reply, Markham looked at the American and was angry to see his expression of contempt.

'There's no need to look like that; it's perfectly obvious from the way you talk to my sister and the way you look at her and try to touch her all the time what you want. As an American, it may not be clear to you that she is in a most invidious position . . .'

'Shut up, Markham,' said Bob and, before the boy could express his fury at being addressed in so crude a manner went on, 'My dealings with your sister are her own affair and no one else's. I don't know what you think Americans are but the last thing I would want to do . . . There's no point discussing it. I'll leave you here before either of us loses his temper. Good night.'

He turned on his heel and strode away towards the sea.

Later, when he had walked up the Troitski Prospekt and pounded along the shore among the sea wrack for an hour or more, ignoring the ache in his legs as the newly-healed bones reacted to the unaccustomed strain, he found that most of his fury had evaporated. He had derived some satisfaction from rehearsing everything he would have liked to say to Markham, but the boy's interference had made Bob face the fact that he was going to have to settle his feelings for Evelyn one way or the other. With all the difficulties of living in Archangel and the problems brought by his broken legs, he had tried to ignore what he felt for her. Now it was clear that he would have to do something.

He had found her desirable from the beginning, but he

was old enough and experienced enough to know that desire died with what it fed on. The powerful emotions she had aroused in him were unsought and inconvenient, but he could no longer pretend that they did not exist or did not matter. He had promised Nikolai Alexandrovitch that he would do nothing about them and believed that he would be able to keep the promise, but that was before Archangel. As he had come to know her better and watched her caring for them all in their pathetic apartment, comforting Sasha when he was afraid of the dark or shivering in the cold he hated so much, Bob had slowly begun to understand that there was something about Evelyn that reached right down through all the accumulated layers of defence and disguise to the man he really was: neither the rebel nor the fearless fighting seeker-after-truth; but the shrinking, unprotected, easily damaged man. Until he had accepted his feelings for Evelyn, he had not admitted even to himself the existence of that man or his needs. Having admitted it, he would never now be able to deny it, and if he lost her . . .

Bob stopped himself there, refusing even to contemplate the possibility. There would come a time when it seemed possible to tell her, he was sure. Having walked and thought himself back into some kind of rationality, he turned and went back to the flat.

As soon as he got back, Evelyn looked up. He saw that she was blushing as she searched for words to tell him something. At last she said:

'Bob, I don't know what he said to you, but if it was anything like the things he said to me this afternoon, I am really very sorry.' She pushed some loose strands of her untidy hair behind her ears. He looked down into her pale face with its firm cheekbones, delicately arched eyebrows and deep, glowing brown eyes, and wondered how he could ever have thought that he disliked her. Her dark eyes looked into his as a friend's might, and her beautifully shaped lips, a little cracked by the endless winter, smiled. He forgot what she had said to him and his mouth opened to say all the things he wanted to tell her. Then her expression changed to one of doubt and he was dragged back to the matter in hand. His voice was warm and a little hesitant as he spoke.

'Eve, he made me so angry that I could not answer him properly, but tell me something. *You* aren't afraid of anything I might . . .?'

'No, of course not, Bob. We are friends, aren't we?'

'Something like that; I told Nick I'd look after you and I'm doing my best to fill his place.'

'I know, and I am grateful, Bob. I'm only sorry that it's let you in for such a distasteful scene. I tried to explain to him, but he's just so pigheaded. I'm sorry.'

'Don't be. It's this place, I think. As soon as we all get out of here we'll all be more sensible and get everything sorted out.'

'Yes,' she said grateful for the unemotional way in which he was taking her brother's embarrassing intervention. 'Yes, living so cramped like this makes us all a bit peculiar.'

For the next four days their life was peaceful and relatively easy. Dick came once or twice to the flat but he behaved with some circumspection. He made himself speak politely to Adamson, and as soon as Evelyn realised that her brother was concentrating more on Dindin than on herself she ceased to tense up when she heard his voice calling from the foot of the stairs and watched them both with amusement.

Then, when she and Dindin were clearing away the remains of breakfast on the morning of the fifth day, she heard Baines's heavy tread on the stairs. Sasha went to open the door to him and called out:

'Good morning, Mr Baines. And what can we do for you on this fine day?' a phrase that he had been practising with Dick whenever he came to the flat.

'Morning, Alexander Andreivitch. Miss Evelyn, I came to tell you that the thaw's started and the river's breaking up. It's a sight like no other you'll ever see. You oughtn't to miss it.'

'Thank you, Baines. How good of you. Well, shall we all go? Bob, do you feel like an expedition?'

'Why not? Dindin, Tallie?'

'Of course, Bob. Let's go. And then we can find Dick later and get another lovely cheque out of him.'

Bob looked surprised and turned as though to ask Dindin what she meant, but the excitement and urgency he could feel in the room was such that it did not seem the right moment. Instead, he helped Sasha exchange his soft felt shoes for the thick outdoor boots he had brought from Shenkursk, and then pulled on his own. Together with Mr Baines they clattered down the steep, twisting wooden stairs and out into the street.

'Yes, it does feel much warmer,' said Dindin, pulling off her gloves and rubbing the air between finger and thumb. 'Look, everybody's going to the river.'

It was an exaggeration, but the street was certainly full of people all walking in the direction of the Dvina. Evelyn's face contracted in what looked like a spasm of fear and Bob, who seemed to watch her all the time now, said quite gently:

'What is it, Eve?'

To his relief, she laughed.

'It was silly of me, but just for a minute or two, it felt like that morning when we went to the Taurida Palace. Do you remember? At the beginning, when the Revolution seemed exciting and full of freedom – and innocence.'

He said nothing: there was too much that was unresolved between them for him to be able to talk to her freely about his ruined illusions. As they neared the river, they could hear a repeating sound like a series of explosions. Tallie pulled at Baines's sleeve and when he bent down towards her, she said softly:

'It isn't guns, is it? Have the Bolsheviki come?' Baines gave a great bellow of laughter and said:

'No, of course not. It's the Dvina, bursting out of the ice. Just you wait and see.'

They hurried forward and reached the river bank just as a chunk of ice nearly eight feet across split off from its parent, and as the churning river swelled underneath it was thrown up into the air between the two opposing sheets of ice. They crunched and growled as they bit into the rearing pillar of ice and then released it to crash back into the swirling water, throwing up a spouting fountain in its place.

As she watched the elemental struggle between the living

water fighting its way out of the grip of the moribund ice, Evelyn felt suddenly exhilarated by its power. She turned to see if Bob shared her excitement.

He was staring as though absorbed in the astonishing, violent spectacle in front of them, but she felt that he was trying to tell her something. He was breathing heavily and the hand gripping her own was tight. Not sure how to help him, instead she gave expression to a half-formed thought.

'I'd never understood until today what they meant when they talked about "the forces of Nature".'

At that he looked down at her, and there was an extraordinary expression in his eyes, which she had never seen before. His voice was dry as he said:

'Hadn't you, Eve? No, I suppose not.' Then, still gripping her wrist, he urged her away from the river bank and all the other people. When they were alone and out of earshot, he took her other wrist and looking down at her lovely puzzled face said, with teeth clenched:

'God knows what Nick would have done to me if he knew what I was about to say to you, Eve.'

For some reason that she did not quite understand, Evelyn was frightened rather than angry. In order to control the sudden fear, she looked up at him, and said:

'Nikolai Alexandrovitch understood everything.'

'Do you, though? Not quite, I think.'

'Then explain it to me,' she said, her own breathing irregular and blood coming into her pale cheeks.

But he was beyond explaining anything to anyone. He dropped her wrists and put both hands on her neck, pushing up her chin, and kissed her full, beautiful mouth.

She could feel his hands strong at the back of her head, and the soft gentleness of his lips on her own. His body was touching her all over and as the blood began to pound through her and her heart to thud, she was tempted for a moment to put her hands on his head and hold him even closer. But as the impulse formed so did the pictures of Johnnie weeping on her breast; of the man in the Vyborg with his hands at Dindin's neck. She thought of the way Sergei had made her respond to him and then used that as a weapon. Unaware of her thoughts but alive to the slightest movement of her body, Bob said:

'I want you so much Eve. I hardly dare say it because none of the words is right, but I want you.'

'Don't touch me!'

'What?' he said, still reeling from the emotions she had aroused in him.

'Take your hands off me!' Slowly he recognised that he had failed, and, as he saw horror in her dark eyes, he backed away a little, his hands held out by his sides.

'Eve, don't. Don't look at me like that. I'm sorry if I frightened you. You don't have to be like that. I won't touch you. Calm down.' Then as she continued to breathe jerkily, her lips lifting away from her teeth and her eyes accusing, his frustration got the upper hand over his gentler instincts and he almost shouted at her:

'I won't touch you. Stop it, Evelyn. Jesus, but you're enough to . . .' He shook his head and turned his back on her. Looking out towards the sea, he gathered up the remnants of his patience and said:

'You've had a rough time in more ways than one. I do understand that. But for Christ's sake, I'm not going to rape you. You don't have to go off the deep end like that: just telling me to stop would have been enough.'

'I'm sorry,' she said, her voice quieter now, but still shaking a little. He turned back, remorse battling with everything else, and looked ruefully at her:

'Well, we do have a problem, don't we?'

'We?'

'Yes, Eve. We do. Don't run away from me into that old coldness. I care about you, Eve, and . . .' She interrupted before he could get any further.

'And I, you,' she said. 'More than I had ever expected I could. But why must that involve such . . . such beastliness?'

'Jesus!' he said again, half in supplication, half in anger. 'Forget it. And don't look at me like that. I'm not going to leap on you. I won't so much as touch you.'

18

As Archangel shed itself of its long-held ice, private dumps of unspeakable debris that had simply been thrown out of the houses during the winter to freeze immediately into inoffensiveness began to melt. Ironside's army set about moving most of it, but some remained to add to the multifarious smells and germs of the town. They were not helped by the mosquitoes, released by the new wet warmth to prey on inhabitants and invaders alike. At first the bites were merely tiresome, and the swellings they produced painful but not dangerous; but as the heat increased towards the end of May, even before the sea ice had broken up enough to allow any ships down through the White Sea, the danger became acute.

Evelyn knew nothing of it until she summoned one of the Russian doctors to look at Sasha, who had been fractious for several days and then developed a terrifyingly high fever that made him shudder as though with cold, and cry and mumble in delirium. The doctor looked across the child's makeshift bed and said with pity in his voice:

'Malaria.'

'I don't know much about that,' said Evelyn, desperately trying to sound calm and not let her terror show, 'but I thought it was a disease of the tropics.'

'It was. But they tell me that it was rife in Salonika and many of General Ironside's men were serving there and it is in their blood for ever. The mosquitoes have now transferred it to the population of Archangel.'

Evelyn could not speak, but Bob asked her questions for her:

'What must we do?'

'The first thing is to get nets to put over all the beds. It will be too easy for one of the insects to bite your son and then fly on to you or the others and infect them. Then you should give him quinine. There will soon be a shortage of that like everything else now, so you should try to get your stocks quickly. Keep him warm, restrict his diet to liquids, and wait. He is not in danger if you are sensible. Do you understand?'

Evelyn nodded, her face showing little of the torment she felt, but Bob had seen her hide other overwhelming feelings and he knew.

'Doctor Samenev, where do I get the quinine?' he asked, not even bothering to explain that he was not the child's father.

'Try all the druggists in the town; if they have none, then you must just ask the army. I don't know if they're going to let civilians have any, but you will have to ask.'

Evelyn relaxed infinitesimally as she understood that she could leave the search for quinine to Bob. In spite of their difficulties he was, as he had once promised, doing his best to be like Nikolai Alexandrovitch, and she knew instinctively that she could trust him. Deeply thankful that she did not have to face this anxiety alone, she said goodbye to the doctor and as soon as he had left she helped Bob carry Sasha's bed into the main room. They put it close to hers and she sat down and picked up the delirious child, cradling him in her arms. Bob watched her for a moment, pity for them both twisting his strong face into an almost harsh-looking mask.

'I'll take Dindin and Tallie with me. Then they can come back here as soon as we've gotten any quinine and I'll go on to collect all I can find. And some nets.' Then he put out one of his hands as though to touch her before he remembered and quickly disguised the gesture.

'Don't be afraid, Eve. We'll get him right.'

She lifted her face and the expression in her eyes appalled him.

'Evelyn, what is it? You mustn't give up hope.'

'I'm not. It's just – oh, don't you see? This is what always happens. I have only to care for someone and then something terrible happens. If he dies . . .'

'Stop it, Eve, at once. He won't die. I have to go now if I'm to get the pills, but I can't leave you like this. You'll do him no good. Remember what Nick used to say about guilt?'

Evelyn took a sharp, deep breath and tamped down the sparks of hysteria.

'I'm sorry. Of course you must go. I won't do it again.'

But it was not so easy. While Sasha shivered and sweated in her arms, she could concentrate on trying to cool him. She laid him back on the bed and wiped the sweat off his broad forehead, murmuring comfort to him. But when he slept and there was nothing she could do for him, she would feel terror gripping her at the thought that he might not live. Watching his pallid face as he moved restlessly from side to side, she was taken ineluctably back to her old fears. She loved the child, had loved him ever since she had been allowed to start teaching him. In her mind she rehearsed all that Bob had said to her about the dead of the Western Front, and tried to remember the anger in his voice in case it would stop her tormenting thoughts. But it did not. The fear that her affection was dangerous lay deeper than thought or memory or reason. Somehow it had become embedded in the very fabric of her self.

The shivering child relaxed and the sudden stillness terrified her. She put her fingers to the pulse in his wrist. It still beat. She became determined that he would not die; if there were anything she could do to ensure his survival, she would do it no matter the cost. She would not speak of the recurrence of her old fears; she would try not even to allow herself to think of them.

Dindin and Natalie came back with the first batch of quinine pills soon after twelve. It seemed a pity to wake Sasha out of his still sleep, but they had to do it. He came back into consciousness and pain, and started to cry even before his eyes opened. But he was no longer delirious and his first words were:

'Evie, Evie, make it stop hurting.'

She smoothed the tumbled, black hair away from his frighteningly white forehead and said:

'Sashenka, I'll do my best. Now you must take these three pills.'

'I don't want to,' came the petulant answer and he turned his face away from her. Steeling herself, Evelyn said:

'Little Dove, you must if I am to make it stop. Come along. No, darling, don't cry. Sit up here against me. Look, Tallie has brought you some water. Now try to swallow. That's right, tip your head back and they'll just slide down. Now, take a sip of the water. Good boy.'

But he gagged on the mouthful and spat pills and water out on to the bed. Patiently Evelyn coaxed him to try again and at last he got the pills down.

'Don't go away.'

'No, we'll all stay with you. Try to sleep again.' She laid him back on the bed and looked at his sisters with sadness in her brown eyes, but she made her voice hopeful when she said:

'The doctor said there was nothing to worry about so long as we keep giving him the pills. So you mustn't be afraid.'

'No, of course not, Evie,' said Dindin, cheerfully. 'We met Dick on the way back from the druggist's and he told us the same. What was it he said, Tallie?'

'That lots of chaps he knows have had it and it's not very pleasant but there's no danger. Then he said he'd come here in a little bit to take Dindin out for lunch. And Dindin said . . .'

'That's enough,' said her sister, sharply enough to break into Evelyn's concentration on Sasha. She looked up.

'Going out to lunch, Dindin? With Sasha as ill as this, are you sure?'

'Well, why ever not? I'm not a nurse. There's nothing I can do to help him. You've been trained in the hospital. You can do all there is to be done. Why shouldn't I go out with dear Dick? He understands how cruel all this revolutionary nonsense has been and the sort of life I ought to be living . . .'

'Oh, Dindin, stop it. I know you long for balls and reviews

245

and theatres, but really! At a time like this. You might at least . . . Oh, never mind. Go and titivate and have your fun.'

'I'll help, Evie,' whispered Natalie, putting her hand on her cousin's knee.

'I know you will, Tallie. Thank you. We'll make him better.'

Dindin flounced out of the room and they heard her go downstairs as soon as Dick's voice called up from the hall.

'She didn't even say goodbye,' said Tallie, surprised. 'Or come to see how Sasha is.'

'I think she must be as worried as we are, Tallie,' said Evelyn, not convinced by her own statement. 'Perhaps it's just difficult for her to sit here not being able to do anything to help him. Oh, listen. Is that Uncle Bob?'

'Hello, you two,' he said, coming into the room and dumping a large pile of fine white netting on the table. 'I saw Dindin whisking off in the opposite direction with Markham. What's she up to?'

'Oh, the selfish creature just went out to luncheon. She . . .'

'Hush, now, Tallie.'

'All right, but she is selfish.'

Evelyn tried not to agree, but over the next few days as she battled to keep Sasha cool during the savage bouts of delirium and fever and warm enough when his temperature suddenly dropped, she could neither control nor conceal her anger.

Dindin was rarely in the flat except for dinner and at night, and she almost always brought Dick or one of his friends up the steep stairs when they escorted her home. Trying to tell herself that if it helped Dindin's anxiety to live in such a whirl of activity that was her right, Evelyn did her best to be charitable. She also tried to be glad when she noticed that Dindin had regained much of her old prettiness. Since Dick had started to finance their larder, food had been more plentiful and Dindin's pink cheeks had begun to fill out again. She had begun taking extra care with her appearance too, and would examine herself approvingly in their one looking-glass. One afternoon when Evelyn had had a particularly difficult time with Sasha and knew that she was dishevelled and sweaty in the close heat of the attic, Dindin said to her:

'Evie, I can't think why you've let yourself go like this. You used to be so good-looking, but now in those clothes and with your hair like that you might be a kitchen maid. It's no wonder that Dick is ashamed of you.'

Pushing the heavy dark hair, which was beginning to come unplaited, away from her sticky face, Evelyn said only:

'Dindin, with Sasha so ill my looks matter nothing. I wish you could just concentrate on the important things and . . .' What was the point in going on? 'Never mind. Go out and enjoy criticising me with my idiotic brother. Go on, off with you.'

Bob, who had just come quietly into the room, stood aside to let Dindin out. Ignoring for the moment what he had overheard, he said:

'How is he, Eve?'

'I think the quinine's beginning to take hold. Samenev warned me it would take some days. But he's frighteningly weak, Bob.'

'Samenev seems to know his job all right; if he's satisfied I don't think you should worry.'

'No. I do try not to. Where's Tallie?'

'She was a bit tired after our walk and is lying down.'

'Oh, right. Thanks for taking her out. You're being so good to us all.'

He smiled at her. Since Sasha's illness they had both managed to ignore the scene at the river.

'You deserve some help, Eve, with Dindin carrying on like that. Don't believe too much of what she says, will you?'

'No, of course not. And anyway, what does it matter what I look like or what Dick says about me, especially now.'

Bob came much closer to her and hesitated, trying to find words to tell her that with the last vestiges of fashion and adornment abandoned she looked far lovelier to him than she ever had in the silks and velvets she had worn in Shenkursk, but not wanting to sound as though he was renewing his pursuit of her.

'Evelyn, circumstances may have stripped you of the

trappings of young-ladyhood, but your face, your eyes, your lips, are as beautiful as they always were and always will be.'

She laughed at that. 'Bob, your kindness doesn't have to extend to compliments. I'm just so thankful that you're helping to keep Tallie all right – and sitting with Sasha so that I can get out.' She dipped her handkerchief in a bowl of water by the bed and wiped the child's forehead again. 'I only wish that I could get them away from here. Much as I hated the winter, this sticky heat is almost worse. I don't see how Sasha can get better in this place.'

'I'm looking into it, Eve. The US troops will be leaving soon, and . . .'

'When?' she demanded, her face whiter than ever and her large dark eyes staring at him.

'Soon. I don't know when exactly. What's the matter?'

'Are you going too?' she said at last. At that he put a hand on her shoulder and said:

'Eve, you can't think I'd go and leave you all here, with Sasha ill as he is. I'm going to get you all back to England if it's the last thing . . .'

'Don't say that,' she said hurriedly, hit by a new fear. He smiled.

'All right, I won't. But you must trust me, Eve. I will get you back.'

She did now trust him, but she could not imagine how he was going to fulfil his promise. There were no ships available to the refugees who wanted to leave Archangel by sea; and the railway led only south, directly into the path of the Red Army. Evelyn thought it might be possible for her and Bob to get the Suvarovs across land to Murmansk, but Dick had told her that there were refugees stuck there in no better situation than hers.

Bob saw her doubts and renewed his determination to find a way to get her out of Archangel. He went out as soon as he could to talk to one of his contacts in the US headquarters, who quickly put paid to any ideas he had of getting them all out on an American ship, but told him of an Archangel resident who had a sea-going ketch which he might sell. Bob got the man's address at once and sallied forth to negotiate with him for the boat. On inspection, it proved to need considerable repairs and so Adamson fought a spirited battle over the price and eventually agreed to pay half the total then and half when all the repairs had been done and he had had a chance to take the boat out for sea trials. He and the owner shook hands and he went triumphantly back to Baines's.

Evelyn's face was almost peaceful when he walked into her room, and her whole body seemed to have relaxed.

'He's better,' said Bob, not even making a question of it.

'Yes, the fever's broken. His temperature is nearly normal. Samenev has just left and he said it ought to be just a matter of time now. Sasha woke a few minutes ago and he said he was hungry. Isn't that wonderful?'

'Wonderful,' he answered and, slightly surprised to see Dindin at the makeshift stove, said kindly, 'What are you making for him, Dindin?'

'A kind of milky slop, but it's what Samenev ordered. I just got back in time to make it. Tallie grated the bread-crumbs.'

'Well that's terrific. And I've got some good news too. We'll all be out of here within the month. I've bought a boat.'

Evelyn looked up from the book she was helping Tallie to read and the face she turned to Bob showed nothing but weariness and some anger.

'What's up? I thought you'd be pleased for God's sake.'

'Bob, it's too important to joke about.'

'It's not a joke. I've bought a ketch and as soon as it's been overhauled we'll be off.'

'Oh, don't. How could you possibly afford to buy a boat? I know that Dick is generous enough about the food, but he could not possibly have given you enough for a boat.'

'I don't know what you're talking about. It's nothing to do with your brother. And of course I can afford it.' He saw that she was genuinely puzzled and, becoming less annoyed and more surprised himself, he went on: 'Why d'you think I couldn't afford it? Didn't Piotr or Georgii ever tell you any-thing about me?'

'Plenty of things, but . . .'

'But not that. Well, you ought to know: my family has always had more than enough money and much as I hate the stuff, I've plenty too – far too much. But at least it's coming in useful now.'

Evelyn thought of her assumptions about his background, of her care to protect him from the knowledge of their poverty in Archangel and reliance on her brother's money, of his shabby clothes, of his hatred of the Petrograd rich, of his political opinions, and shook her head.

'What's the trouble? Have you been judging by appearances, Eve?'

At that she smiled ruefully.

'Yes. Why didn't you tell me?'

'I thought you knew. Everybody else did. It was no secret. Besides, what does it matter? It has nothing to do with who I am.'

Dindin turned, a dripping wooden spoon in her hand, and said:

'It would have mattered quite a bit this last year. Didn't you know how worried Evie was about money? Until kind Dick arrived, in any case. There wasn't going to be enough to eat. He came just in time. How could you have been so selfish?'

'No, Dindin, don't,' said Evelyn, seeing that Bob's strong face was suffused with an unaccustomed and most painful blush.

'Eve, why didn't you tell me?'

'I didn't want to worry you. There you were with your legs so bad and I thought you were far from well-off – it would have been so unkind to whine at you when there wasn't anything you could have done about it.'

He suddenly sat down, an expression of horror in his eyes.

'Eve, you don't think that . . .' Then he broke off and looked at Tallie, who was staring inquiringly at him. But Evelyn stretched a hand across the table to touch his.

'No, Bob. It wouldn't have made any difference. I asked Samenev. Truly. It's the mosquitoes; nothing we could have done would have prevented it. You mustn't think that.' They were speaking very quietly, but Sasha woke up just then, thirsty and rather miserable. To distract him from his woes, Evelyn told him the news.

'Uncle Bob, have you really got a boat?' he demanded, his faint voice strengthening with every syllable. 'Will you be able to find the way in it? Isn't it very difficult to drive a boat?'

'You sail a boat, Sasha, or steer it. Driving's for carriages and motors. I do know how to. And Eve has done some sailing too, haven't you?'

'Only a bit – in Tony's little dinghy – and never very far from the shore. I won't be much help to you, I'm afraid.'

'Well there'll be time to practise. As soon as the repairs are done, I'll have to take her out to test her seaworthiness and I'll need a crew – it'll serve both purposes. Although I am having her rigged for single-handed sailing, I shall need help – and time off to sleep.'

'Can I see it, Uncle Bob?'

'When you're stronger, Little Dove,' murmured Evelyn, laying one of her thin hands on his clammy forehead to check his temperature. 'You have to stay in bed for a bit longer. Doctor Samenev insists. Now, here's Dindin with your food. She'll feed you.'

She stood up to allow Dindin to take her place and moved out into the corridor with Bob.

'You were right, I was taking Dindin too seriously. I think she really was worried about him. It just takes her a different way. She is as pleased as Tallie and I that he's beginning to get better.'

'Do you think she'd sit with him tomorrow morning?'

'I'm sure she would, but why?'

'I'd like to take you and Tallie to see the boat. She needs quite a few repairs, but I'd like you to see her. It'd do you good to get out and smell the sea.'

'All right, if he's still without a temperature in the morning.'

19

Tallie was as excited as though she were going to a panto-
mime when they set off towards the docks, and Evelyn
looked across her small dark head at Bob in deep gratitude. This pleasure was the first that Tallie had shown
since Sasha's illness. Bob smiled back painfully, feeling
that he deserved no gratitude at all from Evelyn and still unable to understand his own insensitivity. Had it not been
for his ridiculous reluctance to use any of the money his
family's trust fund had paid him, he would have been able
to give Evelyn practical, necessary help months ago. Looking back, he could not understand why he had never asked
her how she was buying the food they all ate. Struggling
to cope with the pain in his legs and his fears for the future,
he must have simply assumed that Baines was providing
it, or that Andrei Suvarov had made some kind of arrangement.

Fortunately his uncomfortable, humiliating thoughts were
interrupted just then by a burst of raucous cheering and the
brazen sound of a military band.

'What's happening, Uncle Bob?' asked Natalie nervously.
He answered in his most reassuring voice.

'It's the relief troops from England, Tallie. They've come
to take the place of the Americans who are leaving. Don't be
afraid.' She pushed her small, damp hand into his and together with Evelyn they walked towards the marching troops
and waving, clapping people. Evelyn pointed out to Natalie
the magnificent figure of General Ironside, standing huge

and handsome with the bearded Russian generals and the mayor of the town waiting to take the salute.

They watched until the military formalities were done, when the mayor came forward with bread and salt, which the commanding officer of the new troops ceremoniously ate. The Russian town had welcomed the new wave of invaders with all the power of its ancient traditions and the British had signified their acceptance of the responsibilities of friendship.

But Bob knew and Evelyn guessed that there were less happy feelings on both sides. Very few Russians from the town had come forward willingly to join the army that was fighting the Bolsheviki on their land; the British command despised most of the Russian officers, who seemed to spend all their time and energy composing unnecessary Orders of the Day in absurdly flowery language, or hatching plots and plans that they were entirely incapable of carrying out. Many of them treated their men in a way that shocked the British and Americans, and provoked mutinous riots among the regiments under their command.

Bolshevik leaflets were continually appearing in the town, plastered on to the sides of the houses, drifting along the muddy streets, deposited anywhere and everywhere to exhort Russian and foreign soldiers alike to leave their commands and cease the fighting. Spies were thought to have infiltrated almost every part of Archangel life, and anonymous or pseudonymous articles appeared in the town's newspapers criticising the Intervention and trying to alert the populace to what must happen when the invaders deserted those who had befriended them.

The one hopeful sign that co-operation was possible was the existence of Dyer's Battalion, a group of Russian prisoners who had been formed into a labour battalion under a young Canadian officer named Dyer. With care, training and efficient discipline, he and his fellow officers had turned the surly and rebellious rabble into a fighting unit. They had been allowed to see action on various of the small fronts during the winter, and had acquitted themselves well. Poor Dyer had been killed, but the spirit he had instilled seemed to continue and Dyer's Battalion was an achievement of which many of the British were proud, although some of the officers did not entirely trust the men even then.

But Ironside had confidence in them and they and their Allied officers were to go down the Dvina with the relief troops to try to crush the Bolshevik forces in the region so that a peaceful evacuation could be successfully carried out.

Evelyn watched them march past to the sound of their own regimental band and wondered what would happen when they faced their own countrymen in a major battle. It was one thing for 'White' Russians like Sergei Voroshilov and Georgii Suvarov to fight the Bolsheviki, but these men, whom she had once heard called 'the very riff-raff of the Revolution'?

'D'you think they'll fight, Bob?'

'God knows. But it is a great gesture to send them.'

'You sound almost admiring.'

'You can't help admiring it,' he said, not explaining exactly what he meant by 'it'. 'I disapprove of the Intervention with every bit of me, as you know, but now I can see both how it happened and that parts of what they do are admirable.'

'Such as?' asked Evelyn, not sneering, but wanting something hopeful to admire.

'Oh, this business of Dyer's Battalion. I suspect that left to themselves the Russians would have shot them – or sent them to be worked to death on one of the islands at the mouth of the Dvina. But your people have fed them, trained them, made them fit and adequately healthy, given them a band, given them status. It *is* hard not to admire, even if it fails in the end.'

'I suppose so, although I can't help thinking of that phrase of Marshal Bosquet's. But then none of this is quite war, is it?'

'Not exactly, but I've a feeling it'll become more like it before your boys get to go home. All the more reason why I want you all out of here before it happens. Come on, let's by-pass this lot and get to Petrovitch's.'

Evelyn did not answer, suddenly realising that if there were to be a battle, Dick might have to fight. With all these new, fit relief troops, his C3 health status might save him, but if it did not then she would be back with all the old fears. She shivered.

'Eve, are you all right? You can't be cold on a boiling day like this.'

'No, I'm not cold.'

'Come on; come on,' said Tallie, getting even more excited as they reached the sea.

They turned into the boatyard, which was full of decaying boats, piles of timber, and old tarry ropes. The smell of the place was oddly exciting, compounded as it was of freshly sawn pine planks, varnishes, oils and tar, all overlain with the salty tang of the sea. The sight of Bob's yacht, high above the landing-stage in its wooden cradle, made the idea of escape seem much more credible and Evelyn began to believe that they might actually get away. But the size of the boat bothered her.

'Bob, you mustn't rely too much on me. Tony's dinghy was titchy compared with this, but I truly don't understand how you think we can cross the Barents Sea and the North Atlantic in it.'

'Eve, I'm not planning to. Look,' he said, taking an old map out of his pocket and spreading it out on the top of a damp, odorous fish box. 'We'll get out of the White Sea and then in reasonably easy stages creep round the coast to Norway. See: then we'll hop from Hammerfest to Tromsö, on to Narvik, Mosjöen and Trondheim. Then round to Bergen. I think we could then cross the Atlantic and get to the Shetlands, but it's probably wiser to sell the boat in Bergen and get an ordinary commercial steamer down to Newcastle.'

'But it'll take weeks,' she protested as she took in the scale of the map and the immense length of the Norwegian coast-line.

'Probably about three. Perhaps four,' he agreed, apparently unworried. 'But it'll be far better than rotting for all that time in Archangel. And this is just the right time of year – the ice is at its least now, and we'll be able to sail for as long as one or other of us can keep awake since there'll be no real night to stop us.'

'I suppose so,' said Evelyn at last, but her face showed how daunted she was.

'Don't worry, Eve. You're right that it'll take time, but there's no reason why we shouldn't make it. I've sailed bigger boats than this and I promise I'll take you out to practise before we set off for Bergen.'

The old boatman appeared just then, a smoking pipe between his teeth. He patted the rough planks of the yacht's side and said in a heavy accent:

'Good ship, yes? She'll take you safe to Norway.'

'Thank you, Mr Petrovitch,' said Evelyn formally. 'But how long will it take for you to get the repairs and the new rigging finished?'

'Two weeks, perhaps three. Who knows? Is better when I get materials, yes?'

Adamson spoke sternly to him in Russian and they moved off together to Petrovitch's cluttered office, leaving Tallie to scamper around the legs of the cradle and Evelyn to think about getting home at last. There was comfort in the idea, but not as much as she had expected. True, she told herself, trying to stamp out the sudden doubts, it would be wonderful to get away from Archangel. But for the first time she began to think of what England held out for her apart from safety from the Revolution.

Could she go back to the old life? In the past she would never have so described it, but now it seemed to have been one of deadening boredom, punctuated by the dim pleasures of rainy tennis parties, dreary dances and patronising, enervating good works. How could she slot back into the tramlines that seemed to have been laid down for her at birth? She should find a suitable man to marry, from a family known to her parents, learn to run a small house and its servants in the way her mother had done so that she would be suitably qualified to take over her husband's parents' house in due course. Then would come children, increasingly matronly responsibilities in some village, opening vicarage fêtes and giving talks to the assembled women; and above all seeing that her children too were properly trained to take their place on the same dull tramlines. There must be more to life than that.

Of course she would have Sasha with her, and by now he seemed more than ever like her own child, and there would be Dindin for a time and Natalie. They would add something. But what of Bob? She had been afraid that he might go back to the States and leave her in Archangel and thought it was the prospect of living there without him that was so upsetting. Now, at last, she understood that being anywhere without him would be to live in a loneliness from which she would never emerge.

Until Sasha's terrifying illness had smashed into her self-absorption, she had not even noticed how much she relied on the big, shabbily dressed, untidy American. His unsuitability and his occasional mockery had seemed so important that she had not seen beyond them to what he was really like – or how much he meant to her. His sarcastic dismissal of all the shibboleths with which she had been inculcated had once hurt her, but now she understood that it was that very dismissal that had allowed her to see how unsatisfying her life had been. Like Nikolai Alexandrovitch, Bob knew what was important, and it had nothing to do with conventional manners or correct dress.

Bob had broken through the battlements that had surrounded her, and through the gaps he had made she had been able to see a world in which she would be able to live as herself, not just as a counter in some meaningless, convention-ridden game. To go back to the emptiness of her old existence, having caught a glimpse of what life could be, would be tormenting.

At that moment he came out of Petrovitch's office and tood blinking in the bright light and rolling the torn sleeves of his cream-coloured peasant shirt up over his muscular, tanned forearms. As she watched the sun glinting almost like gold on his thick fair hair, Evelyn felt that she had never seen him properly before – it was as if cataracts had been miraculously removed from her eyes. At last she could look at him without the fog of misunderstanding and misdirected emotions that had made it impossible to see the man he really was. The tremendous masculinity that had once seemed so threatening now promised to be a rock to which she would be able to cling through storm and tempest.

He walked towards her, unaware of the immense, almost volcanic, changes that were taking place within her. She was being forced to feel every sensation she had denied – and to see the last few months from his point of view instead of her own. She had thought him another burden she had to carry, furious with him for trying to turn their growing friendship into something else, for trying to take advantage of her in the cramped, forced intimacy of their situation. Evelyn actually flushed as that thought swam up into her mind. Looked at through his eyes, the picture was rather different, and she recognised belatedly that it was she who had been exploiting him, relaxing against the friendship he offered and refusing to see that it could never have been just friendship. She had been as blind and selfish over Bob's feelings as she had once been over Johnnie's.

As he came up to her she smiled at him and tried to tell him with her eyes that she understood and was sorry, that she would be to him whatever he wanted. He looked down at her, not understanding what she wanted, and raised one of his thick fair eyebrows. When she did not explain, he said once again:

'What's the trouble, Eve?'

Trouble! How could she answer that? Perhaps he no longer wanted her; she had probably killed all the feelings he had for her by her idiocy. Quite unable to speak, she just shook her head and turned aside to find Tallie. Bob looked after her, puzzled, then up at the yacht. Perhaps she was worried that in so confined a space he might try again to make love to her and that she would not be able to control him. He sighed in exasperation; why did she think that men were ravening beasts? Couldn't she understand that he had got the message, that it just wasn't in him to force himself on a reluctant woman, however much he might have wanted her – even if he could spare the time from navigating a yacht that size through some of the most treacherous seas in the northern hemisphere? The thought of such a scene suddenly made him laugh and broke the tensions of the moment.

He collected her and Tallie and, calling farewells to old Petrovitch, they walked slowly to the tram stop and so home.

When they climbed the twisting stairs, they found Dindin entertaining Dick and another British officer to tea. Both men leaped to their feet as Evelyn walked in and she said almost impatiently:

'Oh, for goodness sake! Don't bother to get up. Sit down and have your tea.'

But they waited, cups in hand, until she had taken off her light shawl and sat down by Sasha's bed. He was asleep again, breathing heavily in a way that bothered her. She put her fingers to his thin wrist and felt his pulse: it was irregular and oddly faint. Evelyn looked up towards Dindin to ask how long Sasha had been like that.

Dindin was edging her chair very close to Dick's and gazing meltingly up at him through her eyelashes. Just so, thought Evelyn annoyed, had she looked at Andrei Alexandrovitch in the old days. Hadn't the realities they had all lived through done anything to teach Dindin dignity, or concern for anyone except herself? Did she really feel nothing for her brother? Then Evelyn took herself to task and acknowledged that even in the middle of her anxiety for Sasha she was envious. If Dindin had been in the absurd situation in which Evelyn now found herself, she would have simply stroked Bob's arm and said straight out, I am sorry I stopped you from kissing me that day at the river. There is nothing I should like better now than for you to seize me as you did then. I have discovered that I love you. But, being herself, she could not. If he did not want her any more, she could not lay herself open to the possibility of agonising rejection. It might serve her right for her insensitivities in the past, but it would not be bearable. In any case, there were more important things to worry about. She pushed it all away and said:

'Dindin, how long has Sasha been asleep like this?'

'Oh, most of the afternoon. Why? Samenev said sleep is a great healer.'

'Did he come while we were out?'

'No. Come on, Eve. What are you making such a fuss about?'

'Do you want him, Eve?' asked Bob, quietly coming over to stand beside her. She looked up at him, grateful for his calmness and his sensitivity.

'Please. I've never seen anything like this. I don't want to do anything that might . . .'

'Hush now, Eve. I'll go right now.'

The two young men followed him out of the room about ten minutes later, leaving Dindin to take her cousin to task for driving them away. Evelyn was too tired and worried to answer and just waited for the doctor, never taking her eyes off Sasha's face. His skin seemed to her to be more transparent even than during the worst of his fevers.

When Samenev came he banished Natalie and Dindin from the main room before he examined Sasha, and then he made Evelyn sit down.

'What is it, Doctor? What are you afraid of?'

'Now, now. There's no need for hysteria.'

'No, I know. But please tell me.'

'It's not the malaria. The quinine has dealt with that. But he seems very much weaker than he should be. There's no real cause for alarm, but he'll need careful nursing to get his strength back. His heart seems to have been weakened by the strains of the illness – and . . . And he is struggling.'

'You told me there was no risk.'

'There is no risk from malaria nowadays. His constitution has been much weakened; we must just keep him quiet and cool and hope that he regains enough strength.'

Evelyn dropped her face into her hands. She felt two strong hands on her shoulders and knew that Bob was there, supporting her as he had done for so long, ready to do whatever she needed. She leaned back and looked up into his face, not caring that there were tears in her eyes.

20

Evelyn scarcely slept that night, getting up again and again to check Sasha's pulse, bathe his forehead, comfort him when he woke and was fretful, and by morning she was exhausted. She was up and dressed by the time that Natalie and Dindin came in to help with breakfast and neither of them noticed anything, but as soon as Bob appeared he said at once:

'Is he no better?'

'I'm not sure; but he's no stronger. Oh, Bob . . .' Just in time she remembered the presence of Sasha's sisters and stopped herself from expressing her worst fears, but she could tell from the direct sympathy in his eyes that he knew what they were.

'Have some coffee, Eve. It'll give you strength. I don't suppose you got much sleep.' She smiled waveringly and sat down at the table.

The coffee was strong and hot and as she obediently drank it, it did seem to put some life back in her. She had just put the big cup back on to its saucer when the door opened and her brother stood there, his normally pink face a little pale, and his determined chin jutting forwards. Dindin bounced up from the table at once and went running to him.

'What is it, Dick? You look different. What's happening?'

'We're off this evening – down the Dvina.'

'Not to fight? Oh, dearest Dick, no,' Dindin wailed. Evelyn heard the protest and wondered in curious detachment how Dindin could be so concerned about one healthy young man when her own brother, defenceless and very ill, lay almost at her feet.

'There's no need to take it so hard, Dindin,' he said, putting on a patronising voice that Evelyn recognised. 'There's just going to be a bit of a putsch against the Bolos to drive them back so that we can arrange the official evacuation. No need to fret.'

Dindin showed no signs of regaining calm. Her face was the dirty white of the ice that had covered the river all through the winter and her dark eyes looked almost like holes cut in the whiteness. Evelyn got stiffly up from the table, looked back over her shoulder to check that Sasha was all right, and then went to her brother.

'Good luck, Dick. You'll forgive me, I know, if I don't come to the river to see you off. I can't leave Sasha.'

'No, no, of course not. Poor little chap. How is he?'

'Very weak still.'

'Well, goodbye, Evie.'

'Goodbye, Dick, and the best of good luck.' She leaned forward as though to kiss him but he stuck out his hand. She took it and he shook hers firmly, before turning back to Dindin. Evelyn thought suddenly how poverty-stricken their privileged, comfortable, Yorkshire life had been in that they had never been able to touch each other or express any real feelings. She looked for Bob, who was standing close behind her. He put his hands on her shoulders and said over her dark head:

'Good luck, Markham.' The boy turned from Dindin and his face stiffened as he saw how his sister was standing.

'Thanks, Adamson. I know I can trust you to look after the girls while I'm gone.'

'Of course, you can rely on me. Presumably you have no idea how long you'll be away.'

'None. But Dindin tells me that you're trying to get some boat or other ready to take them all out of here.'

'Yes. It doesn't look as though the formal evacuation will come before the fall and Eve needs to get home, don't you?'

Dick said nothing, but was obviously struggling to put some feeling into words. Bob helped him out. 'I take it you don't disapprove, Markham?'

'Indeed not. But, I say, Adamson . . .' He broke off, looked across at his sister and their cousin and then said: 'Could I have a word outside, old boy?'

Bob could feel Eve tense under his hands and he leaned towards her to whisper:

'Don't worry, Eve, I'll see to it. You wait here.' He followed her brother out into the corridor and waited, a little amused, as the boy blushed and obviously searched for a way to broach what was clearly a delicate matter. In the end he threw out his rounded chin and his chest in the way Bob had seen before and said in a clipped tone that reminded the American of Evelyn in Petrograd, though with more hesitation than she had ever shown:

'I have accepted my sister's assurance and of course yours that there is nothing – er – untoward between you two, but your living here under the same roof as Evelyn is, well, to say the least of it, irregular. And, I don't like to have to say this . . .'

'Come on Markham, spit it out,' suggested Bob, who was leaning against the tatty wooden wall with his arms crossed and an expression of half-amused superiority on his face.

'I rely on you to take her straight to my father's house in Beverley when you reach England, and well, not to be alone with her. I mean without the Suvarovs, between landing and getting to Yorkshire. Please don't think that I don't understand how in your flight from Shenkursk it happened that you all had to share this flat, and I'm damned grateful, believe me, that you're taking her home, but in England it will naturally be different. I assume that you will speak to my father then.'

'Markham,' said Bob kindly enough, 'my relations with your sister are her affair and no one else's. I hope you haven't talked like this to her again.' When the boy shook his head, Bob carried on: 'Good. She's been through too much to have to listen to arguments of propriety and convention, still less with whether or not she wishes to marry me. I guess that's what your last cryptic sentence meant.'

Richard Markham decided that he had never been so embarrassed in his life and was furious with Evelyn for landing him in this dreadful situation. His voice sounded almost strangled as he said: 'Well, yes, that was rather what I meant.'

'Look, you can't compel feelings just to suit some crazy British idea of what is decent . . .' Bob stopped there, recognising that Richard Markham was trying to do his best for Eve and so he tried to explain: 'In the years we have known each other we've gotten to be friends, but that's been in the middle of this whole mess. There is no knowing what will happen once we're back in normal life. But if you're still afraid that I'll seduce her deliberately to ruin her reputation, I can swear that nothing is further from my thoughts.'

'Good of you, Adamson,' was all Richard could manage to say.

Then they went back so that Richard could say goodbye to the girls, and Bob, watching Evelyn's small embarrassed smile, knew that she had guessed at least part of the conversation. When they were at last alone that evening she said to him:

'Thank you for being so patient with Dick this afternoon.'

Bob smiled at her with a new gentleness and said:

'It wasn't so hard. He was trying to do the right thing for you, and I'm with him on that.' Then, in case she shared some of her brother's embarrassment, Bob changed the subject: 'Did you notice Dindin at supper?'

Trying to control the ludicrous, inappropriate feelings that were seething in her mind, Evelyn shook her head meaninglessly.

'I know. I hadn't realised they were quite so close. I suppose he has been here quite a lot while you and I have been out; and he has taken her for rather a lot of walks since Sasha got ill.' After a moment she controlled her voice and went on. 'I thought he was just trying to be helpful, but obviously it was not quite so altruistic. I just hope that he recognises how vulnerable she is now. He may be amusing himself . . .'

'Oh no,' protested Bob. 'That wouldn't square at all with his notions of propriety.' But Evelyn did not smile. There was too much at stake for her. He could hear bitterness in her voice when she said:

'It's different for men.'

There was an arrested look in his dark-lashed hazel eyes as it dawned on him that she, too, might have thought he was trying to seduce her for fun and would then leave her as soon as he had had what he wanted, but before he could find words careful enough to ask her, Tallie had called out from her bedroom:

'Evie, *Evie!* Please come!'

During the next few days, as Evelyn tried to persuade herself that Sasha was regaining some of his desperately-needed strength, Bob watched her and tried to find a way to talk to her. But he could see that she was too worried to listen to anything. All he could do for her while Sasha was so ill was to speed on the boat-builder and to chase Evelyn herself out of doors at least once a day while he sat with the child. She resisted leaving him as he became progressively weaker, but accepted Bob's point that it would do Sasha no good at all for her to become cross and difficult through lack of fresh air and exercise.

Two days after Dick had left for the battle, Evelyn took Tallie and Dindin down to the river. They knew that the furthest point of the advance was miles from Archangel, but in the hot, thick air of July there was nothing to muffle the boom of the guns. While Tallie paddled in the river, wincing at the sounds, Dindin stood like a figurehead looking down the Dvina, an expression of unfulfilled yearning on her face that made Evelyn forget all her irritation with the girl and want to strangle Dick.

'Dindin,' she said carefully, 'don't be too afraid for Dick. I'm sure he's not in too much danger.'

'How can you say that?' burst out the girl. 'He's facing those cruel, wicked Bolos – and he might be . . . he might be killed. What would you have said if someone told you not to worry about John?'

'Isn't that a little different? You haven't known Dickie for very long, Dindin, and in very artificial circumstances. You can't know yet how each of you will feel when we're back in England.'

Dindin, who had heard nothing but patronising advice in that, turned back to stare blindly down the huge, slow-moving river and said:

'I love him, and I belong to him.'

Evelyn felt suddenly faint and put up her hand to her forehead.

'Dindin,' she said as calmly as she could, 'What . . .? I mean, has he said anything . . . does he feel the same way?'

'No,' she said in a far-away voice. 'But I know he loves me. He used to kiss me when he came while you and Bob were out and someone like him would never do that if he didn't mean to tell me he loved me. Besides I could not feel like this if we weren't both in love.'

The violence of the anger she felt surprised Evelyn, but she could not shake it off. It was true that she had wanted Dick to distract Dindin from her imagined feelings for Bob Adamson, but that Dick, who had taken such a sanctimonious line with his elder sister, should now arouse this sort of feeling in a girl as unprotected as Dindin seemed unforgivable. Knowing so much of what Dindin must be feeling, Evelyn felt sorrier for her cousin than she had ever felt before and she wanted passionately to protect the girl from the doubt and misery she herself was experiencing every day. But the rage coursing through her must have coloured her voice, for when she tried to explain to Dindin that she must not build hopes that were too heavy for such slender foundations, the girl burst out:

'Well, you wouldn't let me fall in love with Bob when I wanted to and I need someone.' Tears poured down her cheeks. 'It isn't fair, Evie. My brothers are fighting each other and may be dead now; Sasha is horribly ill; my parents are stuck in Shenkursk and they will probably be killed too. All the men I might have married are dead or far away. I haven't anyone. I just didn't know it would be like this. It's even worse now. And if he's killed what will I do?'

'Dindin, I am so sorry,' said Evelyn, trying to make her cousin sit down on the old pier beside her. Then she put an arm round her shoulders. 'But you mustn't be afraid. Although there have been lots of wounded in this campaign, hardly anyone has been killed. I am sure Dick will come back to you. And you are family, Dindin; we'll always look after you. I've just been so worried about Sasha that I didn't think how afraid you must be about – about the future. I am so sorry.'

In Evelyn's mind, the knowledge of what her brother had done so irresponsibly and selfishly nearly outweighed her fears about the battle that was being waged so audibly down the river. As soon as she had taken Tallie back to the flat and found Bob there, she asked him to go out with her, leaving the children in Dindin's charge. She told him what she had learned and to her dismay his first reaction was to laugh.

'Bob, it's not funny at all.' He sobered quickly and said:

'For Dindin, no, not funny at all. But what a little tick to order you and me around so piously and at the same time start kissing the first available woman.' He felt Evelyn stiffen alarmingly at his side and in a quite different tone said: 'Now what's the matter?'

'It's all so crude, Bob. It's so horrible and what Dick has done is so wicked that it makes . . . Oh, I don't know how to put it.'

'I wish I understood what goes on in your mind,' he said after a long pause, and then, exasperation getting the better of his determination to remain coolly friendly while she needed all her energies to deal with her anxiety over Sasha, added, 'or that you could bring yourself to tell me.'

Evelyn stood and looked at him. If only she could. Her lips parted as though she was about to speak. Then the thought of his embarrassment if he had to tell her that it was all over for him paralysed her. Tears of frustration welled into the corners of her eyes and he saw them.

'I didn't mean to worry you again, Eve,' he said, contrition battling with anger in his voice. 'Don't think about it. I know you can't. Come and see the boat anyway. They've started varnishing.'

'That sounds as though they must have nearly finished,' she answered, relieved to have so easy a subject to talk about. 'Thank God, we'll be able to get Sasha out of here.'

'Yes. Tomorrow – or perhaps the day after – we'll be able

to take the boat out for a trial. Will you at least trust me enough for that?'

'Oh, Bob, of course I trust you. I've told you so often. What can you mean? Oh, help, look at the time. I must get back. Samenev said he'd come at five.'

The doctor looked graver than he had yet done as he pulled the sheet back up to Sasha's chin and Evelyn did not dare ask him what the prospects were. He rubbed his beard for a moment or two and then turned to her and said:

'It is getting dangerous. You must watch him carefully. If . . . if he gets any weaker or he has trouble breathing you must send for me at once. Do you understand?'

'Yes, Doctor. Do you mean . . .? Is he . . .?'

'It is possible. Try to keep calm for his sake.'

'Calm!' she almost shouted, and then moderated her voice: 'But what can I do? Isn't there some medicine he should take? Oh, can't you do something?'

'Nothing. It is the body fighting back against the weakness. We have to wait to see if he will win.'

'Will you talk to his sisters? I don't think I could.'

'Of course. Be brave now.'

After that Evelyn did not even undress to go to bed once the girls and Bob had left her. She just sat by Sasha's bed in the mocking light as the night hours dragged themselves out so torturingly slowly. His face was almost grey and his lips were pinched and cracked. He had been conscious for shorter and shorter periods in the last few days and as she watched him then she gave up hope.

Soon after midnight, his breathing, which had been laboured but almost regular, started to change. Suddenly alert, she bent forward to feel his pulse; it was odder and fainter than ever. Forcing herself to leave him for a few minutes, she went to the curtained cubby hole where Bob slept.

He woke at the first touch of her fingers on his face, and sat up instantly.

'Eve, what is it? Is he worse?' Her face answered him and he threw back the bedclothes.

'You go back to him; I'll go for Samenev. Go on back to Sasha. I'll be as quick as I can.'

She did as he said and sat down again by Sasha's bed. The noise must have woken him out of his semi-conscious sleep, for she saw his dark eyes gleam in the white light.

'Go to sleep, baby, I'm here.'

'Don't leave me ever, Evie,' he said in a hardly audible voice.

'I won't, Sashenka. I won't ever leave you.' She thought he had drifted back into unconsciousness, but in a few moments he spoke again.

'I wish Piotr was here.'

Evelyn felt as though someone had her heart in a vice and was slowly tightening it. Doing everything she could to keep the sound of tears out of her voice, she said:

'Do you miss them all so much, Little Dove?'

'Only Piotr. I wish he was here.'

It was anguish for Evelyn to be unable to give the child what he so much wanted at such a moment. She picked up his thin, floppy body and held him in her arms.

Because her left hand lay over his heart, she knew the exact moment when it stopped beating.

When Bob came back with Doctor Samenev twenty-five minutes later, they saw her holding the child to her breast, while her cheek lay on his hair. Samenev tried to take Sasha from her, but she tightened her arms defensively.

'I must examine the child.'

Without raising her head, Evelyn said:

'There's nothing to see now.' The doctor did not understand and in a voice of exaggerated patience said:

'If I'm to help, I must examine him. Lay him on the bed now, there's a good girl.' But Adamson was quicker.

'Eve . . .' he began, but could not go on.

'Yes,' she said, looking at them at last. 'He's dead.' Then her face seemed to break up before their eyes.

'He's dead.'

There was a cry from the doorway and Bob turned to see Dindin supporting her little sister, who seemed to have fainted. Both girls were barefooted and in their skimpy white nightgowns. The doctor went to help them, muttering:

'Lucky I've plenty of bromide. They'll all need it now.'

Galvanised into action by the sound, Bob walked slowly towards Evelyn. He wanted to comfort her, to hold her as she held the child, but he did not dare touch her. Gently he spoke to her.

'Eve, let me lay him on the bed.'

She did not answer, but neither did she resist as he lifted Sasha's limp body away from her. He put it down on the bed, straightening the limbs and then, as carefully as though the boy could still feel, he closed the eyelids. He stood looking down at the child. Feeling in his pocket for a handkerchief to wipe the corners of his eyes, he turned back to Evelyn.

'Here,' he said, the pity roughening his voice. 'Take this.' He offered her the square of linen.

Obediently she took it and tried to staunch the tears that she could not control. When she took the handkerchief away they still fell.

'It seems so unfair,' she murmured as though to herself. 'What had Sasha ever done?'

'Ah don't, Eve.'

'I'm sorry.'

The doctor came back just then, carrying his fat black bag and saying:

'Poor girls – well at least they'll sleep off some of the shock. And now, young lady, I want you to take a dose too, and then Mr Adamson and I will make some arrangements.'

'You're going to take him away, aren't you?'

'I must. In this season, it is not possible to leave him here.'

Bob shuddered and watched anxiously as Evelyn got up and went to the bed. She brushed Sasha's dark hair away from his pale forehead and then bent down to kiss his face.

'It's cold,' she whispered. 'Oh, Sasha, my baby, I'm so sorry . . . so sorry.'

She took his hand and rubbed it between her own as though to warm it. Then she laid it on his chest, brought the other up to cover it and moved away.

Bob released the breath he had been holding and went to pick up the body. As he lifted it, he said:

'Eve, I shall come back as soon . . . as soon as I can.'

She nodded and went back to her chair, to sit staring out of the small dusty window. When she heard them go slowly down the steep, wooden stairs, she whispered to herself: 'Shall I ever be allowed to love anyone?'

When Bob got back, his mind full of the horror of carrying the empty body of the child to Samenev's hospital mortuary, where it would be disembowelled and eviscerated in the post-mortem, Evelyn was still sitting where they had left her. She turned at the sound of his step and what he saw in her face drove all his own misery out of his mind.

'Eve,' he said, his heart breaking for her. 'Eve, don't. It's over for Sasha now; all the pain. He's free now.'

'But don't you see? I did it. If I hadn't been in Russia, I don't suppose they'd ever have let the children come to Archangel, and if they hadn't he'd never have got malaria at all.'

'Eve,' he was beginning as he groped for words that might comfort her. He knelt down beside her chair.

'Don't be angry with me now!' she cried out as she saw his face. 'I couldn't bear it.'

'I'm not angry, dearest child. I couldn't be,' he murmured, cradling her exhausted body and stroking her hair. 'Lean against me, Eve. I can't stop it hurting, but I want to help.'

'John, Tony, Sasha: who else is going to die? Oh, help me, Bob. Why does something awful happen to people I love? What's going to happen to you?'

He had thought so much about what she might one day say to him and what he could say to her that it had never occurred to him that she would admit her feelings at a moment when he could neither make love to her nor ask her to marry him. With his very real sorrow for Sasha mingling with the relief that she cared as he had always hoped she would come to care for him, he held her as gently as he could and said:

'Evelyn, nothing's going to happen to me. Listen to me

and believe it. I love you. I won't leave you ever, for anything. I promise you that, and you can trust me. Don't try to say anything. Just rest against me now. The pain will ease.' He rocked her gently until she relaxed and then he carried her to the bed.

He sat beside her for the rest of the night, and every time he saw her eyes open, he took her hand and talked to her until she could relax again.

21

They were allowed to bury Sasha the next day, as soon as Samenev's post-mortem was over.

When they set off for the cathedral, the temperature was well over seventy-five degrees and to Evelyn it seemed the cruellest of ironies that Sasha, who had hated the darkness and the cold of the winter almost more than any of them, should be buried on this cloudless, hot, sunny, perfect afternoon. She felt a little better once they reached the cathedral, for although its exterior was white, gaily painted with frescoes, and topped with glittering golden domes, the inside was cavernous and dark. Candle flames flickered on the dark gilt mosaics and incense-smoke wreathed above them.

There were no seats and as she knelt down on the cold, stone floor, Evelyn was thankful that she was able to do this small thing for Sasha: to remember him in this formal way. John had had no funeral and the knowledge of his smashed body lying undiscovered in Flanders added horror to unhappiness. Kneeling there with her cousins on one side and Bob on the other, his shoulder almost touching her own, she tried to lay aside all the feelings of anger and resentment at fate to remember the happy hours she had spent with Sasha, with her brother Anthony, and with John. It seemed the only way to give anything back. She was not sure that she believed in any kind of afterlife, but just in case there was another world she wanted to launch Sasha into it with cheerfulness, not on a tide of lamentation.

Bob was so close to her that he could feel the sudden relaxation in her tense body and he was glad. During the morning, as he grappled with the practicalities of interment in Archangel and tried to find some way of getting a message through to Shenkursk, he had got back some of his sense of reality and no longer felt as though it was their own child who had died. The sharpest pain was over for him, but it had left him with a mess of regrets, and a determination to get Evelyn out of Archangel and away from the place of Sasha's death as soon as possible.

When the service was over, they emerged into the blinding sun to walk beside the coffin to the Russian cemetery. There they watched sadly as the small grave was filled in. Natalie suddenly pulled off her black ribbon-band and dropped it into the grave. Evelyn did not ask why, but put one arm round the girl when she stepped back, and hugged her warmly.

At last the pit was filled and smoothed over. Natalie and Dindin turned away, leaving Evelyn to stand, looking at the sticky earth and trying to come to terms with her desolation. She felt a hand on her arm.

'Bob. Thank you for . . . everything.'

'No need for thanks, Eve,' he said, putting an arm comfortably around her shoulders. 'Come on, this is a miserable place and it has nothing to do with our Sasha.'

'No,' she agreed. 'I was just trying to remember him as he was before . . .'

Bob squeezed her shoulders and then released her. Together they left the grave-side. As soon as they were outside the cemetery gates, Dindin said:

'Are you going straight back to the flat?'

'Yes, of course. Poor Tallie is very tired, aren't you *duschinka*?'

The little girl nodded and pressed close to Evelyn, but Dindin tossed her head and said:

'Well, I'll see you later. Captain Johnson told Dick he'd look after me, and he invited me to tea today.'

Not feeling up to the task of dealing with Dindin's untimely exuberance, and in any case wishing her to have any distraction she could, Evelyn did not try to stop her. When Dindin had left them, Evelyn murmured:

'Bob?'

'Yes, Eve, I'll come back with you.'

It was just as well that he did, for Tallie had to be carried for the last mile and Evelyn could never have managed it alone. But before that, they had to walk past the cemetery that had been set aside for the Allies' military casualties. Evelyn averted her eyes, but Tallie said:

'Uncle Bob, why are they taking coffins out of the ground?'

'Oh, Tallie, they can't be,' protested Evelyn. 'It just looks like that.'

'No, Eve. They *are* digging them up. Our army is pulling out, as I told you, and it's an American tradition that we never leave our boys in foreign soil. They always get taken back to the States if it's possible. Normally, of course, they'd have been taken back at once, but with the sea iced-up, they couldn't be.'

It seemed very macabre, and Evelyn did not want to think about it. They walked on in silence until Natalie could walk no further. Then Bob carried her and when they reached Baines's house, they put her to bed and lit the spirit lamp under the battered old *samovar* Baines had let them have. When it boiled Evelyn made tea and, as she handed Bob his cup, she said:

'Bob, you've been so good to me.'

He took the cup from her and smiled, thinking how extraordinary it was that even now, pale and puffy-eyed, she still seemed to him to be more desirable than any woman he had ever known.

'Eve, what I told you last night is true. I won't change, I won't disappear – unless you send me away.'

'It seems so dangerous to believe it . . .' she began, but he stopped her, his hand to her lips.

'No, Eve, there is no danger, no risk. I'm here, I'll always be where you need me. I'll show you, soon, why there's no need to fear.'

She was about to say something when the door burst open

and they saw Dindin standing there alone, an expression on her face that reminded Evelyn horribly of Sergei Voroshilov.

'What on earth is the matter, Dindin?' she asked.

'There's been a dreadful mutiny.'

Evelyn was surprised to see that there were tears in her cousin's round, dark eyes, in spite of the cruel anger that twisted her plump lips.

'But, Dindin, there have been hundreds of mutinies this year. Ironside must have had more practice at defusing them than any commander in the history of warfare.'

'Not like this one. It's much, much worse. It's Dyer's Battalion.'

'I suppose that was only to be expected – a battalion of prisoners, who were probably Bolos themselves,' said Evelyn, trying to reason the sudden dread out of her mind.

'They shot ten of their officers.'

'Dead – or just wounded? Dindin, tell me.'

'I'm glad to see that you care a bit, after all. Three British officers dead, four Russians; the rest wounded. One of them was shot seven times, but he swam the Dvina to raise the alarm. They're bringing him back to the hospital today.'

'And what was the upshot, Dindin?' asked Bob. 'Has the whole battalion mutinied? How did they stop it?'

'I don't know. Johnson just said that about a hundred men had gone over the line to the enemy and that they've caught a few of the ringleaders. I hope they'll shoot them.'

'Surely not,' said Evelyn, swinging sickeningly from horrified anger at the mutineers to disgust at the prospect of such barbarity.

'It is the statutory punishment for mutiny in all armies. Bob knows that, and he'll tell you. And these Bolo swine have killed their officers.'

'But they were Bolsheviki in the beginning. Did they swear allegiance to us, or promise not to go back to their own people?'

'I don't know, Evie, but why should you care? They're our enemies. Johnson didn't say anything about what they'll do to the mutineers, but he did say that he didn't think any prisoners would be taken in the next battle – they're all too angry and they'll shoot any Bolsheviki they get.'

'But what if Piotr's one of them?' came a small, sad voice from behind Dindin. Evelyn got up at once.

'Tallie, we don't even know that he's in their army. There's no reason to think he's anywhere near Archangel.' As she spoke, Evelyn remembered a phrase from John's letter and she cursed the governments who led their people into wars that so brutalised the men that they did such things.

'Why should you care anyway?' demanded Dindin. 'He betrayed his family and his country. He put us in this dreadful state. It's his fault that Sasha died.'

'Evie?' came Tallie's voice.

'Yes, what is it? Don't you feel well, Tallie?'

'Oh, I'm all right. It's just . . . Do you think that when we've won the battle, anybody in Shenkursk will get away?'

'Oh, Tallie, I don't know,' said Evelyn, wishing now that she could strangle Dindin for saying such things in the child's hearing. 'I wish they would. But they wanted to stay. They could have come when we did, but they wanted to stay so that when everything gets back to normal you and Dindin will be able to go back there.'

'But if they do come, will there be room on Uncle Bob's boat?'

'Yes, of course,' said Bob putting decision into his voice as he tried to remove the anxiety from Natalie's eyes. What neither he nor Evelyn mentioned was the fact that Andrei Alexandrovitch and Natalia Petrovna would have to apply for official permission to go to England. Evelyn had sought it for Dindin, Sasha and Natalie as soon as they reached Archangel and the consul had handed her all the necessary papers nearly two months earlier. She had also got permission for Georgii just in case he should find his way to Archangel, but there had been no news of him since the day he had left Shenkursk with Sergei.

'Do you think we'll ever see them again – or Piotr?'

Distressingly reminded of Sasha, Evelyn tried to comfort his favourite sister.

'Oh, little one, of course you will,' she said, wishing that she could be so sure. 'When this horrible war is over, they will come to England or you will come back to Russia, and we'll all be together again. I'm sure of it. Bob, will you take Tallie back to bed? And explain it all to her? He's very sensible, Tallie.'

'Yes, I know. Goodnight, Evie.'

As soon as the door had shut behind them, Evelyn tried strenuously to remind herself of all the things that Dindin must be suffering and said in as neutral a tone as possible:

'Now, Dindin, Bob and I have to take the boat out tonight to try her out and I'm going to have to leave Tallie in your charge. We may not be back until late morning. You will stay here and look after her, won't you? I mean, no going out with Johnson or any of the others? And see that she stays in bed. She's very tired.'

Dindin shrugged.

'I'll do my best. But I'm hardly trained as a nursemaid.'

'She is your sister, Dindin. And you heard just now, she's worried about your parents.'

'Do you think I'm not? Why are you always so vile to me? You make me slave here, leave me behind when you and Bob go all over the place. I don't have any fun. You criticise whatever I say or do. It's not fair.' Evelyn took a step backwards, shocked by the sudden outburst.

'Life is not exactly fun for anyone just now,' came a deep, drawling voice from the door.

'Oh you always take her side nowadays, Bob. I can't think what Piotr would say if he heard you. I mean the things you two used to say about Evie . . .'

'That's enough. Stop it.'

'I won't stop it. She acts as if she owns me and whenever I do anything except wait on her she tells me off. Who does she think she is? She was hired to be my governess and . . .'

'Dina Andreievna,' he said and then went on in Russian: 'What would your brother say to such words? Evelyn has looked after you all, worried for you, worked for you. Your father and Nikolai Alexandrovitch put her in charge of you. Piotr would . . .'

'I don't care,' she said in English, stamping her foot and working herself up into an almost frightening fit of rage. 'If he's as horrid now as he was then he'd just laugh at me and be *glad* that I've been reduced to a servant's life. And that Sasha's dead. That's what he and you wanted, wasn't it? All the decent people of Russia were to be killed or turned into serfs so that pigs like those ones on the train and that brute in the Vyborg could lord it over us. I hate him and I hate you and I hate Evelyn and I don't want to go to England and I can't bear to stay in Russia and I . . .' She burst into a fit of hysterical weeping, leaving Evelyn to look helplessly at Bob.

He jerked his head towards the door and, wondering a little at her obedience, Evelyn left him to cope with her cousin as best he could, while she went to see that Natalie was all right.

Later, after an uncomfortable meal, during which Dindin made her hostility to Evelyn quite plain, Bob looked across the table at her and, with a smile that seemed new, partly diffident, full of affectionate complicity, and infinitely appealing, said:

'Well, Eve? Shall we go?'

'Certainly. Dindin, will you be all right?'

'I suppose so, if you have to go. Captain Johnson promised to come round and tell me what's going to happen to the mutineers – and that'll make me feel better.' Despite all her good resolutions, and her real sympathy for her cousin, Evelyn's lips tightened as she heard the pettish, vengeful, grudging sound of Dindin's voice. But she managed to say nothing and turned away to put on the thick, dark-blue jersey that Baines had lent her and change her shoes.

'Don't be too cross with Dindin, Eve. She's . . .' began Bob as soon as they had left the house. Evelyn turned to him at once and he smiled involuntarily as he saw what was in her face.

'I couldn't be, Bob. It would be too unfair. I was just like that – I used to think those sort of things and if I didn't say them I'm surprised.' She was silent for a minute or two and then went on: 'But I wish that Dindin didn't have to go through all that hell to learn what's what. And I don't want her to hate herself when she discovers how . . . how misguided she has been.'

'She's been through quite a bit already.'

'I know.'

'And so have you, haven't you, Eve? But it's nearly over, and then we can begin properly.'

'Haven't we already?' He smiled at that.

'Eve . . .' She waited, doubtful and a little worried. Then he went on, his hand very tight on hers. 'Did you really mean what you said by the river that day?'

She was at a loss. They had been so often to the river.

'What did I say, Bob? I've said so many things I didn't mean and wish I'd never uttered. What did I say?'

'That you thought I was trying to seduce you because I'd overheard what you said to your brother about . . . about John's last leave.'

'That's what I mean about hating yourself,' she said immediately, glad to have the chance to explain to him. 'I meant it then, but now . . . I am so sorry for all those things I said and did that . . . Oh, I don't know. It's too difficult to say. Why did you ask?'

'I'll tell you a bit later. We've got to concentrate now on getting her out of the harbour. Come on, Eve.'

It was a beautiful evening. The massed rolling clouds that were so much part of Archangel's white nights had cleared with the wind and it was a sky like pale greenish-blue crystal that slanted up from the horizon. The deep gold sun was low, and spilled its reflection across the dark sea in a shower of light. To be out of Archangel and sailing towards freedom, even if it were only a temporary escape, felt like bliss itself to Evelyn. As Bob called out to her she smiled at him and shook the heavy plait of dark hair back off her shoulder as she pulled obediently at one of the sheets.

They sailed on for a good hour and a half before Bob hove-to in the lee of a relatively high cliff, well out of sight of Archangel. He came along the deck. Evelyn, who was obediently coiling up a length of rope so that she could put it away in one of the lockers, looked up.

'Eve, I've got to talk to you. I swore to myself that I'd say nothing until we got to England, but it'll all be even more complicated then and here, at least, we've a chance to be on our own for a bit. Come and sit down.'

She took his outstretched hand and went with him to sit on the cabin roof, looking out towards the slowly sinking sun. He held her long, slim hand in both of his, tracing the veins in it with fingers that quivered slightly. After a while he laid her hand on his knee and looked up, saying with some hesitation:

'Evelyn, I've been so clumsy every time I've tried to tell you that I love you, that it's hard . . .' Blushing, but determined to make up to him for some of the things she had said, Evelyn put up her free hand and touched his tanned cheek.

'I'm so afraid of losing you now that I don't know what to do or say and for me that's strange. I feel like a boy of fifteen.'

'Bob,' she said with some difficulty, realising that she could no longer expect him alone to make the effort. 'The last few weeks I have been facing the thought of what it would be like to go back to the old Evelyn Markham and live her life without you, and I know that the only way you'll lose me is if you tell me that I've got to leave.'

'Do you mean that?' he demanded and reading the answer in her eyes, he flung his arms round her and kissed her. For a moment she was frightened; he seemed almost violent. As she flinched, he drew back a little and gently brushed her eyebrow with his lips.

'I didn't mean to scare you. Promise you'll say if I do anything that does that?' When she said nothing, trying to hide her face against his chest, he lifted her chin between his finger and thumb and said:

'Eve, it's like making love in a foreign language. You're the first of your species I've ever met. You must tell me.'

Trying not to think that if he really loved her as he said, he would know what she was thinking and feeling, she nodded. Then he took her down into the cabin.

At first she could think of nothing but her shyness, but he was so matter of fact, and so gentle, that she slowly learned to relax in his arms. It was then that the fear came. He knew at once that something had happened and stilled his hands.

'Evelyn, tell me.'

His voice held a note of command to which she tried to

respond, but she did not know how to tell him. Looking down at her in the glow of the golden sunset, he tried to imagine what she was thinking. At last he said:

'What are you afraid of? Not me, surely?'

Taking a shuddering breath and looking out of the little round porthole, she said with some difficulty:

'Not of you. For you.'

At that he pulled her close to him and said into her cloud of dark hair:

'Evelyn, I told you I'd risk it. This is not the time to talk of anyone else – all that is over. Let me show you why.'

She had done so much to hurt him in the past months and she wanted so much to be able to love him that she turned in his arms and let him teach her the secrets of the universe.

When she could think and see and hear and feel something other than the whirling, thundering seas of sensation within her, she swallowed a little nervously and said with a kind of determined courage that he recognised:

'I love you.'

He was so moved that she had brought herself to say it that for a while he could not answer.

22

The next morning, rather late, Bob woke her and was amused to see the confusion with which she acknowledged him and what had happened, but he loved her and so hid his smiles, saying only:

'If we're to get back this morning, Eve, we'll have to leave soon. There's no wind, so we'll have to use the engine. I must go up on deck and see to things.'

She waited until he had closed the cabin door behind him and then slid out from under the thin sheet that had covered her and dressed as quickly as she could. She had not forgotten Sasha and the pain of his death would always remain with her, but the nightmares had gone and the two worlds she had inhabited with such difficulty seemed to have become one. Something very like happiness vibrated through her as she followed Bob up on to the deck and as he turned from hauling up the anchor he caught sight of her expression. His own face seemed to mirror it and she walked quickly up and touched his hard cheek.

If it had not been for her cousins, patiently waiting in Baines's horrid house, Evelyn would have been tempted to ask Bob not to turn the yacht back to Archangel but to set off there and then into the blazing white horizon. But they were and so she steeled herself for the last days in Archangel.

They reached the harbour-mouth just before twelve, slipping slowly between the big military carriers and few timber barges that were anchored on the still, almost oily-looking water. There was no one in Petrovitch's yard, which seemed odd, and Evelyn and Bob looked at each other, puzzled, as they made the boat fast at the jetty and clambered down on to the hard. He shrugged and taking her arm led her out of the yard towards the Troitski Prospekt.

As they walked nearer the river they were met by milling crowds and a kind of excited clatter of voices speaking in French, English and Russian.

'What is it?' asked Evelyn, absurdly.

'Look there, down the Dvina. Something's happening.'

Together they walked to the edge of the river and looked southwards to see a flotilla of boats and barges steaming towards the main town jetty.

'They must have come from the battle. Come on.'

As they walked nearer and nearer they could hear shouts of triumph in the excited multilingual jabber. As soon as they reached the edge of the tumultuous crowd, Bob asked a civilian spectator what was happening. The Russian answered in adequate English:

'They've thrashed the Bolsheviki at Seltso further down the Dvina – look at the prisoners they've taken. A man I was talking to just now said they had nearly three thousand.'

'Thank God they did take prisoners. What about casualties?'

Evelyn's pallor and shaking voice must have struck the man for his voice was much gentler when he said:

'Not much more than a hundred of yours, *baryshnia*; more of the Bolsheviki, I think.'

Evelyn felt Bob's hand close comfortingly on her left wrist and he said in a matter-of-fact voice:

'Come along, Eve. We'll find someone who can tell us about Dick before we go back to the children.' She smiled gratefully at him and went with him through the thick crowd towards the river.

Bob saw an officer whom he knew slightly and went off to ask for information, leaving Evelyn to stare in horrified interest at a string of barges that were being pulled towards the jetty. On each one was a kind of cage of wooden poles full of exhausted, dirty-looking men in unfamiliar shabby grey uniforms. Some of them had bloody bandages round their heads or arms; some were slumped against the stout poles of the cages, their arms hanging outside. But the worst thing, a sight Evelyn had never thought to see in Russia, was a group of men, lying against their comrades' shoulders, coughing and choking as though there was some terrible obstacle in their throats. There were marks that looked like burns around their noses and mouths and many of them had their hands at their throats as they fought for air.

'Gas?' she whispered. 'Who has gas here in Archangel?' She was just about to go to look for Bob when she caught sight of a man lying flat on the bottom of the cage, obviously unconscious, the tell-tale marks of the gas on his face and a filthy, stained bandage round his shoulder. At first she thought she must be mistaken. There was no reason for him to be in Archangel. The last news they had had of him had been when Bob left him in Moscow. Then he was a civilian. Why would Piotr Suvarov have left the centre of things to come and fight up in the Arctic? It could not be possible. She bent down so that she was on a level with the man and could not be in any doubt. It was he.

The one clear thought in the whole, whirling muddle of emotions that seemed to have taken over her brain was that they must get him out. They could not leave him in Archangel. Once the British had departed, he would be at the mercy of the Whites and however great the justification for some of the stories she had heard of their vengeance, however hot her anger at what the Bolsheviki had done to Russia, it was not in her to leave her cousin to such punishment.

Walking swiftly forward to stand with her back to the cage as though she could somehow conceal Piotr from the authorities, Evelyn looked wildly round for Bob. She saw him almost at once and, even as she started towards him, she wondered how she could so easily have recognised the back of his head in the middle of that huge, shifting, polyglot crowd. When she reached him and touched his arm he looked down at her with an infinitely reassuring smile and said as he covered her hand with his own:

'Crowe here says that your brother's fine. He'll not be

back in Archangel for a few days yet, but there's no danger. And he's not been wounded.'

'Thank God,' she said, genuinely relieved but too pre-occupied to say any more or thank the officer who had given them the news. 'Bob, will you come? There's something . . . Please come.'

'Hold on, Eve. Thank you, Crowe. We're most grateful. See you later. All right, Eve, what's the trouble?' It was so unlike her to be discourteous that he could not understand what she was up to, pulling at his sleeve and urging him back to the edge of the river. But when they got there and she silently pointed at the bottom of the cage, he knew at once. Evelyn watched the blood drain out of his face and for a moment was afraid that he might even faint. Putting a hand on his, she felt its clamminess and said quietly:

'Bend down, Bob. Let the blood back into your head.'

A poor imitation of a smile stretched his lips.

'I'm not going to faint.' But as he looked down at the boy's face the sickening dizziness in his brain did not recede. In his illness and pain, Piotr looked as vulnerable as Sasha had been. As well as the burns of the gas, the recent campaign with inadequate food and not enough sleep had left its marks in his face. Huge yellowish-grey shadows lay in sinister half moons under his closed eyes, and the lashes lying against them looked almost luxurious in their glossy black contrast. Piotr's hair was roughened and at first Bob thought it must be filled with dust, but then he saw that its colour had deceived him: there were grey and white streaks among the black.

Squeezing pity, horror, fury at the British, hopeless unhappiness chased themselves through Bob's mind as he looked down at his friend. With his hand clenching and unclenching on Evelyn's, he said through his teeth:

'We have to get him out of here.'

'I know. I've been trying to think how.'

At that he turned away from Piotr and looked at Evelyn, gratitude and love and doubt all fighting in his eyes.

'Don't look at me like that,' she said very quietly. 'Of course we have to take him out. But how? Even if we get him away from here, we can't think of hiding him at Baines's. Dindin is mad enough and full enough of hate to betray him.'

'Do you think so – I mean if she were actually faced with him in that condition?' Bob asked.

'God knows, but we can't risk it. If we can get him out, you'll have to get him to the boat. I'll keep Dindin quiet and bring her and Tallie in time for the evening tide. Can we leave so soon?'

'Yes. You've got your passports and the Suvarovs' . . . Oh, Christ, what do we do about Piotr? Even if we get him out of here, he'll be arrested at once if we land him in England without permission. And we couldn't get him to the States – and anyway it'd be just the same there. What . . .'

'Don't flap so, Bob,' interrupted Evelyn, putting a hand gently on one of his. 'I got papers for Georgii when I got the rest. We can use those. No one will know – once we've got that filthy uniform off – which twin he is. Stop looking so tormented, Bob. We're drawing attention to ourselves. God knows how you're going to get him away from here, but we must.'

'Don't worry about that. I'll find a way. In amongst this lot, there's bound to be some confusion. You go back and see what you can do with Dindin; warn Baines that we're off tonight; Dindin can tell her various admirers quite innocently and there'll be no cause for suspicion. They all know we've been planning to go as soon as the boat was ready.'

'All right, Bob. See you later. If you need . . . No, look, I'll go back to the girls now, but we'll come to Petrovitch's tonight with as much food as we can collect. Good luck.' He took her hand in a brief, hard grip.

'Oh Lord,' he said suddenly. 'We'll have to avoid Murmansk with him on board and I wanted to call in there for water and more charts. Can't be helped. Don't look so worried, Eve. I'll see to it.' She was glad to see that the confidence was back in his eyes and the blood in his face as she turned away to push through the dense crowd, whose excited relish at the sight of the prisoners made her feel sick.

When she had gone, Bob turned once more to look at his

friend and flog his mind into working order. It felt as though it was full of sawdust and every time he tried to think, the sawdust seemed to swirl up and block each nerve and brain cell. As he stood there a Russian voice, speaking bitter and broken English, interrupted his thoughts: 'Come to gloat, have you *Tovarisch*?' Bob looked up quickly to see a slight, dark Russian in the uniform of a hospital orderly standing sneering at him. Looking round to see who else was near, he said in quiet Russian:

'Far from it.'

'Your Russian is good, Comrade. Where and why did you learn it?'

'At the Smolny Institute, Comrade, with friends of mine and I think, perhaps, yours.' Adamson looked at the orderly, suspicion narrowing his eyes; then he decided to take an immense gamble. 'Particularly that man there, the gassed one on the floor of the cage.'

'Are you English?' demanded the orderly, equally suspicious.

'No, American. And you, Comrade, what are you up to in the uniform of the invaders?'

The man's contemptuous glare softened slightly.

'There are many things a man can do in the camp of his enemies.'

'Will you help?'

'Depends. What do you want?'

'I have a boat at Petrovitch's yard. If you can get him away from here, we can look after him there.'

'Why should I risk my position with the invaders to save one man who from the looks of him might die anyway?'

'Because Suvarov is of great value to the Revolution,' said Bob, although the words threatened to stick in his throat. An increasingly violent dislike of this cautious Bolshevik was growing in him and he did not trust the man one inch, but there was no alternative. A hospital orderly was the only possible hope of getting an unconscious man away from the cages.

'Very well, leave it to me,' said the orderly. 'Go to the yard in case there's trouble with old Petrovitch, but there shouldn't be: he's one of us. I'll get this man Suvarov . . . Yes, Suvarov, to the boat and then we can talk about what to do with him.'

No, we damn well won't, thought Bob. When you deliver him that's the last you'll have to do with him, you snake. But he smiled slightly and nodded. Then he turned away, wondering how Evelyn was managing with Dindin.

When she had first got back she had been faced with a scene that horrified her. Dindin was sitting with her head on the table, sobbing, while Tallie stood white-faced and trembling beside her. Evelyn's immediate thought was that they had somehow heard the news of Piotr's capture, but then she saw that that was impossible. Tallie heard her and ran across the room to fling herself at Evelyn's legs and say:

'Evie, Evie, please help me. I don't know what to do.'

'What is it, Tallie? Calm down. Just tell me,' she said, her heart wrung by the white distress on the child's pretty, triangular face.

'Dindin went to the execution of those mutiny men early this morning,' she said, stumbling a little over the words in her anxiety to get them out, 'and there were lots of other people there to see what was happening, but it wasn't as nice as she thought it would be.'

'*Nice!*' The disgusted syllable was forced out of Evelyn before she could stop herself. She had always hated the very idea that the mutineers were to be executed; that sightseers should be allowed to watch such a thing seemed barbarous; that her own cousin could have brought herself to do so filled her with horror. Hadn't she had enough of death and pain and misery? 'Dindin, how could you?'

'Evie, don't be angry. It was . . . awful. I didn't know; I didn't understand. I . . . Oh, Evie.'

Recognising real distress and shock, Evelyn forced herself towards her cousin and even gave her shoulders a small hug.

'Do you want to talk about it?'

'Not really,' she said, sitting up and pushing the wet and draggled hair away from her swollen eyes, but then could not help herself. 'They were to be shot by other Russians – ordinary soldiers, but they hadn't given them enough bullets, you see, in case they mutinied too, and so the mutineers weren't killed at once. They just hung there tied to their posts with wounds, but not dead. In the end the other officers who were there had to go along with their pistols and finish them off. It was terrible. They looked so . . .'

'Hush, Dindin,' commanded Evelyn, almost as tormented by the picture Dindin had painted as the girl herself, but determined to help her to find a way out of her misery. 'Nearly everything that's happened in this war that isn't a war has been terrible. This is only part of it. You won't ever forget it – and you should not – but you must put it away from you now. We're sailing away tonight on the evening tide, and you must try to think of that and of getting to your new home. Dick is all right – we heard this morning – and he will be back soon, when Ironside evacuates this place. Soon we'll be in England and we will all learn to start our new life together until you and Tallie can come back and be with your own family again.'

Dindin snivelled and rubbed the back of her hand across her eyes.

'I'll try, Evie. But I can't think of anything else.'

'Now, don't be silly. We're all going to have to help Bob tonight and you'll need to be strong. Why not go and pack up your things now. Perhaps you'd do Tallie's too while I do something about food. I suppose you haven't eaten anything?'

'No, I'm sorry,' she whispered and that humble apology told Evelyn just how much the execution had changed her cousin.

'Are we really going tonight?' Natalie's quiet, patient voice brought Evelyn back to her present responsibilities.

'Yes, Tallie. We'll be getting out of this horrid place on the tide tonight. Aren't you pleased?'

'Yes,' she whispered, still very white, 'but we're leaving them all behind and . . . we may not see them again.'

'Oh, Tallie,' murmured Evelyn, taking the child into her arms and wanting badly to tell her about Piotr. 'When it's all over we will be together again. I am sure of it. Now if you go and help Dindin, I'll pack up my things and Bob's and we can get off.'

As soon as she had packed she went in search of Baines to tell him they were all leaving and to thank him for what he had done for them. Speaking even more gruffly than usual, he said:

'I was sorry to hear about the little chap.' He saw tears in her dark eyes and thought how different she was from the stiff-necked young woman who had come to his house so many months ago. 'Don't take on. Shall I ask one of the boys to help get your bags to the dock?'

'That would be very good of you, Mr Baines,' she said, trying to regain her composure. 'In fact, if he could escort the girls, then I could go on ahead and pick up some food for the voyage. Would that be all right?'

'Of course. Oh, there's that Johnson come to see Miss Dindin again.'

Evelyn only just managed to suppress the exclamation that rose to her lips. He was the very last person she wanted to see at that moment. Nevertheless she gathered herself together and said:

'Captain Johnson, how fortunate! The boat is ready and since we've heard about the battle and that Dick is well, there's really nothing to wait for. We're off tonight.'

'Ah, excellent. I think Miss Suvarov needs to get away from here. I heard a rumour . . . I don't like to say this, but did she go . . .?'

'Yes, I am afraid that she did. And not surprisingly it has upset her dreadfully.'

'I'd better go up and see her, if that's all right with you?'

She could not think of a way of stopping him without arousing his suspicions.

'Certainly. Would you give her a message from me? Tell her that one of Baines's men will escort her and Natalie with the bags to the dock, and that I am going on ahead to collect some provisions?'

'Yes, of course I'll tell her, Miss Markham, but please don't worry about the Suvarovs. I'll bring them along myself.'

At least she would be able to warn Bob in time to get Piotr hidden below decks, thought Evelyn as she smiled at the tiresome, chivalrous Englishman and hurried away.

23

Evelyn hurried to Petrovitch's yard and as soon as she got there she saw a cart piled with Bolshevik corpses pulled across the entrance. Beyond it was Bob in conversation with a man in orderly's uniform. He had his back to her, but Bob saw her at once and came hurrying towards her.

'What have you done?' she demanded, her voice made harsh by shock and by the fear that gripped her.

'Don't, Evelyn, don't,' he said very quietly, touching her briefly. 'One of the hospital orderlies, who is a Bolshevik, has brought Piotr here. We've got him on board. It was the only way I could think of to get him away without suspicion. There's no point trying to rescue him if we bungle it at the outset.'

'But can you trust him? You're sure we won't find the Military Police arriving before we get away?' she whispered back.

'It was the only way,' he was beginning, when the orderly turned. Evelyn said sharply as she saw him:

'Dobrobulyov! You!'

'You know him?' asked Bob.

'We met at the hospital. He was everywhere.'

'So, it's Nurse Markham,' he said in his thickly accented English. 'Excellent, Suvarov will need nursing: he looks very ill to me.'

Evelyn moved swiftly towards the small gangplank, but his voice stopped her and she turned back to face him again.

'There is a price for my help, Comrades.'

'Of course,' said Evelyn trying not to sound sarcastic. It had only just then occurred to her that even if they succeeded in leaving Archangel this man could still ruin them by reporting them once they had gone. A single telegraph message from Archangel's headquarters would have police alerted at every port in north-east England.

'Well, out with it.'

Dobrobulyov felt in a pocket inside his grey tunic and brought out two thickish envelopes.

'Simple enough: we just want you to deliver these two. The names and addresses are on the envelopes. All you have to do is conceal them somehow while the Customs clear you and the boat and then get them to their addresses.'

'And if we fail – not deliberately, but through some accident?' asked Bob carefully. Dobrobulyov smiled coolly.

'The only accident that would save you then would be one that had sunk the boat and drowned you all. We shall know from the actions the two Comrades take and the answers they will get to us somehow whether they have received these instructions. If they have not, it won't be too late to get a message through to the authorities in England that they should investigate the Suvarovs, the Markhams, and a journalist from the United States. I think you would have trouble wriggling out of that one, Comrade. You will be questioned in any case, I expect, by the Foreign Office. You must be careful.'

The rescue of Piotr Suvarov had taken on a very ugly aspect. There was treachery somewhere in it now, not simply bending an inconvenient but irrelevant fact of war. Bob watched Evelyn's stricken face, and wished that this horrible choice had never faced her. There was nothing he could do to help. That he too was faced with the same choice did not seem to matter. He would do whatever he had to, but she had already been through too much. It wasn't fair, the child in him cried out, but there was no answer. Her voice surprised him in its firmness when she spoke again:

'And you, Dobrobulyov, how will you fare when the Allies leave and you are left with the vengeance of the Whites?'

'Well enough. If Archangel gets too hot for me, I'll melt away. It's not my home, you know. I'm here only to do a job. He's different,' he said, jerking his sharp chin towards the yacht, which looked incongruously graceful as it pulled gently at the ropes that held it to the quay and rocked on the swell. 'He's ill – won't be strong enough to escape on his own feet for months, if ever. He needs nursing. Frankly I couldn't give a tinker's curse – that's what you say, isn't it Adamson? – whether he lives or dies. He's of no particular value to the Revolution, whatever you say. But those packets – they're different. I have to get them to England and I've been waiting for an opportunity like this for months. Well? We haven't all that much time.'

'Of course we'll take them,' said Evelyn, not even looking at Bob. There was no choice. She could not leave Piotr to the vengeance of his countrymen. If it had been only the Inter-vention Army, she might have had doubts, but with the stories she had heard about both Whites and Reds echoing horribly in her mind, she was not going to risk his life.

'How wise of you Nurse Markham. I wish you a pleasant voyage.' She winced at the sneer in his voice, but waited until he had picked up the shafts of his dreadful cart and pulled it out of the boatyard. Then she turned to Bob.

'We had no choice,' she said, 'and we can always hand the letters over to the Foreign Office when we get back, and try to explain. I'm sure they'll understand.'

'We'll have to hide him from Dindin until we're well away from here,' he said doubtfully, not sure at all.

'It may not be quite like that,' Evelyn said, and then told him of the execution Dindin had witnessed. He was as hor-rified as Evelyn had been.

'D'you think it will have changed Dindin's mind about Piotr? Was the shock enough?'

'I think it might have been. I almost told them this after-noon – especially Tallie, who loves him as much as Sasha did. But it didn't seem quite safe. And I needed her to tell Johnson that we're leaving. He's going to escort them both here. I couldn't stop him.'

'No, you were right to say nothing, I'm sure.'

Together they went on board and climbed down into the cabin, where Evelyn went at once to her unconscious cousin and stripped the ugly and stinking uniform off him. She wished aloud that she had some medical equipment with her and bent to tackle the filthy makeshift bandages that covered his shoulder.

'There should be a box in that locker there – the cupboard by your right hand,' said Bob. 'I never sail without some kind of first-aid kit. Petrovitch did the best he could.'

Evelyn found the box and saw that at least there was antiseptic and a roll of lint, together with a few bandages. She turned to smile briefly but with real gratitude at him and did what she could for her cousin. When it was over, and the groans that had begun to issue frighteningly from between his livid lips had stopped, and he was back to coughing again, she brushed the hair away from his forehead and whispered:

'You must make it, Piotr. You must live.'

'It might be easier if he did not,' said Bob and the sadness in his voice took away any cruelty.

'I know,' she answered. 'But easiness isn't the point.' There was so much in her mind that she could not explain it all to him. The years since John had died had taught her that nothing could ever be certain, but they had also taught her that whatever was done to you or to other people by fate or enemies or war or revolution, you had an absolute obligation to keep your humanity intact.

For that reason, if for no other, she would have done anything in her power to save Piotr. To have consigned him to murder by his own countrymen, would have been to sink to their level. To refuse to save him merely because the price of his life was to import into England letters containing seditious ideas would have been to concede victory to the Bolsheviki. It was only when ideas or theories were considered to be more important than people that men like her cousins or Sergei Voroshilov could wish to kill each other. It was only when ideas made people into 'enemies' that wars could rampage through the world, killing, laying waste, torturing, starving and sending people mad. In any war, she now believed, there could be no real victor. And if risking trouble with the authorities of her country was the price for saving one man from his own, she would pay it.

Wishing yet again that she could talk to Nikolai just once more, hating the knowledge of what might be happening to him, Evelyn touched his locket. Before Bob could say anything, Piotr began to stir. They both looked down at his bunk as his eyes opened and focused. Evelyn smiled in reassurance and said:

'You're going to be all right, Piotr. We'll get you away from here and you'll be all right.'

He moved his tongue around his lips as though he was thirsty, and then put a thin dirty hand up to his head, before saying in a tone of exhausted astonishment:

'Evelyn? How are you here? What's happening? And Bob?' Then a smile came to his face and he said hoarsely:

'So Bob couldn't resist, after all. I'm glad.'

She was not sure what he meant, but she said in her most professional manner:

'Don't try to talk. The gas has attacked your throat and lungs and you must concentrate on breathing as well as you can. Don't waste your strength.' The tired, heavy-lidded eyes closed as she spoke and he drifted away again. Evelyn pushed herself up off her knees at the side of his bunk and turned to Bob, who was watching her with an expression that drove the breath out of her lungs for a moment. Her hands went out to him.

When she could speak again, it was difficult to remember what it was she had meant to say. Then she shook herself out of the mood.

'The others will be here any minute now. Let's go on deck. There's nothing more we can do for him now.'

They went up to wait. The sea glittered almost like elaborately cut sapphires in the bright sunlight and Evelyn looked out from the shore towards freedom, longing to leave Russia at last, but terrified of the voyage ahead. She had lived in Archangel long enough to know how dangerous the sea could be and she could not help thinking of all the disasters that might overwhelm them. They might capsize. They might lose themselves and miss the anchorages where they expected to pick up food and water. They might run into heavy weather and . . . She tried to take hold of herself and find some courage.

Bob had assured her several times that the navigation would be relatively simple and well within his competence. He had picked up plenty of information about the tides and currents, the hazards they were likely to encounter, and the way that sailors experienced in those waters dealt with them. But in spite of all his reassurances, Evelyn was beginning to panic – and then Bob smiled at her.

She realised that she had been chewing her bottom lip unconsciously and made herself relax. Then she walked towards him. He gripped her hand and whispered so quietly that no one else would have been able to hear:

'Don't be afraid, love. Whatever happens, I'll get you home.' Her hand moved in his and she started to speak, but he was before her. 'And then we'll talk about what we're going to do for the rest of our lives. We'll get it right this time.'

'Yes,' she answered suddenly almost as confident as he. 'We will get it right.'

At last Dindin and Natalie appeared at the gate of the boatyard, escorted by one of Baines's Russians and Captain Johnson. Evelyn exchanged glances with Bob and climbed quickly down on to the quay to offer the Englishman her hand.

'It is good of you to have brought them, Captain Johnson. Thank you so much.'

'Not at all, Miss Markham,' he replied. 'Now, can I help you load some of this stuff?'

'No, no. Please don't trouble. It's all quite light. If you could just help me get it out of the cart then Igor Vasilievitch can take the cart back.'

Together they unloaded the cart and then Evelyn thanked both men carefully and said goodbye to them. The Russian shook her hand and went at once, pulling his empty cart behind him, but Johnson stayed, chatting to Dindin and teasing Natalie. At last, Evelyn sent Tallie on to the yacht and began to pass the bags up to Bob, who was waiting at the top of the companionway. When Johnson at last dragged himself away from Dindin, warmly clasping both her hands and promising to visit her in England, Evelyn shook his hand again and waited until he, too, had walked through the gate.

'Phew, I thought he'd never go.'

'Oh, Bob, why are you so horrid? He was charming to bring us here and say goodbye.'

'Yes, Dindin, of course. Now, will you pass up those last bags, please?'

When they had everything loaded Dindin was at last allowed on board. The gangplank was pulled up, and Petrovitch unwound the ropes that held the yacht to the Archangel jetty. Evelyn did her best to coil the ropes neatly as she pulled them up across the side.

The strip of water between the yacht and the jetty widened. Bob turned the wheel and the yacht took the wind in her great sails and came alive. Evelyn stood with the Suvarovs on deck as they waved to old Petrovitch and said farewell to the Russia they had known all their lives.

Tallie was pressing close to Evelyn, and Dindin was in tears. While Evelyn was trying to think of something that might comfort them both, Dindin said in a voice so different from usual that Evelyn put an arm round her shoulders:

'Do you think we'll ever see any of them again?'

Infinitely relieved that Dindin seemed to be able to think sanely about her family again, Evelyn said warmly:

'Yes, I'm sure we will. When all this madness is over they will come to England or, or send for you all and you'll be able to go home . . . and besides . . .'

'But it won't ever be as it was before, will it?'

'No, Dindin, I don't see how it ever could go back,' answered Evelyn, accepting that the moment to tell Dindin about her brother had not yet arrived. 'But would you want it to, really? Back to the Okhrana, spies, unjust courts and savage punishment for speaking out against the Government, and starvation and riots and all that cruelty?'

'Not those, no. Of course not. But the old things, the good ones. Skating on the Neva, dancing at the palaces along the embankment, the opera, whizzing over the ice in Papa's sleighs, summers in Finland, winters in Petrograd, Easter service in the Kazan Cathedral. All the old life with all the family together? Will we ever be able to go home?'

'I hope so, dear Dindin.'

By then Bob had steered the yacht through all the moored transport ships and cargo vessels and they were heading for the open sea. As the land dwindled behind them into a thin pencil-line in the hazy distance, Evelyn took a deep breath and said:

'Let's sit down for a moment.' The two girls obediently sat on the bench to the right of the wheel, and, smiling briefly up at Bob, Evelyn went on: 'There is some good news. Piotr escaped from the battle. He's down in the cabin. We are taking him back to England – to safety.'

Before she could say anything else, Natalie stood up and glared at her sister. Then she cried out:

'Dindin, aren't you pleased? It's Piotr – don't you care at all?' Then she ran to the companionway and went down into the cabin. Dindin looked after her for a moment and then said to Bob and Evelyn, more calmly than they had ever heard her speak:

'Of course I care. Don't you think that after yesterday I haven't seen him tied half-dead and groaning to some execution post in some vile barrack-yard every time I think of him. Why didn't you tell me? Did you really think . . .?' She broke off, in tears again, to fling herself on Bob's chest.

He held her with one arm while he kept the other on the wheel. Evelyn left them together. In the cabin she found Natalie kneeling on the floor by Piotr's bunk, gently if clumsily sponging his forehead with cool water.

Evelyn stayed with them for more than an hour, trying to get used to the increasingly sickening movement of the yacht and not to listen to the conversation that buzzed down through the boards of the deck. At last she heard footsteps coming towards the companionway and waited for Dindin.

Natalie heard them too and said:

'Here's Dindin, Piotr.' He opened his tired, battered-looking eyelids and said in that cracked, rasping voice that hurt Evelyn whenever she heard it:

'Good.' Watching Dindin, Evelyn saw that she was still in tears. Then the painful voice started again: 'Who else? Sasha? Did he get out?'

Both his sisters looked at Evelyn. Summoning up her dwindling emotional courage, she said as quietly as she could:

'He's dead, Piotr. He was ill and he just died – very quietly. I mean, he wasn't killed. No bullets.'

Piotr closed his eyes again and they might have thought he had lost consciousness if it had not been for the deepening lines between his eyes and the slight quivering of his jaw. Before anyone could say anything else there was a sharp shout from on deck:

'Eve, get up here, would you? There's too much ice about – I need a lookout.'

Scrambling up from the floor, Evelyn said, 'Look after him, you two,' and climbed up on deck. Bob greeted her with a tenseness that was quite foreign to him and a quick command:

'Get up there in the bows, Eve, and keep a damn sharp lookout for ice. Some of these chunks are big enough to send us to the bottom. Sing out when you see one and stick your hand out so that I can see where it is. OK?'

'Sure,' she said, and went forward, leaning carefully against the cabin roof.

The passage up through the White Sea towards the Kola Peninsula was terrifying. Her heart lurching, sinking and rising almost as much and as often as the bows of the yacht, Evelyn kept her eyes on the treacherous lumps of ice that dotted the green sea like mines. At times Bob only managed to sway the yacht by a few inches from the small bergs that bobbed and floated so innocent-looking yet so dangerously in their path.

But eventually, exhausted and with their minds ringing from the tension, they rounded the flat coast of the peninsula, and sailed out into ice-free sea. Bob called out to Evelyn that she could come back, but it was a while before she could combat the dizzying weariness brought by relief. Then, stiffening the muscles in her legs, she hauled herself up by the sheets and stumbled back to him.

He greeted her with a warm hug and a quick, hard kiss. Then he said:

'We'll need something to eat if we're going to keep going. Will you do something about it?'

'Yes, of course,' she said and went below. A quick glance at Piotr made her say: 'Dindin, will you get some food for Bob? And you and Tallie, if you're hungry. Don't bother to try to cook anything: some of that sausage and bread would be best. We'll try to make something hot when we anchor. I must see to Piotr.'

She did not wait to see whether Dindin was going to obey, but went at once to raise Piotr's shoulders and help him breathe. He coughed and gasped in pain for several minutes until the spasm passed. Then he lay against her shoulder, too exhausted to speak. She laid him down again on the thin pillows, and turned to reassure Natalie.

It was hours before she dared to leave Piotr, and he only regained consciousness just before midnight, long after the girls had gone to sleep. Then he looked up at Evelyn and said:

'They said you'd be looking after the girls. Thank you.'

For a few moments she did not understand. Then she whispered:

'They?'

'My parents; in Shenkursk. I was there last week. They said they'd sent the children to Archangel with you.'

Dizzy with relief that they were safe, hardly daring to ask the question that had been tormenting her for so long, Evelyn said:

'They're all right then? Thank God. And . . . and Nikolai?'

'Yes, he's fine. Troubled, of course. Aren't we all? But safe and well.'

She put her head down on the side of his bunk and let the blessed relief flood through her mind. Then she felt his hand touch her head and looked up again.

'Thank you, Piotr. I must . . . Will you be all right if I go up and tell Bob?'

'Of course.'

Not until she stood upright on the deck watching Bob at

the wheel, bracing himself every now and then against the swell, did Evelyn realise how confined the cabin had been. She stood silently watching his figure outlined against the low sun and the dark green-blue of the sea until he noticed her.

'Eve, I've been waiting for you,' he said, holding out his hand.

She went to stand beside him, her shoulder just touching his.

'Bob,' she said, 'Piotr was in Shenkursk and he saw them all. They're all right. Nikolai is alive.'

She felt his arm heavy on her shoulders and knew that he had been as anxious as she. After a while, he moved a little away from her so that he could see her face. For a moment he said nothing, just watched her; she looked fearlessly back at him. In the end he spoke:

'I never thought I'd see you look so happy.'

'Isn't it peculiar? Before all this, John, the War, the Revolution, losing Sasha, Nikolai, Piotr, the letter – everything – when I should have been happy I was not, and now when there are still so many reasons to be worried and miserable, I seem to thrum with happiness.'

He laughed out loud and reached to hold her close to him again. Into her hair, he said:

'What an incredible word, Eve. What does it mean – "thrum"?'

She smiled a little too.

'I don't know. I've always supposed it meant to vibrate and hum slightly – like the string of a cello or something. Anyway, be intensely moved – but nicely and quietly – by something marvellous.'

'Well if that's what it means, Eve, then I am thrumming too.'

'Truly?'

He let her go suddenly, and for an instant she was paralysed with her old fear that the happiness was an illusion, but she was able to move again when he said:

'Brace yourself, my love, I've got to put her about. Get ready with the jib – and keep out of the way of the boom.'

The big yacht heeled over gracefully and passed within only a few feet of a small hill of ice so far from the rest in the White Sea that it must have calved from some glacier in the Arctic. Evelyn watched it drift safely to the stern of them and said musingly:

'It should really be called 'Floating Icebergs' shouldn't it, not 'Floating Islands' – the pudding, I mean. It looks just like that.'

For some reason that absurdity, the triviality of her vision, set the seal on his delight. In the middle of revolution and war they had discovered that they loved each other and were now picking their way through a sea of emotion as full of disastrous obstacles as this one; they faced goodness-knew what problems when they reached England, if they ever did reach it, with a Bolshevik escaped prisoner; yet she was sure enough of herself to enjoy for a while such a trifle. He would never have been able to explain it to anyone who had not lived with them through the whole terrible time, but it was with real fervour that he said through his clenched teeth:

'Eve, I love you so much.'

She leaned against him, thoughts of all kinds rushing through her mind: happy most of them; others bearable. She no longer pined for the reassurance that he would never leave her. For once it was enough that they were there to-gether. Nikolai was safe for the moment. They had not man-aged to save Sasha, but they had brought Piotr away from almost certain death. And now they were sailing in the light of the low, red-gold sun, on their way home.

'Look Bob, the sun – it's sinking.'

She stood with his arm around her and watched the sun lower itself down behind the horizon, leaving a smaller and smaller segment, so vivid and brilliant that it looked as though the brightness might spill out of the circumference that bounded it. At last it sank below the horizon, but its warm, red glow still lit up the sky and was reflected back by the thick white clouds that hung above the yacht.

Evelyn felt a tremendous exultation flood through her, and said vaguely:

'It's almost like a promise, isn't it?'

Bob did not answer, and she was so surprised that she turned to look up at his face. She could see that his mind was no longer in tune with hers.

'What is it, Bob?' The urgency of her voice got through his preoccupation. He looked down at her.

'Look over there, at those low clouds. That's rain there. Damn.'

She followed his finger and saw in the distance a pewter-coloured shadow that joined the sea to the massed clouds that seemed to be spreading fast throughout the sky, and even beginning to hide the comforting red glow of the sinking sun. It was a most curious sight and it seemed frighteningly sinister.

'Fetch my oilskin, will you, Eve?'

'Of course.' She turned down the companionway, trying not to wake any of the three Suvarovs, and grabbed the first two oilskin coats and sou'westers she could lay her hands on. When Bob saw that she had two of each, he said roughly:

'No. Get below, Eve. We must go through it if we're to reach the first anchorage, and there's nowhere between that and us where we could safely lie-a-hull. But I want you out of the way.'

'Don't make me go, Bob. Please. And you're bound to need help with something. Let me stay.'

'All right,' he said after a while. 'But you'll get damn wet. God, here it comes.'

It was like plunging into a tremendous wall of spiking water. The rain beat down on their exposed hands and faces, almost as sharply as needles; and with it came the wind, hitting them hard, and sending the yacht bucketing through the waves. Evelyn, cowering on one of the benches at the side of the cockpit, wishing that she had not insisted on staying with him, stared across at Bob, hoping that he would not look as frightened as she felt.

He turned for an instant, as though he could feel her scrutiny. To her astonishment, she could see that his eyes were alight with excitement, and, although he had his tongue clamped between his teeth, there was a triumphant smile on his lips. He must have seen her fear, for he turned his eyes away from the compass for just long enough to bawl through the cacophony of wind and thrashing, slapping water:

'Afraid, Eve?'

Not trusting her voice, she nodded her ugly sou'wester at him. He laughed, a joyous sound that reached her in spite of the racket.

'Don't be. You'll get used to it. And I'm here.'

She shuffled along the bench, which was already awash with seawater, until she was near enough to touch him. He braced himself against the swell, took one hand off the wheel and gripped hers. They were both wet and cold, but there was such strength in his hand that for a moment all her fears died, and she really believed that they would reach Bergen alive.

It took them another two hours of battling with the wind and the water before Bob was able to turn the yacht into the tiny, but completely sheltered, cove where he had planned their first stop. Then, almost beyond tiredness, they dropped the anchor and turned to struggle with the wet and stiffening sails. The mounds of canvas were horribly heavy and seemed to Evelyn to be the most unyielding material she had ever touched. But at last all the ties were secured and the sails safely stowed, and the two of them could go below.

So worn out was Evelyn that when she fell into the bunk that had just been vacated by Dindin, she could not stay awake long enough to say anything to any of them. The words were just beginning to form in her mind when sleep rolled over her like some immense cottonwool blanket. Bob kept control of his conscious mind a little longer and explained to Dindin what had happened, where they were, what she and Tallie could do to help while he and Evelyn slept, and when he wanted to be woken. And then he too slept.

Dindin woke him five hours later and he went up on deck as quietly as possible, hoping that Evelyn would sleep on, so that she would be in a fit state to take the wheel from him later. The rain had poured itself out and although thick clouds still covered the sky, they were white and innocent again. With Dindin's help, Bob raised the anchor and the sails and they sailed on past the dull, rocky shore.

There were no trees to be seen and the only green anywhere was the thick moss that seemed to pour in rivulets down the crevices of the rocks. Every so often they passed a temporary-looking settlement of Laplanders, and Tallie would wave at the curiously dressed people who emerged from their houses to watch the big yacht slip by. Once a group of children waved back and Tallie's face lit up with pleasure.

For most of the time she was dreadfully bored: too small and light to be able to help with any of the jobs involved on deck, and banished to the cabin whenever there was more than the slightest swell, she spent most of her time sitting and watching her brother. But he slept for hours at a time and even when he woke could not really talk to her and did not want the drinks of water or tinned milk that she wanted to fetch for him.

Evelyn woke at last, to see Natalie carefully wiping Piotr's face and murmuring to him all the endearments she could remember hearing from her mother. There was a sad smile on his thin face as he submitted to her care and for a few moments Evelyn simply watched them. Then she remembered her obligations, flung back the quilt that covered her and staggered out of the bunk. Tallie looked round.

'Has the storm really stopped, then?' asked Evelyn, her voice a little thick and unsteady.

'Yes. Uncle Bob and Dindin are up there now. But they didn't want me to get in the way, so . . .'

'So, you came to look after Piotr. You're a good girl, Tallie, and it's such a help to know that he's in safe hands.'

The child smiled more happily and turned back to her patient. Piotr smiled over her head to Evelyn.

'All right, Piotr? Can I do anything for you?'

He shook his dark head against the rough pillow and she left them together.

Later in the day she took over from Bob while he went below again to sleep and she grew in confidence with every hour of good weather, letting her hands relax on the wheel and ceasing to fight the swell. As she learned to sway with the deck, keeping an eye on the compass and altering course a little first one way and then the other, she came to feel almost happy, and relinquished the wheel reluctantly when he came up again to relieve her.

While the weather held they fell into a routine of four hours on and four off. Dindin took charge of the tiny galley, producing hot food whenever she could, but more often handing up a plate of hard, dry bread and sausage to whoever was at the wheel. She learned how to keep the kettle only half full so that she could hold it over the rudimentary paraffin stove and produce hot tea in all but the roughest weather.

Then, six days out from Archangel, they reached the rocky, fissured coast of the North Cape of Norway and the weather changed. Evelyn was in command when the wind suddenly veered and she had to fight to keep the wheel from wrenching itself out of her grasp. With larger and larger walls of green water rearing up behind her, threatening to crash down on the deck and overwhelm them all, Evelyn yelled:

'Dindin! Wake Bob.'

He came scrambling up on deck, took one look at the sea and called out:

'Stick with it, Eve. I must reef.'

Looking behind her every few seconds at the towering waves, she gritted her teeth and clung on to the wheel as he clawed down the folds of heavy canvas until the sails were reduced to small triangles. The effect on the steering was immediate and Evelyn leaned forward against the wheel to catch her breath. When he had made the sails fast to the boom, he inched his way forward and touched her white face.

'Can you cope for a bit longer, Eve?'

She gulped, nodded, and then said:

'But what about the sea? Look.' He looked back at the waves and then down again into her face.

'Yes, but she's managing, Eve. Look, hang on. I must check the tides and channels.'

He went below to consult the charts he had collected in Archangel, calculated a new course and then went to relieve Evelyn, slipping on the steps of the companionway as the yacht turned momentarily into the wind, and rapping his chin most painfully on the top step.

That was a bad beginning to a terrifying forty-eight hours, by the end of which all three of them had bangs and bruises and grazes from the falls they had taken both on and below decks. Dindin had been vilely sick and was completely exhausted, Tallie had succumbed to her own peculiar burden of terror, frustration and boredom in a screaming fit, and Piotr seemed iller and paler than ever. By the time they limped into Hammerfest, the northernmost town in the whole world, Evelyn would almost have preferred to drown than sail another yard.

Bob, fighting his own weakness and appalling doubts about the whole expedition, decreed that they should spend at least three days in the port, recuperating, re-stocking the boat with food and water and, if possible, finding a doctor who spoke a language that one or other of them knew to look at Piotr.

They achieved all his aims and on Thursday 29 August sailed out of Hammerfest on their way to Tromsö. They were past the most dangerous stage of their voyage and from Tromsö onwards planned to call in at real ports every few days. The isolation of the country between Murmansk and Hammerfest had been one of the most frightening of Bob's anxieties and that at least was over. Navigation would be difficult as they threaded their way through the islands off Narvik, but at least they were within relatively easy reach of civilisation – and a seagoing civilisation at that – for the rest of their journey.

Nineteen days out of Hammerfest, exhausted, bruised, their eyes burning from the salt spray, with their hands cut and blistered from the ropes; cold, damp and very hungry, they brought their ship into Bergen at last. As Dindin helped Bob moor her and they all waited for the harbour-master to complete his formalities, Evelyn felt the beginnings of an immense contentment.

Bob, turning from his task of checking the last fender, saw her face and understood that she was at peace at last. He slipped into a seat between her and Tallie, and whispered into Evelyn's ear:

'Now all we've got to do is to decide whether to get married here or wait until we get you back to Yorkshire.'

Tired though she was, Evelyn put back her head and burst out laughing. He realised that it was the first time he had ever seen her laugh.

'Let's do it here,' she said. 'And then there'll be no fuss.'

Author's Note

The Author would like to thank the Trustees of the Imperial War Museum for allowing her to consult document collections in their charge, particularly the diaries of Major E. M. Allfrey and Commander T. St.V. Tyler RN, which describe the events in Archangel in 1919, and the diary of L. C. Pocock, which gives a graphic eyewitness account of the February Revolution.

Other, published, eyewitness accounts that give vivid pictures of the events that form the background to this novel are: Claude Anet's *Through the Russian Revolution* (Hutchinson, 1917), Rhoda Power's *Under Cossack and Bolshevik* (Methuen, 1919), R. H. B. Lockhart's *Memoirs of a British Agent* (Putnam, 1932), Ariadna Tyrkova-Williams's *From Liberty to Brest-Litovsk: The First Year of The Russian Revolution* (Macmillan, 1919), and Edmund Ironside's *Archangel 1918–1919* (Constable, 1953).

Apart from the historical facts of the two revolutions in Russia in 1917 and the subsequent Intervention at Archangel, all the incidents in this book are figments of the author's imagination, as are all the characters, who bear no relation to any real people, living or dead.